RABBITS

'Darkly funny as *Saltburn*, but with kilts'
VAL McDERMID

'*Rabbits* pulls you in and doesn't let go.
A dazzling, compelling novel'
JOHN NIVEN,
author of *Kill Your Friends*

'The leap from journalism to fiction is not always an easy
one, but in Rifkind's case, my only frustration is that
he took so long to take the leap. A darkly funny, often
disturbing, hugely entertaining story that sneaks around
behind the crumbling façades of wealth and masculinity to
smoke a joint and shoot some shit'
TIM MINCHIN

'The best 2 a.m.-whisky story of madly evocative
nineties' youth: parties in crumbling houses, and a sense of
time running out. This book is fabulous company – you'll
cancel your own parties to get to the end.
A queasy, hilarious joy'
CAITLIN MORAN

RABBITS

Hugo Rifkind

First published in hardback in Great Britain in 2024
by Polygon, an imprint of Birlinn Ltd.

Birlinn Ltd
West Newington House
10 Newington Road
Edinburgh
EH9 1QS

9 8 7 6 5 4 3 2 1

www.polygonbooks.co.uk

ISBN 978 1 84697 670 4
EBOOK ISBN 978 1 78885 662 1

British Library Cataloguing-in-Publication Data
A catalogue record for this book is available on
request from the British Library.

Typeset in Adobe Caslon Pro by The Foundry, Edinburgh
Printed and bound in Great Britain by Clays Ltd, Elcograf S.p.A.

For the actual rabbits, who didn't deserve any of this.

PART ONE

I

WHEN THE SHOTGUN WENT off under Johnnie Burchill's brother's chin, word had it, the top of his head came off like the top of a turnip lantern. Then it got stuck, by means of a jagged triangle of bone, into the upholstery of the roof of the Land Rover. A thing like that spreads around. The story, I mean. Not the head.

I'd just turned sixteen. It was 1993. Man, that was a great year. Well. A big year. The girls wouldn't start at our school until the next September, which seemed pretty exciting at the time, but actually that would turn out to make life slightly less fun, rather than more.

Or, at least, it would for me. I was from Edinburgh, and I'd been to a day school before, so I knew girls already. As a concept, at least. Some of the other guys had been boarding since they were seven, though, and had basically never spoken to a woman who they weren't related to. Not that you'd always have realised this, to meet them. I mean, you would with some, like Wee Geordie Meehan, who went beetroot even when he spoke to the cleaners. Others, though, were as confident as anything, although in that particular boarding school way, which often meant talking about wanking a lot, or putting their cocks on your shoulder from behind when you were working in the library. In retrospect, I guess some of them were just lonely because their parents were in places like Dubai. Still. Time does not heal.

It was a couple of weeks before Easter, anyway, when they found Johnnie's brother, Douglas. He'd been in the Land Rover, which had gone over the edge of the ravine in the rabbit field, but they reckoned he'd been dead already. Gun between the knees, wheel goes into a pothole, brains go on the roof. He was nineteen. Stupid way to die.

'No way,' said Alan, when I told him at ice-skating. 'We nearly did that last month. Johnnie and me. And Barf. And this guy from the farm called Dean. Barf was driving. I was in the back with the gun. Hugging the thing. We nearly went into the same ravine! It came out of nowhere.'

'How does a ravine,' I managed to ask, 'come out of nowhere?'

Alan said it was dark and they were stoned, which was actually a really good answer. I didn't know Johnnie all that well back then, but I knew he always had drugs. Alan said it had been 3 a.m. and they were properly baked, the tingly way you get with that chalky hash they ship in at Leith which Alan said had been packaged with acid: when you close your eyes and it's all marching ants, and all the sound goes weird, and you might as well be a dude on a boat. And Barf had been driving because he also lived in the countryside and had known how since he was twelve. He'd asked Johnnie what the dip was up ahead, and Johnnie had said, 'Nothing much,' and Barf had only realised at the last minute that Johnnie was totally wrong.

'Okay,' I said, 'but that's not all that similar. Because Douglas was by himself. Or that's what I heard from Chobber from Glenalmond, who heard it from Nelly, who got it from Marcus's dad because he's mates with Fusty's family. And they're next door.'

'Still stoned, though, aye?' said Alan.

'Oh aye,' I said, in a familiar sort of way, even though Chobber hadn't mentioned whether Douglas had been stoned or not, and I'd hardly smoked that much hash yet myself. Really, I hadn't spoken to Alan much more than I had to Johnnie by that point, apart from making him laugh once in maths by telling him that when Mrs Ellson got cross, she looked like Chewbacca having an orgasm. I found Alan a bit intimidating. He wore Doc Martens instead of school shoes and had quite long hair. Also, he had something impressive going on with art. I longed to be like that. Although I didn't know how.

All that, though, was about to change. These days I feel like I don't know anything: not about life, or about Scotland, or my own place in either of them. I don't mind admitting that. Who does? Back then, though, I knew it all. Or, I was about to. You know that thing you have, when you're a wee kid and getting bigger, and you start to think there's another world out there, where everything is better and more exciting, and all the people are more attractive and interesting and better in every way?

Well, I had that, and I was right. And soon, I'd be in it. And it all started the week after, at the best party I'd ever been to. At least, so far. Since then, I've probably been to better. Although not for a while.

★

Actually, I'll talk about the party in a bit. First, I should probably explain the ice-skating thing. You noticed? The way I said 'when I told him at ice-skating' and just left it hanging there, like ice-skating was a thing you can just mention in a conversation and everybody goes, 'Oh aye, right enough, we all do that, nothing weird there, Tommo, move along.' No. Even a year before, I never went ice-skating, except sometimes with this kid Steve from my old school on a Wednesday afternoon when we were small; only he started playing ice hockey and I didn't, so that didn't last long.

What happened, though, was that I got posh. Like, I was posh before, compared to some people, but now I was posh compared to everybody. Actually, that's not true. That's something else I was about to learn. *Almost* everybody, though. My dad's a writer, and he used to be the sort of writer that nobody gave a shit about, but then he became the sort of writer that people gave lots of shits about. And because of that he had to travel to London a lot, even to America, and it was a bit difficult having me stay at home, what with my mum being in the hospital so much. I also had a sister called Annie – sorry, *have* a sister call Annie; weird way to phrase it – but she was about to do her finals at Nottingham in Extremely Hard Maths. Also, to be honest, I was being a bit weird at my old school.

Not 'killing-the-neighbours'-pet' weird. Not 'penis-on-the-shoulder-in-the-library' weird. I was mopey, though, and a bit sad, and I'd moved up to the senior school and I wasn't in a class with any of my friends.

That school – my first school – was massive. It was called Robert Acton's College, and it was the biggest school in Edinburgh; there were about two thousand people there, and when you were nobody special, you felt like you were nobody at all. We all wore these brown blazers, and when it rained they smelled of shit. In fact, I remember once a teacher pretending he hadn't sneaked off to the pub when we all got back on the coach after a trip to the National Museum of Scotland, and this guy at the back said, 'I smell bullshit,' and this famously dim girl said, 'No, that's just wet blazers,' and everybody laughed and only she didn't understand why. Thinking about it, the school and the museum were about the same size. There were endless corridors, and a rule that you had to walk on the left, along this green marble strip inlaid into the floor, because there were just so many damn people desperate to be anybody, and some mornings it all made for a smell of bullshit like you would not believe.

If I'd thought that being nobody was bad, though, being somebody was even worse. All of a sudden, kids I didn't even know started pointing at me, and saying, 'My mum reckons you're a millionaire now,' and, 'How've you only got a quid for lunch like the rest of us?' and, worst of all, 'Airhellair' instead of 'Oh, hello' because that's what the butler says in the thing my dad wrote. Man, that butler. You'll have seen it. He solves crimes. How annoying?

There was this sneering thing in *The Scotsman* about my dad after the TV company bought the first butler book, and it called him 'a writer of mediocre airport fiction', which I always thought was odd because I don't think any of his books are about airports; the covers all have women in shawls on horses. What they meant, I suppose, was that he wrote books that people buy in airports, although for a long time they didn't buy them anywhere, much. Only then he wrote the first butler one, and loads of people bought it, and then he started writing scripts, and then he was never there.

This, too, was bad in ways I hadn't anticipated. To be honest, I'd thought it was annoying before, when he was at home all the time in his study, coming out and shouting stuff like 'They're screwing me, Kath!' whenever he opened a letter which told him just how many of his books with women in shawls on the covers people were buying in airports, which was hardly any. But it was a lot more annoying when he suddenly wasn't there at all, and neither was my sister, and it was just my mum waking up each morning, saying, 'Tommy, darling, could you get the bus today?' and going back to bed again. And I would, and I'd wander around being invisible and not really talking to anybody, unless I could find Steve and that lot at lunch. But then the show started on TV, and I couldn't even do that any more because of the 'airhellairs'. Bullshit.

Probably there are kids who are used to this sort of thing, like the fat ones, or the ones with weird faces. One boy, for example, looked like a *Thunderbirds* puppet and couldn't ever catch a ball, and you'd always see his mum picking him up from school and she looked like a *Thunderbirds* puppet, too, and Christ, that guy's life? Awful.

I'd never been like that, though. I was just normal. Only now I wasn't, and I didn't know what to do about it. And I kept thinking, well, that's that now, I suppose I'm going to be one of them; wrong turning, and this is my life for the next four years. So, I'd just go and sit in the toilet instead, where you could close your eyes and lean back, and the porcelain on your neck was all cold but the drips and gurgles of the pipes were like a magic invisible choir of beeps from a spaceship, or perhaps dripping stalactites from a cave. Or at the very least something else from somewhere else. And the longer you sat there, the more it seemed like you were, too.

After a while I was staying there even when the lessons started, especially when it was maths or geography. Not long after that they sent a letter home, and in a way it sort of made me feel warm and nostalgic watching my dad open it, because he hadn't been that cross about a letter in ages. Only, not long after *that* he sat me down and started this really long speech about how he wanted me to think about going to this other school, called Eskmount, which was much smaller and a boarding school, 'and a cut above, because we have options now'. The clincher for me, I think, was when he said, 'Of course, you'd have to leave your friends,' and I wondered whether any of them would notice and realised I didn't care all that much if they did.

Looking back, though, that's really quite a crap explanation of why I went ice-skating. The point is, at my new school, during the Christmas and Easter holidays, it's just what you did. Not most kids, obviously, because most kids lived out in the countryside, like Johnnie Burchill or Geordie Meehan. There were a few of us who lived in Edinburgh, though, and we were members of a thing called the Normandy Club at Murrayfield ice rink. I think it was started, like, fifty years ago, by a pushy mum from one of the other posh schools; she who got in touch with all the other mums who wanted to make sure that their kids stayed posh even during the holidays. There were a few of us from Eskmount, along with kids from Loretto and Fettes and St George's and Merchiston and Glenalmond, all of which were 'a cut above' all the schools that they aren't.

Mainly you smoked and played video games in the arcade.

There were girls there, too, and everybody knew everybody else because they'd all met when they were eleven at these Scottish Country Dancing lessons in a New Town church hall run by a woman called either Beryl or Meryl, which is a whole different level of niche posh Edinburgh madness that I'm afraid remains beyond me. The girls, also, weren't like the girls from Acton's. They wore wool sweaters and jeans, but never tracksuits, and they all had long straight hair, and they always wanted to go round and round the ice with their arm through somebody else's arm, talking. And by 'somebody', I mean Alan.

On most planets, I guess, Alan would have been too cool for ice-skating. Somehow, though, it didn't work like that here. He'd stand there, camouflage collar up, breathing steam until the girls came over. It never took long. Me, I'd mainly hang out by myself or sometimes with this guy Peter, who had been at Acton's and then went to Lothian College, which is another one of those schools which is a cut above, but honestly not that much above, in this particular case. He was the sort of kid who has no chin and wears a smart shirt under a jumper, even for fun, and we didn't have much in common. But his mum knew my mum and knew she wasn't okay, and so on my first day she'd told him he had to say hello. It was sort of like an arranged marriage. Maybe, in time, love could have grown? I wasn't that into him, though, and he had a couple of other nervy friends in grandpa clothes, so he wasn't that into me, either.

Sometimes Alan and I would say 'all right' at each other, but mainly I'd just watch him and watch the girls. How, I'd wonder, can I make them want to skate around arm-in-arm with me? I'd think about the warmth of their arm through my arm, and maybe the cold, thrilling chill of their ice-rink hair as a gust blew it into my face. And it was weird that I felt like I knew exactly how that would feel, even though I had never yet experienced it. That'll be a mum thing, I guess. Bit unsettling.

There was this one girl, Emma, who isn't important to this story at all, but I noticed her early on because she had a loud laugh and this fringe that was always in her eyes. One time she was skating with Alan and they both fell over. And they laughed and laughed, sprawled on the ice, and then he got up and pulled her up, and he had one hand on her wrist and the other on the back of her thigh, against these tight green jeans she was wearing. I can still see it. I'd never touched a girl like that. How, I wondered, did people get brave enough? Was it really all from Scottish Country Dancing?

Next week, I'd think to myself, I'll just go and join their group, skate on up to Alan and be a part of it. Only how? What would I say? Why would they want to speak to me? So, I never did, because I didn't have the guts, even after I started sitting next to him in maths. Or, at least, not until Johnnie's brother, Douglas, got shot in the head. Silver linings and all that, eh? Sorry, that was a terrible thing to say. Can we pretend I just didn't? Honestly, I'm actually quite nice. Girls sometimes used to say that. Not back then, obviously, because I never spoke to any. But afterwards. For a bit. Even when I wasn't.

2

ALAN WASN'T THERE ON the first skating day immediately after the head-brain-gun Land Rover fandango, which is when I overheard the story from Chobber, who was one of those skinny, evil kids with curly hair. Bet his penis has seen shoulders aplenty. Later, though, I'd retell the story like he'd been telling me, directly. Actually, he was in the arcade telling a whole group of people, and I was standing nearby pretending to play Double Dragon. Don't bang on about it. Same thing.

The next day, though, I was there early because I had nothing else to do. My dad was in America again, Annie was in Nottingham and my mum was in hospital, and most days were boring and the mornings were the worst of all. Even the cat had better places to be, and she was almost as old as me. Plus, Mrs Russell, the cleaner, was due in, and that was always excruciating because she was bound to find evidence I'd been either wanking or smoking. So, even though Normandy Club didn't start till ten, I'd normally leave the house a bit before nine and get a couple of buses, sitting at the back where the maroon pleather seats were warm and the diesel vibrations thrummed right up your arse. Which was not, by the way, why I sat there. I think? And I'd be at Murrayfield in time for a bacon sandwich and a sugary tea from the café half an hour before anybody else got there.

Generally, though, I wouldn't eat it in the café. Instead, I'd go right up to the back of the empty indoor ice hockey stand and watch while the kids filed in. The seats were orange and plastic, and quite often a bit rickety and broken by people who'd got a bit overexcited watching the Edinburgh Pretend Americans, or whatever they were called, losing to the Glasgow Shitbirds. I'd sit in an empty row, with my skates up on the back of the one in front, and I'd watch my smoke sail out high up over the ice and feel all poetic about it. I was dead poetic as a teenager. At Acton's, in the primary school, I wrote one which won a prize. It was about war.

This time, though, Alan came up to join me. I noticed him coming a mile off and nodded at him, and he nodded at me, and then it felt like it took him another three minutes or so to hobble up the stairs because he had skates on, too. I didn't know where to look. Excruciating. There's only so much attention you can pay your own cigarette, right? Clump, clump, slipping around. He still looked cool, though. Big baggy black jeans and an army jacket, and a tatty white T-shirt with a pendant dangling around as he stumbled on up. Undercut hair sailing in the draught. I ought to look more like that, I thought to myself. Although not exactly like that. Obviously.

Eventually he sat down beside me.

'You know Johnnie?' he said. 'Johnnie Burchill?'

'Yes,' I said. 'I mean, of course.'

Johnnie was in my house at school, as well as my year, so I ought to have known him better than I did Alan, who was only in the latter. Johnnie and I had never been in a dorm together, though, and I was new and found him a bit intimidating. Although he smoked in the tub room, too, and I'd been smoking for almost a fortnight now, so I was thinking that next term I'd get to know him a bit better.

'You heard about his brother?' asked Alan.

'Yes,' I said again. 'Of course.'

Then I wondered whether I should have brought it up myself, straight away. I'd worried it might be disrespectful of the dead, but maybe it was more disrespectful not to? Then Alan asked whether I'd spoken to him, meaning Johnnie, obviously. Not his dead brother with half his head stuck in a roof. No. And I just shook my head regretfully, as if me calling Johnnie could totally have happened, but in this instance just hadn't.

'I suppose they're not answering the phone,' said Alan. 'Can I have a fag? Thanks. I can't get through to him. I don't really know what happened, except for what was on the news. It's terrible. I'd call Flora. Only she's in Val d'Isère. I'm wondering if I should go up.'

What was this? Who was Flora? Also, what the fuck was Val d'Isère? I didn't know any of this stuff. I did know more about what had actually happened than Alan, though, thanks to Chobber. So, I told him, and he told me his own stories about driving around stoned in Land Rovers, too. And I didn't have any stories about that sort of thing yet, but I did have a story about inhaling deodorant through a towel on the roof of the fives courts with Nigel, a certifiably weird but actually quite nice kid in the year above who was into Dungeons & Dragons, heavy metal and Satanism. So, I told him that instead, and before long we were three fags in and definitely having a conversation.

After that we went down onto the ice and kept on chatting, even though there were a bunch of girls around, and all of a sudden it was like they'd noticed I existed. Nobody wanted to put their arm through my arm, true enough, but I did make that girl Emma and one of her friends laugh by asking if a muddy stain on the ice was the blood of the people who came here on Wednesdays. Then I made them laugh again later, when a bunch of us went off into town to McDonald's for lunch, and I said I didn't want a McChicken Sandwich because the sauce looked like spunk. And after that I sort of stopped talking because two jokes in one day about bodily effluence is probably enough if you're just starting out.

Then, when Alan and I left to walk to our bus stops, he asked if I was coming to Charlotte's party on Saturday, and I had to admit that I didn't know who Charlotte was. And he said, 'You just had lunch with her, you space cadet. She was the one in the hoodie,' and I said, 'Oh,' and blushed, even though I quite liked being a space cadet because it made me feel like Robert Smith from The Cure. Then he said, 'Johnnie was meant to be coming. Come along, we're meeting beforehand in the Tron at about five.' And I said, 'Sure, yup, see you there,' even though the Tron was a pub, and I hadn't been to one before and I wasn't at all sure they'd let me into it. And then I went home. Peter, by the way, didn't talk to me at ice-skating that day at all. In fact, since then, I'm not sure he ever has.

★

15

The Tron was an old man's pub just off the Royal Mile, and distinctive for no particular reason other than it was traditionally the coolest place in Edinburgh to pretend you'd been drinking in when you got back to school after the holidays. The first time I heard people talk about it, I assumed it must be all sci-fi and neon, like the film. It's not, though. It's tweedy and varnished and blue and named after the Tron Kirk across the road. No idea who first went there. I don't mean ever. Probably some old guy? I mean, as in, who decided it was the sort of place that people like me ought to go.

Anyway, there was an upstairs bit at ground level, but that was normally closed. Instead, you went down a staircase into a warren of varnished wood, tweed chairs and the smell of fags and 70 Shilling beer. Although I didn't know that was what you did at this point, obviously, because I never had.

I got into town early. Up at The Mound, I got off the bus at about three. Cold as misery because I deliberately wasn't wearing enough clothes under my jacket and the air was all chill and thin and pale and thoroughly Edinburgh. First, I went up Cockburn Street, where the shops all sold hemp hoodies of the sort Alan and Johnnie sometimes wore, and I looked at a few but decided pretty quickly that one of those might be a bit much. It's not like there were rules exactly, but each year at our school only had two or three people who dressed like that, and it was making a bit of a statement to decide unilaterally that you were one of them. I didn't want to suddenly be cool. I wanted to have always been cool, but in a way that people were only just noticing. These things are complex, right?

Instead, I went to Flip, this huge shop for students in which everything was cheap and second-hand except for some of the T-shirts, which were just cheap. I bought a green army surplus one and a white army surplus one, and a thick red-and-black lumberjack shirt. Then, at the counter, I bought a black shoelace necklace with a CND sign. After that I went to the changing rooms and put them all on, layered over each other, and stuffed my old T-shirt in my jacket pocket. Then I looked at myself in the mirror for a while before taking the necklace off and shoving it into my pocket, too. Then I bought some more cigarettes and spent a good quality hour aimlessly wandering around the shops on Cockburn Street again, browsing the aisles of crystals and essential oils and dreamcatchers and clothes made out of multicoloured nets for girls. Faintly wishing I had enough money for some Yubi-Gold legal high herbal cigarettes, while also wondering if they might be the least cool thing in the world. Trying to remember which shop it was that everybody at school said would sell you real hash over the counter if you knew the right password.

By the time I got to the pub, Alan was already there, along with this guy from the year above us and two other boys I recognised because they'd been at skating with him once; I'd wondered who they were then, only they'd never come back again. It was like they'd been ambassadors, just visiting, from a cooler and altogether more salubrious winter holidays ice-skating club for private school teenagers about which I did not yet know.

Other than that, the place was empty. The barman flicked his eyes in my direction and yawned. Maybe I looked older than I thought.

'This is Jamie,' said Alan, nodding at this blond kid with a big smooth face. 'And Will,' he said to the other guy, who had one of those flat, handsome granite faces that people sometimes have, which make you think they play rugby a lot and can be really confusing when they don't.

'Layman,' said Jamie, in an English-sounding voice. 'He's shagged, like, nine girls.'

'Cool,' said the other guy, I think speaking for all of us.

'Will Layman,' said the Layman. 'It's not nine.'

'Well, seven, then,' said Jamie.

'Tom,' I said. 'Tommy. Tommo. Whatever.'

Christ, I thought to myself. I should sort that out.

Alan told the group I was a friend of Johnnie's, and the way he said it I was almost starting to believe him. Then the guy from our school said that the thing that had happened to Johnnie's brother, Douglas, was really bad shit, and we all nodded gravely.

'Oh, he was a great guy,' said Jamie enthusiastically. 'And such a cunt?'

This made me frown, but nobody else was frowning, so I stopped frowning and went back to nodding gravely, which seemed to be the way to fit in. Somebody went to the bar. I asked for cider, which I still feel was a mistake. Jamie started telling us a story about Douglas. This one time, he said, there had been a party at Fusty's castle. Douglas had been there, obviously, because Fusty's estate was next door to his and Johnnie's farm, just by Auchternethy in Perthshire, and they were best friends, even though Douglas was at our school and Fusty was at Glenalmond, which was a totally different one. So, there were lots of people there from both schools, but also all these girls from St Leonard's, which is like St George's but in St Andrews. As in, it's a school. St Leonard's, I mean. St Andrews isn't. That's a place. With a school in it. Keep up.

They had a Portaloo at this party because the Fusty family, the MacPhails, are very rich. The castle belonged to Fusty's uncle, although most people thought he was Fusty's dad, although I'll come to all that later. Once, he'd been called Fusty, too, because his name was Philip and his surname started with 'MacPh—' and he smelled. And some kids learned that from their parents, I guess, and so Little Fusty got called Fusty after Big Fusty, because nothing changes ever.

Anyway, Big Fusty MacPhail, being horrible, wouldn't let them in the house. But he also owned a building firm, a big one that builds houses all over Scotland, so he had Portaloos going spare. This wasn't all coming from Jamie, you understand. Bits of it, I've pieced together since. Such as the uncle thing and where the Portaloo came from, although you maybe don't care about that at all. The point is, two girls went in the Portaloo, maybe to snort speed, and then Douglas and Little Fusty rolled it down a hill.

'Woah,' said Alan.

'They were all blue!' said Jamie, like he was delighted about this. 'Hair, clothes, everything. Soaked blue. And one of them was that Vanessa. You know? Total slut. Do anyone. And she was in a white shirt, and you could see everything. But blue!'

'It's weird how it's blue,' I said, not having heard people talk about women like this before.

'And then,' said Jamie, 'they shagged them. Douglas and Vanessa, and Fusty with the other one.'

'While,' said Alan, who sounded unconvinced, 'they were blue?'

'Maybe,' said Jamie.

'You weren't there?' said the guy from our school.

'No,' said Jamie. 'But it's a really famous story. You must have heard it before.'

3

IT WAS GETTING DARK when we got to Charlotte's
house for the party, and it was a surprise. As in, the house
was. Not the darkness. That always happens in the evenings.
This isn't new.

The house, though, was just by Niddrie. Alan had said
that before, and I thought he'd meant Longniddry, a pretty
village out in East Lothian. Niddrie isn't like that. Niddrie
is a housing scheme, full of low-rise blocks covered in that
grim grey pebbledash harl with satellite dishes out the back.
It's like, you get bits of Edinburgh where the pavements
are all soft red and grey flagstones of the sort you'd buy in a
garden centre, and you get bits where the pavements are the
sort of rough concrete you can imagine smashing your teeth
out on while somebody in a very shiny tracksuit kicks you in
the back of the head. I don't want to be a dick about it, but
I don't think people from Niddrie went to the Normandy
Club all that much.

Charlotte's house, though, wasn't like other houses in
Niddrie. We had to get the bus to this long street with a
dogshit park on one side and this really high stone wall on
the other. Windy, grey, Edinburgh, March. One of those
days when you can really see why the Romans left. Nobody
about, although it was the sort of place where you look over
your shoulder a lot, in case somebody suddenly is. I was

watching the others to see what they thought about it all, but Alan knew where he was going and the other three, I now realise, didn't know enough about Edinburgh for any sort of self-preservation spidey sense to be tingling. Not like me. I was well streetwise, already. Remember, I'd been at a day school.

Just along the wall there was a gate, and through the gate there was a gravel drive. In the morning, I'd see that inside the wall, on the house side, there was no end of shite. Rubbish, hunks of wood, flat white enamel bits of cookers, all that. Charlotte lived in the big house. People who didn't live in the big house used it as a dump. It's a lesson, that. Until then, or thereabouts, I'd always assumed people with more money had nicer things. I now know that sometimes they just have more expensive things, which might have stopped being actually nice fifty years ago.

It was big. Too big in the dark to see, as I would the next day, that the top had an eagle at every corner, and the front ones had no wings; one of them didn't even have a head. Light spat out of the cracks between the curtains of the big windows, along with the heartbeat of miscellaneous American rock music. Alan rang the bell a bunch, and nobody answered. Then he banged on the window, and Charlotte threw open the door. Pretty girl. Angry mouth. Black dress over a white T-shirt and DM boots. Holding a bottle of Diamond White. Oh, she's that one, I thought.

'Oh God,' she said, panicked. 'More.'

★

Inside, it was nuts. The hall backed into this big, curving staircase, and these two kids I didn't know were coming down it while having a sword fight with actual swords. Swords, mark you. Big old grey ones. Both of them were smoking at the same time, which looked hard. As in, English for 'difficult'. Not Scottish for 'intimidating'. Which is maybe not the way you'd expect it to go with swords, but there you go.

You know those houses that are so posh that everything looks red? This was one of those. The carpet on the stairs was red. The floorboards were reddish brown. The curtains were thick like tapestries and red, too, and so were the smug faces in the oil paintings of dead wankers in ruffs on the walls. Maybe I'm exaggerating. I guess some stuff was green, too?

More than that, though, there was the smell of the place. Maybe it's a false memory, because in the context you'd think I'd just have been smelling Marlboro, spilled beer and the Body Shop White Musk of the girls. Still, it's there in my mind, very firmly, as something different and new. Polished oak and old books, firesmoke and tobacco, a hint of sherry, a hint of dog. Gun oil drifting from hidden cabinets, and waxed green leather wafting from a closet in the hall. The smell of the crushed, threadbare armrest of a sofa owned by the same family since 1924. The smell of the shabby posh.

'Booze,' said Alan, and he and I peeled off from the other three and went left into this fuck-off big living room with a wooden floor. There were portraits on the walls and a fireplace with an ancient curling stone in it, which I would soon learn was obligatory. At the far end, there was a big rug rolled up into a sausage, I suppose so it didn't get damaged.

People were sitting all over it, though, so that plan didn't seem to have worked out too well. We'd bought booze in a wee shop on the Royal Mile. Or rather, Alan and the older guy had, for the rest of us. I'd only even tried to get drunk once before. That time I'd mixed vodka with Fanta, only I'd drunk it all too fast and immediately puked it all up again. Then I'd had to spend all night just pretending. Really annoying. This time, I'd gone for Coke. It seemed a safer bet.

Girls were running back and forth holding bottles, and boys were holding cans of beer. This one older guy from my school, Ruaridh, came past holding three beers, stacked end on end with the top one open. He had a hand on each join, and when he drank it was like he was playing the saxophone. I recognised some people, but Alan knew everyone. There were, I suppose, too many people there. We got talking to these two girls from Kilmanton, which was a girls' school in East Lothian that had a reputation for only letting in aspiring nuns, but these two weren't like that at all.

One of them was this girl called Zara, and she was big. Not fat. Scaled up. Deep voice and hair she kept throwing about, like she was a horse's bottom and being bothered by flies. She had this baggy, beige, V-necked jumper on, which she also had to keep adjusting, so as to not be obscene. The other, Annie, could have been a ballet dancer. Thin as anything. Tight brown jeans, long hair tied up at the top but flowing beneath, like a samurai.

Zara started touching Alan. Hands on his shoulder, his arm, his side. Girls and Alan, always with the touching. Annie was nice enough, but she didn't seem overly inclined to touch me. I didn't tell her she had the same name as my sister. I didn't think it would help.

'You boys,' said Zara, mock-scolding, 'are so late.'

'We were in the pub,' said Alan, and there was something thrilling about it. Lads. Lads who go to the pub and are late and make girls with deep voices affectionately roll their eyes. Lads like me.

'Scandal,' said Zara. 'Did you hear?'

We hadn't heard. Even Alan had only been here for two minutes, and I was literally born yesterday. So, Zara told us this story about Charlotte's older sister Marie, who apparently existed, and the way she'd been shagging her boyfriend Luke upstairs a couple of hours ago. Their dad had gone upstairs and stepped really loudly on the creaky step, just in case, but had walked in on them anyway and started shouting. He'd kicked her out, only then he'd gone out and she'd come back.

'Woah,' said Alan.

Personally, I found various aspects of this story didn't quite add up.

'Tell me,' I said, 'about the creaky step thing.'

'Excuse me?' said Zara.

So, I explained that it just wasn't clear how it was supposed to function in this story. He'd stepped on it by mistake? On purpose? It was a signal? How did we know about it? Had the dad come down and announced the entire tale to the group? Because Marie can't have heard it, or she'd have stopped. Unless that was the whole point? That she could have stopped shagging but rudely hadn't? Or what?

'Is he always like this?' asked Zara, like I was a misbehaving pet.

'I'm sorry about him,' said Alan. 'Weirdo.'

'He's hilarious,' said Annie, as if properly noticing me for the first time, and I thought to myself, well, hey, it's an identity.

Then Alan asked if that meant Charlotte's parents were coming back, then? And Zara said they might be, nobody was quite sure, but it would be fine, they'd just go upstairs. Which, to me, seemed flatly contradictory of the whole step/sex scenario, but also like no sort of parenting I'd ever come across before. Although, that said, my mum was in hospital with tubes coming out of her nose, my dad was in Hollywood, and I lived with a cat. So, I couldn't pretend to be an authority here.

Look, am I conveying this? Are you getting how it was? Parties are hard to describe. You want to tell people what happened, but really all that happened was that groups of people ran around talking to each other, and boys occasionally went 'Raaagh'. I drank a bit. Charlotte, whose house it was, appeared and disappeared, alternately looking thrilled and stressed. At one point a couple started snogging on the rug, him sitting on it, her sitting on him, but everybody shouted 'Whoo!' at them until they went upstairs. Possibly, quite a lot of people were going upstairs. Annie smoked long, thin, pink cigarettes in a packet that said *Richmond* on it, and she gave me three or four, but I didn't know how to start kissing her, or even if she'd want me to. Alan and Zara kept going away from each other and then coming back, like magnets. The way she watched him across the room reminded me of a cat watching a bird, but I don't think he watched her. After a while Annie asked me who I was looking for the whole time, and I pretended I didn't understand, and she went off to dance with these other girls and a tall boy called Paddy who I briefly daydreamed about fighting. Maybe with swords.

Barf turned up. He was this sallow, solid, floppy-haired boy from another house at school who hung around with Alan and Johnnie a bit, but never really spoke. He was also in my class, and we'd sat next to each other in geography for a term, but I didn't know him well. People used to say he was scared of women, and he kind of seemed to be, backing away from Zara and going to hide with some lads. The music was coming from a portable CD player thing, which was initially totally dominated by this guy called Will – not Layman, another Will – who kept playing Metallica over and over again, but then a gang of girls chased him away and put on the music girls like, instead. When they played 'Sit Down' by James, we all sat down. I was sitting next to Annie, who gave me another thin, pink cigarette. She gave one to that Paddy guy, too.

It was ten, or maybe a bit later, when Johnnie arrived. He came in with this girl, and this guy, too. The guy was older, too old to be at school, and had a checked shirt and a Barbour on; he looked as angry as a beetroot that was having a really grim day. He came in and slumped into a chair, doing this weird thing where he pinched the top of his Chinos and tugged, so his fat, angry knees didn't snag the material. Johnnie was wearing huge black jeans and a hemp hoodie that was exactly like the one I'd nearly bought, which made me really glad I hadn't. He had the hood up, and he looked wasted and amazing. I was still on the floor at that point, smoking my thin, pink cigarette. I could watch. It was fine.

Why was Johnnie so charismatic? *Was* he so charismatic? Thinking back, it's not impossible that I just had a crush on him. He was hard, but he was pretty. You know? Shouldn't say that about a guy, but he was. He had floppy brown hair that always did the right thing, and he was small but neat, like a kickboxer. His face was precise, but too angular to be girlish, in a way that was helped by this scar he had on one cheek, like an Action Man. His clothes were always falling apart, but in exactly the right way, which meant his bollocks never quite hung out. More than that, though, he just seemed to embody . . . well, everything. Everything that this new world of mine was about. Or, at least, everything I wanted it to be about. He knew guns, drugs, hillsides, girls who would lead you by the hand into barns. If Alan hovered above it all, as if forever destined to be somewhere else, then Johnnie rose up right out of it, like a mushroom from its mycelium base. Even today, when I miss it all, I miss it all through him.

Right then, though, it was the girl who really caught my attention. Everybody's attention, really. When they came in, she was squashed up against him, like a possession. She had a big green jumper on and ripped-up jeans, and this streaky scarlet dyed hair down to her collar, and an open bottle of red wine dangling from the neck in her hand. The stereo was playing something by the Violent Femmes – the one about not being able to get just one screw – and after a second or two she pushed herself away from Johnnie, stumbled into the middle of the room and started to spin around, like a top.

At first, people cheered. Then it got scary. The bottle was still in her hand, not spilling a drop because of what I'd learned in physics was called 'centrifugal force'. It was nearly hitting people, though; the very end of it was between two of her fingers, and you could tell it was going to go. When it did, it hurled into a group by the wall and then down to the floorboards, not smashing, somehow, but belching wine all over the floor. The girl stopped, watched it go, pointed and laughed. Then her arms went up, and her head went back, and her eyes went even further back, and she started to topple. That was when Alan leapt in, grabbing her around the middle.

She slipped through his arms, straight down. The big green jumper stayed with Alan, though, perhaps sucking up a T-shirt, too, and for a moment she was just a bare torso, white-pink belly and white-pink breasts introducing themselves to the room. Like a secret revealed. Breaking open a fruit.

Then she was on the floor, and the girls descended upon her. Geese around a piece of bread. It's all burned into my mind, even now. Not just the breasts. All of it. Even Johnnie fades to grey. I'd never seen anybody like her before in my life.

★

The older, furious guy was Fusty. The girl was Flora MacPhail. At that point I thought she must be Fusty's sister, but I'd learn later she was actually his cousin. Complicated. We'll come to that. They lived next door to Johnnie, whatever that meant in the countryside, and at one point she'd been Johnnie's girlfriend, too. I figured this all out half an hour later, smoking a joint in the back garden with Johnnie, Barf and Alan. Johnnie made it, with this hash and tobacco plucked from a little engraved silver tin. I was worried I'd do something wrong, but you can't, really. Smoking is smoking. It was a relief.

Johnnie seemed keen to avoid both of them. Even though he'd come with them and to my mind now belonged with them, forever. It was confusing.

'She's acting like it was *her* brother who died,' he was saying bitterly. 'And he's acting like I'm his dog.'

'They're just worried about you,' said Alan. 'Probably.'

'Worried about her dad, more like,' said Johnnie. 'Worried about what I might say.'

'Shit,' said Barf non-specifically.

'Flora's dad?' said Alan. 'What's it got to do with him?'

Johnnie shrugged. Then he looked directly at me. 'How's he here, anyway?'

Alan looked uncertain. I had the joint. I sucked on it. I said absolutely nothing. Lives turn on these moments.

'He's a mate,' said Alan eventually. 'Isn't he? Should I not have . . .'

'Nah,' said Johnnie. 'Tommo, I'm sorry. I'm being a dick. You're okay, man. Pissed. Good to see you.'

'I'm really sorry,' I said, passing the joint back to him. It was the first thing I'd said in ages. 'About . . .'

'It was his,' said Johnnie, turning the spliff around and peering at the burning end. 'He had it in his pocket. With the tin. The police gave it to me. I guess they thought it was just baccy. Dead man's hash, eh?'

I thought about this. I could feel this bar of tingling,

white fuzz stretching around the back of my head from ear to ear. I quite liked it. Dead Man's Hash. Good band name.

'Flora freaked out,' said Johnnie. 'We smoked some in the car. Only told her afterwards. Fusty didn't want us to. Hate that prick.'

'It's good you made it down,' said Alan quietly.

'Wanker,' said Johnnie. 'He said he was going to leave after dropping us off. He'd better.'

★

We smoked a lot. Then we went back inside to drink a lot, too. There was a lot more snogging going on by then. That girl Annie was on the rug with that guy Paddy, but she clocked me when I came back in. Everybody did. Or, at least, that's how it felt. Dead man's hash. Four lads, smirking in from the garden, red-eyed and with a secret, and one of them basically a celebrity. I liked that. I liked being someone, and for once not because of the fucking butler. Since then, I've learned that I'll often think that everybody is staring at me when I've been smoking hash, and usually they aren't. That night, though, I really think they were. Yeah, I liked that. I liked it a lot.

4

I SLEPT ON A landing, outside the room that Alan and that Zara girl were in. Me and Barf. Like we were medieval vassals, or pets.

I was sleeping under a curtain. I could tell it was a curtain because it still had a rail on it, with rings. I'd found it on the stairs, where it had conceivably fallen from a window. Other people had brought sleeping bags, but I hadn't thought of that. It was made of this thick brown velvety stuff, but I was still freezing. I got up, and shivered and stretched, and put on my shoes. Then I went downstairs. It was about 9 a.m.

Flora was sitting at this messed-up wooden table in the kitchen. She had a blanket around her shoulders and was drinking a cup of tea.

'Morning,' I said.

'Hello,' she said.

The kitchen was a mess. Not because of the party. More like, it was always a mess. The floor was cracked grey flagstones and the walls were rough-painted plaster. It was like a cave. My mum was always complaining that our kitchen was from 1981, but it was a shitload nicer than this one. It wasn't cold, though. There was a green Aga against one wall which looked older than the Moon.

'I think, uh, Johnnie was looking for you,' I said. 'Last night. Really late.'

'He found me,' said Flora, and I saw that the make-up around her eyes had spread around, making her look like a racoon. 'Who are you?'

'Tommo. Tom Dwarkin. No one, really. I'm a friend of . . . people.'

'That's nice,' said Flora, breathing into her cup. 'To be a friend of people.'

I didn't know what to say to that. I went over and warmed myself against the Aga.

'Sometimes,' said Flora, 'I think I prefer the morning after, rather than the party itself. Everything is still. Everybody is out of their armour. Revealed. You know?'

I thought of Flora being out of her own armour last night. Maybe I blushed.

'I know what you mean,' I said. 'But I've got a headache. Actually, two headaches.'

'This one time,' said Flora, like it was a secret, 'I had three headaches.'

I laughed. Then I said I wasn't sure I'd have room for three headaches, and she asked if I was saying she had a big head. And I said not necessarily, because one of them could have been at the front, maybe in her nose, and then she laughed. Then she asked if I wanted a cup of tea, and I said, 'Yes,' and she said, 'So make one, then,' and I did and sat down.

'Sorry,' she said, 'who are you?'

'Tommo,' I said again, deciding that was the one to go with. 'I'm at school with Johnnie and Alan. And you're Johnnie's ex, right? Flora. And you live in the castle next door.'

'You know too much. It's creepy.'

'Yes,' I agreed, to see how that went, and she laughed again. Then she said it wasn't really a castle. Then she said that Charlotte had gone out to get a ton of bacon, but there was some here already and we should get into that before everybody else got up. Although I said I had to go in a minute, actually, because I needed to visit my mum.

'In a castle?' she said.

'In hospital.'

'Is she okay?'

'Well, no,' I said, smiling a bit. 'She's in hospital.'

'She could be a nurse,' said Flora.

'She's not a nurse. She's a civil servant. But she's got this thing. This autoimmune thing. It's quite bad.'

Flora didn't say anything.

'It's not AIDS,' I said suddenly.

'That's . . . good?' said Flora carefully.

'At least, I think it isn't AIDS.'

Then Flora said she thought I'd know if my mum had AIDS, and I said she was probably right. Then Flora said her grandad had died six months ago, and I immediately said, 'Of AIDS?' and Christ, where did that come from, although she just said, 'No.' Then she asked if my dad was any good at cooking, because hers definitely wasn't, and I said my dad wasn't here, either, because he was working in America.

'It's just you?' she said uncertainly.

'I should go. It was nice to meet you properly.'

'Wait,' said Flora. 'Some girl told me I passed out last night and showed everybody my tits. She's a bitch, though. Do you know if that's true?'

'I didn't see anything like that,' I lied. Then I found my

jacket, took a very thin pink cigarette from a packet on the floor in the hall and let myself out into the eye-stabbing chill of the March air.

★

The Western General was about as far away from Niddrie as you could get. I had to sit on a bus all the way into the Commonwealth Pool, and then on another one all the way out again. And when I got there, she was asleep.

I hate hospitals. Everybody does, but maybe I hate them more. When I was a kid, my friend Duncan's big brother had some issue with one of his bollocks, so he had to go into the Sick Kids for a couple of weeks. I was staying with Duncan one weekend, which meant we had to visit him. There were all these kids there, obviously, but they were all together, and I was jealous of them. Then I got home and realised that they probably had issues with their bollocks, too. And I wasn't jealous after that, and I lay awake most of that night, thinking about hospitals, never wanting to go to one again.

I was never jealous of anybody in my mum's hospital. It was too warm and too quiet and smelled of disinfectant, but in that way that makes you realise there are worse smells lurking underneath. Everybody on that ward seemed to be a mad old lady, and they all had tubes coming out of God knows where. And you'd walk down the ward and all the beds were surrounded by these really thin hanging blue sheets on rails, and they'd wisp at you, like cobwebs in horror films, as if they wanted to stick to your arm hair. And you'd wonder who else they'd stuck to recently, which mad old people who were never going home, and then you'd wonder what the point of anything was if you had to come and die in a place like this.

She wasn't dying, though, my mum. At that point, I don't think they'd even figured out what she might die of, and I remember actively not wanting them to; it felt that as soon as they did, she might. Either way, she was just asleep, with a blue, webbed blanket up to her chin and an oxygen thingy under her nose. So, I dumped my jacket on the chair by her bed and then went down to the café to get a bacon sandwich. By the time I got back, she was awake again.

'You've been smoking,' she said immediately.

'I was in the café!' I shouted.

'Before that,' she said, grinning. Honestly, mums are a nightmare. I'm holding a steaming bacon sandwich and she's got nozzles in her nostrils and, still, somehow, she knows. There was a big box up by her head with lights on it, and every few seconds it went beep. She didn't seem to mind, though, so I tried not to, either.

'Are you okay?' she said.

'You're the one in hospital,' I pointed out.

'With your dad away, I mean. And Annie. You're alone at home. Just before your exams. It's just such bad timing.'

'Ach, stop,' I said.

Then my mum started telling me about a call she'd had from her sister Julie, who lives in Bristol, and that I could go and stay there if this happened again during the holidays. But I wasn't going to go to bloody Bristol. Aunt Julie was this massive overbearing feminist academic lady who was married to a much smaller academic called Martin, and all they ever wanted to talk about was sex.

They also had this horrid little dog called Basil who licked the dishwasher and your face and also its own arse, and come on, sod off, no.

There weren't many options in Edinburgh because my parents weren't from here. They weren't Polish, either, although my dad did always say that 'Dwarkin' had emerged from the name Dworkowicz in the 1870s, when his own grandfather got off a boat in Southampton. My dad had grown up in Peterborough as an only child and stayed there; my mum's family were from Manchester. They came up here when Annie was about a year old, because my mum got a job in the Scottish Office and my dad reckoned Edinburgh might be more conducive than East Anglia to writing books about women in shawls on windswept hillsides. These days, though, my dad couldn't be here because of the work, and he needed to do the work so he could pay for my mum's care, and basically everything ticked along smoothly so long as my mum's white blood cell count remembered to only plunge through the floor in term time. Or through the ceiling, perhaps. I always forget. Whatever direction, either way, in which it had just gone.

'I'm fine,' I told her. 'I'm having a good time. I went to a party.'

'Oh, that's nice,' she said, and she sounded exhausted. 'A birthday?'

'Maybe,' I said, pondering this for the first time.

'You didn't take a card?' she said, annoyingly.

'It was this girl. Who I know from skating. She lives in Niddrie.'

As expected, this made my mum say, 'Niddrie?' and I

said, 'Yes, Niddrie,' and she said, 'Niddrie?' and I told her it was this big old house behind a wall, and she said, 'Oh, but that's the Costorphines.'

I shrugged.

'Bill Costorphine,' she said. 'You'll have seen him in the news.'

I shrugged again.

'Lord Costorphine,' she said. 'The judge.'

'It didn't come up,' I said.

'He once put his hand on my bottom ,' said my mother, thoughtfully, 'at a drinks party at the Scottish Office.'

'You what?'

'I stuck a cocktail stick in his arm.'

'What are you even talking about?'

Then she asked how I knew them, and I said about the skating thing again, and that Charlotte was a friend of Alan's from school, and she said, 'Which Alan?' and I said, 'Alan Campbell,' and she said, 'Mungo Campbell's boy?' and by that point I was getting a bit annoyed, partly because if Alan's dad had once put his hand on her bottom, too, then that was actually going to be a really big deal. Also, though, it was because my new friends were exciting and special, and it somehow ruined things that she knew who their parents were. It made me think that their parents might be going, 'Oh, David Dwarkin's boy?' when they heard about me, and I didn't like that at all. Then I felt guilty for feeling annoyed, on account of the hospital and tubes and stuff. Then the machine started beeping a bit faster, and a nurse came in and did something with her drip.

A little bit after that she fell asleep, so I wandered down to the shop and bought her *The Scotsman*. When I got back, she was still asleep, so I read it myself. The front page was about a helicopter crash by an oil rig. Apart from that, it was all about the election. The Conservatives were screwed, especially in Scotland, and there was a big fight going on about the NHS and some girl's ear. Also, the Duke of York was getting a divorce. And then, on page seventeen, there was a story about Johnnie's brother.

I'd skimmed half of it before I even realised it was him. The article called him 'landowner and farmer Douglas Burchill', which seemed a grandiose way to talk about an eighteen-year-old kid who once turned a girl blue by rolling her in a Portaloo down a hill, but I guess these newspaper types know what they are doing.

Apparently, anyway, there was some issue with the gun that had killed him. It wasn't legal. First, it hadn't been licensed, and second, it hadn't been the sort of thing you even could license, anyway. The paper called it a 'pump-action shotgun', which made me think of *The Terminator*, and apparently they'd been banned about twenty years ago. There was a quote from the Procurator Fiscal saying they weren't going to be procurating anybody, though, because they couldn't establish its ownership, and you can't prosecute a dead guy, anyway. Still, the police were using it as a public reminder that anybody with old firearms ought to register them, pronto.

I think that was probably the first time I properly thought about Johnnie's dad being dead. Alan had mentioned he'd died when he was small, but it hadn't sunk in. Now his brother was, too. He and his sisters were one parent away from having no parents. I sat there in the chair, watching my mum's green blanket go up and down, listening to the beeps and the distant sound of slamming doors and shouts. And I wondered what that was like.

5

I DIDN'T GO TO Douglas Burchill's funeral, but Alan told me it was awful. The ceremony was in the village and that was okay, he said, but back at the house Johnnie drank too much, too quickly. He tried to punch Fusty and fell over, then got dragged away by Fusty's real dad, who was Flora's dad's brother-in-law and unexpectedly massive and scary because he'd been in the SAS. Then he came back and started arguing with a bunch of distantly related Australians until the soldier got involved again, and for a moment Alan had genuinely worried he might take a swing at him, too. Johnnie's little sisters, who were twins and only about ten, kept crying and pulling at him until Flora took them away.

There was, said Alan, some sort of legal drama going on with the farm. Apparently, it was actually owned by fifty million members of the family, and a handful of outside investors, too. They'd all wanted to sell for years, but Douglas, who had inherited the controlling stake from his dad last year, wouldn't hear of it. Now Johnnie had it, so they were all hassling him. Or something like that. Flora's family were involved in some way, too, and everybody was very angry with everybody else.

'To be honest, I could have done with you there,' said Alan, at the side of the rink. 'For a bit of support.'

'Sorry, man,' I said. Wondering, neither for the first time nor the last, exactly how I'd stumbled into being whoever he suddenly seemed to think I was.

★

The new term started a week or so later. We went back on the Sunday because boarding school never misses a chance to ruin a weekend. My dad got home the night before and picked up my mum from the hospital. She was a bit better by then, but the major change was that they'd figured out what was wrong with her, which was something called multiple sclerosis.

'Is that bad?' I asked my dad, once she'd come in, looked around the kitchen and then gone to bed.

'We'll have to wait and see,' he said briskly, which I suppose meant he didn't know. Later, quite a lot less briskly, my mum said I could ask her anything I wanted. But I didn't want to ask her anything.

The next day, my dad helped me put my trunk in the boot and drove me over to school. We lived just east of Holyrood Park, in another one of those 'garden centre flagstone' bits of Edinburgh. According to my dad, who was always going on about this sort of stuff, it had once been a real village and the last stopping point in or out of Edinburgh, a place of inns and stagecoaches and stamping horses and men in triangular hats. Now, what with roads and cars, it was thoroughly absorbed into the city proper. Eskmount, though, was only half an hour away. This made my life quite different from all those kids who had to come in from the middle of nowhere. Or, you know, Oman.

'Look, I'm really sorry you were by yourself so much,' he said, in the car.

'It was fine,' I told him, and I wasn't even lying. Both of my parents had kept asking me what I'd spent the whole holiday doing, and there was simply no way of explaining to them that most of the good bits had involved McDonald's, cigarettes and not quite ice-skating. I just kept telling them I'd done a lot of revising. I think they thought I was being evasive to make them feel better.

'Your mum said you went to a party,' said my dad, watching the road as we crawled towards Portobello. 'At Bill Costorphine's.'

Oh, here we go, I thought.

'You know the girl?' he said.

Not really, I told him. She was a friend of friends. From school. Alan Campbell and Johnnie Burchill.

'With the brother?' said my dad. 'God, horrible story. I didn't realise he was your age. It was in the paper.'

'In LA?' I said, perhaps a little pointedly.

'Poor kid.'

'Mmm,' I said, vaguely wondering if he meant him, or me.

'Impressive house,' he said, after a while.

'Eh?'

'Costorphine's place,' he said. 'I've heard. What did you make of the staircase?'

I thought of the two boys I'd seen, having a swordfight on it.

'It was okay?' I said cautiously.

'Pevsner,' said my father, 'is effusive.'

These were not words I knew.

'Pevsner?' said my dad. 'Nikolaus? The architectural

historian. He wrote a whole essay about it. It's supposed to have particularly fine rococo scrolling on the instep. Did you meet Costorphine? Was he there?'

I told him I didn't know, which was an answer he found extraordinary. He'd gone out, I said, but he might have come back. Maybe he was upstairs. Nobody was sure. It was a bit wild.

'Aren't we high society these days?' said my dad, sounding amused. 'Your poor old dad goes off to work, and you're in Bill Costorphine's house!'

'You,' I pointed out, 'were in Hollywood.'

My dad said he was in a hotel. And once or twice on a set. It wasn't ever that much fun. Los Angeles was an industry town.

'No parties?' I asked.

'Just one. Boring. Work thing. All business. Everybody is American. Nobody that interesting.'

'Oh.'

'Although,' he said, 'have you ever heard of a man called Robert De Niro?'

★

When I was a kid at Acton's, I thought that boarding schools were basically castles. Which shows what I knew, because only part of Eskmount was a castle. That was Smethwick, which was Alan's house. Pretty dark place. Johnnie and I were in Esk House, which was a warren of blue-painted corridors above the school offices and the dining hall. The car park outside was all posh because it was the school's main entrance. On the first day back after the holidays, it was full of kids and parents lugging luggage around. All the boys were in kilts because that's what we had to wear to go back to school, because somebody somewhere very important was evidently on drugs.

Sometimes upper and lower sixth-formers got their own rooms, but I was still in fifth form, so I was in a dorm. These were ramshackle and varied and had kids from all three years below; the biggest had nine or ten people in them. You moved dorm each term and you never knew where you were or who you were with until you turned up at school and looked at the noticeboard. This could be stressful. You didn't want to be with wankers; and by wankers I literally do mean wankers.

That term, though, I found I was in Beagle, which was this tiny little dorm with only three people in it. This would have been great news for a winter term because it was one of the few dorms with radiators in it, presumably because it once used to be something else. Even for a summer term, though, it wasn't terrible. It was halfway up a weird little staircase, quite removed from everywhere else. The only thing above was a dorm called Tower, which was right at the top of everything and had a reputation for being lawless because no member of staff could ever be arsed to trek all the way up there. Don't expect these names to mean anything, by the way. Alongside Beagle and Tower, there was M, K, F, Jerusalem, San and Frontal. Only sometimes were there reasons. Tower also had a big cupboard in it with a stepladder at the back, which you could climb up to a trapdoor to the roof. It had a Yale lock on it, but a few years before this mad kid called Yarmond had scaled the drainpipe outside, unscrewed the thing from the inside and taken all the pins out. So, now you could unlock it with a screwdriver, or nail scissors, or basically anything.

The best thing about being in Beagle, though, was who I was with, which was Johnnie. In charge of us, at least nominally, was Nigel, who was that kid I told you about already who was into Dungeons & Dragons and Satanism. He'd been in the junior school, too, and people said he'd smelled of roll-ups since he was nine, so this frankly made him an odd choice to be in charge of anything. Although he was good-natured, too, Satanism notwithstanding, so it could be that the housemaster had decided he'd give Johnnie an easy ride in a difficult term.

That said, the distribution of kids around dorms seemed pretty random at the best of times, to the extent that some people said Toad had a habit of drawing them up the night before term started when he was pissed. Toad, by the way, was the housemaster. He'd always been called Toad because somebody once said he looked like a toad, although I couldn't see it myself. You might have also thought that, what with him being Toad, Esk House would be known as Toad Hall. But it wasn't.

*

Johnnie turned up while I was sitting on the bed in my dorm changing into a pair of jeans. Barf was carrying the other end of his trunk, but then he had to go because he was in Pothle, which was the crap house for freaks. He and his dad had picked up Johnnie because they came past his house anyway and had a big car.

'This is okay, eh?' Johnnie said. 'You, me and Creepy Luci?'

'Luci' was what we all called Nigel. Short for 'Lucifer'.

I was relieved. I'd been thinking about that look I'd got from Johnnie at Charlotte's house, when he'd asked why I was there. Like a laser. Clean through my head. Although now he seemed to assume I was a friend of Alan's, just like Alan assumed I was a friend of his. And I was beginning to realise that they both only need to assume it for another week or two and it would be true.

Luci turned up after that, looking awkward with his dad, who was a bald vicar. The moment he'd gone, Luci opened his trunk and put up a Megadeth poster on our wall. I mean, why not? Then the bell rang for House Triple, which was what we called assembly because the bell rang three times to let you know it was happening.

Triple happened in the third-form day room, which was a smallish hall with desks along the sides, where the twenty or so kids in that year in our house sat to do their prep. Red walls, cheap woodwork, black rubber on the floor that the school had apparently bought in a job lot from a closing-down cardboard box factory. It was a bit invasive when the rest of the house barged in, with all the little kids forced to abandon their desks so that older kids could sit all over their shit. People would do it quite self-righteously, too. Like, older kids had sat all over their shit when they were small, and now it was their turn.

You look around the room and take in the changes that have happened over the holidays. Who has a new haircut, who has new glasses, who got fatter or thinner. Who had a new jumper, even. This stuff stands out. Decor-wise, I noticed, they'd replaced this crappy metal plug box thing by the door, which had had a loose wire on it for the past six months that tripped the fuse for the entire floor whenever you kicked it. They'd also put a wooden panel over a splintered dent in the plasterwork that had been there for even longer; it had happened when a boy called Hutch from the First XV had done a judo throw on this kid from Pothle for a joke. This is all the stuff I was looking at, anyway, when I realised that basically everybody else in the room was looking at Johnnie. Like he had two heads. Or, perhaps, like he had one head, but with the top blown off.

Toad noticed it, too. He had been droning on about it being an A-level and GCSE term, as if we didn't know, when he stopped and looked at Johnnie. Then he looked at everybody else and gulped. Like, visibly. As if he had not thought, in advance, that this might happen.

'I think we all know,' he said, 'that the Esk House family lost a member over the break. And so, if Johnnie will forgive me, I think we should have a moment's silence.'

Johnnie didn't say a word. Nor did anybody else. Some people put their heads down. Johnnie stayed totally still but closed his eyes. I looked around. After about forty seconds, this little third-form kid called Ian did a fart, but people broadly managed to hold it together.

'Right,' said Toad. 'Well, that's about it. I don't think I have more news. Except, oh, we have a new payphone downstairs. I expect it will be a bit noisy for now. But in time, a cubicle shall be erected.'

People went nuts. Screaming laughter. A teacher says the word 'erected'? Come on.

'I don't know what "cubicle" means to you!' he shouted. 'But to me it means a box!'

Worse. Real *Les Mis* rebellious vibe. Toad shook his head and walked off down the corridor towards his flat. Once he'd gone, things broke up, with everybody catching up with everybody else. Johnnie, though, pulled up his hood and walked off towards the stairs, passing this big blotchy mirror that was screwed into the wall. Looking, from his reflection, like he hated everybody in the world.

★

The next evening was eventful, although I remember the next morning really well, too, because we didn't wake up and we definitely blamed the system.

Waking up ninety teenage boys, you see, is a complex process. Nobody has a diligent mum or dad to hand, and you can't just expect them all to have alarm clocks. What's your error rate going to be in that scenario? Thirty per cent?

Instead, by means of a rota, one individual kid was each week tasked with waking up all the other ones. It's funny, but writing that down, it seems to make less sense, rather than more. Still, it's what we did.

What with this being an unpleasant task, and Eskmount being an old-fashioned boarding school, the kids who had to do this stuff were always in the lowest year. Me, I never had to do it. I joined the school too late. I'm told, though, that it was as stressful as anything. There was a bell, an old-fashioned electric one that you triggered with a button on the stairs that looked like a light switch. You rang it at 7 a.m., then again at 7.15 a.m., and then finally at 7.25 a.m. The last time you had to ring it three times, so as to indicate House Triple, the roll-call before everybody went down to breakfast. And after the first two rings, you had to run around the entire house, knocking on every door, opening it and shouting what the time was. This included not only the dorms but also the individual bedsits of sixth-formers. Wee Geordie Meehan told me that lots of them would leave notes with elaborate instructions about kettles and coffee machines, and they'd all move their furniture around, so you had to grapple behind wardrobes and stuff to find the light switch. Or they'd instruct you to physically wake them up.

'In their manky sheets,' said Geordie. 'Or they'd be aw "I missed ma fuckin' breakfast, thanks tae you!" and so you'd be dreadin' them.'

Geordie was from a farm in Ayrshire. Maybe you got that? The point being, though, bell-ringing was a stressful, high-precision operation and things often went wrong. And, in this case, the thing that went wrong was that the third-former in question – an incredibly small boy called Niall – forgot all about our wee, stupid dormitory altogether. So, nobody woke us up. Not for Triple, nor for breakfast, either.

We were all still snoozing away when Toad kicked open our door in the middle of first period. First, he shouted at us all to get out of bed, but Luci was only wearing a T-shirt and no pants, so then he shouted, 'Cover yourself up, for God's sake, Nigel!' which made Luci run around in a panic to and from his tallboy cupboard thing for longer than you'd believe. Johnnie was openly sneering. I was doing that thing where you know you can't laugh and it makes you shake like you're on a spin cycle. Toad didn't like that at all.

After that he screamed at us for ten minutes solid, about Luci betraying his trust and the two of us needing to focus on our GCSEs. Honestly, for ages. You'd think he might have wanted to go easy on Johnnie this term, what with everything. Maybe this was all supposed to be a big, character-building show to indicate that he wasn't. Or maybe he really was just a lunatic. Because that happens, right? By the time we got dressed and out and down the avenue of ragged elms to the classroom at the end of school by the Chapel courtyard, it was well into the second period of double maths. So, Johnnie went off to third set and I went off to the top one, walking pinkly through the class and squeezing into my seat next to Alan.

'Waaaagh?' said Mrs Ellson, like an angry Chewbacca this time, and she gave me four sides then and there. Sides, by the way, were this traditional Eskmount punishment that involved mindlessly copying bits from a Latin textbook onto special blue A4 paper. Honestly, the more I think about that place, the weirder literally everything about it actually was.

★

The other big thing I remember about the first day back is the fight that Johnnie had. That was later, though. First, there were lessons, which were just lessons; teachers trying to make us feel stressed about the exams. I wasn't, really. I'd switched from Scottish Standard Grade to GCSE when I'd moved schools, because Eskmount was teaching us how to fake it as English people. This should have left me a bit behind, but I'd had basically no friends for the past six months, so I'd had a lot of time to work. It was all easy except for the boring bits, which were impossible. I didn't care. Is this even interesting? I'm pretty smart. It was fine.

Then, sport. Alan and Johnnie were both great at cricket.

Alan was in the First XI despite only being in fifth form, which was unusual. Johnnie wasn't, but everybody reckoned he would be next year. We hadn't done cricket at Acton's, so I was thrown into this insane multi-year hockey league for everybody else who didn't make the grade. That was pretty rough. There was this whole crew of upper sixth-formers who were into death metal, but in a much more scary and less endearing way than Luci was, and they'd wear terrifying T-shirts with skulls on them and charge around shouting about Satan. This one time, some really small kid in the year above got literally knocked out by a ball the moment he stepped onto the pitch.

It was funny, in a way, because the kid was called Payne, and the mental death metallers loved shouting 'PAIN' at him. This time he ran onto the pitch and Eugene, this huge, insane and, I feel, somehow Russian bloke with terrible skin, roared, 'PAIN,' and hit the hard orange ball at him, and it socked straight into his forehead. Really loud. Payne was running, and it was like a wrestling clothesline. Wham, flat on his back. I'd seen kids get concussed before, mainly in rugby, but that was totally different. They'd stand up and run around in random directions, shouting mad shit about their mothers or lunch. This kid just lay on his back until the ambulance came. He was okay in the end, though. Look, I'm getting distracted. I just mentioned all that to tell you about Eugene. He comes up in a minute. In the fight.

After tea, which was what we called supper, we had prep, which was what we called homework. After that, you had an hour and a bit until Evening Triple, after which you had to go to bed. People would chat, or hang out, or watch the one telly each house had between the lot of us. The cool kids, though, would go and smoke at the Dump.

The Dump was a patch of overgrown wilderness behind the really pretty walled garden that sprang out of the side of Smethwick Castle. Once, I think, there had been a skip there, hence the name and the occasional rubble, but now there were just some straggly trees and bushes snaking back to the fence that separated us from this forlorn local park. You could be seen crossing the hockey pitch to get there by any teacher who cared to look, but once you got there you couldn't be seen from anywhere. Once in a while, a couple of the teachers would turn up, sometimes with a car at each end, to catch whoever they could. Everybody called this a 'raid'. Like it was *Boyz n the Hood*.

Wild garlic grew there, which meant that in the summer you could always smell which kids had been there the night before. You kinda knew, though, anyway. I'd started going the term before. Not with anyone. Just by myself, to see what it was like. It was dark during the winter, though, and all you could see were the little red dots of everybody's Marlboro. Quite a few of the sixth-form girls would go, too, although you weren't always sure which ones they were. It was like some secret Renaissance sex club, where everyone wore masks. Just without the sex. Or the masks.

That night, I went by myself, too. Johnnie had already gone off with this huge and quite smelly kid called Tank from the year above, and I hadn't wanted to be all 'Hey, we're friends now! So, I shall come, too!' I had been hoping he'd ask, but he didn't. Maybe he'd forgotten I might want to. I gave it ten minutes, so as not to be needy, and then I went over myself. Now it was April, so it wasn't dark when we got there, but it would be by the time we left. There were maybe thirty kids there. Everybody looked up to see who I was, in case I was staff or some evil prefect. Nobody seemed to mind that I was just me. Johnnie was in a huddle by a bush with Alan and Barf. I joined them. They said hi, like it was normal. Funny, how hard my heart was beating. I can still remember how it felt. Like I'd already had a fright.

Eugene wasn't there yet. He was easy to spot when he was, partly thanks to the leather jacket he'd wear in the evenings, all messed up and studded. It had a skull on the back, which Luci had done with paint. He was a really good artist, Luci. Although not in the same way that Alan was, because all he'd really do was stuff like skulls. He'd do them on jackets and DM boots for anybody, in exchange for the right amount of fags or vodka. Later that term, this girl called Matilda in upper sixth, who everybody fancied more than you'd believe, asked him to do a portrait of Kurt Cobain on the side of her cherry reds, and he got really stressed, spending like a fortnight on it and totally screwing it up.

The other reason Eugene was easy to spot was that he was a head taller than everybody else. And that head was huge, like it belonged to Jaws from *Moonraker*, but with a spidery white scar on his chin from when he'd sledged into a barbed wire fence as a kid. My point being, he definitely wasn't there at first, but once the light fell, you could suddenly hear his voice booming around, talking about death. I was over by Alan and Johnnie by then, and at first it was just background noise. Gradually, though, phrases started drifting through the air, and it was pretty obvious which specific death incident he was talking about.

'Nobody,' Eugene was declaiming, 'shoots himself in the mouth. Nobody. You don't have long enough fingers. So that's murder, my friends. Hardcore.'

We all fell silent.

'Unless you're a spastic,' said Eugene, and then he did a brief impression of Johnnie's dead brother, with a disability, shooting himself in the mouth.

'Jesus,' said Barf, in disgust.

We could see each other, but not Eugene. He was maybe twenty metres away. But so loud.

'Gun through the teeth?' Eugene was saying. 'That's an assassin. Like a cock. Suck it, bitch.'

'Sick, man,' said somebody else, but approvingly.

'Okay, look,' said Alan uncomfortably, 'shall I go and . . .'

He trailed off. Johnnie didn't say anything, so at first I thought he was giving us all a cue to just pretend it wasn't happening. Can do, I thought. Only then Barf shouted the words 'Scar-faced cunt' really loudly, and I realised that wasn't how things were going to pan out.

Eugene wasn't bothered. Shouting abuse at older, stronger boys at the Dump was an ancient tradition.

'I don't know who you are, man,' he shouted back, 'but you'd better run.'

'Wait,' said Johnnie, but to us. Then he stooped down and picked up a couple of half-bricks from the rubble on the ground. One in each hand. You know those bricks with the circular holes in them? Those. These, he hefted for a few moments, thoughtfully.

'Mate . . .' began Alan, 'you don't need to . . .'

Johnnie smiled at him. Then he turned on his heel and

threw one of the bricks, overarm, in the direction of Eugene's voice. He was over among us in seconds, with other kids from his year trailing behind.

'Motherfucker,' he said, sounding shocked. He had a hand to his chest. 'That could have knocked my teeth out. Which of you—'

'Me,' said Johnnie quite calmly.

Eugene stared at him. Then he shook his head and seemed to realise he had an audience.

'I'm going to hurt you,' he said, in that overblown mid-Atlantic Hollywood way of his, but meaning it, too. 'I'm going to make you beg for the sweet release of—'

'He's his brother, you prick,' said Alan, who had this unshakeable confidence, even then.

'Leave it,' said Johnnie.

'Whose brother?' said Eugene, bewildered.

'Douglas Burchill's brother,' said Alan. 'The dead guy?'

'Oh,' said somebody back in the darkness. 'That's Johnnie.'

Eugene frowned. Then he peered at Johnnie. Then his big cartoon-war-criminal face crumpled into uncertainty.

'Look, man,' he said. 'I was just messing about. I, like, respect your position. I can see that was bad. But you threw a brick. That's not cool.'

'I respect your position, too,' said Johnnie, very seriously, and then he used the other brick to hit him in the face.

6

FOR ME, I SUPPOSE, that was the first time I properly understood Johnnie. The first time I had him marked out, like I would from then on, as a person only tenuously bound by the usual rules. Because it was unusual, the brick thing. Casual violence was pretty frequent, but it was usually ritualised, as a process of semi-traditional abuses and humiliations of younger boys by older ones.

Down at the bottom of the scale was 'bedposting', which involved tipping somebody's bed upright while they were still in it, trapping them against the wall. Sixth-formers would often rampage through the dorms doing that on the last night of term. Or, indeed, any other night.

There was also 'run the gauntlet', which involved older kids wrapping pillows around hockey sticks and forming a tunnel of thumps, through which younger ones had to run. There was 'trunking', which involved being put in a trunk – helpfully, everyone had a trunk – and slid down the stairs. There was the 'brown-eye rub', where somebody would wipe their arse on your white shirt or sheet, although that had fallen out of favour by my day, and I'm not sure I ever saw it done. And there were a variety of other ways you could be locked in things, dunked in things, hung out of things, tied to things, or have various items of clothes embarrassingly added or removed. I missed out on most of it by arriving late. Little was driven by actual animosity, and younger kids, I suppose, consoled themselves with the thought that one day they'd get to do it to somebody else. Before he'd been a monster, in other words, Eugene had probably had a pretty rough time himself. I mean, you'd hope.

None of that, though, helped anybody process a younger kid smashing an older one in the face with a brick. Twice, actually. Once as he stood, and then again when he was on his knees. That had no category. It didn't map on. So, nothing happened. You know that bit in *Scum*, when Ray Winstone knobbles that kid with the pool balls and batters the other kid in the washroom, and then the screw comes along and the kid is all covered in blood and woozy and the screw shouts, 'Name him! Name him!' and the kid just mumbles, 'I slipped, sir,' over and over again? Well, it was like that. Johnnie walked off, and Eugene got picked up and taken to A&E, minus two teeth. Teachers asked questions to which they already knew the answer, but they didn't get the answer they already knew, so they chose another one. Within an hour, officially, Eugene had been hit by a cricket ball. But everybody knew.

Perhaps that was why the headmaster never mentioned Douglas, even once. He was this very smooth guy, the head, in a big-eared Prince Charles sort of way. Everybody thought he had ambitions for politics. We had School Triple every day, and it would always be a speech about morality, or life-lessons, or the Character of an Eskmounter. I'd heard he bloody loved it when people actually died. Three years earlier, people said, some girl went off a cliff on a skiing holiday, and he'd got a whole week out of that. But there was not a sniff about Douglas. No lessons, no platitudes. Maybe the head had written the eulogy already but then had to throw it away. Poor guy.

For Eugene, anyway, it wasn't that bad to lose two teeth from a brick. In fact, it was pretty cool. Also, Johnnie did still have a dead brother. So, in a way, Eugene looked good for saying nothing, and he still got to walk into breakfast smirking the next day. Look, we're a complicated tribe.

It was maybe two weeks afterwards that Johnnie got taken away by the police. We all thought we knew why. Even the next day after the bricking, people were covering their mouths and shouting 'Psycho!' at him when he walked past, a bit like the way they used to shout 'Scarfaced cunt!' or sometimes 'Huge-eeen!' at Eugene. But about ten days after all that had happened, a Tayside Police Rover pulled into the car park outside Esk House during morning break, and two coppers got out while a bunch of us stared out of the window from Jerusalem dorm, and then Toad sent a third-former to go and fetch Johnnie from the tuck shop and bring him back to the office. And I did wonder, at that point, whether hitting somebody in the face with a brick might have consequences, after all.

He was back before lunch, though, and I found him smoking in the upstairs tub room. A tub room, by the way, was a communal washroom. Tubs were baths, and this room only had showers in it, but it was still a tub room. Look, I don't make the rules. He was pale and twitchy, stubbing out one fag and lighting another.

'And?' I said, trick-clicking my fake Zippo to light my own, as you did.

'It's fine,' he said, although he didn't look fine, and I waited for him to say something else, but he didn't. There were a few older kids in there, but they were mainly lower-status older kids you didn't really need to worry about. The only exception was Fleece, who was this rugby-mad kid in Luci's year with really curly hair, and he asked Johnnie if he was going to jail. And Johnnie said, 'Not yet,' and he said, 'Psycho!' and the other kids sniggered in a slightly scared way, and then they all went off for lunch.

'Seriously,' I said, once they were gone, 'what happened?'

Johnnie sighed. I hadn't finished my cigarette, but he'd now finished his and he obviously wanted to go.

'I mean, how did they even find out?' I said. 'Somebody must have called them.'

'It wasn't about Eugene,' said Johnnie.

I didn't say anything.

'It was about my brother,' he said.

Doesn't make sense, I thought. He can't be dead again.

'They *think*,' said Johnnie sardonically, 'that there was somebody else in the car. When it happened. When the gun went off.'

So, obviously, I said, 'Who?' And Johnnie looked angrier than ever, but also now somehow scornful, and he said, 'Maybe me.'

★

By May you'd walk to the Dump in the light, smoke in the light and head to bed in the light, too. 'It's ten o'clock, light outside, and they're sending us to bed,' Luci used to grumble. Those long Scottish evenings, though, were something. Ethereal. Spiced with tobacco and garlic. At the Dump, the light was green except for where it cut through the foliage in yellow shards. The hour after prep was a no-man's land, too, authority in retreat. You could wear your own clothes by then, but the norm was a strange, sartorial goulash, with school trousers and T-shirts, or half a tracksuit, or white rugby shorts and a sweater. Lots of hats. The girls had less strict uniform rules – any white shirt, any long skirt – and, come evening, they'd accessorise with boots and scarves, moving among us like smoking Amish.

The only sport-free afternoon was Wednesday, when we had the Combined Cadet Force, instead. This basically involved a whole bunch of marching about in scratchy green uniforms and learning how to strip and reassemble a gun, which sounds more fun than it was. They were SA80s, and the school had about a million of them locked up in a building called the Armoury, and I never did figure out whether they could actually fire anything or not. CCF ended just after half-term, anyway, with a thing called the Annual General Inspection, when we all had to stand out on one of the rugby pitches for an hour or two while the headmaster, and his ears, and some visiting bigwig army wanker would very slowly walk up and down, looking at our boots. Every year, a couple of people would pass out, always in the same way. They'd go from the knees first and then pitch face forwards, elbows bucking back. That first year I was there we were studying the First World War in history, and I remember reading about how people in the trenches would collapse when they'd been shot, and it was pretty much the same. Each year, a bunch of kids stood by as stretcher-bearers.

After the AGI we had Wednesdays free, supposedly to revise. Normally Alan, Johnnie and I would sneak out towards the sea wall, behind Musselburgh race course. Sometimes Barf would come, too. Cockenzie power station loomed down the coast, and this was a place of lagoons and mudflats, where they turned the ash into landfill. Ugly as sin. Sometimes the flats were pools and sometimes they were just fields, but there was also a stage in between where they were grey like the moon, and soft and terrifying, and surrounded by signs saying, DANGER OF DEATH, KEEP OUT, although of course we would not. Stand still and you'd sink, probably forever. Barf was the bravest, basically strolling, like he was bored. I was terrified, although less so when I did it myself than when I watched Johnnie make the run. He'd scurry like a rat, tripping, falling and rolling, down to his knees and back up again. Sneering, somehow, all the way. Probably it was also because of the history lessons, but to this day whenever I think of the Somme I think of there. Boys running. Barf facing down the guns. Alan stuck, twisting on a fence. Johnnie's cold arm sticking out of the mud.

Exams came and went, and they were nothing unexpected. I revised hard for a week, filling my head up with Macbeth, geography, chemical bonds and Aggressive European Nationalism in the 1930s, but I pretty much knew it all already. Alan was conscientious; Johnnie, not so much.

The day after exams finished, the school packed our whole year off to this army camp for a week, I suppose as a way of making sure we didn't cause too much chaos with nothing to do. That was a place called Cultybraggan, and people used to talk about it in hushed tones of dread. They search your bag on the way in, people said, which meant everybody's major concern was where to hide their fags. People would hide them inside Pot Noodles, or wrap them up in the paper from bars of soap. Legend had it that one kid had hidden a pack of twenty individually stuffed down the middle of packets of Polos, but I actually tried that once and the holes were too tight. Mine went in a shoe. It was fine.

All week, in those stupid, scratchy uniforms. The camp itself was cold and weird, built during the war for captured Nazis. Scrubby grass, ugly buildings, all these chickens hopping around. You'd sleep in these freezing, half-tube buildings called 'billets' with corrugated iron roofs. There were kids from lots of other schools there the same week, but they all seemed to be volunteers, unlike the conscripts that we were. This meant they were clean, neat, precise, while we were a ragtag bunch of disasters. The place was run by real army NCOs, and they were a lot less nice than teachers. When we weren't marching, we were running. One day there was an assault course, which would have been fun if it wasn't for the way you had to keep doing the whole thing again and again until you could get around in under three minutes. I was with Wee Geordie Mcchan, and we were properly shit at getting over the high wall. There was also canoeing, during which all the terrifying squaddies kept making us capsize in water so freezingly Baltic that your chest would seize up and you'd shiver for the next three hours. I'm serious. It was fucking awful.

My big memory of it all, though, happened after the canoeing. We were all a mess by then; beaten down and trembling. That afternoon we had a class called 'Survival', which sounded ominous, but it was all happening in one of the corrugated billets, which was an immediate relief, because there's a limit to how exhausted you can get without going outside. This one had bagpipe music coming out of it, which was a surprise. This fat, merry, red-faced sergeant major met us at the door. 'In ye come, lads!' he shouted, but nicely. 'Swing your arms! March tae the pipes!' So, we did, and inside there was a screen set up and, best of all, seats. Which meant we were going to be sitting down.

We sat. The music ended, the lights dimmed, and the screen started showing us a Bugs Bunny cartoon. Weird, yes, but definitely the best bit of the week so far. You could feel yourself calming down and warming up. It was a break, it was civilised. Nobody was shouting at us, and it was all going to be okay. Five minutes in, and the assault course and freezing reservoir were both a distant memory. And that was when the jolly sergeant major pulled the plug, plunged us into darkness and opened up with a machine gun.

Blanks echoed off the corrugated iron roof. So loud. People were on the floor, holding their heads, but I was transfixed and staring. Flash. Flash. Flash. The soldier, flickering, arm drawn back. And then, through the strobes, arrived a flapping chicken, descending onto the shoulder of this small, quite prim Glaswegian kid called Michael. The lights came on. Michael looked at chicken, chicken looked at Michael. At least one of them was screaming.

Then he had to kill it. Or, technically, we both did. I don't know why the sergeant major picked me. I suppose it was the way I was just sitting there, staring. Either way, I had to hold the thing down. I can remember the feel of it, all warm and fluttery. A tiny mad heart, beating fast, not mad enough not to know exactly where all of this was headed. Michael had to twist the neck and pull. He didn't twist enough. It got really long – a foot long, maybe – before the chicken was dead. Then we had to pluck it. Somebody else tried to tug the guts out of the head hole, but couldn't. They came out the other end.

Then there were more chickens, so other people could have a go. Johnnie and Barf both did theirs in seconds; bodies under the arm, fingers round the head, flap, flap, all done. The smell, though, once the things came open. I'll never forget it. Not like chicken. Like vomit, and darkness, and despair, and the unforgiven underside of everything. Somewhere in one of them, the jolly sergeant major found a tiny yellow egg. He ate it. Honestly, was your school like this? How mental do think you'd have been, if it was?

★

Afterwards, we went around the back of our billet and smoked. It was drizzling, but at least you didn't have to worry about getting caught. For all the talk beforehand, smoking was actually something the army didn't seem to care about at all. Every drag I took, I could smell my hand. Musty and brown, like it would never get clean. Honestly, the bastards. An exam on Macbeth before all that. Fie, my lord, fie.

'But you must have killed something before?' said Barf.

I shrugged. Flies. Ants. Maybe a bee.

'A rabbit?' he persisted. 'A pheasant?'

'Why would I have killed a rabbit or a pheasant?'

'Or a fish.'

'A fish?'

'They're not like us,' said Alan, who was a bit green, too. 'They're hicks, Tommo. They're a whole different thing.'

7

BOTH OF MY PARENTS were home when term ended because my mum's various scleroses were either multiplying more, or perhaps less, depending on what the good one was, and the bastard detective butler was taking the summer off, too. They made a big fuss about how wonderful this was, so I did, too, even though I was only there for two days before shoving my kilt and sleeping bag into a rucksack to go to Fusty's twenty-first birthday party.

'Sorry,' said my dad, as he drove me through Holyrood Park towards Waverley station. 'You're going where? With whom?'

'The MacPhails. A place called Auchnastang in Perthshire. Although I'll probably stay with Johnnie's family next door.'

Then my dad said, 'Philip MacPhail?' and I said, 'You know him?' because Philip was Fusty's real name, and I'd forgotten his uncle was called that, too.

'Only by reputation,' said my dad. 'Brr. Bit of a shark. Worse than a shark. Remember all that hoo-hah with the halls at the polytechnic? The body on the building site?'

I did not. But I did know that MacPhail owned a construction company. From the Portaloo stuff.

'And you're at school with his son?' said my dad, getting that look.

'It's his nephew,' I said. 'But no.'

My dad sighed.

'I actually know his daughter,' I said, and I thought of Flora and the one conversation we'd had, and I wondered if that was even true. 'Through Johnnie Burchill and Alan Campbell. It's a bit like the last party, actually.'

'Campbell?' said my dad. 'As in Mungo's boy?'

'Oh, you know him, too?' I said, feeling a bit harassed now.

'Moray Place,' said my dad. 'I suppose they have a lot of books?'

I had no idea what he was talking about.

'I was at a party with him once,' said my dad quite wistfully. 'With my publisher. I think he was the literary editor at *The Scotsman* then. Of course, no time for the likes of me.'

'I haven't met him,' I said, feeling somehow embarrassed for the both of us about what he'd just said. 'It's Johnnie who is Flora's friend, really, not Alan. Although he is, too. And so am I.'

Then my dad put on the voice he'd use when he was finding things amusing for reasons I didn't understand and said this was awfully complex. And I got a bit annoyed and said, 'Not really, actually.' Then my dad said he'd forgotten how Byzantine teenage friendships were, and I didn't say anything.

'Byzantine,' said my father. 'As in, from Byzantium. You've heard of Byzantium?'

'Of course,' I said, because Byzantium was this hippyish bar above a bookshop and bric-a-brac market on Victoria Street where you could buy beer without ID, along with toasted cheese sandwiches, for about two quid. Johnnie and I had spent a Sunday afternoon in there, just before exams.

'There's less of that sort of thing as you get older,' said my dad sadly.

'I suppose there would be,' I said, wondering if I'd go completely insane when I was old, too.

★

Alan was at the station, leaning against the wall by John Menzies, like he was waiting for somebody from *NME* to come along and take a photo. I jumped out the car and waved off my dad, trying to shake the feeling of being a kid handed from one grown-up to another. A beige, plasticky train took us to Perth and then a grimy Gleneagles Stagecoach took us to Auchternethy and beyond.

That part of Perthshire isn't quite the Highlands yet. It undulates, rather than soars. There are pine forests and fields, and roads are studded with bristled pancakes that were once rabbits that were just too slow. Alan, who had done the journey many times before, knew exactly which lay-by we had to get off. It was nowhere, really – by a field, by a forest – but on the other side of a barbed wire fence was a track, and on that track was a rusty yellow Renault with the windows open, blasting The Lemonheads, and in the car was Johnnie, smoking a Regal Filter. Still sixteen, he couldn't drive on the road but this, already, was the farm.

Obviously, we could have got off half a mile down the road, nearer the house, but then Johnnie wouldn't have been able to show off his car. It had cost him £40 at an auction in Crieff a year ago, with a week left on the MOT. Douglas had driven it back for him, and it was his in which to roam the fields until it gave out altogether. Johnnie said he'd done that with his last car, too, which had lasted eighteen months. By my maths he was going to have a bit of an issue six months from now, what with Douglas not being around to get him another. Although I didn't say that out loud. I went in the back, with the bags.

The castle was literally next door, which meant seven seconds of illegality crossing the A823 and then into fields on the other side. Johnnie didn't usually joyride the tracks and fields on the MacPhail side, but nobody minded him rattling along the tracks to visit Flora, provided he stayed out of the way of the tractors. We did three sides of a rapeseed hillside and then went through a gate in a massive ten-foot-high hedge onto a gravel driveway, and there was the castle, squatting over us. These days, I'd know it as a late, restrained Scottish Baronial, veering towards completely preposterous around the odd attic window. Back then I'd have just called it 'massive'.

There were already loads of cars and all sorts of people rushing around carrying balloons, tables and crates of glasses. There was a marquee at the front, on a huge oval lawn bounded by the driveway, with the front of it facing directly towards the house. By the front door we saw Fusty standing on a chair pinning up bunting, with a blonde woman in a pink cardigan looking up at him crossly. In turn, Fusty was scowling at the bunting, in a manner that suggested he hated it and blamed it for all of life's misfortunes. Then the woman swivelled her head and looked at us crossly instead. I suppose she looked a bit like Flora. Well. A cross between Flora and the Queen.

'Around the back,' she shouted.

Alan wound down his window. 'Afternoon, Mrs M.'

'Don't call me that,' she said.

'Afternoon, Emma,' said Alan instead.

'Hello, Alan,' she said. 'Johnnie. Philip, say hello to your friends.'

Fusty glanced at us and said nothing, feasibly logging us in the same category as the bunting. Johnnie was stony-faced. Mrs M didn't seem interested in me at all.

Flora was, though. We parked as instructed around the back, where everything was a bit more brickish and industrial. More cars, a tractor, a quad bike. Flora came out of a back door in jeans and a jumper, and Alan and Johnnie both got a hug.

'I remember you,' she said, and then I got one, too.

'And I remember your breasts,' I wanted to say but, of course, didn't. Her hair smelled of pine. She told us to go and help them set up the bar in the marquee, sounding quite a lot more like her mother than I'd anticipated she ever could. Although by the time we got there, somehow, Johnnie had faded away.

★

He turned up much later, when the party was about to start. We were in a bedroom upstairs, all green and frilly, getting into kilts and shirts and socks. I had the kilt and socks from school, obviously, but my dad's silver-buttoned Bonnie Prince Charlie jacket had hung on me like a tent, and a blithe stroll into one of the shops that sold the things on the Royal

Mile had revealed them to be horrifyingly expensive. In a flash of inspiration, though, I'd found one in Armstrong's – this weird old second-hand shop where they mainly sold fancy dress and leather – for £15. The lining was brown and it smelled of mothballs, but I realised now that the same was true of the jacket Alan was wearing, and of Johnnie's, too. Theirs had been in their families for generations. Mine had just been in somebody else's.

Johnnie said he'd gone for a walk to see the loch, although he was slurring and his lips were wine-red. By then I had a buzz on, too, from the beer we'd drunk in the bar and the spliff we'd had in the car, and from the shots we'd both taken from the cut glass decanter of whisky that our room had on the mantelpiece. It never feels like that again, does it? That feeling you get, when you're that young and a party is about to kick off. The way the hairs on your neck go up and stay there, and your pulse quickens with delicious anxiety, and you're half-desperate to dive in and half-wishing the whole thing could be over and done with already.

First it was evening, and then the sun set over Auchnastang, and then it was dark. There were drinks, then reels, then dinner, then a disco. I suppose reels after dinner (lamb) wouldn't have done anybody any favours. I largely sat them out, even beforehand, mainly because I didn't know what to do. Also, Alan was stuck to Flora like glue by then, somehow, and Johnnie kept going outside with this lean, chuckling guy called Dean to smoke weed. Girls usually liked Johnnie because he was doe-eyed and cool and the scar under his eye was in exactly the right place, but that night Johnnie didn't seem very interested. Turned out Dean lived in the village and worked on the farm. He was nice enough, but after the third trip round the back of the marquee I left them to it, because there was a whole new world inside and I wanted to see how it worked.

Fusty was a year older than Douglas would have been. His friends were here, and Flora's friends, but also adults of a strange sort of Scottish rural aristocracy. At least half of them sounded English. The men were sometimes fat and sometimes hard army trim, in tartan trews and patent shoes, or sometimes those weird, embroidered slippers with heels. Big MacPhail himself, Flora's dad, was the Platonic Form of the first type: red-faced with sandy Hitler hair and a belly like a Space Hopper. He had that mannerism I'd noticed before from Fusty, of pinching his trousers below the pockets to tug up the legs whenever he sat down. How does a thing like that get passed down? Surely not unconsciously. Surely somebody has to copy somebody else.

That whole night, I saw Big MacPhail dance only once, crisply but unsmiling, as if it were a duty. Not long afterwards, I came out of the toilet when he was outside it, chatting with some other similar sort of bastard, about to go in.

'Mr MacPhail,' I said, holding out a hand. 'I'm Tom Dwarkin. Thanks for having me.'

'Don't think I want to touch that,' he said, and his sidekick roared and perhaps I went a bit pink.

The women mainly had pearl earrings and hair like Peter Stringfellow. There was one more incongruous-looking pair on his table, who were obviously family of some sort, and a couple, but whom I couldn't place at all. She was small, mousy, almost invisible, in an austere dress that, when you concentrated, made her look like the ghost of a Puritan. He was huge and glowering, with a Brian Blessed beard. They never seemed to speak, not even to each other. Periodically he'd stand up and go meaningfully outside, like he was security. Later, I'd learn that this was a man called Iain. And that he actually was security. In a way.

A small handful of people, a generation up, centred around an elderly woman who had the same regal hair as Flora's mum and a stare and a chin like an American president. This was MacPhail's mother, Flora's grandmother. Not so long ago, I supposed, they had been the stout parents themselves, and before that the wild and excitable teens, in parties much like this one, generations before.

Flora, by the way, was in a shimmering blue dress that looked like underwear. She had messed-up Courtney Love make-up on beneath her scarlet hair, and where others wore heels, she wore Doc Marten boots. She must have looked like nobody else for miles, and yet she didn't seem out of place. I honestly couldn't say for certain whether this is a memory, or just something I've told myself is a memory because of everything that was to come. But despite looking like she'd come from another, trendier, hip London planet, she definitely acted like she belonged on this one. The dutiful hostess daughter, kissing her mother's friends on the cheeks and tinkling demurely up to well-trussed men. No, I'm sure it's a memory. I can see it now.

The older generation danced differently to the young, more precisely, like showponies I'd seen on telly doing dressage at the Olympics. My age group were more haphazard and savage. With some reels you'd get one group meeting another, generations intermingling, leering gents spinning blushing teenage girls, or strapping lads accidentally clotheslining old grannies. There was a strange egalitarian feel to it, by which I suppose I just mean that the kids all drank and smoked, and the adults didn't mind. At one point I did a thing with Alan and Flora both, the three of us in a line, stomp, stomp, stomp, clap, clap, clap. That was okay. Mainly I just sat and watched.

Fusty danced, too, dutifully, shirt slick and translucent with sweat. There was a girl he seemed attached to, horsey, lots of teeth, but he didn't seem to like her any more then he had the three of us, or the bunting. Sometimes he'd snap at her when she got the steps wrong. I knew that Flora also had a couple of much younger siblings, both girls, but they were nowhere to be seen.

The last reel was an eightsome. In hostess mode, Flora wanted a group, and she shoved me together with a girl called Trixie: dark, freckled and green-eyed in a black velvet dress. I could smell her perfume. It was like she was somebody's mum.

'I don't know what I'm doing,' I said to her, and she took my hand in the thrilling damp porcelain of her own and said that she didn't, either. At one point I had to go in the middle of a circle and dance alone. I channelled Elvis. Apparently, this was good. When it was her turn, she let her curtains of hair do the work, flicking it this way and that, while spinning and keeping her green eyes on me. Then the dance finished, and her hand was in mine still.

We were on the same table, too, with Flora's friends. Trixie, I was starting to realise, was as drunk as a lord. Drunker than a few, actually, because there were surely some here. Quite a lot of what she said was a bit annoying, and much of the rest didn't make much sense. Up close, I could occasionally see that the things she had done with her make-up were making her look older than she was. She was at school with Flora, down south, and lived in a place called Dorset. She'd never been to Scotland before, she told me, pouring the red wine so badly that the white tablecloth made me think of a nosebleed. She smoked Marlboro Lights, because everybody did. When she took them from her mouth, her purple-brown lipstick left a line. When I leaned over to pour her wine, a mothball smell came from under my arms. Her bra strap was green, too.

After the meal we danced to 'Deeply Dippy' by Right Said Fred and 'Black Betty' by whoever that was by. We were right up close, and her hair in my face felt cool and wonderful, as expected. And then, by the time the DJ started up with 'Insanity' by Oceanic, we were somehow out behind the big, high hedge that separated the driveway from the fields, and her squirming tongue was in my mouth and mine was in hers. She tasted of cigarettes and wine and, feasibly, just a touch, of vomit.

'I've got a boyfriend,' she whispered, breaking off, and then her hand went up between my legs, all the same, and mine went up between hers, too. My ridiculous silver jacket cuff buttons snagging on her tights. With me wondering, with every inch my hand progressed, exactly what I was supposed to do with it when it got to the top.

★

Much later, I slept in the room where we'd got changed, along with about twelve other teenagers. The room was a chaos of limbs and kilts and sleeping bags and taffeta

75

dresses scrunched back into bolts of cloth. It was my first experience, that night, of the way these people's parties are exercises in degeneration. You start all trussed up and shiny, hair neat, dress straight, laces on kilt shoes wrapped up to the knee. Then, past midnight, the collars are all open and there are bodies on the driveway and piles of vomit under every hedge. Lots of weddings are like this, I suppose. But the posh train young.

Trixie had abandoned me once we'd gone back into the tent, sashaying across the dancefloor into memory. Part of me was disappointed, but I also didn't actually want to spend the rest of the night with her when there was so much else to soak in. Johnnie had reappeared, this time with a bottle of whisky. For a while I was a booze lad, involved in some drinking game with him and a variety of men up to the age of about seventy. There was a burned cork, you repeated rhymes, you got it wrong, then you marked yourself like an American football player.

Eventually Flora's dad joined the table, and Johnnie abruptly peeled away. Ten minutes later I went to find him – Johnnie, not Flora's dad – and he was stretched out on four chairs by the dancefloor, quite asleep. We carried him upstairs, me and Alan and two other guys I didn't know from Fusty's old school. We had him under the arms, they took his feet.

'Tragedy, what happened to him,' one of them said.

'Mmm,' I said, wondering if he just meant tonight, or everything.

The party ended not long afterwards, with 'Auld Lang Syne'. The room formed into a circle, and everybody held hands. Then, for the chorus, people just ran at each other, in crashing, bashing, thundering chaos. Then they crossed arms for verse two and did it again. There were people on the floor and shoes all over the place. It was basically your one last chance to really mess up any old granny who had escaped you in 'Strip The Willow'.

After that, disintegration. Fusty spent a while barking at people about an afterparty down by the loch, but then the rain came. Alan and I smoked a couple of joints in Johnnie's car and then headed into the house. He went to find Flora. I roamed the house, which seemed to be full of tartan living rooms in which young men with massive thighs were smoking cigars. I drank a whisky, and another, and another, and I crawled off to find a patch of floor next to Johnnie, who was out cold in the bed. Somehow it was 3 a.m.

8

IN THE MORNING, ONLY about five hours later, I found Flora in the kitchen. Big woollen jumper, feet and bottom curled into the same wooden chair, sipping a huge mug of tea with both hands. She looked well scrubbed. Head-girlish. Like a swimmer.

'Déjà vu,' she said.

'I'm not much of a sleeper,' I said, wondering whether to make a joke about AIDS. This was a nicer kitchen than the last one I'd seen her in, all pastel wood and blue and white tiles. There was an Aga and a big wooden table, because all these people's kitchens have those, but this was the sort with curtains, too.

'You're not leaving?' she said. 'Already?'

'No!' I said. 'I mean, how? No wheels.'

Flora grinned. 'I have wheels.'

The wheels, it turned out, were a quad bike. The body was go-faster red with a black leatherette seat, and it had gauntlets over the handlebars with a smart-looking walkie-talkie thing on the wrist. Flora left me standing in the yard out back, next to Johnnie's car, and then roared out of a shed on the thing, nearly making me shit myself. Then she told me to climb on the back and I did, gripping behind my bottom onto a black metal rack strung with frayed spider grips.

'Waist,' she said, over her shoulder, so I gingerly put my arms around the rough boiled wool of her jumper. My wrists were on her hips and her hair was in my face. I did not feel like Marlon Brando. Then we were off, with a jerk, and I realised that if I'd held on anywhere else, I'd now be lying on my back in the mud.

First, we took the gravel around the house and by the marquee. Maybe we were going faster than Johnnie's Renault ever had, or maybe it just felt that way. We were going in the opposite direction to the day before, away from the loch and the road, through a forest of fir and up a gentle hill and then, suddenly, a steep one. This, I'd learn, was the north of the estate, where the Grampian mountains carve down in a pioneering spit through Glen Tilt, like a jagged Highland spear. Improbably, we were out of farmlands and fields already and onto a moor dotted with purple heather. I was only in a T-shirt and shivered in our motion breeze, despite the early yellow sun.

'You can see half the world!' shouted Flora, spinning a half-turn and cutting the engine, and I realised we'd come to a ridge, somehow above everything, looking down over the valley. Ahead, beneath, there was the sweep of the forest, then the castle, then the loch, then the road, then farmlands beyond.

I lit a cigarette, struggling in the breeze, and offered her one, too. She said no, thanks, too early.

'Wow,' I said, looking out.

'So, Trixie?' she said, leaning into my ear, the chill breeze suddenly replaced by her mouth's thrilling warm one.

'Yeah,' I said. 'I mean, a bit. She said she had a boyfriend?'

'Like, *eight* boyfriends,' snorted Flora, and I sensed I shouldn't admit that this immediately made her more attractive, rather than less.

The wind was too strong for smoking; my cigarette was growing long and orange and pointy, so that it felt ungainly, like an urban mistake. Perhaps the end would blow off, start a fire in the heather. Didn't that happen? Fires? Flora's hair was redder than the tip, and when she moved her head it splayed across her air-blushed face, making it soft-focus, like Vaseline on a lens.

'That's Burnside,' she said, suddenly, pointing to the fields beyond Auchnastang.

'Where Johnnie lives?' I said.

'It was all joined together once. Same estate. But some Victorian was terribly modern. So, the son got ours, and the sisters shared theirs. Ages ago. And that's why ours is still just ours and will be forever, and theirs has always been owned by about fifty thousand people and is a big old mess.'

'You're related?' I said, still struggling with this because I knew she'd been Johnnie's girlfriend once, too.

'Distantly. Maybe I'm his immoral aunt. Sexy, huh?'

'I guess,' I said, knowing she was joking, but also thinking it definitely was, yes.

Basically, she said, one of the Victorian sisters who inherited Burnside had been Johnnie's grandad's aunt. While the brother, who kept the castle, had been her and Fusty's great-grandfather.

'But Fusty's not your brother?' I said, still struggling to map this out.

'Cousin,' she said. 'First cousin. His mum's my dad's sister.

So, technically, he's Fusty Bonnar, not Fusty MacPhail. Although they changed it when he was about fifteen. After he came to live with us.'

I asked if something had happened to his parents, thinking this might give him an excuse for appearing to be such an awful wanker, although she said they were fine. They'd even been at the party. His dad was Iain Bonnar, the big, bearish, security-type guy, and his mum was Elspeth, the Puritan ghost woman who had been by his side. Bonnar worked for Flora's dad sometimes, but he was also the managing factor at Burnside, which was Johnnie's farm, as the latest in a long line of people who had done that job since Johnnie's dad had died. They lived in a little cottage, between the farms.

'But he's the heir,' said Flora. 'Fusty, I mean. Since Delilah was born. That's when they decided. Because it's just me, her and Mary. All girls, see? And Mummy can't have any more. And it has to be a boy. So, one day, all this will be his. Not mine.'

'That's fucked up,' I said, and Flora gave me a sharp look. 'Sorry,' I said. 'Isn't it?'

'It's families.' Flora shrugged, looking out at the low, daffodil sun, and I thought about Fusty's parents in their lonely cottage, while their son lived in a castle with another family altogether, who all knew that one day their castle would be his, and not theirs at all. Then I thought of my own family, which was just made up of people, with zero discussion of what would go to whom or why, and not much even to go, anyway. Did owning stuff like mountains and fields make you happier than we were? Maybe. Although Fusty didn't exactly strike me as happy. Also, nobody in my family had ever shot their own head off, even once.

That was when she grabbed my arm and pointed with her other hand.

'It was right there,' she said, and it was like she'd been reading my mind. 'Where it happened. Above that ravine. Just along from the barn.'

★

And then, for the first time, I went to Burnside. Alan drove us there after bacon rolls, with me in the passenger seat this time and Johnnie green-faced and foetal in the back.

How to describe Burnside, particularly after Auchnastang? Definitely not a castle. Pretty once, perhaps, but not really anything so special at all. Put it this way, I doubt Pevsner was effusive. I remember it as a large, harled, yellow house, although the paint had deep, damp, dark V-shapes at every corner. The harl, in patches, had suffered flaking and baldness down to the grey stone beneath. Burnside was crumbling, though, not rotting, and I'd see enough of these houses over the next few years to learn the difference. You might say it had a structural deficit. As in, the money that needed to go out simply didn't match the money coming in. Nor had it done, I'd learn, since Johnnie's dad had died.

Inside, the floors were covered by threadbare tartan, and the walls, while all fairly freshly painted, had that old, damp horsehair plaster thing going on, which made them lumpy and irregular, turning the corridors in particular into something like those odd, whitewashed caves you get in Spain. It was cosy, though. You could feel, I suppose, the efforts being made to hold it all together. You could feel the love.

Johnnie's mum was out when we arrived, doing something to do with horses, but Johnnie said she'd had a couple of friends around the night before and there were eight or nine empty wine bottles on the kitchen table.

'A couple?' said Alan, as we went in the back and four thousand brown and white terriers yapped at our knees.

Johnnie shrugged, and I thought of all the wine bottles in my own kitchen, too.

I remember the smells. Wet dogs and wood fires and cigarettes and stews of red wine and meat. This kitchen – always with the kitchens – was brown and wooden and seemed like the sort of room you could bring a sheep into for a bit, and it wouldn't really stand out. From the window you could see a high wall, like the one by the Dump at school. Once, I'd learn later, this had been a walled garden, but today it had horses in it.

'Do you want some food?' said Johnnie weakly. 'Or . . . bacon?'

'We had bacon already,' said Alan. 'Go to bed.'

He did, and I went to the toilet. Wooden seat, porcelain cistern. Above it, framed on the wall, was a crocheted tapestry thing of a sad-looking pheasant. Beneath it, in the same frame, was a poem written in script, which began, 'Never, never let your gun / pointed be at anyone'. I also remember the last: 'All the pheasants ever bred / won't repay one man dead'. And I remember wondering whether they still even noticed it, and if so, why the hell they didn't take it down.

Alan and I ate more bacon, anyway, sandwiches on white

83

farmhouse loaf, and sat at the kitchen island smoking our
way through an open packet of Peter Stuyvesant that was
next to the kettle. I wasn't sure about this, but Alan said
there were thousands of boxes of the things up in the attic.
Johnnie's mum turned up on fag three, and I immediately
stubbed mine out.

'Och, don't be daft,' she said, giving Alan a hug. She was
a small, wiry woman with a dark bob and looked a lot like
Johnnie. Her name was Jenny. Muddy blue jeans, a blue
padded gilet and a knotted handkerchief around her neck
like she was a cowboy about to rob a bank. God knows where
all the wine had gone, but there was no evidence of it having
gone into her. She wasn't stopping, she told us, because she
was off up to Brenda's for the Sunday thing (?), and then
she was picking up the girls, but she hoped the party had
been good, and were we all staying tonight because there
was a pheasant casserole, and how was Alan's mother? Oh,
and also, where was Johnnie, and had everything been okay?
Because it wasn't always these days, excuse me while I get a
tissue. You get the idea. She didn't cry, as such. It was more
that her eyes went shiny, and she looked furious about it.
I liked her. When she left, she gave me a hug, too, and I
thought of my own mum, and how bony she'd become, and
the way I hugged her now like she was a bunch of delicate
lightbulbs in a bag.

*

Jack Burchill had died when Johnnie was nine, Douglas
was about twelve and the twins were basically toddlers.
There was no particular story to it; he'd been in a little

Suzuki jeep and simply rolled it off the road one night, somewhere up towards Aberdeen. Posh Scots are always dying in cars. I suppose it's because they spend so much time in them. Once, they criss-crossed Scotland on horses and in stagecoaches and had to worry about highwaymen, potholes and red deer straying onto the road. Now they do it in cars, and the major dangers are being shitfaced and kamikaze sheep.

Instead of to bed, anyway, Johnnie had gone to sleep in the drawing room, on a big threadbare sofa with rather camp wooden legs and a covering like it thought it was in Versailles. The room was unlike the rest of the house, being smart and spartan with a polished floor, like an island of stillness and propriety, only slightly disturbed by having the boozy, unwashed carcass of Johnnie in it. Alan flopped into an armchair and dozed off. I, for wont of anything better to do, did the same. When I woke up, Johnnie wasn't there any more and Alan had his head thrown back, like he'd broken his neck.

I wandered back to the kitchen, yawning, just as Jenny was coming in with the girls. They were about eleven years old and twins, but they looked nothing like each other. Marianne was freckled, curly and red-gold, like a little lion. Tabitha was dark, like Johnnie and his mum. They weren't interested in me at all, and nor was I, particularly, in them. Jenny made me tea, and we talked of school, and then Johnnie turned up from outside, looking farmerish, stomping mud from his boots. He was sullen with his mum, which I didn't get at all, because she was so easy to talk to. Then we woke up Alan, opened some beers and started watching a VHS of *Blackadder*. And then it got dark. We drank more beers, Jenny went to bed, and Johnnie disappeared for a bit and came back with a gun.

'Coming out?' he said, and we did, creeping on tiptoe across the stones outside the house so as not to wake the twins.

Actually, that reminds me, I should call the twins. Marianne, particularly, because she's a student in London now, which is where I live, too. 'We won't lose touch?' she'd say to me years later, after the funeral and after the trial. And I promised we wouldn't, and I've kept to that. Although I'm not sure it makes either of us very happy.

★

'It's less heavy than the guns at school,' I said stupidly, as we rattled down some muddy track in his Renault. I wasn't comfortable. Burnside, Johnnie, a car, a gun on my lap – come on. This was too much.

'It's just an air rifle,' said Johnnie. 'Mum's been a bit weird lately about the proper ones in the cabinet.'

'No shit,' I didn't say.

I was in the back. Alan was riding shotgun – for want of a much better phrase – but he'd passed the thing back to me so he could skin up. Outside, it was ebony Scottish night, with a dark grey smear of cloud visible to the west. As far as I was concerned it was all just fields and tracks, but I realised eventually that we were heading for the lay-by where Johnnie had picked us up the day before. Waiting there on a bike was Dean, the farm guy from the night before. He had this tight, angular, twisted face. One cheek sunken in because he was sucking it. The headlights in the dark made it look like a pit.

'All right, boys,' he said, dumping the bike behind a hedge.

'All right, Dean,' said Alan, getting out and climbing in beside me so that Dean could sit next to Johnnie up front. Alan sounded more Scottish than usual, I noticed.

We drove, we smoked, we killed. Johnnie had a big, heavy-duty torch which plugged into the cigarette lighter, heavy like a toolkit and with a mirrored face on it the size of an ashtray. Dean would blare it out the window as we bumped through the fields, turning swathes of midnight grass into a bright June green and going 'Oi!' whenever he saw a rabbit, which would prompt Johnnie to hit the brakes. Sometimes they'd be running – hopping, really, like miniature kangaroos – but more often they'd be transfixed for a moment or two, staring back at the light with their eyes glowing red. The sheep would do the same, but their eyes glowed green. But we didn't shoot the sheep. Dead rabbits went up front, facing forwards on their bellies, secured under a spider grip stretched across the bonnet. When the light shone out the windscreen, it went through a thicket of their ears.

I think we shot quite a few. With the air rifle you had to be pretty close, otherwise you'd only wound them, and they'd hop miserably away. In practice, this meant about twenty feet. You only had one shot each time, as well. The gun clacked, rather than banged, and then you had to pull it in, break it double and stick another pellet into the breach.

Sometimes Dean would shoot, sometimes Johnnie would, leaning bodily across him to hold the gun out of his window. Alan rolled the joints, and I smoked them and watched. 'Yabastard,' Dean would say when a rabbit prematurely hopped away. And then 'Goanyafucker' when Johnnie shot one, and it flipped onto its side, legs scrabbling, white fluffy underbelly flashing in the light. If Johnnie got to them first, afterwards, he'd shoot them again, point blank, right in the head. Dean would grab them with his hands, holding head and back legs, and just kind of . . . stretch them straight. If nobody was talking, you could hear the crack of their necks, like a dry branch under a foot.

'I told you,' said Alan. 'These hicks, they're savages.'

I grinned. Although they let me shoot one a little after that and, with the drugs, and the night, and the bodies all strapped to the bonnet, it felt like nothing at all.

Before long we had about seven and I was stoned dim-witted. That sort where everything is happening above everything else, like your body has been squeezed by a huge, gentle fist and your head is bulging over the top. Alan made Johnnie stop, and then he climbed out the window and lay starfished on the roof while Johnnie drove around.

'You'll fall off,' I shouted up at him.

'*You'll* fall off,' he snapped back quite prissily, although I was in the car and couldn't fall off anything, so that kept us laughing for about fifteen minutes. Johnnie stopped the car and we all got out, falling to our knees, crying with it. By the time the laughter subsided, I was even more lost than before. Every breath came in and out. The back of my head made of foamy plant oasis. Eyelashes like aerials in the night. I lay on my back and watched the dark clay smears race across the blackened sky, some faster, some slower. Had they driven off and left me, I'd have curled up and gone to sleep right there. Cheek on the grass. Maybe died. And happily, too.

Gradually, I became aware of silence. Pushing myself up

on my elbows, I saw that the car was still close, lights blazing into nothing, but the three of them were fifty metres away, all looking in the same direction towards the distant lights of some sort of building on the other side of the valley.

'Hey!' I shouted, but they ignored me. I got to my feet and staggered towards them, stumbling on hillocks and rabbit holes. 'What's going on?' I managed, as I drew close.

Alan looked back at me over his shoulder.

'It was here,' he said quietly.

'What was?' I said stupidly.

Johnnie was smoking the joint furiously, staring, saying nothing.

'Oh,' I said. 'Oh, I'm sorry.'

Dean was uncomfortable. 'Let's get on,' he said.

'That bastard,' said Johnnie, looking towards the lights. 'You think he's sorry?'

'Of course he is,' said Alan awkwardly. 'Come on. They were friends, man.'

'Oh,' I said, suddenly realising what the distant lights were. 'That's the castle.'

Johnnie raised the air rifle to his shoulder and pointed it towards the house, impossibly far away. Then he pulled the trigger.

'Bang,' he said.

Then he reloaded the gun and did it again.

9

THEY PUT MY MUM into a medically induced coma at the end of the summer, on the last night of the Edinburgh Festival. Probably I was looking at fireworks at the time. They have these amazing ones each year as part of the Military Tattoo at Edinburgh Castle, and they end with this tumbling waterfall of light pouring down from the battlements and the rock to the gardens below. It looks like gems, or jewels, or magic, and I appreciate that at this point you may think I'm banging on excessively about fireworks in order to avoid having to think about the coma thing. And you may be right.

I was at Alan's house, anyway, where his parents were having a party. That whole summer, I'd seen a lot of Alan, and almost nothing of Johnnie at all. Flora, I knew, had gone Interrailing. So, Alan and I mainly hung out in Edinburgh instead, and it wasn't actually too bad.

Alan's crowd, I came to realise, weren't quite the same people as Johnnie and Flora's. These were Edinburgh girls who knew their way around the Waverley Centre and how to take buses, even though their fathers might be members of the Faculty of Advocates. They weren't wild like Flora's friends, and they didn't have horses, or wear striking, baffling fashions, or have one foot in London. There was, though, a bookish, arty strain there which I found a little easier to navigate. Annie, with the thin cigarettes from the party, was there one time, although I don't remember speaking to her. Some of the others I recognised from ice-skating.

Often, Alan and I would turn up at lunchtime in the neo-Gothic oddity of the café at the National Portrait Gallery, knowing that some of them would have been spending the morning there, with pads and sticks of charcoal, gearing up for A-levels. Alan would chat away, in his easy manner, about the lineage that all those endless Scottish portraits of Jacobites and aristocrats owed to Dutch and Flemish artists of centuries earlier; how every rosy-cheeked blush of a Raeburn was actually a lift from Vermeer. I wondered how he knew this stuff, and whether he had to practise. Then one afternoon this girl Claire was talking about El Greco, having bought a postcard of his *Christ Blessing* from the National Gallery down the road. 'It looks so medieval,' I said vaguely, because it did, and she said, 'Exactly! Even though it was much later! That's such an interesting perspective! Was he doing it on purpose?' And I thought to myself, wow, this shit is easy as anything.

I liked speaking to Claire. Sometimes when I go into a gallery café even today, even in London, I'll find myself instinctively looking around for her, because the whole point of cafés in galleries, surely, is that people like her might be there. She was only our age, but she always seemed slightly older. A bit like Alan, I suppose. She had this constant and slightly performative need for coffee, although she always called it *café*, like she was French. That was a bit annoying, but she also had this way of tightening her eyes and peering at you intensely while you spoke, making you feel you must have just said something pretty damn profound, even if you were pretty sure you hadn't. One day I tried doing it back at her, while she was deliberating about whether or not to get a cheese toastie, and she asked if I had a headache. There's a knack to it, I guess. Still, it was flattering. She had a face that always made me think of the Second World War, for reasons I never understood at the time but in retrospect were probably to do with lipstick. I think she and Alan already had something going on at that point, although I didn't know how that squared off with whatever he'd recently had going on with Flora, so I didn't mention it, and neither did he.

In the afternoons, we'd all sometimes buy wine and idle away hours in a circle on the grass in Princes Street Gardens. Until then, park drinking had mainly meant vodka and Fanta, but we were with girls now, and sophisticated, so wine it was. White, mainly. Usually, we'd even buy cups. Really grown-up. And at night, at least once it was August, there were all the festival bars, full of festival people. At Acton's, the culture had dictated that you were supposed to loathe the Edinburgh Festival and everybody it brought in, to the extent of there being a bit of a cult of walking up and down the Royal Mile saying 'Piss off, I live here' to as many students with flyers as possible. These girls, though, saw plays and talked about them. One time, Claire and her friend Gina took the two of us to see these students doing a version of *Hamlet* set on a space station. It was terrible. We'd been to the pub beforehand, and then Alan and I had a spliff on the walk through the Meadows, and then we smirked and giggled throughout, and we went on to utterly fail to have the sort of conversation that Claire had definitely wanted to have about it afterwards. No more plays after that.

For a while, I suppose the four of us were a bit of a gang. Like, there were always other people floating around, but maybe we were the core. Gina, Claire's friend, had a filthy laugh and played women's rugby, and once, when this student guy kicked a bottle at us in the Grassmarket, she punched him so hard in the chest that he fell over. She always wore a neckerchief, which along with her short blonde hair made her look so much like both of the twins from Bros that I honestly sometimes have to remind myself these days that there weren't two of her. Sometimes, while Claire and Alan flirted and talked about Gauguin, Gina would put me in a headlock and challenge me to get out of it. I never could. She was pretty cool. A few years later, she'd move to Australia. Although maybe you saw that coming.

Some nights, anyway, we'd hang out with them, and other nights it would just be me and Alan, while the girls were off seeing plays, or being with their families, or doing whatever it was that girls do when they're not flirting with boys or putting them in headlocks. They seemed to have to go home more than we did, and earlier, too. Stricter parents, I suppose, or maybe it was just different with girls. There was this pub called the Tilted Wig where we'd normally end up; one of those places that you could see at a glance was entirely full of quite posh underage kids, but somehow got away with it. The usual meeting place beforehand was Greyfriars Bobby, the wee statue known to everyone as 'on the dog'. As in, 'I'll meet you on the dog at seven.' This one time, the morning after a heavy night, I woke up on Alan's floor with DOG 630 written on my hand, and I couldn't remember why. He had the same on his and, given that we were still together, it just seemed improbable that we could have been meeting each other. So, we went there, just to see, and eventually these two lads we knew from Glenalmond turned up, equally baffled, with the same written on theirs. It felt endless.

★

'Have you spoken to Johnnie at all?' I asked Alan, as we walked back towards his house, on one of those long, open festival nights, which had started as an early afternoon and was fast turning into an early morning. Apprehensive because I'd called a few times, but he hadn't once called me back.

'Nah,' said Alan. 'I mean, I spoke to his mum. But you know what he's like in the summer.'

'Mmm,' I said, quietly relieved. Then I decided to be brave. 'I mean, no. Because I didn't know you last summer. Remember?'

'Oh, right,' said Alan, sounding surprised. 'Well. He goes a bit feral. Very farmy. All guns and mud. Him and Dean. I think they're renovating some cottage this year. They'll be drinking beer and knocking down walls all day.'

This made me wonder whether we should go and join in for a day or two.

'Could do,' said Alan. 'But him and Dean. I dunno. Guns and mud. It's not my thing.'

Alan's house was in Moray Place, and I was too young back then to know how big a deal this was. If you don't know Edinburgh, it's this circus of massive townhouses smack in the middle of the New Town. Most of them are flats these days, but Alan's folks had the whole five floors and had done ever since his great-grandad came back from being in charge of somewhere in the Himalayas.

Alan's mum, Leonora, was a bit terrifying. She was from some big Glasgow Italian family and was tall and very beautiful, and she wore gold earrings and beige cashmere polo necks and was always sweeping in and out of rooms, usually witheringly cross about something.

It was his dad, though, who made me really uncomfortable. Mungo Campbell was a literary critic for *The Scotsman* and an occasional theatre producer and restaurateur, and if those things don't sound like they should all go together in a single person, then don't blame me. As tall as Alan, he was bald, but he had quite long hair at the back, and he always wore red trousers and a checked shirt, and he was always chortling away at something, but somehow not nicely.

'And who is this one?' he said to Alan, the first time I met him. He had one of those Edinburgh voices where the Scottishness is almost, but not entirely, imperceptible. It was quite late at night, and he was sitting in a palatial front room with a blonde woman and a rat-faced little man. They were drinking sherry that I could smell from the door.

'Tom Dwarkin,' I said. 'How do you do?'

'Ho!' he said, slapping an armrest in glee. 'Dworkowicz's boy! Literary royalty!'

I didn't know quite what to do with that. In my experience, grown-ups weren't openly rude, but this did sound quite a lot like 'writer of mediocre airport fiction' cuntiness to me.

'Fuck's sake, Dad,' said Alan, which immediately made everything quite a lot worse.

'So profane!' said Mungo. 'And in the presence of the son of a veritable bard, as well. Joining us for a sherry?'

'Oh, do,' said the blonde woman, and the rat-faced man sniggered.

There were social behavioural codes I didn't know going on here, I realised, and one of them was whether or not somebody like me was allowed to tell his friend's dad to shove his sherry up his red-trousered arse. Before I could say anything, though, Alan quite curtly declined and said we were going upstairs.

'Of course you are,' said his father grandly, and he made himself go cross-eyed while miming an elaborate smoking gesture. He just means cigarettes, I thought to myself, but then he flashed us a peace sign and I must have blushed pink as a ham.

Pretty much the second we left the room, I could hear him pretty openly explaining to his friends who my dad was and how it wasn't his thing, heavens, no, but how fortunate it was for some that Americans had no taste at all. Not so much like he thought I couldn't hear; more that he didn't care if I could, or even reckoned I somehow deserved to. And I thought of my dad, and the nervous, impressed way he'd talked about meeting Alan's dad, and I didn't like that at all. And so later, when I came back downstairs to use the vast and ancient porcelain loo, I deliberately did a bit of piss on the carpeted floor.

★

I spent quite a lot of time there that month, all the same. It was a bonkers house, seemingly with a drawing room on almost every floor. There was an open staircase up the middle with a raised circular glass roof, like a Victorian arboretum. Alan's room was up the top, with a sink and a telly and a Nintendo and a Gibson electric guitar in it. There were posters of art on his walls, which I found quite intimidating, and a skylight that opened out just beside the big glass roof and onto a whole secret world of slate valleys and lead. Shuffle along to one end, and you had a direct view to a very small bit of Edinburgh Castle. We went up there often, but I had a terror of tripping over my own feet and plummeting through the priceless glazing and down past five storeys of banisters below.

Leonora was usually around, although never in the same room as Alan's dad and never with the same people. Generally you could tell which court was hanging out where by the accents. Leonora's people were Glaswegian and sounded it. There was her sister, whose name I forget, who was identical to her but a bit smaller, and her brother, Marco, who was a solid guy with short black hair and wore the same sorts of tweedy clothes as Mungo but somehow in a way that always made him look like he'd made a terrible mistake. They were too new, too neat, too tight; can't really explain it. The collar sat all wrong around his wide neck, and those mustard cords should not have had to strain around his bum. He was Homer Simpson going to church. Their father had owned a bunch of shabby cafés and takeaways on the West Coast which Marco had redeveloped, very successfully, into bistros. Later, I'd learn, he looked much happier in an apron.

It's not, you understand, that I was never in my own home that summer. Both of my parents were there, what with the hospital having kindly released my mum and the TV network having done the same with my dad. For the first half of the holidays, I almost felt like a bit of a gooseberry, so pleased were they to have each other back. She'd be up most days, dressed, even in jewellery. They'd go to restaurants for lunch and sometimes to plays in the evening.

'I'm monopolising your mum,' my dad would say almost shyly over breakfast, and I'd make a joke about it, trying not to let on that I didn't really care because whatever this multiple sclerosis thing was, it didn't seem to be the end of the world; and I was sixteen, with better things to do, and she was going to be around forever, because when you're sixteen that's the deal. Perhaps there was some lingering hospital angst there that stopped me from ever staying over on Alan's floor, although that might just have been horror at the thought of morning small talk with Mungo. Often I'd find myself walking hazily home alone at 1 a.m. or so, back through the blackened pastures of Holyrood Park and past the bottomless void of Duddingston Loch. It was mine, and it was magic, and I never passed a soul.

She was sick again, though, by the time the festival started. Not terribly, at first, but enough that her shirt-dresses and earrings went away again, and her pink fluffy dressing gown came back. Some lung thing, which had started with an infection and wasn't going away. Although the main symptom of her disease, it sometimes seemed to me, was a proliferation of white plastic around the house; a rail by the door, a step by the toilet, a seat of some sort in the bath. In the good months, the remissions, all this stuff was banished to the garage. In the bad ones, though, it would reinvade and apparently reproduce, constantly seeming to generate more of itself from the nexus of her bedroom, which became a place of jugs and pots and commodes and God knows what else. I certainly never said it, and I'm not sure I even consciously thought it, but I didn't like going in there, not at all. It was as if the hard white surfaces reflected too much of me and too much of her; our souls and our smells. I felt forever dirty, squeamish, external, nicotine drenched. I stayed away. Not all the time. Not even most of the time. But still. As much as I could.

★

Anyway, there was a party. Remember? The night of the fireworks. The Campbells had one most years, I was told, because although you could only see the castle itself from that secret spot on Alan's roof, the fireworks might as well have been directly overhead. There were hundreds of people there, all braying and drinking and wearing knitted ties at each other.

Unlike the MacPhails, the Campbells held parties which arrived almost without any heralding buzz at all. Like everybody had just dropped by, randomly, with booze and glasses seemingly materialising all by themselves, much like the medical supplies at home. As with all their parties, it was 10 p.m. before Marco arrived in a van from one of his restaurants, packed out with wheels of brie and pizzas and great troughs of carbonara and bolognese. Gangs of shrieking volunteers would troop downstairs to bring it all back up. That night, half the guests were still down in the street when the fireworks went off, with the rest all on the huge, open staircase, gazing up at the glass. Alan and I raced up and up, bursting into his room and through his skylight onto the slates, and it was like a war.

I'd thought the party might wind down after that, but instead it grew. The voices were deafening; the telephone rang constantly and nobody cared. Leonora and Mungo were, as ever, holding different courts on different floors; hers a whirl of frilly blouses and hairspray on the ground floor, and his more of a dandruffy yammer spilling out of his oak-panelled study into the drawing room on the first. Mungo himself was resident on the landing, shouting sentences into people's ears above the din – 'not even truly historical, virtually Mills & Boon' – that sounded very plausibly as though it might be about my dad. I didn't like that very much. While Leonora, by contrast, still looked through me like I was barely even there.

Sometime after eleven a handful of Alan's friends arrived, not exactly after the pub – because this was magical Festival Edinburgh, where the pubs never closed – more taking a break from them. Not Claire and Gina, because I remember that Claire was off on a French exchange by then, which in that strange, teenage way meant that Gina had ceased to exist, too. I forget who it was, exactly, but it was all boys and they definitely included Jamie and Will – sorry, The Layman, who I'd met that time in the Tron. Layman lived in some castle in the Highlands but was staying out Haddington way with Jamie, who was making a big fuss about needing to sober up before driving home, I think as a way of showing off that he had a car. With two teenagers in that house it had been fine, but now there were five or six of us and we were this jarring presence, destabilising things, with big-haired women in shirts with ruffs looking at us a bit like we might mug somebody. So, we all trooped up the stairs, past the ringing phone and past Mungo on his landing – 'of course, technically he's more of a valet' – and took up residence in Alan's room.

Somebody had hash, and, after a hurried, urgent conference, Alan ran downstairs again and came back with a big, empty plastic Coke bottle and some tinfoil. The hash guy put a cigarette burn near the base of the thing, filled it up with water and then burned the stuff on tinfoil over the neck of the bottle while letting the water drain. When the bottle was opaque with milky white smoke, he took off the foil, put his finger over the hole and handed it to Alan, who knocked the whole lot back like he was drinking a Guinness. Then the hash guy took it back and filled it up again. At which point Jamie, I'd imagine, started to realise it might be some time before he was driving anywhere.

★

It was a bit much for me. Not sure why. Hadn't eaten enough, maybe. I sat down hard on the end of the bed, nodding a bit. I wasn't quite sure what was going on. I could hear a phone ringing, far away. Ring, it went, ring bloody ring. The dulled chatter of the party was pushing at the sides of my head, like underwater pressure on a reef that was also a fairground. I wondered, was there such a thing? Who would even go there?

'Clownfish!' I said delightedly, having thought about this for a while.

'Shush,' said Alan, who was speaking to Layman. Although, whatever they were talking about, I didn't see why we couldn't all talk about my thing instead.

'No way was it an accident,' Layman was saying. 'No way.'

'Look, leave it, man,' said Alan. 'He's our friend, yeah? And you can't just come in here and—'

'Johnnie,' I said suddenly. 'But he wasn't arrested. It was just questions. And we thought it was about the brick, but it wasn't.'

'Just shut up, Tommo,' said Alan, much more savagely than I was used to, and I held up my hands, breathed out and thought 'sod this', before going off downstairs to find some cheese.

Which was a bad idea. The downstairs, I mean. Less so the cheese, although that was hardly a silver bullet, either. I remembered that half-wheel of brie had ended up in the dining room, and I planned to eat quite a lot of it. Somehow, though, I just wasn't very good at getting through the crowds. Everything was an elbow. 'Excuse *me!*' people kept saying sharply. Eventually I got to the dining room, found the brie on a sideboard next to a chair and sawed off a wedge, but it wasn't quite what I needed. There was this sugary chutney stuff next to it, and that seemed more promising. Cince?

'Quince!' I said, out loud.

'Excuse me?' said a lady in a gilet.

'Quince,' I said again and pointed, and she smiled uncertainly and moved away. 'Quince' was a word, right? But did it mean . . . vagina? Had I just said vagina? Had she moved away from a man saying vagina? I sat down in the chair. I wasn't sure the quince was helping. I was cold and stoned and panicky.

'Quince,' I said weakly. I felt a bit like I was shitting. It would be very bad, I reckoned, if I was shitting. But I sat, and I breathed, and eventually I realised I wasn't. I ate some brie. I ate some quince. Absolutely quince. I was sure of that.

On the sideboard, I suddenly saw, was an open can of Coke. It was half empty, but I drank it anyway. That was better. Maybe I'd go back upstairs. Maybe I'd go home. Instead, though, I just sat there, wondering why my parents had never had parties like this, even when my mum was well. Or had they? There was a memory there, hazy, of being small and in my bed. Noises, voices and glass on glass. Distant and quiet, then louder. My mother coming through the door, in a triangle of electric light. Silhouetted at first, almost sashaying. Leaning over me to check I was okay. A necklace, like a pendant, hanging right down in my face. Red glass catching the gleam.

I opened my eyes. Mungo was there, his face right in mine, as pale as the brie. Maybe he's having a whitey, too, I thought, but he wasn't.

'For God's sake,' he said. 'There you are. We've been all over the house. Your father called. She's at the hospital. I've got you a taxi.'

10

HANG ON, THOUGH. YOU'LL be thinking I'm a total sociopath. There I was at the start of all this, telling you about the amazing year I was about to have. And now here I am with a mother in a coma, like that wasn't even a major fly in my ointment, and my dad is clearly about to crack up, too. All I can say is that the one didn't really have anything to do with the other. I was sixteen. You've been sixteen. You know.

I don't really feel like telling you much about the hospital, either that night or any other. There were beeps and tubes and . . . look, I'm just not doing this. She'd been awake when they brought her in, but by the time I got there they'd knocked her out because that was the only way to fix the lung thing. The obvious question was exactly when they were going to wake her up again, but apparently that was a bit unclear. My dad told me straight away that he wasn't going back to London for a bit, and I didn't say anything, and then he said I didn't have to say anything, and I still didn't, and then, a couple of days later, he asked why I wasn't saying anything. Honestly, it was confusing.

A couple more days later, my sister, Annie, came home. The night before she arrived, my dad went into a mad panic and cleaned the house all over, which was a bit annoying because he'd never in the past bothered with that sort of thing for me. Annie had left Nottingham by then and was in London, doing a summer placement training to be something called a management consultant. She said it was hard to take time off.

'What actually is a management consultant?' I asked that first night, after she'd taken my dad's car and come back with pizza from the good place by the Commonwealth Pool.

'Don't be rude, Tom,' said my father, for some reason.

'It's like you tell people how to run their companies,' said Annie. 'When they come to you for help. Basically.'

'But you don't know how to run companies,' I said. Because it seemed unlikely that she would. At Nottingham, as I mentioned, she'd studied Extremely Hard Maths.

Then Annie said this was why they were training her, and I said it would make more sense to just train the people who actually needed the help, to cut out the middleman. And then Annie told me I was being a horrible little shit, and my dad said she was right. And I had a vague feeling we shouldn't all be talking to each other like this, now of all times. But I don't know, maybe I was.

We're pretty different, me and Annie. It's not that we don't get on, but she's five years older than me, which at that point was too big a gap for us to have really hung out. At Acton's she'd been head of the maths club and head of the debating society, which you might imagine would have conferred some glitzy status onto me, even before the demon butler entered the equation, but only if you've never met a teenager or, in fact, been one. Once, also, when I was still little, she won a maths competition on that children's science TV programme presented by that guy with the wacky hair and stupid glasses, and they gave her a BBC Acorn Electron computer. And you know what? She didn't even play Frogger on it. She just used it to do more damn maths. Totally fucked up.

At university she started running marathons for fun, and she's probably kind to animals and keen on world peace, and if you're wondering at this point why I'm not more like her, then congratulations on thinking exactly the same thing as basically everybody else I'd ever met until I started meeting people like Johnnie and Alan.

That week, though, I dunno. It was like she was a stranger. Maybe it was my fault. Every morning she'd go running and she always said she'd take it easy if I wanted to go with her, and I'd just roll my eyes and say nothing at all. Every afternoon she'd drive my dad's car over to see Mum, and I'd usually go with her, although that was awkward, too, because on the way back she'd be all distraught and haggard, with her frizzy hair all over the place and her eyes as red as the hair was. And I'd be basically fine.

'I suppose you're in shock,' she said one time, as I fiddled with the radio on the way back.

'I'm not in shock,' I said, not looking up.

'Or you're on drugs,' she said. 'Oh God. That's all we need. Him to be on drugs.'

'Shut up.'

'I mean, you do actually understand what's going on?'

'I'm not an idiot.'

'Go on . . .'

'She's ill,' I said. 'It's a lung thing. They're making her better. It's not complicated.'

Then Annie said she wasn't going to get totally better, because it wasn't just a lung thing. And it was important I realised that. And I said she wasn't going to be asleep for ever, though, was she, and Annie said no, hopefully not, and I said well, then, they were making her better. And then I turned up Forth FM because they were playing that Stiltskin song from the jeans advert that I quite liked, and for some reason this made Annie so cross that she literally slapped the steering wheel.

'Seriously, what's wrong with you?' she said.

'Maybe I've just spent a lot more time at the hospital than you have,' I said, enjoying how savage it made me feel. Even though it was rubbish, and I knew it was rubbish because she'd actually been glued to my mum's side the whole time when she first started getting ill, quite unlike me. But it shut her up.

Other times she'd ask questions about school, but they were odd, annoying questions because she had no frame of reference and kept talking about times she'd stayed in youth hostels. Or she'd ask if Dad had been drinking a lot lately, and I'd just shrug. Sometimes she'd try to tell me about her office life in London, but I honestly had no idea why I was supposed to be interested in that. Then, in the evenings, she'd be incredibly and disproportionately cross with me for smoking out the back door once my dad had gone to sleep. I get it now. She thought the wheels were coming off.

She was there for two weeks, and after she'd gone it was just the two of us. At night, he'd drink red wine in his study again, and I'd pretend not to notice again, and he'd pretend to believe I hadn't. And in the morning there would be another bottle in the bin and I'd pretend not to notice that, too. 'You don't need to go back to school straight away,' he said to me eventually, and I must have looked at him with absolute horror because then he said, 'Unless you want to?' and I tried to hide my relief and said that I thought I did.

★

When I was back, I started hanging out a lot more with Luci. I was in the sixth form now, and I had my own dank, crumbling study, and his was just across the landing. It's not that I didn't hang out with Alan and Johnnie, too, because I did, a lot, but Luci was teaching me how to play guitar, and I was spending a lot of time on it, and Alan was too perfect at the guitar for me to really want him to know I was even trying. Plus, there was an egalitarianism to it. I never felt like a hanger-on with Luci, and it was a bit of a relief.

Luci was a strange guy; very close to being the template of long-haired poet that girls were supposed to like, but just a bit too heavy metal to properly carry it off. But he was soulful, and geeky, and interesting, and I felt him engaging parts of myself that I'd spent the last year pretending weren't there. We'd play Nirvana and The Lemonheads over and over again, him on his steel string and me on his old battered classical. He also had a cheap Gibson knock-off and a tiny amp and, after a while, I switched to that. I liked it fuzzy, to cover my mistakes. There was no reason to stop. We'd play for hours.

Luci's study opened out onto the roof, and he'd unscrewed the wooden blocks that were supposed to stop people climbing out and spend half the day out there, meditatively sitting on a cushion, smoking rollies.

After a couple of weeks, I realised he hadn't just been

sitting out there smoking, either, but had been exploring, too. Crawl up the slate and you could slip down into another skylight, which led into a warren of attics, above almost all of Esk House. Quite often you had to carefully step from rafter to rafter, so as to not break through the plaster to the room below. There were parts where we had to go on our knees and parts where we had to whisper because we were over Toad's flat and he might hear. There was also a long, low stretch which ran over a corridor of studies, which was punctuated with white outline rectangles every ten feet or so on the left-hand wall. These, Luci showed me, were panels up in the raised box of each room's high roof window. One night, during tea, we pulled one away in a spirit of experimentation and found ourselves peering down into the study of a kid in Luci's year called Fergus. One along, and we'd have been over the office used by Mork, the deputy housemaster, so called because he looked like an alien. Lucky break. He might even have been in there.

Honestly, it was like fucking Narnia up there. Dark and lonely and precious. Then you'd come down and go into the crowded, screaming dining hall, and you'd walk with a swagger, with a secret nobody else knew.

The other thing you could do via the roof was get out at night. Take a left, slide down a bit, dangle and drop, and you were on the huge, flat roof of the dining hall. From there you could be seen from the dorms, so the trick was to stay low and run. The dangerous bit was a raised parapet at the end, which you had to climb over. On the other side there was a lamppost, a foot and a half from the wall. Between the two you could go up or down. At first, for a while, Luci and I would head out for chips from the local high street every other night. Even potato tastes exquisite when you're not meant to have it.

This one time, though, like a dick, I took Johnnie and Alan up there. It was just before lunch, and the tub room was crowded with smokers, and I guess I was showing off about knowing another place. Luci stuck his head out the window ten minutes later.

'Oh, hello,' he said.

'Um, hi,' I said. 'I just thought they'd like to—'

'Cool axes, man,' said Johnnie, nodding back towards the guitars in the room, although in that nasty Johnnie way that he sometimes had. And I suddenly clicked on something I'd not really noticed myself noticing the term before, when we all shared a dorm. Which was that Johnnie was pretty vile to Luci generally, like he thought he was a bit of a joke.

'Sorry,' I said. 'Should we not have . . . I thought . . .'

'No, man, it's chill,' said Luci affably. 'Put the blocks back afterwards, yeah? Peace and love.'

'Yeah, sure,' said Alan.

'Yeah, peace and love, Nigel,' said Johnnie, and Luci nodded, left his own room and went down to lunch. And I felt like a terrible arsehole, really quite powerfully, for the rest of the day.

★

My dad would pick me up most Sundays that term, and we'd go home via the hospital. It was grim. We wouldn't talk much, although he'd try, and then we'd get into my mum's bleak anaemic cell of a private room and I'd sit there silently, wishing I could go away and smoke.

Everything about me smelled of tobacco back then, maybe because I spent so much time in Luci's room and had gone off washing. Some days it felt like I'd been stewing fully clothed in a warm bath of tea made from Golden Virginia and then dried out on a radiator. My dad never let on that he noticed, but then I never let on that I'd noticed the state of him, which was dire, and bleary, and pungent. In the hospital, though, it was like my mum's old bedroom but worse. As if my smell was bouncing off all the hard, plastic surfaces, amplifying and echoing. Brazen as a ball bearing rattling in a tin. Some days I wondered if my dad mainly took me there to cover up his own vinegary wine smell. She had a mask on and tubes up her nose, but however far under she was, there was no way she didn't know.

Afterwards we'd go home for lunch, or sometimes to a restaurant, and my dad would drink Coke, but I could still tell he wasn't getting much out of it. He was anxious, and I was sullen, and it made him more anxious still. For the first few weeks he'd talk a lot about definitely not going back to London, and I'd say nothing, and then eventually he said he actually had to for just a week, and I still said nothing. Then, in one of those wild, chaotic cock-ups that never would have happened had my mum been conscious, he suddenly realised that the brief week he'd booked to go down south was also my half-term.

He wanted me to come with him, but I told him I'd go to Alan's. I didn't, though. I didn't even ask because I knew Alan was going to Tuscany, for some reason, with his mum. I just went home from school on the bus and stayed there, watching TV all night, ignoring the phone, draining the wine cupboard and making the house smell like me. I'd never actually been much of a drinker, least of all by myself, but that week was different. It was as though my dad had gone but left his drink problem behind, so now I had to do that one, too. It wasn't even a conscious decision. I sort of poured the first glass only half concentrating, and then fell asleep in the living room, and then kept going the next morning, waiting to see what would happen.

What happened was that Johnnie rang the doorbell. Three days in. Maybe four. I came to the door in my dad's dressing gown, carrying around a bottle like Jim Morrison.

'Jesus, man,' he said. 'What are you doing?'

'I'm watching *Das Boot*,' I said, because I was.

What had happened, he said, was that my dad had called Alan's house, and Alan's dad had told him I wasn't there and never had been, and that he must have got the wrong idea. So, my dad called Johnnie's house next, and Johnnie had answered and just bluffed that I was there but asleep. Real instinctive duplicity from that kid. You had to admire it. Then he'd caught the train, to come and find out what was going on.

'Nothing is going on,' I said irritably. 'It's a maritime war classic.'

'Jesus, man,' said Johnnie again. Then he followed me in, almost nervously, and looked around before asking why we had this sort of house.

I stared at him.

'I thought it would be more like Alan's,' he said.

'Pevsner,' I said, 'never mentioned yours, either.'

That was his cue to stare at me. Then he grabbed the bottle

out of my hand and made me coffee, and together we started
to clean. All the windows were opened, and all the bottles
went in a bin bag. Then he made me have a bath, and then
I went to sleep for two hours and slept like a corpse. And
then we went out into the Grassmarket and got properly
shitfaced until about 2 a.m., but in a manner that definitely
felt a lot more wholesome. And then, after another night at
my house, I did go and stay at Burnside after all.

★

That Christmas there was a thoroughly unexpected
development, which was that I started being invited to balls.
As in, black-tie dances, but for teenagers. Weird, yes, but also
a relief because sixth-formers didn't go ice-skating, and I'd
been wondering how my social life was supposed to work.
The first invitation was from Zara, the girl with the falling-
off jumper that I'd met at the Costorphine party a while
back, and it was to the Pony Club Ball in Hopetoun House.
I had Alan to thank, as usual, because she was taking a group
of ten and she'd asked him to bring another boy. Honestly, to
this day I still don't really understand the relationships Alan
used to have with women, and so effortlessly, too. They'd
had a fling, and then they'd stopped having it, and now they
were friends instead. It was fucking weird.

Anyway, the invitation card arrived, and I left it lying
around, which was a mistake because it prompted my dad
to put it on the mantelpiece.

'Why?' I demanded, mortified.

'It's what you do,' he said. 'It's the done thing.'

'Airhellair,' I thought bitterly, but I let it go.

As I'd learn, there was a pattern to these things. First, you all turn up for dinner at about 6 p.m. at the house of somebody you barely knew. Zara's house, in this case, and generally a girl's house, because girls' parents were less likely to know how boys actually behaved. Boys in black jackets and kilts, girls in big shiny dresses, unless they were small and black and velvety. You'd get a glass of wine on arrival, or a beer, and you'd stand around in a living room feeling awkward as hell, half strangled by your shirt, stammering and sober and unable to smoke unless the parents were particularly cool ones. Then you'd eat and drink more. Eyes would meet eyes; girls would blush under their mum's blusher. Somebody, always, would get too drunk, too soon, and it would have to be a secret. By the time you were all en route to the actual dance, in parents' cars, or taxis, or on occasion a minibus, there would, in the air, be the illicit whiff of vomit.

That first ball I went to, the Pony Club, was wild. Some sort of fundraising thing. I don't think many people had ponies. It was a big hall, with round, white table-clothed tables around the walls. There were reels, then disco, then more reels, then more disco. Mainly, though, there was wine, and smoking, and snogging. Never had I seen so many faces pressed into other ones. 'Is this okay?' I remember thinking quite nervously. 'Is nobody adult in charge?' Before long, Alan had paired off with this loud and husky-voiced cousin of Zara's from London, who had spent the entire meal trying to start a mystifying argument about prosecco being nicer than champagne. From then on they were ensconced in a corner, with her frankly excessive mane of blonde hair covering both of most of them, like a veil.

Johnnie wasn't there, but Barf was, with strangers. Actually, there were about a million people I knew there. Even some from Acton's. In the darkness of the disco – Right Said Fred, I think it was – I ran into Claire, of gallery café fame, and who I hadn't seen at all since we'd hung out the previous summer. She had a shawl on, and a silvery, fish-scaled dress that made her look a little bit too much like a mermaid. I asked if her friend Gina was here, and she said, 'No.' Then she asked if Alan was, and I said, 'Um.' And, while I really tried very hard not to openly nod in the direction of him and his brand-new friend, there must have been something in my 'um' that made Claire immediately swivel in their direction and see them.

'Oh,' she said brightly.

We went to the bar, which was in the next room, and we bought glasses of red wine and talked about the stuff we'd done the previous summer, as if we were lifelong friends who hadn't seen each other in years, rather than people who had hung out literally three or four months earlier. Something about that, and the wine, and the situation with Alan, and the way her dress was obviously a really bad idea, made me feel all mature and confident and predatory. Sort of like I was James Bond.

'Shall we go out for a cigarette?' I said to her, after a while, because I wanted to seize my moment, and my chat was drying up, and I desperately didn't want to risk having to talk about El Greco again.

'We can smoke in here,' she said, but she said it with a smirk that made me think we were probably on the same page. So, once we got out in the cold air, and she'd pushed her long dark hair behind her ears, and I'd lit our cigarettes, and a few seconds after she'd sort of pushed her shoulder into mine, I closed my eyes, turned my head and pushed my mouth towards hers. Only suddenly, hers wasn't there. I can remember the cold air on my tongue. Flapping around, like a fish.

'What are you doing?' she said.

'Nothing,' I said. 'Sorry.'

My arms were still by my sides. I had a cigarette in one hand and a glass of wine in the other. I felt pretty ungainly.

'Seriously,' she said. 'Are we not just friends? Do you fancy me?'

I didn't know what to say. The honest answer was, 'Not particularly, but it just seemed the thing to do.' But I obviously couldn't say that.

'Not particularly,' I said. 'But it just seemed the thing to do.'

'God, boys are annoying.'

'I'm sorry,' I said, and I felt miserable. I hate being annoying.

'Let's go back inside,' she said.

Inside, though, it was chaos. Like, batshit chaos. Never seen anything like it before. Music. Strobes. Booze smell and smoke. Mouths against mouths. A battlefield of hands up kilts and frottage through M&S party dresses and woah, Black Betty, bam ba lam. Although the weird thing was, once we were in there, I suddenly realised that Claire was holding my hand. Like she actually wanted people to think we were together, even though we definitely weren't.

'You don't mind?' she said.

'Why would I mind?' I said.

'Okay, you're actually not that annoying,' she said, and her eyes darted towards Alan, and I found myself thinking, and

I know this sounds weird, that nobody had actually held my hand for this long since I'd been a kid.

★

At the end of the night, she went off with her lot and I went off with mine. Zara's house was in the New Town, although it wasn't in such a posh bit as Alan's, and it was also quite a lot smaller. We'd all brought sleeping bags, and the idea was for the eight of us who were staying over to sleep on the floor in her room. Although sleep seemed to be quite a distant plan, all in all, because there were also lots of chocolates, some more wine and a TV and video in the corner. Which meant that by 3 a.m. I was sitting against a wall, far too drunk and buzzing on Dairy Milk, and also trying to watch *Midnight Express* while, under a duvet about five feet away, the husky-voiced blonde girl fairly obviously gave Alan a handjob. There were two other couples in the room – Zara and some rugby type called Neil being one of them – which meant the only two of us left over were me and this vibratingly nervous girl called Mary in Snoopy pyjamas. And, honestly, I was tempted, and I think she was, too, but it all just would have been a bit too awkward. Also, I don't know if you've ever seen *Midnight Express*, but it's about being stuck in a Turkish jail and, if you're paying attention, it doesn't actually make you feel that horny.

A few days later there was the Teenage Ball in Musselburgh, near to Eskmount, and a couple of days after that Alan and I took the bus up to St Andrews for some sort of similar but more studenty thing with Johnnie, too, where the voices were all a degree more posh and the cars a degree more likely to be Range Rovers. Fusty and Flora were at that one, too, although with a bunch of older people I didn't know, and who I found a bit intimidating. I held Flora's attention for a while, all the same, chatting at a table by the dancefloor, but I'd drunk too much by that point and all I really remember is the wine stains on the white table cloth, mixed with cigarette ash, and her telling me I should write to her at school, and me blushing, and then some English-sounding student guy proprietorially taking her away to dance.

I don't even remember whose house I stayed in afterwards, but I do remember that I kept on drinking, sort of quite bitterly, and that I was as sick as a dog. Also, I remember getting the bus home the next day, with Alan slumped against the window beside me. And I remember looking at my own left foot, which was in a Doc Marten boot with a white formal kilt sock poking out the top. And I remember feeling an itch between my toes, tugging at the sock and thinking of the trenches, and also thinking, 'Sheesh, but it's a long time since I took that off.'

11

AT SCHOOL, I'D MADE friends with a girl called Ella. Shit, I'm not telling this story right at all, am I? I keep doing this. Breaking news: there were girls now. Since the start of the year. God knows why they came, or why they stayed once they had. For the boys it was like a bomb going off, but for them? Probably the first day was the worst. Tea was an ungoverned meal at Eskmount with zero staff and only the prefects in charge, and the culture of the prefecture, let's say, was not one of feminist enlightenment. That first meal of the new year, the new girls would arrive altogether, heads down and terrified, and have to look for their tables, all the while being scrutinised, graded and jeered at by a few hundred clammy, furious, confused virgin boys. Pretty special. For the rest of the time, it doesn't quite cover it to suggest they were second-class citizens. They barely were citizens. Think of them as the centre point on a triangle with sides labelled 'immigrants', 'pets' and 'aliens'.

Actually, there weren't that many respectable opportunities to speak to the girls. Do so in public and you would be mocked for being 'sticky', which was a terrible crime. I think the idea was that you were sticking to the girls, rather than generating any literal form of unspeakable glutinousness, but it wasn't a reputation you wanted. *Having* a girlfriend was fine – more than fine; admirable, noble, enviable, heroic – but looking like you *wanted* one was thoroughly contemptible. There were always eyes. Walk with them, talk with them, everybody knew.

Meal tables, though, were neutral ground. Ella was on mine, along with Wee Geordie Meehan – who, like Barf, couldn't speak to girls – and a bunch of other people too young and small to worry about. Technically the head of the table was this huge First XV guy called Menzies – Mingis, the Minglord – from the year above, but Ella was unblonde and bookish and baffling to him, so he always went to sit with his huge, red-faced friends somewhere else. That left me in charge, and I quite liked it. Ella wasn't one of the girls that those boys would lust after, but she had a nice, rosy-cheeked face and short curly hair that was a lot like my own. She was also in my English class, and we'd talk intently about *Hamlet* and Sylvia Plath and the philosophy of *Waiting for Godot*, often for the whole meal, with Geordie barely saying a word. Then, out in the wild, I'd ignore her, because that was what you did.

★

It was a little after the Christmas holidays that my mum first came home. By then she'd been technically awake for a couple of months, but Annie had been right, because it didn't really make her better. What I'd been waiting for, I started to realise, was the point where she came back enough for me to say, 'Oof, let me tell you about the last few months!' and for her to say, 'Yes, I basically missed it all, didn't I? Tell me what it was like.' And then I'd talk about the times we'd thought she'd been about to go, but hadn't, and the exhausted jubilation when she seemed to be coming back. The shivers of the hospital waiting room, when you're as cold as you've ever been, but the chill is your own, coming from within. And somehow, worst of all, the waiting outside for my dad to pick me up when I'd been in and he hadn't been able to face it; that listless fraternity with the wind and the pigeons, the car park moments at the end of the day.

All this, I'd been planning on telling her. I'd rehearsed it in my head and imagined how the conversations would go. Instead of having her back, though, I now seemed to have this new mum, who smiled when I came home, but who was usually asleep, and largely silent when she wasn't. Carers and doctors came and went, but it wasn't exactly like any of them were predicting great, sunlit uplands ahead. And without any prospect of that, I didn't really know how to make sense of any of it. Not time with her, nor even time with my dad, which was somehow even worse.

*

The good news, though, was that by Easter Johnnie had his driving licence. That holiday he'd drive down in the farm's Land Rover a couple of times a week and we'd go out, normally staying at Alan's. If we had hash, we'd drive up around Arthur's Seat when it got dark and hotbox ourselves stupid by the top loch. He'd had a stereo put in with the money he earned on the farm, but heavy bass always blew a loose connection on the speaker on the left. Green Day was particularly bad for that. He kept a screwdriver in the dashboard explicitly to fix it, but one night I'd had enough and mashed it all together with some Juicy Fruit. Did the trick.

When there were parties, also, he'd drive us to them, even if they were in another part of Scotland altogether. Somehow, none of this seemed to take any money at all. Or, at least, not much. Johnnie would fill up his Land Rover with free diesel from the farm – 'red diesel', he called it, because it was dyed red – which meant that a night out cost a packet of fags and a six-pack of beer, or a half of vodka, or a £3 bottle of wine. Sometimes Alan would have booze inherited mysteriously from his parents; sometimes we'd turn up with nothing, wherever we were, and help ourselves. Presumably I also ate food occasionally, although for the life of me I cannot remember what, or from where. There were so many houses, with so many floors on which to sleep, and so few parents, anywhere. Maybe they were off having affairs, or were half dead in a ward; you never asked. Only once, at a party somebody's student cousin threw in her Glasgow flat, do I remember being in a place which ostensibly belonged to no parents at all. Bit of a shithole.

One weekend we went up near Aviemore, for a chaotic blitz of a thing in the massive house of a girl whose parents had something very important to do with either whisky or fruitcake. Or maybe both.

'How are they so fucking rich?' I remember Johnnie asking bitterly, although I guess we both knew that fruitcake and whisky paid better than sheep and mud. The kids up there were all at Gordonstoun and Glenalmond, and they all sounded English, and a decent chunk of them seemed to live in castles. This was Flora's crowd, really, but she was off in Switzerland now, skiing.

Another, we went down to the Borders, near Jedburgh, for something pretty similar in a farmhouse. The kids here were bigger and harder; altogether more obviously Scottish. Ella from school was there, even though she lived in Glasgow, because she was staying with this other girl from school called Catherine who was from Kelso, just down the road. We took up residence on a sofa in the living room, nattering through the madness all around. It wasn't like school. It was fine. At one point she stopped talking and put her head on my shoulder, and I put my arm around her waist, warm against her big Shetland jumper, and I remember thinking how nice that was. Then I stumbled outside with Johnnie for a joint and ended up really quite abruptly getting off with this girl – called Milly, I think, but perhaps Gilly – after an absolute maximum of six minutes' small talk about her New York Yankees baseball cap.

Ella and Catherine left not long after that.

'You're a twat,' snapped Catherine, after Ella walked past me, staring ahead, to their car. And I shrugged at them blankly, like I didn't know what she meant. Boys are annoying. Right?

I don't mean this as an excuse, but something I noticed around then, which was new, was that I was becoming the drunkest person there. Wherever there was. Not everybody would have noticed it, but I did. It wasn't quite like it was with Johnnie, who still needed picking up off the floor three nights out of five, but covertly I was definitely giving him a run for his money. Normally I'd remove myself just in time for a tactical vomit behind a bush, or a private half-hour in a spinning bathroom. I was not showy. I was the old housecat who crawls off to die. My point being, if it all sounds like constant blazing hedonistic delight, then that's probably because that's how I usually choose to remember it. There were other bits, though, and they don't slot into that narrative at all. Objectively, I can see that now. Maybe you can, too.

★

I wrote to Flora quite a lot. She'd told me to, after all. I'm almost certain I wasn't being creepy. I'd started after that thing at Christmas, and I wasn't sure she'd ever write back, but she always did. Maybe my letters were longer than hers, but not by much. I'd tell her funny stories about stuff that had happened; people falling over, teachers losing their shit. I enjoyed the telling; accuracy was not my watchword. I always imagined her reading them aloud in some sort of steamy girls' changing room, all these hot posh English girls giggling along with white towels around their chests and done up in their hair like turbans. Don't laugh at me. It could have happened.

Her writing was beautiful: curvy and smooth. She'd write on proper writing paper, unlike the scraps I'd torn from schoolbooks. She'd detail weekend trips into London, which seemed impossibly glamorous to me, about bands they'd seen in Camden and T-shirts they'd bought on Portobello Road. There was a Portobello in Edinburgh which was full of old people and chippies, but this was a bit different, maybe. She'd also tell me about her plans for next year, and how she might go to India and work in a hospice. I liked the sound of India, but a hospice? With people like my mum?

Once, also, she told me that Trixie had been asking after

me. I remember it very clearly: standing there in the hallway of Esk House and getting an actual erection from the words on the page. That evening I wrote to Trixie; no surname, but I figured there couldn't be more than one Trixie at her school. I couldn't tell you precisely what I said. Same sort of letter as always, I guess, although I remember agonising over whether or not to refer back to when I'd met her at the party. I wanted to sound suave and experienced, acknowledging a sexual experience without it being a big deal. I couldn't phrase it right, though. It sounded either sleazy or like I was showing off. I left it out.

Flora called me the next day, on the phone in the cubicle of Toad's own famous erection downstairs. It's hard to explain how exciting this was. Her actual voice, so different from any other voice I'd heard in weeks. Delivered only to me.

'You wrote to fucking Trixie?' she said incredulously.

'That's bad?' I said.

'Loser,' she said.

Although, a couple of weeks later, I had a reply from Trixie, too. Malthouse, her surname was. The paper was pale blue and smelled nice, and she did a little heart over the 'i' in her name. It was quite short, though, and I guess she could have written it to anybody.

★

The big thing with Johnnie, though, was that all that year he was drifting away. You couldn't miss it. I can't pretend I was working that hard myself, but it was only lower sixth and there were no exams, so the first year of my A-levels felt pretty similar to whatever I'd have been doing anyway.

English was just reading books and talking about them with Ella, and politics was just reading the newspapers like Alan did, so I'd started doing that, too. History was the war, and ancient history was stuff I'd learned aged eleven when I was really into *Asterix* stories and the minotaur. Alan did clever with an alternative swagger, so I did, too. We smoked, we were a mess, we played guitar, we read books, we spoke to girls if we damn well felt like it. All of a sudden I had an identity.

None of that quite worked for Johnnie. He wasn't dumb, but he didn't care, either. He was in two of my subjects and, on a good day, he'd copy my essays. He had headphones in half the time, mainlining grunge or The Levellers. In lessons he'd stare out the window, or sometimes fall asleep. More and more, he was pissing people off, I think on purpose. He'd borrow money and not pay it back. Not that he couldn't, even. He just wouldn't. As if he wanted to see what would happen. He also developed a reputation, far worse, for stealing.

It was odd, actually, the attitude to theft. Clothes, unless known to be particularly cherished (Eugene's leather jacket, say), were considered communal property. Likewise toothpaste, hair gel, books and all other personal possessions, up to and including guitars, stereos and small pieces of furniture. Literally, you could prowl around, take what you want and vaguely mumble to somebody to let somebody else know you had it. Taking cigarettes or alcohol was generally frowned upon, but you could 'borrow' them provided you were open about it and didn't finish them off. The big exception, though, was money. There wasn't much floating around, but it was sacrosanct. You could leave a ten-pound note on your desk, say, and while the Brylcreem or Guns N' Roses tape next to it might disappear, the cash itself would not. If it did, everybody knew there was a problem. And now there was one, and the consensus was that it was him. And now 'Psycho' became 'Klepto'.

'Klepto!' people would shout at him, into their hands, as he walked across the courtyard in front of the chapel. And he'd ignore them, or smirk.

The school tuck shop was known as Flab – you ate too much chocolate, you'd get flabby: seriously clever – and it was this wee shack down by the science block. It was run by this mad old caretaker dude called Jeffers who'd lost half an arm in the war, and half the school would crowd in there of an early evening before tea. Peak *Neighbours* time, and there was a telly above Jeffers' bar. The rugby First XV would dominate the bench against the back wall. By the start of the summer term, Johnnie couldn't go in there any more because he owed too much money to too many of them and was suspected of taking far more.

'Oi, Tommo!' they'd shout at me instead, in their performatively deep, performatively Scottish voices, as I queued for a Chomp. 'Oi, Tommo, where's Klepto? Guy owes me a fiver!' Or worse: 'Did he take my twenty?' And I'd shrug apologetically and pretend not to hear them muttering to each other that we were a bunch of stoner freaks, anyway.

It wasn't actually intimidating. More awkward. Weirdly enough, Barf was in the First XV by then, as a second row. Bit of a chameleon, that one. Though they never shouted at Barf about Johnnie. Just me, really. Alan didn't go near Flab. Alan ate fruit.

The odd thing was, Johnnie didn't need to steal. He was

making money. Every other night, now, he'd do a run out over the roofs for chips or pizza, touring the younger kids' dorms and charging them double for the risk. Often he'd go with Luci because the pair of them had developed a friendship even more unexpected than ours. Well, an association, let's say. Unwashed and a bit reviled, with his long hair and skulls and incense, Luci already had something like the *sui generis* outcast status to which Johnnie seemed to be aspiring. I think Johnnie maybe had just started climbing out of his window to smoke, and then it became a habit.

It caught me unawares. There I was at about 10 p.m. sitting on Luci's floor, hacking away at 'Lithium' on his acoustic, faintly baffled as to where he might have got to if he wasn't with me. And then the pair of them came barrelling back through the window with a pile of cheesy margaritas. Felt a bit peeved, actually. Like I was being cheated on. Twice.

★

Things got worse. There was this big, ginger, rugby-playing prefect guy in our house called Wilson – he probably had a first name, too, but I only remember Wilson – and he was convinced that Johnnie had half-inched a tenner from his desk. He told everybody, which in the veiled customs of Eskmount should have meant that Johnnie either spoke to him and denied it, or quietly replaced the money and said nothing at all. Instead, though, he just walked around smirking. So, Wilson souped him.

Sorry, did I mention souping? I'm not sure I did. It involved no soup. Take half a plastic jug of milk and add . . . well, anything. Tea, coffee, ketchup, salad cream, semolina, haggis, whatever. Actually, soup was totally allowed. It didn't matter. All that mattered was that you poured it over somebody's head.

It couldn't happen at lunch because all the teachers sat at the big top table. Breakfast and tea were run by the prefects, but souping at the former required a rare and frankly unacceptable level of morning energy. Also, Johnnie was a hard person to soup because his movements were unpredictable and he often skipped meals. Wilson got him eventually, though. I didn't see it too clearly, because my table with Geordie and Ella was at the other end of the room. I heard it, though. There was a roar and a scream, and then there were people running everywhere, girls too, swatting collateral goo off their arms.

Wilson was still there, guffawing, still even holding his jug, and I suppose it must have been fifty-fifty that Johnnie would just fly at him, perhaps with a tray, or a plate, or even one of the heavy metal teapots on every table. He didn't, though. He just stood up, flicked his hair back out of his face, drenching everybody nearby, and walked calmly out of the hall while everybody pointed and catcalled 'Psycho' and 'Klepto' at him. Then, that night, he went into the prefects' common room, stole the officially sanctioned six-pack of beer they had in the fridge and left a jug of piss in its place.

Obviously, they knew it was him. The jug, the piss, it was almost poetic. Also, it was a declaration of war. And so, the next day, in the house doughnut queue at break, they came for him. Not just Wilson this time. Maybe ten of them? A cross-section of the prefecture, with a bit of loaned rugby lad muscle. One moment, I was face-to-face with Johnnie, about to ask him if he wanted to come out Luci's window for a fag. The next, he had a pillowcase over his head and was being dragged, backwards, away.

'Hey,' I said stupidly.

Wilson had the back of it, scrunched up in his massive hands, and at first Johnnie was literally being dragged along the floor by his head, hands scrabbling at his face. Then, suddenly, there were people everywhere, pummelling him, punching him, kneeing him in the arms and legs. He was lifted up and his shirt was ripped open, buttons flying. Then his shoes were off, then his trousers, too. Then he was naked from the waist down, and horizontal in the air, with people holding his arms and legs. He was thrashing, mad as an eel on a deck, but he didn't have a hope.

'Mind his cock!' somebody shouted excitedly, and then they were off, bearing him down the corridor, like one of those groups of terrifyingly energetic Royal Marines you sometimes see on the telly, running round with a cannon. He still had his shirt on, and a single sock.

I followed. Of course I did. Everybody did. There must have been fifty people rushing through the house, laughing, shrieking, sprawling, kicking open doors ahead. Then we were in the tub room, and he was being flung – literally, flung – into a bath. It was cold and already full to the brim. No Archimedes geniuses, this lot. He went in back first, head in its pillowcase cracking against the porcelain. Somebody – not Wilson necessarily, I just don't remember – put a hand on top of his head and shoved it under the water, then held it there. His arms and legs went wild.

'Hey,' I said again, which was no more effective than the time before.

Then, abruptly, almost everyone was gone, and Johnnie

came bursting up, face taut against the wet pillowcase like the Turin Shroud. He pulled it over his face and looked around wildly at the five or six of us who were left.

'Bastards,' he managed.

'Why?' I said. 'Why the piss?'

'Just get me a towel,' he said, and I did.

Was I different from the other bystanders? Maybe. What, though, could I have done? I hadn't asked him to mess up his life, and I was no match for a mob. All this, I told myself. While also knowing, without any doubt at all, how relentlessly he would have fought on my behalf, if it had been the other way around.

★

He was expelled with half a term to go. Luci, too, although he'd done his exams by then and didn't give a shit. They'd gone through the attic space and prised away the panel to get down into the little office used by Mork, the deputy housemaster. By that point Johnnie's place in the school was dangling by a thread, and when Mork opened the door, his actual body was also dangling by a rope ladder made out of knotted sheets, with a half-full whisky decanter in his spare hand and Mork's half-full wallet in his pocket. Luci was up top, peering down.

Hardly anybody was sorry to see him go. The grief, the violence, the 'Klepto' stuff; places like Eskmount reject those things, like an immune system. He'd become the grit in the eye. Reactionary mobs always win. Sometimes just slowly.

12

I SPENT THE END of that summer up at Burnside. Annie had decided not to be a management consultant but was now working for some sort of London bank, and Dad was going up and down between there and home, seemingly at random. I told him I wanted to stay in Edinburgh to be near my mum, but it wasn't really true. She was back in hospital. Lungs again, with a side order of kidneys. I'd go to see her a couple of times a week, but never for long. Sometimes she was definitely listening; sometimes you couldn't be sure. Sometimes, after I'd told her something I was totally sure she'd be interested in, she'd prepare to speak, and I'd beam and brace myself to listen, and then eventually it would turn out that she'd only wanted to say, 'Can you close the window?' or 'Is there a blanket on my feet?' Which wasn't, you know, always scintillating. The nurses were old and sad; the place smelled of bleach and was two bus rides away. I hated it.

Johnnie didn't exactly invite me up, but he seemed pleased enough when I invited myself. I guess he was lonely. Alan was off in Italy doing a history of art course. It was only when I got to Johnnie's that I learned Flora had some new boyfriend in London and wouldn't be back for three weeks. And Dean, his farmer friend, was in jail.

'Sorry, he's in what?' I said, when Johnnie picked me up from Perth station in the farm's Land Rover.

'He's in jail,' said Johnnie, fiddling with the stereo. 'He was growing weed in his dad's greenhouse. Totally raided. He got six months.'

'But that's awful.'

'Weed wasn't,' said Johnnie cheerfully, and then he put on 'Sell Out' by The Levellers and the bass went *voooom* and so did we.

Jenny, Johnnie's mum, was pleased, too. He was signed up for sixth-form college in Edinburgh next year, but he had no summer plans at all and I think she had a notion that I might be a good influence. I didn't mind. At least half my reason for going to Burnside had been to sneak my way towards seeing Flora again, but I'd soon almost forgotten this. In the days, we worked on the farm, mainly stripping the interiors out of these damp, dilapidated cottages down by the river. They were a mess, like every building on the farm was a mess. All the windows were cracked, often because Johnnie and Douglas had put them out over the years with their air rifles. Rats skulked in rotting kitchens, birds nested in chimney stacks. Nobody had used any of them for ages. We earned £4 an hour, which adds up, particularly when you've nothing to spend it on.

At first I was a bit perplexed as to who was actually paying us. Didn't Johnnie own the farm? Although, he explained, as we hammered and chiselled and stripped, that his family actually just owned the largest percentage of the company which owned it. The next largest was owned by Flora's dad, who had bought it from Johnnie's dad in the 1970s. It was he who had put up the money for renovations, mainly because he wanted it to have healthier balance sheets when he took it over. There were also a whole bunch of Australian relatives whom Johnnie didn't really know, descended from his great uncle. Day-to-day, the place was now managed by Iain Bonnar, Fusty's real dad. 'He's MacPhail's guy, though,' Johnnie said, a few times. We saw him most days, glowering murderously through the windscreen of a Land Rover. He terrified me, but on the other hand he was giving me £40 a day.

Our main project was a little cottage surrounded by banks of nettles. The whitewash was grey and the roof had a massive hole in it, but it was pretty, all the same. It's fun work, knocking down a house. We had sledgehammers for walls and scrapers for plaster. Sometimes we were joined by this fat old builder from the village called Archie, who was in charge of the team that would eventually be rebuilding everything. He wasn't usually much help. 'Oan ye go, lads,' he'd say, settling himself atop a pile of rubble with a Regal, watching us crack on. One time, when I was clearing some weeds, he told me to get a hoe.

'What's a hoe?'

'Ye city-bred cunt,' he said, but nicely.

Another time, though, Johnnie put his sledgehammer through the plaster in an upstairs room and bees started flooding out. Archie came to life. The trick, he said, was to keep smoking *all the time*, so that the bees left you alone. Actually, it totally worked. Delicately, we stripped the walls until we could see the hive, which was beige and between beams and rectangular, about the size of a lunchbox. You could smell the honeycomb, like the inside of a Crunchie. The bees sounded like traffic.

'Okay, stand back,' said Archie, and then he took a broad shovel and slowly scooped the whole thing onto it. Things went a bit wild at that point. I was backing towards the door, waving my arms. Johnnie seemed to be trying to stare the bees down. Psycho. By then, though, I don't think you could smoke enough. Then Archie took a step towards the glassless window hole and flicked his arms, sending the whole swarming blizzard soaring out onto the skip on the grass out the back.

'Now,' he said, turning towards us, bees in his beard, shovel planted downwards like a wizard's staff, and the sky out the window behind him blackening like a coming storm.

'Now, what?' said Johnnie, sounding uncertain.

'Now we run like fuck,' said Archie conversationally, so we did.

For the next hour we lay about in the sun out the front, until the bees came to terms with living in a skip now. For the rest of that week, though, they were coming back in, buzzing forlornly as they failed to find their home in a wall that wasn't even there any more. I felt bad for them. I wondered what would happen to them, now the world they knew was gone. Archie said they'd die.

★

When we weren't working, we mainly killed things. Systematically. Learning death like a sommelier learns wine. Our staple victims were pigeons. They lived in the rafters of the murky barns in the farmyard and were exactly the right quarry for Johnnie's pellets. You'd aim the first into their fat bodies from down below, and they'd plummet, windmilling feathers. Then you'd pump another in from point blank into the head, and all that would stop. At first Johnnie did most of the shooting, but as the weeks went by, I did my bit, too. It wasn't like the chicken. This was clean and easy. It felt like a moral act, too, because the barns were full of grain from the fields and so were the pigeons. I knew this because after we shot them, we'd carry them to a shed by the house which was home to seven or eight farm cats. Within an hour or two, all that would be left was a scattering of grey feathers and a little golden pyramid of grain. Not even any bones. Cats are savage.

Sometimes Johnnie would shoot the rats that stalked all the derelict barns and cottages, but they were hard to spot between rubble and crates, and they never stood still. One shot would normally do it. The pellet would go straight through, leaving a smooth, red bump of entrails as an exit wound. I wasn't wild about that. We left them where they were. Bald tails.

Crows were much harder, but you had to try. Johnnie said they were vermin, eating smaller birds and pecking out a lamb's eyes. I dunno. Maybe? The trouble was, they were smart. Normally you could walk right up to them, but approach with a gun and they'd side-eye you, cackle and lope off into the next field. I swear, you'll think I'm making it up. But they knew.

Johnnie, though, also had this rusty black Webley Hurricane air pistol that had belonged to Douglas, so once or twice we tried putting it in a rucksack and walking up to the crows while talking expansively of other things. 'I say, old chap, have you been watching the football?' I'd say, in a posh voice, and he'd say, 'Yah, hurrah for the Hearts of

Midlothians!' while giggling and fumbling in the bag for the gun, but the birds weren't having it at all. Keen eye for sincerity, those guys. Eventually, though, we hit on a new plan involving Johnnie's disintegrating Renault. Basically, he'd drive madly across the field, right up close, and then I'd kick open the door and try to pop one. Like a gangland shooting out of *Boyz n the Hood*. It worked precisely once, from about five feet away.

'Fuck, yeah!' said Johnnie, exultantly skidding to a stop.

The crow was a lot tougher than a pigeon, though. It tried to take off after I'd shot it, with one useless, broken wing flapping around. It kept making a noise, but not a loud noise. The binbag-black beak widening and closing. The placid screaming of nightmares.

'Jesus,' I said, shaken, fumbling to load another pellet, but Johnnie was quicker, leaping from the car with a tire iron from the foot well. Bang. Lots of times, actually. Maybe too many.

'A murder of crows,' I said afterwards, trying to be blithe.

'Just the one so far,' he said.

'Yeah . . . but the word,' I said. 'You call a group of crows a *murder*. Like, instead of *flock*?'

Johnnie just shrugged.

In another barn, the one where they kept the tractors, there was a barn owl. It was an amazing, beautiful white ghost of a thing, and the moment you stepped inside it would soar silently out over your head, like a wraith. We never tried to kill it. I'm honestly not sure why not.

Quite often, throughout this time, I'd try to see myself as Flora might, if she were there. That 'murder' line would have impressed her, right? But all the killing? I wasn't sure. I knew they shot pheasants at Auchnastang at Christmas and some other bird in the summer. In my mind it was all loud men who say 'yah' a lot getting together in tweed with Labradors and spaniels. But that, I felt, might be a bit different.

★

For rabbits, anyway, we'd wait until night, when Jenny had gone to bed and Johnnie could illicitly nab the proper .22 rifle from the gun cabinet without her ever knowing. All the guns were licensed to his mum now, although she never used them. I wondered how she could bear to keep any at all, although Johnnie said you needed them on a farm, just in case. It was sleeker than the air rifle, with a telescopic sight, and it smelled impressive and dangerous. We'd head out in the Land Rover, higher and smoother than the Renault, and the big, red ashtray-faced searchlight would light up the sky like we were summoning Batman.

The year before, with the air gun, we'd had to get close to the rabbits to have a hope. Now we could be hundreds of metres away. It was like being a sniper in a computer game, and the fields were ours and the night our kingdom. I loved it. It was late July now and never too cold, and the stars were insane. We'd get stoned, but not stoned stupid. Just to the right level, where the gun was another limb and the bullet was a piece of your mind that could send a bunny toppling down a hillock.

The first night we went out, we got eight, and they looked better lined up on the Landy's bonnet than they ever had on the Renault. Johnnie said that Iain Bonnar paid him £3 a head because three rabbits would eat as much grass as one sheep. Afterwards, by way of a celebration, we drove down to the moonlit river for a last spliff. Maybe it was half-past midnight. We had a couple, sitting lightly on the bumper, blowing smoke towards the white light dancing on the ripples. By the time I'd finished rolling the third I was deep in thought about how often Johnnie had done exactly this, exactly here. And maybe Douglas and Fusty in years before that, and even before that, who knows, maybe Johnnie's dad and Flora's dad, too. Although with whisky and cigars back then, probably, rather than Dean's garden-shed weed. I wondered how much he had grown, and how much trouble he was in. And I was about to ask when I suddenly realised Johnnie wasn't next to me and hadn't been for ages.

I found him around the front of the car, lit by the headlights. He was cross-legged on the grass. Head down, with a lock-knife in one hand and a rabbit in the other. Red-black blood up to his elbow.

'What . . . ?' I began, and then I noticed three dead rabbits stretched out in front of him. The fourth, in his hands, looked like it had been through a mangle.

'Bullets,' he said. 'Iain will see. He'll know we've been using the rifle. I need to get them out.'

I couldn't say anything. Johnnie bent the knife sideways. There was a cracking sound.

'Heart,' he said conversationally. 'Look. Purple. Those are the ribs. Like matchsticks.'

'But, Johnnie . . .' I was quite upset. Thinking of the chicken. Maybe not just the chicken.

'You're the one who shot it,' he pointed out.

'Yeah. But. Is it necessary?'

'Actually, it might not be,' he said. 'Because the bullets and pellets are the same size.'

'Jesus.'

'You're right,' said Johnnie. 'Dunno what I was thinking. And we can't give him this one now, anyway. State of it. He'll think I'm nuts. Too stoned.'

And he stood, and held it by the back legs, swung it into the river. And I felt a drop of gore land on my bottom lip. Tiny, like salted rain.

★

Our only other hobby was dangerous driving. There was a steep road off at one end of the boundary between the farms. The Plunge, Johnnie called it. It wasn't private – it was tarmac, and anyone could use it – but it went nowhere much except the top of a quite random hill, so nobody did. Johnnie liked to drive to the top, turn around and cut the engine. By the time you'd rolled to the bottom, you could be doing thirty or more. He'd do it with his eyes closed sometimes, while I screamed and hit at him. Once or twice, we did it at night, with the lights off. Windows open, wind rushing in, the road and the hedge all pitch-dark, feeling the world rush by, hoping to judge things smartly enough to brake before we hit the corner and the ditch at the end. A few goes in, I started to enjoy it. I was on a learning curve. It's the countryside. You make your own fun.

★

One afternoon Johnnie had been sent off in the Renault to

fetch some bags of grit or sand, or some shit like that, and it was just me and Archie. We were removing a stove; a huge brown rusted metal thing, incomprehensibly concreted into the stone of the chimney breast. It took a lot of chiselling, and Archie had a policy of taking a fag break roughly every fifteen minutes. So, I did, too, and I found myself asking about Iain Bonnar, Fusty's dad. The guy in charge of the farm. So huge and silent, and of such indefinable status. At night when we were out and about, even when it was really late, Johnnie would glimpse the lights of his Toyota roaming around the farm and immediately kill ours, because Iain thought we did our hunting in the afternoons, and with a legal weapon. Also, I remembered him at the party. Hulking, like a bouncer.

'Iain Bonnar has been here about as long as I have,' said Archie. 'Which is near twenty year. Since he married Elspeth MacPhail.'

'But he always looks like he hates it here.'

'Probably does,' snorted Archie. 'All that stuff with the boy? Giving your son tae another man? Weird business.'

I shrugged. It was a weird business to me, too.

Archie confirmed that Bonnar had been in the army. He'd fought in the Falklands.

'Wow,' I said, thinking this seemed about right.

'And then he wis polis,' said Archie. 'Up in the village. Proper bruiser. Right up until he took over here a couple of years ago. And that wis a weird business, too.'

'How do you mean?'

Archie said Bonnar had done things for Flora's dad, even as a policeman. I asked what he meant, and he settled down, turning his fag break into a double fag break, as he did when he had a story. Bit of an old woman was Archie. You could imagine him in an apron, gossiping over a fence.

Once, he said, maybe fifteen years earlier, a convoy of gypsies had parked up in the field by the grain barn. They were there a week, and MacPhail went to see them and asked them to go. They said no, so he offered to pay them. Then they said yes. But two days later, they were still there.

'So, Iain went tae see them,' said Archie. 'In the night. With some other lads. And after that, right enough, they went.'

'Huh,' I said.

Archie said there were stories about Bonnar doing other things for MacPhail, too. Not on the farm. More to do with his property business. Evictions, on a site up on the West Coast. Some sort of entanglement over a car park up in Aberdeen, where a local gang had tried to muscle in, and Bonnar had persuaded them to muscle out again.

'Not a man tae dance with,' said Archie meaningfully.

'Jesus,' I said, thinking of him at the party, not dancing at all.

'And now his boy's in the castle and he's still in his own wee cottage,' said Archie, 'and how he stands it, I do not know. That wife's no' a ray of sunshine, either, eh?'

'But they should be pleased. Fusty is their heir. All that stuff over there. It's going to be his, right?'

'Disnae look pleased, though, eh?' said Archie. Archly, I suppose.

★

Anyway, after a fortnight or so of this sort of thing – work, death, work, death, work, death, slightly camp gossip from Archie, incredibly dangerous driving, work again, death again, still no Flora – a couple of lads came by the cottage to drop off some more gravel for the paths. We were hard at it, smashing out the bricks that had been behind the fireplace.

'Johnno!' called one of them from the window of his big red van, and we put down our sledgehammers and went out to speak with them. Turned out Johnnie knew them because they were friends of Dean's. They hadn't been to see him up in the Perth jail, but they were thinking about it. Johnnie sounded much more Scottish when he spoke to them. Although probably so did I. He introduced me as 'Tommo'. Tommo and Johnno. Super. Like Hobbits.

'Mind that night last year wi' the gun?' said Fergus, who was skinny and ginger. 'That wis grand. So stoned, man.'

'We're out most nights,' said Johnnie. 'Come with?'

'Mental,' said Mark, who was the other one, and that night they did.

It was properly messy. Mark brought acid, Fergus brought speed, and he and Johnnie took both. Me, I didn't fancy the acid. I'd had some mushrooms one Sunday with Luci the term before and I'd found them mundane but unpleasant. My tongue had kept hitting the back of my front teeth and they had felt huge and dangerous, like a guillotine at the end of a cavern. Didn't like it. Although, happily, it turned out that mixing weed with speed was interesting enough, and a great way to break the monotony of smoking it on its own.

Mark and Fergus were smart and fun, nattering gossip from the farm and village. They were both a year older than us. Fergus was settled now, working as a brickie with his uncle. Mark had a place at Napier after the summer to do engineering. He wanted to know about Edinburgh clubs, and I had to bullshit a bit because I'd hardly been to any.

'Not even Pure?' he said, aghast.

'I don't think so,' I hazarded.

Fergus sat in the front with Johnnie. Mark was in back with me. They were an odd mix of reserved and wild. With Johnnie, who they knew, there was an edge of deference, for his car, his farm. One time, when we saw some lights on the road, Fergus asked if it might be Bonnar, and Johnnie said he didn't care if it was, and that was enough for him, as if Johnnie versus Iain Bonnar was a perfectly reasonable match.

Me, I was more of an anomaly. They had a tape – *The Orb's Adventures Beyond The Ultraworld* – and we put it on, and it turned out that driving around the Scottish countryside listening to ambient trance really is more fun than just listening to moaning depressives from Seattle. Within an hour, everybody was baked and jabbering. They'd both whoop every time we shot a rabbit. This one time, when Fergus ran out in front of the car to pick one up, Mark leaned forwards, pumped up the music and started strobing the fog lights. Fergus danced on the spot, knees up, big fish, little fish, cardboard box. This, I thought, was the kind of thing I wanted Flora to know about. For a while, I sketched out how I'd put it in a letter I could write the next day. Then I remembered she was staying with her boyfriend in London, so decided maybe not.

It was maybe 1.30 a.m. when we ran out of Rizlas. Bad planning. For a while we dug in our pockets for receipts and talked of smoking through cans, but we didn't have receipts or a can, so it was all a bit of a waste of time. Then Mark said there was a garage on the other side of Auchternethy that might be open, and Fergus, who was driving, spun the wheel and headed for the road.

'Woah,' I said, alarmed. 'You're not too messed up?'

'Nae bother,' said Fergus.

'It's fine,' said Johnnie from the passenger seat, so I shut up.

The garage wasn't open, though, so Fergus said he'd try the one in Crieff, which was a small town only twenty minutes away along the back lanes. It was pitch-black. Cloudy, no stars. Sometimes a suicidal rabbit would burst across the road in our headlights, but otherwise the world was ours. Crieff, though, was a ghost town, too, all hedges and streets and railings and no life at all.

'Alrighty, then,' said Fergus. 'Perth?'

Perth was fifteen miles away, back the way we'd come and onto the A9, but the music was Underworld now, and Robert Miles, and Josh Wink, and I didn't mind at all. By the time we were onto the big road I was loving the headlights and the tail-lights, all working with the sound. My Juicy Fruit speaker connection had worn loose, but the rattling fuzz was mixed in with everything else.

'Tripping,' said Mark, in a low voice, and I was briefly jealous of him and Johnnie with their acid, not that I was feeling all that terrestrial myself. None of us were talking much by then, although Johnnie sounded more or less normal when he did.

Heading into Perth was like docking on a space station, all lights and wonder.

'Bingo,' said Johnnie, as a BP garage came into view.

'Steady,' Fergus said. 'Polis.' And outside the garage, on the road, there was a white and orange Rover. He opened the window and started wafting, trying to flush out the smell.

'Keep going,' suggested Johnnie. 'Next one.'

Something was nagging at me. A cold line of metal across my face. I sat up and looked out the window at the police car as we passed. On the driver's side was a policeman's face. Quite young. Red cheeks. In my memory he was wearing a blue shirt, like they did in the seventies. Can't have been, though. Maybe he had a moustache, or perhaps I just thought he should. Then I looked down at my own hands.

'Um, guys?' I said. 'I'm holding a rifle.'

'Oh, *Christ*,' said Fergus, and after that we didn't keep going to the next one at all, but instead went straight home.

★

By the time we got back, Johnnie was tripping hard. Bad timing, all round. Fergus left the car at the drive and went one way with Mark to get back to his own while we went the other. Johnnie's footsteps on the gravel were deafening, rolling over the countryside. As we got closer to the house, I made him walk on the grass verge instead. Honestly, I was a mess, too. Like, really badly. But I could tell I was better than him.

'Is it time?' he kept saying, about God knows what.

'Shut up,' I kept saying.

Inside I made him take me to the gun cabinet, so we could lock up the rifle. It took ages. It was funny, and then it wasn't, and then it was again. Big, dark countryside house. Ghosts aplenty. Then I dragged him up the stairs to his attic room and pushed him into bed. His was a big double; mine was a mattress next to it on the floor. In my bag, I had a Walkman. Could I be bothered to find it? What I wanted, really, was to go to sleep listening to it. I wanted Mark's music, though. Not mine. What Johnnie wanted was to talk. He peered over the side of the bed and looked down at me, wide-eyed, like a raccoon in a tree.

'That could have been bad,' he said.

'Which bit?' I said, realising only now how much everything was spinning.

'They hate me,' he said. 'The pigs. And they know me. Arseholes, man.'

'Oh, that bit,' I said. 'Because of Eugene? And the brick?'

'No. Because of Douglas. Because they all know Iain, don't they? And I wonder what he's said.'

'Oh,' I said. 'Right, no. Sorry, what?'

Johnnie lay back and sighed. It was dark, but the curtains were open, sending brown light in from the world.

Douglas had been an arsehole, too, he said. Really, a terrible prick.

'Right,' I said, feeling uncomfortable. Thinking that getting my Walkman might be a bit rude at this point.

'I mean, I feel like I shouldn't say it,' said Johnnie. 'Because he's dead. And because nobody else says it. Any more. But he was nasty. Same as Fusty. As bad as each other.'

I didn't say anything. I was thinking of that story about

the two of them rolling those girls down the hill in the Portaloo. Turning them blue.

'And once,' said Johnnie, 'he tried to kill me.'

'Oh, I'm sure he didn't.' For some reason I said it very politely.

'No, he did,' said Johnnie, and he started to tell me a story. It went on a bit, and I don't think I got all of it, but it was about a really bad and angry week that culminated in something to do with a fox that had been eating chickens and living in the farrier barn next to the one that the cats were in.

'There are chickens?' I said, because this was not an animal I had seen at Burnside.

'Not any more,' said Johnnie to the ceiling.

Then he was quiet. For so long, actually, that I thought he'd fallen asleep.

'Yeah?' I said eventually.

'Sorry,' said Johnnie. 'I should have drunk some booze. Come down a bit. The curtains. They're not . . . there. Are they?'

'I mean, you don't have to tell me all this now,' I said. 'It's cool. Any other time.'

Although then he started talking, like he couldn't stop. This fox, he said. It was, like, three or four years ago. And Jenny, one night, had told the boys that their dad used to shoot foxes but she wasn't up for it, and so she said she was going to call Iain Bonnar. And Douglas had decided that he should do it instead, being the man of the house, so he got hold of the shotgun and commandeered Johnnie as a helper. And they waited until Jenny was out with her horse, and then they went into the barn and blocked the door with a bale, and then Douglas told Johnnie to load the gun and started heaving all the other bales away from the wall until the fox bolted out and tried to squeeze past the bale by the door but couldn't quite fit.

'And I shot it,' said Johnnie. 'Right up close. Dead, straight away. And Douglas went mental. So cross. You know all the horseshoes in there? He threw one. Right in my face.'

That scar, I thought, and I asked why he had been so cross.

'Because he was a dick,' said Johnnie. 'Because he was meant to be the big man, I suppose, but I'd been the big man instead.'

'Right,' I said. 'But he was just cross. I mean, it's bad. But it's not like he was trying to . . . to . . .'

Johnnie said that came next, though. Right afterwards. Because he'd dropped the shotgun, and Douglas had picked it up and pointed it at him.

'Right,' I said again, because it was safe and neutral.

'Blood in my eyes,' said Johnnie, sounding exasperated. 'But I remember. And I started crying. Although I thought, well, he's only pretending. And he can't shoot me, anyway. Because I'd only put one cartridge in. Before the fox ran out.'

I didn't say anything.

'And then I think I heard a click,' said Johnnie.

'You think? A click?'

'And, you know, it makes me think. It could have been me. The dead kid. All the other way around. And maybe that would have been better for everyone.'

'Shit,' I said, and Johnnie sounded like he was crying. And I remember thinking back to that morning, when we'd gone at the fireplace with our hammers, and then that evening, when we'd picked up Fergus and Mark, and wondering if this could really have all been the same day. It felt like a month. Or longer. Like me and Johnnie had been together, living like this, for half a life. I wondered if I should climb up and hug him. I wasn't sure how he'd take it.

Although before I could, Johnnie rolled onto his front and flopped a hand down towards me, and I grabbed it, and he grabbed back. I remember exactly how it felt. Around the wrists. Warrior style. Brothers in arms. I also remember that it made me think of those names in gold on the walls in the Eskmount Chapel, lines upon lines of them, of boys like us who had died in the trenches. I thought of them and their guns, and us and ours, and then I remember thinking that this was a shameful link to make, because they were fighting Germans, not rabbits, and Germans had shot back. And I also remember that when I woke in the morning, pretty early, Johnnie had somehow slid down to my mattress and was curled up against me, like a cat.

13

THEN, FINALLY, THE RETURN of Flora. She turned up with Fusty two days before I was due to be heading home. It was nothing to do with me – Jenny was either borrowing or lending a collection of huge hard, brown leather saddle sort of things from or to scary Mrs MacPhail and they'd come to pick them up – but Flora sought me out as I sprawled on the sofa with Marianne and Tabitha, the twins, watching mid-afternoon *Falcon Crest*, with which both of them, inexplicably, were obsessed.

They were always sweet, those two: light and dark. Tabitha, the dark one, was intense and serious, solemnly asking me questions about the sociological backdrop of Californian vineyards to which I simply didn't have the answer. Marianne, the other, was loud and cheerful, apparently like Johnnie's father had been. With the fierce loyalties of children, they'd adopted me as family almost instantly. Both of them also regarded me as the sage of all *Falcon Crest* wisdom, entirely because the show's matriarch, Jane Wyman, had been in a coma, and so had my mum. And, in the context of seeing my life through the imagined eyes of Flora, the spectacle of me chuckling on a sofa with a couple of small girls probably wasn't all that bad.

'Well, hello,' said Flora, suddenly appearing in the middle of the room, as though she'd star-jumped around the door.

'Oh,' I said, sitting up. 'Hey.'

'Shut *up*,' said Marianne, staring intently at a girl on a horse.

'You shut up,' I said, and then I leapt up and went over to the door.

Flora was in baggy jeans and a big, off-the shoulder sweater, both of which looked like they'd been made exactly to look like they hadn't been made for her, if you see what I mean. Her red hair was longer now, and pinker, and she looked intimidatingly grown-up. I asked how London had been, and she said, 'Complicated,' which was an answer that I filed away approvingly. Then I asked her how long she had been back.

'Just a couple of days,' she said. 'I'm here for the Glorious Twelfth.'

'The, uh, French Revolution?' I hazarded, and she laughed, and I immediately made myself laugh, too, although I wasn't sure why I was supposed to.

Actually, explained Flora, the Glorious Twelfth was what they called the first day of the grouse-shooting season. It was all a bit of a party, and it was tomorrow, and Johnnie and I should definitely come over and hang out.

'As it happens,' I said modestly, 'I'm quite good at shooting these days.'

'Oh, we've got enough guns.'

'Yeah, I don't actually have a gun.'

'Guns are people, Tom.'

'That's a mad thing to say,' I said. 'You're a mad person.'

'No, but literally,' she said.

I blinked, and she laughed, which made me laugh, and then we were laughing together and, wow, that was nice.

Then she said there were a bunch of saddles in the Range Rover that needed to go to the barn and, as we walked out, the rough wool of her jumper touched my bare arm. And then she banged a shoulder into me fondly and reached down and squeezed my hand, and yeah, wow, that was pretty nice, too.

I took two of the saddle things and manhandled them towards the barn I would now forever think of as the one in which Douglas had pointed a gun at his little brother and pulled the trigger. They were heavy, and I went across the yard with one on each arm, like some medieval peasant carrying one of those racks they used for buckets of milk. The barn door was open and I could hear voices from inside.

'Just fuck off,' Johnnie was saying. 'Why would you come here? How do you dare? I don't want to see you at all.'

'Come on,' said the other person, and I realised it was Fusty. 'Come and talk to him. To us.'

'No,' said Johnnie. 'Why? I haven't signed anything. I won't. Just leave me alone.'

'Look,' said Fusty. 'We both . . . we both . . .'

Then he stopped because I was at the door. I dunno, how old was Fusty back then? Still twenty-one? Thereabouts. But he was fat like a man of fifty and dressed in a checked shirt and mustard cords, like somebody's uncle. Face the winning hue of wet brick. There was something about Fusty that made him look like the sort of man who badly wanted to be what Fusty was, if you see what I mean. Ersatz poshery. Roleplay. I can't pin it down. Even from the start, he always creeped me out.

'We both what?' said Johnnie.

Fusty looked at me in irritation before clearly deciding I

wasn't worth worrying about.

'We both lost him,' he said. 'That night. It wasn't just you. We both did.'

'You bet we fucking did,' said Johnnie.

And the way Johnnie looked at him? If he'd had that shotgun? Well. Click.

★

It wasn't until later that I tried to talk to him about it. That night, in the car, out in the fields. The shooting was lacklustre by now and, to be honest, the smoking was, too. We just went out because it was better than staying in. That thing about guests being like fish and starting to stink on the third day? It had taken me longer, but I was stinking, for sure. We were bored with each other. Bored with ourselves.

'Look, man,' I said, as we trundled along some lane or another, 'I don't really get it.'

Then I told him to tell me if I was overstepping the mark, by all means, but I didn't get the issue. With Fusty. Because he was his dead brother's best friend. And he'd be hurting. And it didn't seem right that Johnnie hated him so much.

Johnnie stopped the car. We weren't anywhere in particular, but he stopped it anyway. Then he looked at me. Properly furious.

'What do you know?' he said.

'Nothing,' I said meekly.

'No, I'm serious. How much do you fucking know?'

I thought about this. Then I told him that I knew that

Douglas had died by the ravine. That the police had asked him about it last year, but nothing had come of it.

'Not that,' said Johnnie impatiently. 'All the stuff. The big stuff. You talk to Alan, right? He knows. So, what do you know?'

'Oh, right. I know that Douglas owned the farm? Like, properly? Like you will, but don't yet? Although not all of it, because other people own some of it, too. Including Fusty's dad. I mean, his uncle. Whatever. MacPhail. Right?'

'Go on.'

'Well,' I said, and I tried to get it all in a straight line. 'I know that Douglas didn't want to sell it. But that other people did. Particularly, you know, them. And you think that had, um, an impact on his death.'

'An impact? Yeah, that's one way of putting it.'

I didn't say anything. I pulled two cigarettes from my packet of Regal – three weeks on a farm and I was smoking Regal now – and lit them both at once. Then I gave one to him. Johnnie drew on his.

'They were there,' he said. 'MacPhail and Fusty. They made it look like an accident.'

'Right,' I said, and I thought about this. 'I mean, this is your theory? Or . . . ?'

'It's not a fucking theory, Tommo. I know. Right? I know. But Fusty's real dad is properly in with the police, and MacPhail controls everything around here. So that's that.'

'Come on,' I said.

'Come on, what?' said Johnnie dangerously.

I didn't know what to say. I thought of Iain Bonnar and the 'things' mad old Archie had said he did for MacPhail. But this?

'I mean . . .' But I didn't know what I meant. 'I mean, how? And why? I mean, for what? To make you sell the farm? You're still here. Nobody has sold anything.'

'They'll swoop in. MacPhail is going to have it all. And then that fat bastard Fusty will. And I can't do anything. They've seen to that. And if I try, I'll be toast, too.'

'Jeez, man,' I said.

Johnnie's mental, I thought. He actually is a mad person. It was upsetting.

'But I'll get them back,' he said. 'And you'll help me.'

'What, now?' I said, feeling like this must be some kind of sick game and he was about to start laughing.

'No,' said Johnnie, and he started the car again. 'Not now. But soon.'

Then we drove off in silence, to find new bits of nowhere to drive around, and new, harmless, sweet, beautiful things to kill. Then, after a while, I asked him if that meant he wasn't coming to see Flora for the Glorious Twelfth.

'What's *happened* to you?' he said.

★

He didn't come, although he did drop me off. Picture me, disgorged outside the castle in my jeans and with my rucksack and guitar from a muddy Land Rover onto an immaculate pebble drive. Blinking, amid a sea of men who looked like older versions of Fusty and were dressed like Fusty and sounded like Fusty, too. 'A girl called Trixie once gave me a handjob behind that hedge!' I desperately wanted to tell somebody, but whom?

'There you are,' said Flora, coming down the house steps.

'What the hell are you wearing?' I said, which probably wasn't that charming, but I was a bit upset to see that she was dressed like Fusty, too. She had a checked shirt on, along with these knee-length tweed shorts over massive socks. A waxed green Barbour.

She blushed, but in a way more cross than embarrassed. Then she took me into the house and found me another green Barbour and a pair of green wellies, after which I probably looked enough like everybody else to pass without comment. I thought of Armstrong's, that second-hand shop off the Royal Mile. Had there been Barbours in there? Maybe I should get one, for next time.

Shooting at Auchnastang wasn't a bit like shooting at Burnside. Or rather, while that had been merely shooting, this was Shooting. First, for ages, we all stood around on the driveway, as Flora and her mum floated around with trays of mushy sausages on sticks and shot glasses full of some sort of broth. While she was gone, I had no idea who to speak to or what to say. Men in tweed caps were opening and closing the backs of their cars, pulling on boots and snapping shotguns closed. There were spaniels and Labradors everywhere, and a smell of leather and oil mixing with them, and the sausages, and the broth.

'Who you?' barked a blond man with a comb-over.

'Tom Dwarkin,' I said. Managing, but only just, to resist adding 'sir'.

'Tommo's been staying with the Burchills at Burnside,' said Fusty, coming towards us across the stones.

'Yes,' I said, unable to drag my eyes from his shotgun. It was sticking out over the crook of his elbow, with the gun folded open in the middle. His other arm was its mirror image, behind his back. As a mannerism, there was something very Prince Charles about it. Was that what was always going on with the body language of the aristocracy? Would it all suddenly make sense if you stuck in a shotgun? I was also wondering, simultaneously, if this was the first time Fusty had ever actually spoken to me. I was almost surprised he knew my name.

'Ah,' said Comb-over, 'bad business. Poor Jenny. Fine girl. Should have remarried after Alistair. Man about the place.'

'Poor Johnnie, too,' said Fusty, shooting me a protective, if sweaty, glance, of exactly the sort that a murderer wouldn't.

'The other son?' said Comb-over. 'I heard he was a bad lot.'

'He's had a rough year,' I said, a bit too quickly.

Christ, though, but what was this? My voice didn't belong here, with all the men in green waving their blue-black weapons around and their massive cars and the bounding dogs. It belonged, at best, in Morningside, in a world of soft hands, flowers in the front garden and peering suspiciously at the neighbours. Comb-over sounded English, although probably wasn't. Fusty, too. Johnnie didn't, but he also didn't sound like me. Johnnie was gruff Scottish. Farmer Scottish. Scottish with a gun.

Then Fusty said that Johnnie was a friend of ours, which was odd for two reasons: first, it suggested that Johnnie didn't hate him, which he did; and second, it suggested that Fusty and I were also friends, which we weren't. Although Comb-over apologised afterwards, anyway, and Fusty said it was fine, and I shrugged, too.

'Tommo's actually a friend of Flora's,' said Fusty, as if

retreating from a pose too far. 'I think he's a beater today, right?'

This was news to me. I wondered if beaters were the people who killed the birds once Comb-over and his friends had shot them. Because I could do that now. If I had to. With a stick. Probably.

'I think so,' I hazarded.

'Don't get shot!' jeered Comb-over.

'You neither!' I jeered back, in my stupid, squeaky, all-wrong, joke of a voice.

Then Comb-over roared with laughter and punched me on the upper arm. My God, but small talk with these people was just exhausting.

★

Turned out I was all wrong about beating, too. Actually, you're there to walk through the heather waving a flag and going 'Gaaah!' or 'Breep-breep!' or making some other insane noise, thereby encouraging the grouse to take off, so some toff who has been sitting on his backside until now can shoot them back down again. When they took off, you'd shout, 'Over!' and so would everybody else. Distantly, a little later, you'd hear the bangs. You'd do this over and over again, and each time it was called a 'drive'. As in, beaters are drivers. I don't get it, either.

Either way, the geography of everything means you are head-on to the guns, which was presumably why Comb-over had told me not to get shot, because presumably people often do. You start off quite far away, tramping up some distant hillside. By the end of the drive, though, you're only about fifty metres away, and the little balls of lead shot come pattering down around you, like hail. Then Captain Beater (I don't think this was really his name), who was this ancient guy dressed like the guns despite not being one, would blow a horn, and nobody was allowed to shoot at you any more. Or, indeed, at all.

After the horn went, anyway, MacPhail would be the first over the top, clambering fatly out of his little turf bunker to loudly congratulate whichever of his friends had been doing the most impressive shooting. From where we were, they all looked the same. Tweed body, tweed hat, tomato face in the middle. Altogether, it was nothing like the shooting I'd been doing for the past week. Me and Johnnie, we were ninjas of the night. This was something else.

I liked it, though, because I was with Flora basically all the time. She was half-beater but also half-picker-upper, which meant she also had to control a batshit beige spaniel, which was called Candy despite definitely being a boy. Apparently this was something to do with a book called *Lark Rise to Candleford*. Blankface. Once we were close to the guns, anyway, the idea was that Candy would watch the birds as they flew, see where they dropped, then run to fetch them back, whereupon Flora would dispatch them and put them in her bag. Where this system fell down was that Candy was totally on crack. Half the time he ran the wrong way, which meant Flora had to scream, 'Candy, come left!' or similar. To me, there was no obvious connection between her words and whatever the hell direction the mad bastard spaniel fancied running in. Although it seemed a bit rude to point this out.

Most of the beaters were farmworkers, or older men from the village, and the way they all treated Flora was baffling to me. There she was, clambering over heather and being obviously as amazing as ever, and yet they didn't seem to feel graced by her presence at all. In fact, they seemed to regard it as a bit of a hassle.

'Dear God, lassie,' said this one middle-aged guy with a ponytail, eventually. 'Control yer dug, eh?'

'Eeesht!' said somebody else, sort of in agreement, but she just snapped back at them both to get out of her way. To me, it seemed like a lot of the beaters simply didn't realise how lucky they were that she was prepared to spend the day with them at all, when she could have been down in London, hanging out in nightclubs and looking like she belonged in a fashion magazine. 'She doesn't belong here,' I thought, as she strode briskly around on the land her father owned, periodically telling these people he paid by the day to fuck off. 'She's too vulnerable,' I decided, as she picked up wounded pheasants and broke their necks with a crack.

Weirdly, Fusty's real father – Iain Bonnar – was with us, too. I mean, that *was* weird, right? Class-wise? What with his actual son being out with the toffs? He was in an old Barbour but also tracksuit trousers; you really wouldn't have known he was part of the family at all. Sometimes, you'd see him conferring with Captain Beater, as if in a position of authority. Mainly, though, he'd just blend in, wafting his flag like everybody else. At one point, quietly, I asked Flora what that was all about. She just shrugged. Bonnar never shot, she said. Didn't seem to fancy it. Maybe an army thing.

The dead grouse weren't like our pigeons and bunnies. They were beautiful. Often they'd flutter when they came out of the dog's mouth, at least until Flora got to work on them. I held a few. They were warm and delicate, like you could crush them. The females were drab and brown, but the males were startled maniacs with a flash of red above the eye. The red, I suppose, that Flora's hair used to be. Before it was pink.

For lunch, we crossed the class divide. The last drive deposited us half a kilometre along a track from a green painted log cabin by a loch. Here we found Flora's mum, Emma, in a headscarf covered in pictures of feathers and anchors, along with four or five other women who looked exactly like her. All of them were bustling in and out of the hut, putting nibbles and cups of some warming broth onto a long table covered in a red gingham cloth. There were two little girls fishing on the loch, who I took – rightly – to be Flora's younger siblings. Both of them looked like her and her mum. The smaller one, Delilah, was basically just Flora scaled down. The other, Mary, had a touch more of the Fusty side's flush.

'Mum,' said Flora. 'You remember Tommo?'

'Of course!' she purred, which was definitely a lie because we'd literally never spoken and I could only remember her even looking at me once before, which had been when we'd arrived at Fusty's party, and I could have very easily been staff, or a pet, or mould.

Still, she kissed me on both cheeks and gave my shoulders a little squeeze. She looked very cheerful. Then she told me to help myself to a beer from inside if I wanted, so I did, although I was a little worried that it might be a bad idea, what with all the walking I'd have to do after lunch.

More fool me. Most of the guns turned up a few minutes later in a variety of very slightly muddy 4x4s. No walking for them. They were loud. As in, hipflask loud. 'Vino!' roared somebody, but what they got first was champagne, poured by Hostess Emma and her gang into solid stainless-steel tumblers. Think returning conquerors, greeted by adoring womenfolk. A few broke out rods and went to join the kids by the loch, whipping at the water with pale green lines. Most milled around and drank. Then we went inside, where it turned out that another long, gingham table had been laid for lunch. We sat, we ate. Tomato soup, red wine, some sort of game stew, more wine.

There was a lot of talk of a man called Eric who had apparently been under the impression we were eating somewhere else. 'Eric went to the bloody bothy!' they all kept telling each other, helpless with laughter, as if Eric going to the bloody bothy was well up there with that Billy Connolly routine about the wildebeest who thinks he can fly. Also, was this not a bothy, too? Mental.

MacPhail, at the end of the table, kept roaring about that 'bastard Major', although I couldn't hear enough to know if he meant John Major or an actual major. Flora, who was next to me, was up and down the whole meal, helping her mum and being flirted with by men literally her dad's age, who kept staring at her tweed-covered bottom. They weren't subtle about it, not even in front of MacPhail.

'Eyes up, Neville!' he said to one of them sardonically, and Neville, who had the hairiest ears you've ever seen in your life, just smirked and raised his glass, and MacPhail raised his glass back.

'You old *goat*,' said Flora, and then she swatted at the Neville guy like he was a fly. This made everybody roar all the more. What, I remember thinking, the fuck? I tried to imagine my dad and Annie in this dynamic, and I just couldn't do it. Flora also, though, put a hand on my shoulder whenever she stood up, and quite often put her hand on my thigh when she sat down again. And I guess her parents would have seen that, too. Different rules.

More wine, more laughter. Lots of people started smoking cigars, and somebody roared, 'Peasant!' when I took out my farmboy Regal, although I think it represented a sort of acceptance. The guy sitting next to me – no idea what he was called – was delighted to learn I was at Eskmount, because in the 1960s he had been in Smethwick, which was the castle house that Alan was in. He wanted to know all the right stuff: where we smoked, how you got the booze in, and whether it was still almost obligatory to be shitfaced in chapel for Evensong. (Yes.) 'Never had kids myself,' he said at one point, which I suppose explained it.

After pudding, which was some sort of chocolate mousse, he went off to fish, and Fusty came and sat next to me. I suppose he'd drunk a lot, too. His face was even redder than usual and his eyes intense. Like there was too much eye meat stuffed into the balls. Horribly bright.

'So, how is he?' he said, and I was honestly a bit thrown.

'Your . . . dad?' I said. Because Bonnar wasn't here. Bonnar was eating sandwiches, presumably, with the other employees.

Fusty looked at me with what could have been loathing. 'Johnnie. How is Johnnie?'

'Oh,' I said, blushing, wondering if this made me the same colour as him. 'Fine. Yeah. Doing okay.'

Fusty exhaled. A pursed-lip, spittly rattle of a thing. Not nice.

'Does he talk about it?' he asked. 'What happened with Doug?'

'A bit.'

'He mustn't. And you mustn't, either.'

I was a bit drunk. Was this really happening? Me and him, surrounded by all these people, and him talking like this?

'Because there would be consequences,' said Fusty. 'Very bad ones. For everybody.'

'Look, man,' I said. It came out as a croak, and I coughed. 'Look. I don't know what . . . I mean, what Johnnie says is . . . Like, he's entitled to—'

That was when Fusty grabbed me on the shoulder. Really hard. Fat sausage fingers on my teenage bones. He was right in my face.

'I think you know what I'm saying,' he said.

I hit his hand away. More in shock than anything else. No idea what I was about to say. Really hadn't thought it through. Because I did not, in fact, know what he was saying. But right at that moment, before I could say anything, a tall, thin man with sandy hair burst through the door and roared 'Airhellair!' And, as the place erupted, Fusty turned away.

Holy God, I thought, distantly, even here? Although it turned out that this was the elusive Eric, and he meant it in cold blood.

★

There were two more drives after lunch, and I hadn't sobered up. For a while I smoked as I walked, until Flora told me not to, because of fires. It was hot now, and the Barbour went around my waist. My T-shirt had a picture of Evan Dando on it. Beat flap, went my flag, beat flap. I was a bit freaked out by the whole Fusty thing. A bit, but not a lot. Because what, actually, had he been saying? Johnnie was a nightmare. We all knew that. So, perhaps the fat creepy fuck was just looking out for him. Either way, I still had to climb a lot of damn hills.

The very last drive was around a hillside. Towards the end of it, two wounded grouse came gliding unsteadily around the camber. Not two, 'a brace'. Kept forgetting that. Candy nabbed them, Flora killed them, leaving them on the heather.

'Take those,' she called back over her shoulder, so I did. At first, I held them by their warm and broken necks, but I started to worry that their heads might come off, so I turned them the other way up. Their feet were grey, cold and alien, like some inedible starfish you might see on a David Attenborough documentary. Proper country, me.

Scary Iain Bonnar was above me and Flora was down below, but the topography was curving and twisted, and for a while I couldn't see either of them. I was walking along a little burn, hopping back and forth. There was some sort of white, derelict cottage up ahead, and the bangs and shouts of 'Over!' were very loud now. Any moment soon, I reckoned, Captain Beater would blow his horn.

I stumbled. A brace (yes!) of grouse broke cover beneath

my feet, taking flight, just above the heather. 'Over!' I shouted, flapping dutifully, and then as I rounded the curve, I saw Fusty. Not far away. Ten metres, maybe fifteen, slightly uphill, right by the cottage. He had his gun in his hands, not yet up to his shoulder, and he was turning from the knees, following the path of their flight with the barrel's end as they climbed up the slope and doubled back, waiting for them to get up into clear sky before bringing the gun up. It was smooth, looping, balletic; the most graceful I'd ever seen him. The birds didn't rise, though, skimming off cross-country. And by the time Fusty finished his turn, gun still half up, elbows out, feet poised like a sprinter, he was looking right at me.

'Hey,' I said, holding up my grouse and my flag. Although there were bangs all around now, almost deafening, so he might not have been able to hear.

He said nothing at all, but he seemed to be smirking.

'Bit low, those ones,' I said.

Still nothing. I looked around. I was down in the burn gulley; nobody else could see me at all. Noise everywhere. Gunfire and shouts. The water at my feet. The gun could be at his shoulder in half a second. He was staring right at me. I stared back. 'All the pheasants ever bred ...' I thought madly. Then I thought of what 'consequences' meant. Then I thought of that bit when Willem Dafoe gets gunned down in *Platoon*.

The horn went, long and loud. Silence, like the end of an earthquake. I was in the shade, I realised. I suddenly felt really cold.

'Careful, there,' said Fusty, breaking open his gun. 'Chap could get shot.'

★

The day ended outside Auchnastang Castle, with the day's bag laid out on the gravel. Maybe sixty carcasses in a rectangle, like a really expensive rug. Beaks all one way, feet all the other. Neat. Somehow, it reminded me of the CCF Annual General Inspection at school.

All the guns – and guns, I knew now, were people – went up, one by one, to collect a couple from Captain Beater, each palming him a tenner as they did. Subtly, though. Like they were buying drugs in a club. I looked at the birds, and I thought of the Cultybraggan chicken. Then I thought of everything Johnnie and I had killed this month past, and how they'd all look if they were put on a General Inspection of their own. It would be bigger, I reckoned. All those feathers that had flapped on the way down. All those hopping crows. All those rabbit eyes, reflecting the torch.

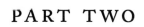

PART TWO

14

AT SCHOOL, NOW IN the upper sixth, I was cultivating an air of enigma. Or, at least, I was trying to. In my memory, I was an aloof, intellectual figure, adjacent to bohemia and bound for greatness. Naggingly, though, the same memory is studded with recollections of hovering at elbows, sniggering at jokes and never quite having the courage to make my own.

Alan was applying for Oxford, and I still wanted to be like Alan, although not too much like Alan. So, Cambridge for me. I'd never been, but I pored through the prospectus and saw that there were grand old colleges which boasted of their ancient alumni and ugly modern ones which boasted of having 'friendly atmospheres'. I settled on a modest, middle-aged, middle-sized college in the centre of town, designed austerely by some manner of puritans, but in warm yellow stone. That'd do. I applied to read philosophy, even though I didn't really know what it was. I had fancied English, but Alan was doing that.

My predicted grades got me an interview, and my interview got me an upgrade to an attic bedsit at Esk House. It was bigger than most, directly above Beagle and swooping with beams. Had I decorated, it could have been quite cosy, but I was confused by how I was supposed to know which posters to put up. Or who I was putting them up for. Alan's room, over in Smethwick, was a perfect balance of the classic and the new; here a black-and-white picture of Madonna from her *Sex* book – not too dirty, she was in suspenders, smoking a fag – and there a bit of the Sistine Chapel ceiling, or a Titian, or a postcard by Edvard Munch. He mocked me for my empty walls, but it seemed like my choice was between copying him or not, and neither seemed ideal.

Suddenly, somehow, I seemed low on friends. Johnnie was gone, and Luci, too, and my habit for individual, intense friendships hadn't left me in good stead. Barf still didn't speak much, and Wee Geordie Meehan only talked about rugby. Alan was a prefect now, which made him wary of going to the Dump, but if he wasn't there, I didn't really have anybody to talk to.

There was Ella, but we'd ended up in the fives courts after a drunken ceilidh in the first half of term, with her hands up my kilt and mine up her shirt and skirt, and it had since all been a bit awkward. I still thought of it almost nightly, but I wasn't sure what to do. On the one hand, there was the obvious appeal of a sex life on school grounds. Maybe even a real one. On the other, though, there was the way she obviously liked me a lot, which was simultaneously arousing and off-putting, in ways I couldn't comprehend. And there was Flora, who Ella wasn't.

Not that Flora was my girlfriend. She was pretty firm on that – she was going to her hospice in Calcutta after Christmas; it wouldn't be fair on the lepers – but I guess this is a good point to mention that I'd stayed the night after the day of the grouse shoot, and we'd ended up in bed. My bed, as it happened, in a preposterous room in her ridiculous house, after a long dinner of dark wines and dark meats at a long, dark varnished table, and then a walk and a joint of Dean's greenhouse weed out behind the hedge that, to me, would always belong to Trixie.

It was brass, that bed, and it was high, and it genuinely had posts going up almost to the ceiling. All the furniture in that room was fluffy and pink, like some mad antique doll house, and the wallpaper was like Louis XIV's shirts. Honestly, the way these people live. As erotic as your gran's curtains. It was a long way from her parents, though, whole floors away, along corridors designed for midnight prowling. She'd turned up once I was already in said bed, anyway, and sat on it, and then lain on it, and then lain on me. It didn't go far. There were rules. She was still dressed, and she'd bat my hands away when they went for her belt.

'I suppose you think it's your turn,' she'd said, not defensively, but not far off, either. Hot breath in my ear. Somehow, it made her a different person. Lower, less awe-inspiring, like I was suddenly seeing her through the eyes of others. This older girl, with a string of slightly younger boyfriends, following a tragic path down to me.

'Of course not,' I'd replied, hoping she'd feel guilty for saying it, even though it was true in a way. Then I'd held her hips as she straddled me, the hot crotch of her jeans against my boxer shorts. At one point I put my hand behind, on her bottom, but it made me think of that Neville guy, so I took them away again. Still, from then on at night, at school, alone, months later, when I wasn't thinking of Ella or Alan's Madonna poster, I'd often be thinking of her, and then. Above me, grinding in the dark, in that exhausted, muted, timeless night. Her smell of expensive wine. The smooth, varnished nail she'd rubbed against my lips. The hard little breaths she made, six of them, packed together, just before she climbed off me and went away.

★

Johnnie, meanwhile, was busy being a bit of a mess. He was at some private sixth-form college in Edinburgh. We could have met up in the cafés of Musselburgh, I suppose, but half the school would have craned their necks through the windows and it all would have felt a bit tragic, like he couldn't stay away. He was living with an old couple in Marchmont who were family friends, and they gave him all the freedom in the world, and he had no idea what to do with it.

A few weekends into term, I signed myself out on a Sunday, having told Toad I was going to the hospital to see my mum. Instead, I went and met him in the Meadows. He had red wine. It was 1 p.m. We sat on a bench.

'It's shit,' he said. 'I don't know what I'm doing there. What do I even need Highers for?'

'University?' I said.

'Come on,' he said.

We were almost wearing the same clothes. The deal with leaving school at the weekend was that you had to wear your uniform, blue blazer and all, but if you wore black jeans instead of school trousers, and you had your DMs, and you shoved your shirt collar down under your jumper, then you could stuff your blazer in a bag and look pretty normal. Johnnie was in the same dark, nothing clothes as me. I didn't get it. He could have had a Mohawk by then. Rock star leathers, whatever. I'd expected more from him.

'Layman is at my college,' he said. 'You know he got kicked out of Sedburgh?'

I didn't.

'Hash and shagging,' said Johnnie.

'Both at once?' I said, impressed.

Johnnie said Layman had been stuck out at his family's place in Craill for the last few months and was thrilled to be back in the world.

'And there are some girls,' he said. 'But nobody can *do* anything. I thought we'd be going to pubs and stuff. Clubbing, even. But none of us have any money and none of them are even allowed. Some get picked up by their parents each day. Honestly. Like kids.'

Had everybody, I wondered, been expelled from somewhere?

Johnnie snorted. 'Probably,' he said. 'Bunch of fuck-ups.'

'Hey, Johnnie,' I said, 'what are you rebelling against?'

'I'm not. I don't mean to. I dunno.'

'You're supposed to say, "Whadda ya got?"'

'Why?'

'It's from a film. I saw it with Alan last summer. Never mind.'

And we drank our wine and smoked his Regals, and then we wandered a little listlessly around the park, not really heading anywhere.

We talked about the farm, for a bit. Johnnie said he was being hassled by lawyers to go to some office on Queen Street to sign some shit, but he didn't want to, and hadn't been calling them back. I said I still didn't really understand what was going on; if Douglas had been trying to keep the farm, then why couldn't his brother try, as well? Johnnie shrugged, and swigged, and said it was complicated. It had been different with Douglas, he said. He was older and went to agricultural college. People respected that. But Johnnie, as the younger brother, was just some kid. Everybody thought he was a waster. And everybody wanted their money. And he had to think of his mum, too, because all her friends were nearby, and if he sold up to MacPhail and didn't make a fuss, then she'd be able to stay in one of the cottages for a while. Maybe even the one we'd done up, with Archie and the bees. Whereas otherwise she'd just be stuck in that old house as it fell apart, with no money to do anything about any of it.

'And it's shit,' he said, 'basically.'

For a while we didn't say anything.

'My mum's not great, either,' I said.

Johnnie sighed. 'Want to talk about it?' he said.

'Not really.'

After that, we drank all the wine. Johnnie wondered how Alan was, which was uncharacteristic for Johnnie. I told him he was aiming for Oxford, working lots. I told him about Ella, but he didn't seem interested. I kept wanting him to ask about Flora, so I could talk about what had happened with her, but he never did. We bought a bottle of vodka up on Lothian Road and drank most of that, too, and then I was sick behind a tree.

'Come on, man,' said Johnnie despairingly, as I staggered about. It was starting to rain.

'I'm sorry,' I said miserably, but he was good about it, gathering me around the shoulders and even coming with me on the 44 bus back to Musselburgh. It was only about 5 p.m. I remember being on the top deck, crying about having not been to see my mum, feeling guilty about how I was treating my dad, and he just kept his arm around me and told me it was going to be okay. That was the thing about Johnnie. So cold, so often, and then you sometimes just got these flashes of absolute focus. Like he was your very own guardian lion.

'We've got chapel,' I said, remembering. 'Evensong. What am I going to do?'

'Here' – Johnnie took a pill from a packet in his jeans and pushed it into my pocket – 'Take that. Later. Not yet. Maybe in an hour? Screw Evensong. Sleep it off.'

'What is it?' I said, peering down.

'Klonopin. Like a bennie? I get them from the doctor. Calms you right down.'

'Thanks, man,' I said, and immediately forgot all about it.

He left me by the school gates, and I made my way gingerly back through the grounds. And then I decided that Johnnie was a bad influence, and I dutifully got dressed for Evensong. But then I fell asleep and missed it, anyway. And, I suppose, looking back, that it maybe wasn't Johnnie who was the mess at that point, but me.

★

He called about the pill a few days later. Some third-former, in tones of hushed and excited awe, came to tell me he was on the phone. Johnnie had passed into myth by then. Like serial killers do.

'Can you get me some more?' he said.

'I haven't even taken it yet,' I said, a bit confused. 'I forgot all about it. You can have it back, if you want.'

'No. I mean, from your doctor? Tell them you're stressed and not sleeping. Can't focus. Brain a mess. Playing with light switches. All that.'

'But I don't want them,' I said, even more confused, and he laughed and called me a tit and said they were for him. So, I asked if he was addicted, but cautiously, and he just laughed again.

'No,' he said. 'But I sold all mine. They're like gold in this place.'

★

It was also that year, I think, that there was a craze among the younger years for fashioning their Remembrance poppies into ninja darts and flinging them at each other. Funny, you go to a place like that, and you think things would get more normal as time went by, that there would be a historical inevitability to it, that you were the legacy of the dark, but the dawn was coming. Looking back, though, I think they might have been even worse than we were. Cartoons of us. Grim. Teams would form; they'd have actual wars. You'd see them running up and down the corridors, with the backs of their white shirts all flecked with pinpricks of blood. Call me priggish, but you couldn't help but think that it wasn't quite what the British Legion would have wanted.

Or maybe it was? Remembrance Day was a huge deal at Eskmount. You'd sit there on the pine pews of the chapel, surrounded by all those names etched in gold of boys who went before, and a piper would play something that sent a shiver down your spine, and you'd sing 'I Vow To Thee

My Country' and 'The Supreme Sacrifice' and, honestly, it was a buzz. Not so much that they'd died for us; more that they *were* us, exactly us, gone before. Less feckless, you'd assume, but perhaps that was wrong, too. Perhaps they'd been exactly as feckless, but had had feck forced upon them. All fecked up, to the end.

★

At the start of December, they called me to Cambridge for an interview. It was faintly annoying because it was on a Monday morning, which meant I had to go down on the Sunday, but it was also a good six hours away by train and they only offered one night's accommodation. So, the night after, I caught a train the other way instead and went to stay with Annie. She was living in Clapham, which meant I had to catch a tube train after the actual train, which meant it took me almost three hours to get there. She lived in a long, terraced street on which every house was exactly the same. I was a bit grumpy when I knocked on her door.

'How was it?' she said, in the hall.

'Fine,' I said, although I wasn't sure it had been fine at all. My main interview had been with a very old woman who looked like an owl, and we were talking about 'mind and body', and she kept saying the name Descartes in different ways, which meant I did, too. Like, first I'd said 'Dey-carr', like I thought you were meant to, but she'd replied by saying 'Dey-cart'. Which meant I said it differently the next time, only for her to switch back to how I'd said it the first time. So, I switched back again, only she did, too.

I didn't know if she was insane or totally fucking with me.

'You can probably say it either way,' was Annie's view. 'I doubt it really mattered.'

Actually, Cambridge had been confusing in all sorts of ways. Dimly, I'd had a notion that everybody there would be a bit like me. I'd expected lots of long hair and general grungyness, bookish people in corduroy sitting around talking about their novels. Instead, the few students I'd seen had been strolling through the butter-yellow quads in tracksuits and rugby shirts. I didn't understand it. Clever people weren't meant to like sport.

'God, you're such a dick,' said Annie, later that night in a huge All Bar One around the corner from her house. 'Clever people can like sport.'

She seemed really cheerful. Like, recklessly cheerful? Does that make sense? Like she was actually pleased to see me. Like we were friends. I wasn't used to it. She'd bought me a steak with chips, and we were both on our third drink. She wasn't even complaining when I smoked. I felt very grown up.

'Only ironically,' I said, thinking of Johnnie and Alan, and how good they were at cricket.

'Okay, so that means you think I'm a moron, then,' she said.

'Totally,' I said, although we both knew this was a lie, because there's a decent chance that Annie is the cleverest person in the world.

Annie took a gulp of her pint and gestured incomprehensibly, swallowing.

'Take your time,' I said.

'You'll be fine,' she said eventually. 'You've got that public school thing, now. My ex-boyfriend had it, too. It fools people.'

'You've got an ex-boyfriend?'

'I've got an actual boyfriend.'

'Christ,' I said, pondering the unspeakable implications of this.

'But my ex,' she said, 'was the one like you.'

'Okay, you're drunk. I see what's going on now.'

'And your friends . . . He was like them, too. Probably. Are they awful? I bet they are. With your whole not-caring thing. Your whole "I can do what I like because people like me own the universe" thing. It's really annoying.'

'You're literally my sister,' I reminded her. 'We're exactly the same.'

'No, no, you're one of *them* now. You've been taught. You've got the superpower. You can be a waster. A hippie. And people just think it's charm.'

That last bit, she said with something near venom. Tipsy venom, but still. I liked the way we were talking. I guess it sounds vicious on the page, but it was intimate, too. Although this time I was a bit taken aback.

'Anyway,' I said. 'I don't think you're right. That's a whatsit. A cliché. Bad things do happen. Worse things, maybe. My friend Johnnie—'

'Don't care,' said Annie, waving her hand around again.

'Oh.'

'Sorry,' she said. 'Came out wrong. Do care. Tell me all about it. Pour out your teenage heart. In a minute. But that's not the point. You've got it. Didn't when you were wee, but you do now. Lots of the guys at work have it, too. Wankers. But I don't. Probably why I didn't get into Oxford.'

'I always just thought you weren't clever enough.'

'Little shit.'

I grinned at her.

'I'll remind you, actually, that I did get a first,' she said, sounding very Edinburgh. 'And I am currently programming an automated yen-dollar-yuan transactional comparison model for the third largest bank in the world.'

'Sorry, but I stopped listening.'

'No, you didn't.'

'Also, you won that computer and didn't even play Frogger on it,' I reminded her.

'Little shit,' she said again.

★

Back at school, I went over to Smethwick to see Alan. In his room with the art and the black-and-white Madonna in her fishnets. His curtains were drawn.

'It went okay,' I said. 'I think.'

'What did?'

So, I reminded him that I'd had my Cambridge interview, and he gave me a look like I'd shat in my hands and passed it over.

'You're going to Oxford when?' I said, trying not to mind this. 'Next weekend, right?'

'I don't know,' he said. 'Maybe. Yes. I think that's right.'

Honestly, it was like I didn't know the guy. Or he didn't know me.

'Did you see Johnnie this weekend?' I asked. 'Or did you not bother? Are we meeting up next week?'

Alan looked like he was going to cry. His skin was grey,

and his eyes were red. His hair was all over the place, but not in a cool way. I'd never seen him like this. Not even that time he'd snapped at his dad.

'Mate,' I said, 'is everything okay? Is this about the pills?'

'What pills?'

'Johnnie? Did he ask you to . . .? Never mind. Look, what's going on?'

That's when he grabbed me on the arm. Really hard. So, I shook him off and asked, again, what was going on.

'How much do you know?' he said.

Oh God, I thought. This again. 'He told me some stuff. That he thinks happened. But it's bollocks, right?'

'He's a psycho,' said Alan.

'Yeah, maybe.'

'He's a psycho, and I've got my own problems. Look, I can't think right now. I don't want to see him again.'

'What, ever?' I said, but he told me he had to sleep and made me go away.

★

The next morning, Alan went home. This wasn't normal, but he did have the interview looming, so I figured they'd just cut him some slack. I tried to call (from the erected cubicle), but the phone in his house just rang and rang. So, I just drifted around at school instead, going to lessons and not doing much else. Wee Geordie Meehan had Luci's old study and didn't mind me going out the window, even though he was a prefect now. Some mornings, when I had free periods, I'd head out there in a duffel coat with a coffee and some books, staying put until mid-morning Triple.

Even meals were getting awkward. I think I told you before that tea was run by the prefects? In my year, I guess as a result of some sort of terrible pastoral error on the part of the staff, they seemed to intersect quite heavily with the penis-on-the-shoulder fraternity. This meant they were wild, and that wildness was manifest in food fights.

I was a head of table now – heady responsibility, this – and I had this tiny, skinny girl called Angela from the year below on my table. She was shy as anything, quiet as a mouse, but she was also blonde with ice-blue eyes, which meant that rugby lads in my year would often come and sit at my table, pretending to be my friends. I didn't mind so much, but she did. The worst were these two guys Glenn and Duncan, who were hearty and huge, and who clearly terrified her. They'd boom questions and she'd whisper replies.

Anyway, this one time, just as the third-former set down the meat tray – bolognese – a whole apple sailed out of nowhere and hit our milk jug, exploding it everywhere. Within seconds, Glenn and Duncan had put the whole table on its side and were shielding behind it, like Butch and Sundance, popping up to fling handfuls of spaghetti over the top. Total chaos. Screaming noise. Canteen blitzkrieg. As the bench behind her fell backwards, Angela, the skinny, blonde mouse, was suddenly on her feet, upright and exposed, and she caught a decent splat of bolognese to the side of the face. Poor girl. Why did they even go there? I don't know how any of them could bear it. Without really thinking about it, I found myself enveloping her in a hug and bearing her down to the ground, as if I were Kevin Costner saving the life of Whitney Houston. She really was tiny, like a child. Then, when it was all over, and the air rang with incredulous, smirking silence, we stood up and she clung to my arm, flushed and exhilarated. Across the hall, from maybe fifty metres away, Ella's eyes met my own. Firing darts, tipped with reproach. And a week after that, Ella was going out with Barf.

★

'What the fuck?' I thought. '*Barf?*'

I couldn't even imagine how they'd first spoken. At the Dump, maybe. There he was, though, suddenly elevated to the sex illuminati. You'd see them walking together back towards the girls' house after meals, side by side, sort of the same size and shape. Or, at least, I would because I always looked out the window.

'So, Barf, then?' I said to her, after an English lesson, walking towards lunch.

She looked around theatrically.

'What, you're talking to me?' she said. 'In public? At school? When people can see?'

'Shut up. You know what it's like. People are . . . you know.'

'You're people. I'm people. It's bullshit. You can do what you want.'

I shrugged.

'He's really funny,' she said. 'And interesting.'

I looked at her in disbelief.

'Aren't you friends?' she said. 'Don't you like him? He likes you.'

'Yeah. I mean, totally. It's just I didn't see . . .'

'Yeah, well,' she said.

'Yeah,' I said.

'You can do what you want,' she said again. 'And so can I.'

'Yeah.'

Two weeks after that, all the rugby lads cheered when Barf walked into tea, and the rumour went around that they'd shagged. I couldn't stop thinking about it. Him and her. Her and him. It kept me up for a whole night. Literally, I lay there thinking about it until the dawn light from the curtain cracks started creeping across my ceiling. I wondered where they'd gone. The fives courts? The music school? Those stone indoor steps which led to Mr Bevan's history classroom (which I'd tried really hard to dub The Stairway to Bevan, but it hadn't caught on)? Probably too cold for the Dump. Unless they were all wrapped up. Layers and no layers. Cold breath in each other's faces. How had I let this happen?

It didn't last. By the end of term Barf was at the Dump by himself, and Ella was walking back after meals with a tall boy called Stuart, who was in the year below and sang in a band. She wore more make-up now and smiled more, too. At tea, our eyes no longer met at all.

★

Alan came back, anyway, for the last week of term.

'I was having these headaches,' he told me eventually. 'Stress, said the doctor. Arsed Oxford right up. Couldn't remember anything. Doesn't matter. I've been okay since then. Maybe I want to go to Edinburgh, anyway.'

'Barf had a girlfriend,' I told him. 'For almost three whole weeks.'

'So?'

'I had a letter from Flora yesterday,' I said.

Alan shrugged.

'Okay,' I said. 'So, never mind all that. Just tell me. Did something really bad happen with Johnnie?'

'I really don't want to talk about Johnnie, either.'

★

Another thing, though. I should have mentioned it before. This conversation I'd had with my dad before all that, before that term had even started. We were walking on Arthur's Seat. I'd just come back from Auchnastang, and my dad wanted to know all about it. Specifically, he wanted to know about MacPhail. And I didn't mind talking about him because it was an excuse to think about Flora. Who, I found, was the absolute antidote to thinking about Ella. Look, it was a system.

'So,' said my dad, 'you remember the plot of episode two, series three?'

I did not.

'The bailiffs who raid the old people's home?' said my dad. 'The disappearing pirate pearl?'

'Oh yes,' I lied.

'Well, don't tell anyone, but that was inspired by MacPhail. A story in the papers. About some heavies he sent to a retirement community near Glenelg.'

'To a fucking retirement community?' I blurted, then apologised for swearing.

'It might not have been true,' said my dad. 'I think he denied it was him. Could have been another party in the process. But lots of stuff like that over the years. As well as that business with the polytechnic. I just don't think he's meant to be a very nice man.'

'He's a big fan of yours,' I said.

'Oh, really?' said my dad, beaming.

★

He was, too.

'Let's go for a drive,' Flora's dad had said to me, that morning after the grouse shoot at Auchnastang. The day after all my weeks at Burnside. The morning after Flora came to my room. Her closed eyes. Her little breaths.

Breakfast, though, had been less sexy. I'd found Flora and her dad both in this sunroom breakfast place at the back of the house; one of those chilly, too-bright conservatories where the furniture was all wicker covered in horrible floral cushions. They'd stopped talking the moment I appeared, exactly like you do when you've just been talking about somebody. Her mum wasn't there. She'd gone to bed early the night before, too, apparently feeling queasy.

Oh, Christ, I'd thought madly. Flora has told her dad about the sex. The not-quite-sex. Whatever. And it's much, much worse than Neville staring at her bottom. And now I'm about to get shot.

He was smiling, though. Not hugely, but definitely not in an 'and now I shall treat you like a grouse' sort of way. He was also looking at me in a way that he definitely never had before, by which I mean not the way you look at a wall, or a sheep, or a part of a crowd, but the way you look at a person when you are actually seeing them and actually give a toss that they are there. It made me intensely uncomfortable.

I'd sat, anyway, and then Flora had pointed out that all the bacon and stuff was on a hotplate on the counter by the door, so I'd had to stand up again. Then I'd poured myself some tea, but it had been one of those posh teas you have to pour through a sieve, so my cup had been full of leaves and I'd blushed bacon-coloured myself. You know those times when you feel like the room you are in is a microwave, but the waves are cooking only you? That. Although Mr MacPhail hadn't seemed to notice any of this. Instead, he told me that they'd have to get me shooting next time, and I politely said that would be lovely, and then he asked me if I'd shot much before, and I'd thought of all the rabbits and the pigeons, so I shrugged and said, a bit.

'But the old man does?' he said. 'Your father? Grouse man? Or just pheasant?'

'I don't think either, really.'

'But Chackerbury?' he said, astonished. 'They filmed there!'

'Daddy,' said Flora flatly, and I suddenly understood what was going on.

I didn't think it was going to be like this. I'd expected snootiness or derision. As per Alan's dad, if you remember that. MacPhail, though, seemed to find it reassuring that I could now be socially pinpointed. Until then, I'd thought of him as a sort of malign American president sort of guy. I'd never seen him without a tie on, and I'd never forgotten his flat rudeness when I'd tried to shake his hand at Fusty's party. Although abruptness, I came to realise, was his way of operating outside his comfort zone. And now I was safe, understood by him and, therefore, in that zone. I had been a vague, confusing hassle, whereas now I was On the Map.

'Of course,' he said, a little later, as we trundled down

the drive in his Range Rover, 'you probably visit a lot of far grander estates than ours. Down south. With your father.'

'I'm not often on set,' I said apologetically, which seemed more tactful than explaining I had literally never been on set, nor ever wanted to visit one, because I couldn't think of the butler without wishing him horribly and painfully dead.

'Shame,' said MacPhail.

'Daddy loves it,' said Flora, with malicious brightness, sitting in the back with Candy. 'He watches every week. With Grandma.'

I craned my neck and nodded at her politely. She was on the other side of this gun rack thing that separated the front seats from the back. There was a shotgun and a rifle in it, just sitting there, on hooks. Although, I was used to guns now, so the stuff that was in the rack threw me less than the fact that she had been banished to the other side of it. You could put Flora in the back? People did that? I wasn't sure what to say. I wasn't good with parents. Also, I was worried I might smell. I hadn't showered because the bathroom next to my insane fairy-tale room had only had a huge, stupid bath in it. And at home, my dad always got cross when I used the bath because it used up all the hot water.

We drove on, with MacPhail pointing at things and me making appreciative noises. It was like I was the Duke of Edinburgh or the guy from the agricultural board.

'Humble, really,' said MacPhail, not particularly sounding it. 'We poor hill farmers. None of your big London money. Only really fund it all via other interests. I'm a property man, you know.'

'Yes,' I said.

'Although, I get my hands dirty, too. Lambing come spring. All pitch in. Don't we, Flo? Little ones up to the house. Forestry over there. Does okay, come Christmas. Rapeseed. No river to speak of. That's down past Burnside, over yonder. Terrible waste. Ah. Here we are.'

He stopped the car in a grassy field. We all got out. Candy bounded away. I felt like a cigarette, but I also felt it would be somehow disrespectful. Also, I remembered Flora talking about a fire risk.

'This is the place,' said her dad, and I peered around. It was just a field. We were halfway up the valley. Below us was the long, straight road that Johnnie and I used to roar down in his little Renault, going forty or fifty without even gunning the engine. Various poles were stuck around the place, with bits of rope tied between them. Not fences. Definitely not sturdy enough to hold cattle. More like they were symbolic of something. *The Wicker Man*? He asked what I thought. I wondered what I was supposed to be looking at.

'It's very nice,' I said encouragingly, although I felt more was required. 'Green,' I added. Dear God.

'Fifty houses,' said MacPhail appreciatively. 'With a proper road, if the buggers agree.'

'The, uh, buggers?'

'Council. Their road. Burnside over there. Flatter land. Better for building. Do wonders for them, too. Jack Burchill was a good friend. Terrible.'

'Can we go?' said Flora.

'Chap has to provide for his family,' said MacPhail and winked at me. Then he strolled off, pushing at poles and squinting at things.

'Lucky family,' said Flora brightly, 'eh?'

'Will he mind if I smoke?' I asked.

'God, no. You're one of the chaps now. Shame it's not a cigar.'

'Anyway,' I said. 'Lucky Fusty. Surely?'

'Ha,' said Flora, as her dad turned around and she waved. 'Fusty. We'll see.'

I looked at her quizzically. And ahead, in the field, her dad spread his arms. Mine, he was saying, like a conquering hero. Although the gesture reminded me also of Flora, the first time I'd seen her. Before her jumper went up. Arms spread at that party in Edinburgh. Spinning until she dropped.

15

I MENTION ALL THIS because at Christmas I had an invitation from the MacPhails. A proper one, this time. To go shooting. This time to be a gun. Because guns are people.

The invitation came in an envelope, on a little cream card which said *Auchnastang* at the top, above a sketch of the house in sepia brown. Where, I wondered, do you actually buy sketches of your own house? Are there sketches of everybody's house somewhere, if you only know where to look? My dad once told me that the big new library on Causewayside had copies of every book ever published, so maybe it was like that.

There were printed words up top – date, time, etc. – and underneath somebody had written, *Family tradition, very informal, thought it might be nice this year to invite some of Philip's friends this year, too*, which threw me because it was signed *Philip* underneath, too. Then I remembered that MacPhail was Philip, but Fusty was also Philip. And I was his friend? Okay.

'What have you there?' said my dad, who had been back since a couple of days after term ended and was keeping erratic hours. Some mornings, I just wouldn't see him. Others, he'd be up and talking horribly brightly about going for walks. Generally, it depended on whether he'd been to see my mum the day before, and how much he'd drunk when he'd got home.

This was one of the latter. He was in his silk dressing gown, drinking coffee. I hesitated, and then I passed him the card. He studied it and sounded amused.

'You shoot now?' he said.

'I have,' I said. 'I mean, I know how to. With Johnnie. It's not a big deal.'

'Do you have the right clothes?' he said, like this was the important bit.

'Informal,' I said. 'Normal clothes.'

My dad said informal just meant it was all friends. No business guests. Or royalty.

'Royalty?' I said.

'What were people wearing last time?'

'I was wearing my Lemonheads T-shirt,' I said, mainly to upset him. 'But I was only a beater.'

'Upstairs downstairs.'

'I hate talking to you about this stuff. Nothing you say makes any sense.'

'I'm on set next week,' he said. 'I'll speak to the costume girls. You're lucky to have me.'

★

It was strange, that Christmas. There were all the balls, like there had been the year before, but suddenly we were a bit old for them. Johnnie didn't go to any, had become scornful of the whole idea. Not that I'd seen him much, anyway. Alan and I did a few, but they were all a bit muted. He was going through an 'on again' phase with Claire, and it was all very grown-up, or at least pretend grown-up, with them kissing each other on the cheek and her calling him 'darling'. She was very familiar with me, which made me feel strangely dignified, albeit in a manner not totally unlike a pet dog who has had his balls cut off.

For each ball she brought along a different friend. Not Gina, because she was away in New Zealand, wrestling pigs or something. Each time we'd go to Pizza Hut beforehand, and she drove her dad's Rover. It was still exciting, in a way, because we'd bundle into the car all cold, and you could smell the girls' perfume and hair even though they weren't anyone's mum, but I wouldn't call it wild. None of us got that drunk, and there was absolutely no sort of orgy afterwards. Like I said. Adult.

'Hey,' I said to Alan, as we sat in our kilts in the back, coming over the bridge from some faintly army-derived ceilidh in Fife one Friday. 'Are you going to that Christmas shoot at Auchnastang?'

It hadn't been the best night. I had a taste in the back of my throat of cigarettes and cheap red wine. It made me feel trampish, rather than roguish. I didn't know what had gone wrong. Claire was in the front with a friend we were dropping off at Juniper Green.

'A shoot?' said Alan. 'What?'

'It's informal,' I said. 'They thought it might be nice to invite some friends of, um, Fusty.'

Alan stared at me.

'Little Fusty,' I said. 'Not Big Fusty. I'm a gun. Guns are people.'

'Fusty's a horrible prick,' said Alan. 'Does Johnnie know?'

'I haven't told him. But Flora . . . I mean. It's not like—'

'It never ends with you,' said Alan, 'does it?'

'What doesn't?'

'A shoot,' said Alan, shaking his head.

'Like, a magazine shoot?' said Claire, over her shoulder.

'He means pheasants,' said the girl from Juniper Green, sounding bored.

'Didn't know you were into that,' said Claire.

'Oh, he's full of surprises,' said Alan.

★

Another different thing about that Christmas was that Claire would sometimes stay over at Alan's, if it was the weekend and her dad didn't need his car. Which meant I couldn't, because even this new grown-up experience of sexless overfamiliarity obviously had its limits. I'd still go back with them, and it was nice because we'd talk about plays and books and films and all that arty stuff she and Alan were into, but there would always be a point in his room at about 1 a.m., after a drink and a spliff or two, when she'd stretch and yawn and climb into his bed, like they were both living some fantasy of being twenty-five or something, and it would be pretty obvious that I should leave. Sometimes, if I had the money, I'd get a taxi. More often, I'd just walk it, like I had done in the summer. It only took about half an hour, although it was pretty weird tackling the darkness of Holyrood Park in my kilt. I didn't mind. If I had cigarettes left in my sporran, I'd finish them off as I walked, never sure where the smoke ended and my breath in the cold began.

'Oh,' I whispered to Alan that night after the army thing, as he took me down through the darkened house and let me out through their cluttered vestibule, 'can I borrow a coat?'

'Didn't you have a coat?'

I had. But that night, as we'd sat on the floor in Alan's room, I'd screwed it up into a ball and quietly kicked it under his bed.

'Must have lost it,' I said. 'At the thing. Stupid of me. I'll call them.'

Alan shrugged and grabbed a tatty old skiing jacket from the rack by the door.

'Wait,' I said. 'What about that one?'

'You want my dad's Barbour?'

'Looks like it might rain,' I explained, although actually the moon was out, and you could see the stars.

★

The coat was perfect. It was worn pale into creases around the elbows and the tartan lining was ripped inside. The big mystery was how Mungo Campbell had managed to mess it up so much on outdoor expeditions that had presumably peaked with mildly drunk afternoon strolls around the New Town.

The rest of my clothes were not perfect. It was a week or so later, and my dad had them laid out proudly on the bed.

'Am I supposed to be Sherlock Holmes?' I said. 'It's not fancy dress.'

My dad was holding a glass of red wine. Not his first. He seemed hurt.

'It's December,' he said. 'You will need a hat.'

It wasn't just the deerstalker hat. The trousers were knee-length, which rang a bell from last time, but they were also really baggy, which didn't. Also, they were snot-green tweed. Everything was. The buttons were shiny horn, and the waistcoat had a gold chain pocket watch. Never mind Sherlock Holmes. I'd look like I was about to deny Oliver Twist more gruel.

'I'm really not sure this is right,' I said.

'Tom,' said my dad patiently, 'I do know about these things. Remember episode three of the second series?'

Actually, this time I did, if only dimly. The butler had exposed a man posing as a Yorkshire industrialist to be an Austrian jewel thief. He'd done this with the help of a gamekeeper, who had captured him in the trenches. But I felt things might have moved on.

In the end, I wore one of his checked shirts under a school jumper, and some brown cords, tucked into his happily green wellies. With the Barbour, it seemed good enough. Although I did take the hat. I would need one. It was December.

I took a train to Perth, as agreed with MacPhail's secretary, where I was picked up by a spotty, ginger guy called Christopher in a little Subaru. It wasn't hard for us to spot each other. We were the only two Barbours on the platform. Had there been a third, it actually could have been quite awkward.

'How d'you do?' he said to me, shaking my hand like we were businessmen. I guess he was about twenty. Then he frowned. 'No gun?'

'I'm a gun,' I said.

'Fabulous hat,' he said, and I immediately took it off and stuffed it in my pocket.

In the back of the car he had a black Labrador, called

Buffy. All I could think about was the last time I'd driven out of Perth, that time with a gun, twitchingly stoned. Christopher didn't seem like the sort of person you'd tell about that. I could feel Buffy's eyes on the back of my head. He knew.

Christopher's skin was terrible. He asked if I'd had many days shooting that year, and I said just the one, in the summer, because I reckoned rabbits and pigeons didn't count.

'Grouse!' he said.

'Yes.'

'Fabulous.'

Edinburgh had been dank and dark, but up here it had snowed, and the low sun was sniping at it from between trees and hills. When I put the back of my hand to the closed car window, I could feel the chill conducting up the hairs. The roads, dimly familiar, were like the world through the wardrobe. I asked Christopher if he had any music, and he said yes and pushed in a tape, which turned out to be Tina Turner. What the fuck, I thought to myself, am I doing here?

The driveway at Auchnastang was full of Land Rovers and Range Rovers again. It was all white here, too, and people stomped around breathing steam, pulling shotguns out of sleeves. Yapping dogs, going mental. Fusty and MacPhail were by the steps, the one looking like a smaller version of the other. Getting out of the car, I thought I recognised nobody else, but then I realised that the guy to our right, in a tie and a padded gilet, was actually Will Layman.

'Hey!' I said.

'Oh, hey,' he said, looking up, and I realised to my astonishment that he was holding a lighter and burning what looked like a long black stick of hash.

'I've got some Rizlas,' I said, looking back over my shoulder at the MacPhails.

'Ha!' said Layman. 'Nice one!'

Then he put the smouldering little black stick into a tin box covered with blue felt and stuck it in his pocket.

★

The hash-in-the-box turned out to be a handwarmer. I seemed to be the only person without one, and I was jealous. Also, I was jealous of their gloves, because I didn't have those, either. MacPhail had given me a gun – beautiful, actually, a 20-bore, which opened and closed with a solid click like an Audi door – but the blue-black metal of it was so cold against my skin, it felt like it was burning. He'd also given me a leather satchel thing full of cartridges. It went on my knees, heavy as a human head, as I sat bumping down snowy tracks in the back of his Land Rover with Fusty, Layman and the Christopher guy. I had my gun open, like I'd seen them all do in the summer. Everybody else was doing this, too. I felt pleased with myself for noticing.

'Dwarkin!' MacPhail had said to me out there on the steps, shaking my hand with apparent delight, as if trying to convince both strangers and me that we'd met more than once. 'Nice to have a bit of showbiz! Delighted you could come!'

Fusty didn't look that delighted. Flora would be a bit delighted, I'd decided. Although I hadn't actually managed to get through to her before coming and, so far, we'd only nodded at each other because she'd been off at the other side of the drive being leered at by old men and doing doggish things with her doggish dog.

'Here,' said MacPhail, and he held a little wallet out towards me, which seemed to be filled with those plastic strips you get in collars, each in their own little section.

'Excuse me?'

'Take, take.'

'Toothpicks?' I said, pulling one out.

'Funny man!' he said. 'Number?'

I looked, and it had a seven on it.

'Splendid,' said MacPhail and took it back, and I got into the car thinking this was the weirdest and perhaps crappest game ever.

What it meant, though, was that I was to be gun seven, out of eleven. Alongside Fusty, Layman and Ginger Chris, there were a handful of men of about MacPhail's age, one of whom I recognised from the summer as Eric Who Went to the Bloody Bothy. In tow were various women, children and dogs, including Flora's mum but not including Flora, because she was off with Fusty's dad Iain Bonnar and the beaters. Everybody piled into the various Land Rovers and then piled out of them again, a few miles into the hills.

'Number one at the top of the hill!' roared MacPhail, pointing, and we all began to trudge.

I put my hat back on. It was snowing now, but softly, and large crisp flakes you could catch on your tongue. Cold enough to rip into your lungs, particularly when walking, carrying and sweating in your layers of brown and green. Too cold, too hot, never right. Spot seven, where I belonged, was a post sticking out of the snow on the slope. Christopher below me, some old guy above, his wife standing alert behind. I'd seen them by the cars; he had the least convincing wig I'd ever seen. Almost Elvis. I guess he thought he was channelling Robbie Burns. The hillside curled; down to my right you could see the edge of a copse of trees. There was chatter as people took their places, and then all was still.

Looking down, I saw that Christopher had closed his gun and was intently scanning the land ahead. I loaded mine and did the same. The sky was the same colour as the snow. Everything was subdued, oddly coiled. Those boys in the trenches, I remember thinking, did they do this, too? Before the war, I mean? Did that remind them of this?

A dog barked. In the distance, I could hear sticks hitting against other sticks and what sounded like a chicken with an urgent message. A man shouted, 'Over!' and a single bird came towards us, not far uphill, not too high. I watched it, not sure what to do, and then the old geezer shot it out of the sky. I could see the flash of his gun against the white. It was a cock pheasant with a green head and a long tail, and its neck snapped into a 'U', like it had hit a window.

After that, it all kicked off. The pheasants came over in singles and groups, and the guns spat death at them. Or, at least, everybody else's did. It was bloody impossible. I knew vaguely that shotguns were a different business to the rifle we'd used for rabbits; that rifles were about things that stayed still far away, whereas shotguns were about things closer up, moving around. Knowing that, though, didn't mean I could actually do it. All around me, birds were plunging out of the sky like men in that Weather Girls song. It was all so fast, and I could feel myself start to panic.

'How d'ye do?' said Elvis, as we trudged down the hill afterwards.

'Bit rusty,' I said.

For the next drive, I was on the edge of a big, flat stretch of ice: a flooded field. Christopher was still next to me; I guess because he was number six. Fifty metres away, I could see the Eric guy, right at the edge of the ice. He was on one of those walking sticks which turns into a seat, gun under his arm, swigging from a hipflask. It was about 10 a.m. Strong.

This time, before the shooting started, a lone, startled rabbit went scrabbling across the ice from Christopher's side to mine. As I watched, he raised his gun to his shoulder and followed it. Then he put his gun up and nodded at me. So, I squinted down the barrel and shot it.

The noise was deafening, not just the shot but also the impact on the ice, like somebody had thrown a tray down the stairs. It kept going, too; a creaking, echoing, twanging sound as cracks spread. Over the other side, I saw Bloody Bothy Eric spring up, slip and fall on his bottom.

'Who the devil was that?' shouted a voice which I think was MacPhail's, although I didn't look to see. I was staring at my rabbit, smeared across the ice in a comet of red.

'Rabbit!' called Christopher.

'Bloody idiot,' shouted MacPhail, and then the birds started coming, but this time not very many.

★

After that drive we met by a loch so we could all drink meaty broth out of special metal cups and MacPhail could shout at people. My crime, it turned out, was to have fired prematurely, which meant the pheasants had taken fright and flown off in the wrong direction, apparently towards some particularly irritating little valley. Shooting before the first bird, I gathered, was a big no-no.

'Especially just for a bloody rabbit,' said MacPhail.

'I'm so sorry,' I said miserably, but he was stalking off already, speaking to Bonnar about exactly where we'd have to go now to kill all the things we hadn't just killed, or nobody would kill them at all, and otherwise what would be the point of their even being alive? There was a spaniel bounding around beside them, and I suddenly recognised it as Candy. Flora, I realised, was behind me, in a huddle with Fusty and Layman.

'Hello,' I said, walking over and lighting a cigarette.

'It's a disaster,' said Flora dryly. 'Some idiot shot a rabbit.'

'Ah,' I said uncomfortably. 'That was me.'

'Yes, darling,' nodded Flora, who obviously knew this already.

Fusty was in beetroot mode.

'Are you stupid?' he said. 'Fuck are you even doing here, anyway? You've ruined the day.'

I felt about five years old. I wondered if I should leave.

'No, he hasn't,' said Flora. 'I was joking. It's fine. Don't be so rude.'

'Chill, man, it's only shooting,' said Layman, and his own comfort seemed bottomless. I can remember exactly what he looked like. Which is odd, given I was in a bit of a flap, but honestly, I can see him now. There in the snow, with his Barbour off. Trim but firm. His clothes – the whole tweed drill – hung like they had been made for him, but they were old, so couldn't have been. Hair tucked behind the ears, under a flat cap that matched everything else. A brown check shirt on, and a blue woollen tie, everything perfect, not an inch going spare. The confidence, to be eighteen years old and voluntarily wearing a tie, and to be looking amazing in it, too. Never in all my life have I belonged somewhere so obviously and fundamentally as he belonged there. It's been years, and I still think of it. I wonder if it's when it all began to change.

We stood there. They were all still talking, but I couldn't think of a way to join in. My tongue felt a foot thick. It started to drizzle. Without thinking, I put my hat on.

'Wow,' said Flora.

'It's my dad's,' I said, taking it off again.

'What fun,' said Fusty, in a really flat, nasty way, and he walked off.

'Prick,' said Layman.

'Look, don't worry about the rabbit,' said Flora. 'We used to hunt hares here. Well, not me. But the family. At the end of the summer. It was a big deal. Huge shoots. Really grand. The Duke of Edinburgh came to one. There's a picture in the house. Upstairs in his study. So many people. Women in hats. Year after year. When Dad was a boy, I think it might have been the most famous hare shoot in Scotland.'

'Huh,' I said. 'I've never seen a hare here. Not ever. Where did they all go?'

'We shot them,' Flora explained.

★

The kit was a surprise. I don't just mean the guns and the cartridge bags. All the other stuff. The handwarmers. The elaborate gloves, with fingers that came on and off. The sticks that turned into chairs and the endless supply of flasks, all metal wrapped in leather, which appeared from pockets and went around, full of whisky, or gin, or some sort of gingery thing I couldn't place. Even the boots. I thought they'd all be green Hunters, like the ones my dad had aspirationally bought a few years ago, which I had aspirationally borrowed. But there were all kinds of other things going on, with zips and furs and elastic and gators. Likewise the coats, which were only all Barbours on first impression. Look closely, and there was Gore-Tex and tight herringbone tweed. Layman's coat, I noticed, had a little tarnished bronze bird logo on one collar. The trick seemed to be to wear clothes that were almost like everybody else's, but which were also subtly different. Although not so different as my hat.

For the last drive before lunch, we were in a gulley. A few picker-uppers had arranged themselves behind us with their dogs, and I recognised one of them as Archie, with whom I'd knocked down the bees' nest in the summer. He was in a camouflage army surplus jacket and had a snub-nosed, greying black spaniel that stayed constantly behind his left foot. I think it might have been the best-behaved dog in the whole place.

'Hello,' I said.

'Ah,' he said, 'it's the wee laddie who didn't know a hoe. And who shot the rabbit.'

I grimaced and gave him a cigarette, and he grinned. I asked him how come he was here.

'I'm allus here for the pheasant,' he said. 'Near forty year.'

'Christ,' I said. 'How old are you?'

'Not the grouse. Too hot. Tramping around. But the

pheasant. Aye. Whole village used tae dae it. Good money. And your dinner. But it was grander back then.'

I kept hearing that, I told him. And it seemed pretty grand now.

'Down Burnside, too,' he said. 'Fine shoots, there. Although not for a wee while.'

Then he asked if I'd shot much, apart from the rabbit, and I said no, literally nothing. He asked if I knew what I was doing, and I looked over my shoulder and admitted that I didn't have a clue. So, when the birds came that time, he stayed with me and talked me through it. Anticipate the flight with the end of your gun, slowly bringing it up. Always two feet ahead. When the stock gets to your shoulder, shoot, but don't stop moving even then. The first two, I missed, all the same. The third dropped like a rock.

'That's it, sir,' said Archie. He hadn't called me 'sir' before.

Later, I killed another.

★

Afterwards, I trudged across the snow with Christopher, heading towards the bloody bothy for lunch. I had my gun under one arm, like you were meant to, and my pheasants in the other hand. Their heads were between my first two fingers, dangling by their necks. I wondered how long they would stretch. Then I made myself stop wondering that.

'Right species this time,' said Christopher cheerfully.

'Fuck off,' I said, feeling cheerful enough myself to risk it. 'Actually,' I added, 'these were my first. Ever, I mean. I haven't shot pheasants before.'

'Pheasant,' said Fusty, appearing behind us. It was like he was correcting me.

'But I got two,' I said.

Then Christopher said that the plural of 'pheasant' was 'pheasant'. Which seemed unlikely. Then he said they should blood me.

'Here,' said Fusty, grabbing one of my birds. Then he jabbed a finger into it, and it came out red. Then he wiped it across my cheeks, left, right.

'Stop it,' I said.

'It's tradition,' he said, like it was a warning, and Christopher laughed, and I shrugged. And I could feel the wind on those two wet stripes all the harder, somehow. It made my cheeks sting.

By the time we got inside the bothy, the blood was all dry and crusty, although everybody said I still wasn't allowed to wash it off. Most people were already there. MacPhail was at one end of the table, sitting next to his wife, Flora's mum. She looked a bit different from how I remembered. Softer and redder, like she was getting a double chin. Flora and Layman were ensconced at the other end, and I had to sit in the middle, between Christopher and Elvis. They squeezed up to make room. People were up and down all the time. You helped yourself from a hotplate on a counter at the side.

'Congratulations,' Elvis said, as I settled down with my plate. 'Splendid. I first shot here in 1952. Although it was all very different then. As was I!'

'Hare?' I said.

He looked at me in horror.

'That you shot?' I said quickly. And then – and I honestly still can't believe I did this – I put two fingers up on either side of my head, like bunny ears, and waggled them around.

'Pheasant,' he said. 'And partridge. Although that might have been at Burnside. Which is next door, you know.'

At the young end of the table – the one I wanted to be at – it was all sounding quite raucous. I think everybody was already a glass or two down. In a bid to show I knew my onions, blood on my face or not, I told him I knew Burnside because I'd shot there in the summer. Which was sort of true.

'They still have shoots?' he asked.

'Well, no,' I said, casting an eye towards Flora, who was giggling about something I hadn't heard and had her arm on Layman's arm. I wondered if she'd seen my bloody cheeks. I wondered what she thought about them. 'It was very informal,' I added.

'We'll have shoots there,' interjected Fusty. 'When I take it over. We have extensive plans.'

Flora looked up.

'Are you combining the estates?' said Christopher.

'Only on paper,' said Fusty. 'Each to their own.'

'Dad,' called Flora wryly, 'Philip is empire-building again.'

'I don't think they've done a proper shoot for twenty years,' said Elvis.

'The place is a ruin,' said some other old guy. 'Totally mismanaged.'

'Maybe we'll have one next year,' said Fusty recklessly. 'I doubt I'll be in the big house by then, though. We've been speaking to an architect from Edinburgh. It's expensive, obviously, but money well spent because it really is virtually a ruin. We'll put a lot of birds down, too. Good to have my own place! At least, until I move back into the—'

'Oh, do shut up, Philip,' said MacPhail loudly, from the far end of the table.

Everybody went quiet. Yikes, I thought.

'Life is full of surprises,' explained MacPhail to the various men around him, and next to him Flora's newly fat mum went pink and looked down. And, by the time I turned my head the other way, I could see that Fusty had also changed colour, but to purple. And behind him, at the side of the room, I saw Bonnar, his father. Not saying a word. Quietly loading sausages onto a plate.

★

After the last drive, we stood around outside the house, drinking sherry that Flora's mum had brought out on a tray. I suppose I'd like to be able to tell you that I noticed her moving awkwardly, something in the roll of her hips, a swelling cashmere bump. I'd be lying, though, because I was actually looking at the pheasants. There were loads of them, more than there had been grouse, all laid out in a square. And my rabbit lying next to them at the side, like it had wandered into the wrong school photo from the comprehensive next door. I also remember that it was growing dark. Waxed jackets under a waxing moon.

My cheeks were tight and scratchy. Would sherry, I wondered, dissolve blood? Flora and Layman were still chattering; I hadn't really spoken to either of them all day. MacPhail was laughing loudly about something, standing proprietorially with Bonnar and Captain Beater by the quad of the dead. People were packing up, replacing wellies with brogues. I watched, and I saw that everybody went along the line of the three of them, shaking hands like it was a wedding; MacPhail first, then Captain Beater, then Bonnar, who would give them a pair of pheasants. Sorry, a brace of pheasants. Of pheasant.

In a panic, I suddenly realised that I'd only brought one tenner. Apart from that, I only had a fiver and some change. What to do? Could you palm somebody change? Was that mental? Could I borrow a tenner off Fusty and then give it straight to his dad? Maybe that was even worse. Fuck. In the end, I only gave Bonnar the fiver. He didn't show any sign of noticing, but I kept thinking of him later, counting it all out, seeing the blue among the brown. I couldn't imagine him telling anyone, though. So, there was that.

★

Christopher offered me a lift back to the station.

'Just a minute,' I said, and I side-stepped him up to the house, where Flora and Layman were going inside.

'Hey,' I said to him, for the second time that day.

'Hey, man,' said Layman, turning by the door. His tie was loosened now. I could feel the warmth floating out of the house. Aga warmth. A promise of drinks and fires and evenings.

'Are you off?' said Flora.

'Yeah,' I said. 'I suppose. I mean, I could—'

'But it's Christmas Eve tomorrow,' said Flora.

I thought of a quiet evening at home, my dad drinking in his study, me in front of the television. The trip, tomorrow, to the bright, bright hospital wing, to see my mum saying nothing at all. From inside, past them both, I wondered if I could smell cooking. I thought of an evening in the Auchnastang kitchen. Big pots on the table. That absurd guest room. Bodies in the sheets. Flora came down the steps, put a hand on my shoulder and kissed me on the cheek. I think it was the first time we'd touched all day.

'It was really nice to see you,' she said.

'You, too,' I said, and then they both turned around and went inside.

In the car, I scratched off the blood with a fingernail, although I scratched a little too hard and drew some blood of my own. Then, at the station in Perth, I put my pheasants in the bin.

16

FOR HOGMANAY, BARF WAS having a party up at his parents' place, which was somehow both very close to Aberdeen but also very far away from Aberdeen, on account of the way all the roads went in the other direction first.

I'd assumed we'd all head up in the red diesel Land Rover, as per normal, but from Boxing Day onwards I kept leaving messages with the old people Johnnie lived with, and he kept not calling me back. 'He's heard about the shoot,' I thought. 'He hates me now.'

Eventually I called at a time he was actually there, and he came to the phone sounding irritated and said he wasn't going to Barf's because Layman was having a party for all the college lot in his flat.

'Oh, right,' I said, thinking that Johnnie couldn't be that cross about the shoot if he was still hanging out with Layman. And wondering whether Flora would be there, and feeling a bit thrown that neither of them had mentioned it. All of which deepened considerably when Johnnie said, 'So, I guess I'll see you guys another time,' and I realised, in a cold panic, that he didn't actually want me to be at Layman's party.

'Look, is everything okay with you and Alan?' I blurted. With the first subtext being 'please tell me this is about him, not me,' and the second subtext being, 'because if it is, screw him, please invite me anyway'.

'Ah, shut up,' said Johnnie, who wasn't one for subtext, and that was that.

What to do? I didn't want to call Alan. Because, well, might not he be going to Layman's, too? He wasn't getting on with Johnnie, but I was pretty sure that he was also friends with Layman himself. I'd met them together. Layman had been to his house. So, I was half worried that he might have not wanted me to come, either, which would have killed me, but I was also worried about just going with him, anyway, and getting there, and Johnnie looking at me in that evil Johnnie way of his, and then having to spend the whole night thinking that people were talking about me, and laughing about me, because I was just some try-hard interloper who didn't belong in any of these places, anyway. Could it just happen like that? My whole new life, ending as suddenly and inexplicably as it had begun? All these places I'd never go again. Burnside. Auchnastang. Even Moray Place. Maybe this was my life now. Just here, alone.

In the end, though, Alan called me and said he was driving up himself to Barf's because he'd got a car for Christmas. Layman and his party weren't even mentioned.

'Oh, wow,' I said. 'Yeah. Amazing. Totally. Thanks so much.'

'Calm down,' he said.

Alan's car was an old blue Mini estate van. Rickety as hell but very cool. We set off in it a little too late on Hogmanay: past 5 p.m. Claire was coming, so I had to lie in the back, in dog mode. By then, I didn't mind.

They'd come into the house to pick me up, and the sight

of her had stiffened my dad's spine from the damp, dejected curve in which it now spent most days when he was here with me. She had her lipstick on, with her dark hair and pashmina tumbling around up top, and tight dark jeans down below. My dad had offered them both a glass of wine while I rolled my eyes, and to my surprise she'd said yes, so I had one, too. Alan had passed because he was driving. Then my dad had given us another bottle for the party, and she and I had it open before we got to the Forth Road Bridge. We were basically back-to-back, with me facing the wrong way, passing the bottle over our shoulders. Periodically she'd light cigarettes for me and Alan. We listened to Simon & Garfunkel and Counting Crows and all sang along as we trundled up the orange glow of the A90 towards Dundee. Forget being a dog; now I felt like a gay best friend. Half an hour in, I didn't want to be at Layman's stupid party with stupid Johnnie and stupid potential Flora, anyway. They should see me now, I thought. Tommo has options.

At Forfar we hit the snow and Alan sounded worried.

'It's only a wee car,' he said.

'Could we die here?' said Claire, doing a breathy, wide-eyed starlet impression that wasn't very Claire at all.

'We have sleeping bags,' I said, and then I steered my voice towards pompous, and channelled Uncle Monty from *Withnail & I*. 'Night must fall,' I added. 'And we shall be forced to camp.'

'Oooh!' she said, very much in the spirit of things.

'Shall we have a spliff?' I said, because this was getting exciting.

'Not yet,' said Alan, playing dad.

At Stonehaven we turned onto the A957, and it all very

nearly stopped being funny. The road was clear but only just, and the snow was almost a blizzard, battering against the daft vertical Mini windscreen in flakes the size of doilies.

'Okay,' said Claire, 'so, remember that film with the Russian band and the guitarist who froze to death? And the way they drove around for the rest of it with him stiff on the roof?'

'I wish I was fatter,' I said. 'Because I'll be the first to go.'

'Are you calling me fat?' she said, and I squeezed her shoulder from behind, and she reached back and squeezed my hand.

'It's not actually funny,' said Alan because, insanely, we still had about thirty miles to drive. We were freezing, even though the heater was up full. In the back of the car I found this knackered old sheepskin hat with earflaps that Alan wore sometimes, and I stuck it on and didn't take it off. That did the job for about three minutes. After that, I broke out the sleeping bags and put one over Claire, like a stole, and all but got into another. She had the car's interior light on and was peering blearily at a road map and a scrap of paper with directions on it. Everything outside was snow, field and single-track road. There were no other cars. Somehow, we'd been on the road for five hours. Genuinely, I started to wonder if we were going to see in 1995 in a lay-by. If we could even find one.

We made it, though. A few seemingly random turns later, we were outside this huge, pillared gateway and a driveway stretching away, incongruous at the side of the road in the middle of bugger all else. You know those pillars with balls at the top? These were those, but they only had one ball. Like Hitler.

'Right,' said Alan, pulling over and cutting the engine.

'What the fuck?' said Claire, who was one of the lads now.

'Spliff,' said Alan firmly, and we smoked it right there in the car, watching the snowflakes twirl in the silent headlights. After that, inevitably, the bastard thing wouldn't start again, but Claire and I leapt out and pushed it up the slippery drive, feeling like giggly superheroes, while Alan gunned the engine, and eventually it roared into life. Then we both piled into the back and sprawled behind the seats, while this huge, mad pile of a country house loomed up ahead. And I thought again about Layman's stupid party and his stupid flat, and I reckoned it couldn't possibly compete with the magic of this.

★

The actual party, mind you, was a bit of a letdown. There were fifty-odd people there and a grand total of about seven of them were girls. That's Barf for you. Post-Ella or not, it seemed he still didn't talk to women. His house, though, was totally nuts. Maccleaugh? Mucclough? Something like that. The main bit in the middle was similar to Auchnastang, but higher and dirtier. On either side, though, there was a wing of almost the same size. The one to the left had dead-looking creepers all over it. In the morning, I'd see that it also had missing windows and only half a roof. Apparently the top two floors were literally inaccessible, what with the staircase having collapsed sometime after the war.

The body of the house wasn't in great nick, either. The whole party seemed to be happening on the ground floor, which was made up of these giant flagstones, worn concave by centuries of Barf and his insane ancestors stumbling drunkenly around on them.

Most of the school First XV were here, which meant there was a lot of beer and shouting of 'Oi-oi' and suchlike. I'm not really sure who everybody else was. They were from Gordonstoun, maybe, where the royals go. It's up there somewhere. Or Glenalmond. Probably not Rannoch, because they were all debauched Layman types, sent there after being expelled from somewhere else because it was in the middle of nowhere and there weren't any drugs.

In the hall, on a table, there was a quite small portable CD player, turned up far too loud and playing *Blood Sugar Sex Magik* by the Red Hot Chili Peppers. So many people were smoking so many Marlboros that you could barely see the roof or the stairs. Atmospherically, I suppose it was a bit like that first party I had been to at that house in Niddrie, but with way more testosterone. As if that first one had gone on and on and become the foundation of a whole new cult, after the boys had eaten all the girls.

We found Barf himself in a drawing room, in the middle of a crowd shotgunning beer, gesticulating incoherently from an armchair.

'Dude!' shouted Alan, pushing through. 'This is nuts. You okay? Your parents here?'

Barf shrugged helplessly.

'They're away,' shouted Glenn, the meathead from my table at school. 'On business, he says.'

'Hey!' shouted this other kid Steve, who I vaguely knew

from Pothle, and who I wasn't all that keen on. 'Listen to this! Barf! Barf! What does your dad do?'

Barf shrugged again. He opened and closed his mouth, like a dying fish, as if he'd forgotten how it worked.

'Your dad!' persisted Steve. 'What's his job?'

'Come on,' I said. 'Leave him.'

'Yeah, we know what your fucking dad does,' said Steve, to me. 'Butler boy.'

'Oh,' Claire said, sounding shocked, but I didn't say anything at all, and it was actually like Steve had already forgotten he'd even spoken to me.

'Barf!' shouted Glenn, joining in. 'Why is your house so shit?'

'What. Is. Your. Dad's. Job?' shouted Steve.

'I don't know,' said Barf weakly.

'Fucking brilliant,' said Steve, in glee. 'He doesn't fucking know!'

'Come on,' said Alan, and we picked our way to the far corner of the room and set up our own little camp. Not quite in defiance of everything else, but almost. After a while, it was like our own little party inside the bigger one. Rugby lads would wander into our world sometimes to share a joint, then wander away again. It was almost deferential. Midnight came and went without anybody remembering to sing 'Auld Lang Syne'. Sometime afterwards, improbably, four or five other cars turned up, mainly full of girls, I guess from another party nearby. They were all dolled up, relatively speaking, and incongruous as anything among all the drenched lads with their tops off.

None of them seemed surprised. I guess they knew what they were here for. In fact, the only thing that seemed to throw them was our little smoky corner, with Alan in his combat trousers and me in my sheepskin hat, and the crimson-lipped art school princess sprawled across both of us, close as a litter, like she didn't have to choose. You'd see them looking, nodding our way, asking each other questions and not knowing the answer. Like I said, it wasn't the best night, but I liked that. There was status there. 'Any moment now,' I kept telling myself, 'one of them will come over and leave her tribe for our own. Like in an American high school film, when a cheerleader sees the light.' But they never did.

★

'Sorry, man,' said Barf to Alan, as he saw us off the next day. It was about 11 a.m. We were out the front, getting into our car. Cold Highland morning. Sky so clear it hurt your eyes. He was still in the same clothes and looked like death. Inside, people were drinking again. If they'd even stopped.

'Don't sweat, man,' said Alan. 'Total adventure.'

'Hey, Barf,' I said, 'what actually does your dad do?'

'I don't know,' said Barf, and he trudged back inside.

★

School started a week later, and I was drifting like the snow. I no longer wrote to Flora and I'd also stopped calling Johnnie. I barely spoke to Ella. In fact, I wasn't doing much apart from revision, and I wasn't really doing much of that because I couldn't figure out how. Cambridge had made me an offer of three As, but I also seemed to be able to cover every important bit of every subject I was learning in a morning, and I genuinely wasn't sure what to do the rest of the time.

The only interesting thing I remember happening in that first half of term was that a friend of little Angela's told me she was keen and wanted me to walk her back after tea. So, I did, and she still didn't say a word, and neither did I, and thereafter mealtimes were, by some dark magic, even more excruciating than they had been before.

Probably that was why, in the second half of term, I ended up chumming along with Alan on a CCF expedition in the Ochil Hills. He was a prefect, so he had to go and be in charge, but there weren't enough prefects, so he took me, too. How to describe an expedition? I guess they were sort of like the Duke of Edinburgh Awards, minus the awards. You had to do them twice a year for the first three years, sleeping in tents and cooking on paraffin. It was supposed to teach you how to read a map and stuff, but there was always just one geeky kid who did that while the rest of you basically just learned how to walk up steep hills while constantly smoking. The first time I did it, this one guy from my technology class developed a skill of sticking a fag up one nostril so he could march along with his thumbs under his bag straps. Hey, it's a skill.

That day, anyway, the walk was pretty simple: a six-mile trek along a gravel path to that night's campsite. Being authority figures – I know – we had to wait in the minibus for an extra couple of hours while all the kids set off, so we could follow them up and find any who had got lost, or fallen into ditches, or simply lain down and given up.

This waiting entailed hanging around with Legohead, the chemistry teacher who was nominally in charge of the whole thing, so called because he was totally bald and his head had this weird bump right on the top of it. Legend had it that he'd got it from getting a beaker stuck on his head in some sort of horrific chemistry accident, but in retrospect it was probably just a birth defect.

At school, he was one of those teachers who gets bullied half the time and is randomly vicious the rest. His classroom had an attic in it where he kept the textbooks, and the guys in the year above us once stole the ladder when he was up it and wouldn't let him down. Proper raging. Here, though, he was actually quite a good laugh, telling us about his time at Newcastle University, where he'd been in a band playing Pink Floyd covers and stuff. Funny, when teachers were suddenly human. Really shook you. He was wearing a woolly hat, so maybe that helped.

'Right, bugger off, you two,' he said, when the two hours were up. 'I'm going to the pub.'

It was cold and grey, but dry at least. We only had little rucksacks, too, because Legohead had let us leave our tent and sleeping bags in the bus. The path was slate and crunched underfoot. We smoked, but only a little, because we were grown-ups now. Alan was talking about school, and the brutality shown towards younger kids, and how much more sense it made once you realised that the whole place had been designed for an age of Empire, where important toff life skills involved knowing how to completely do over defenceless brown people far away without feeling too bad about it.

'Like my granddad probably did,' he said. 'And that's still

what we're basically learning. I mean, come on. Have you never noticed that literally everybody is white?'

'There was Ranjit,' I said, thinking of a boy who had left last year. 'And that guy Paul in fourth form is Jewish. Does that count?'

Alan said there had also been a kid from Swaziland in the junior school for a term once. 'Although everybody used to say,' he added vaguely, 'that his dad was some sort of prince. Jesus, fuck. Would you look at that.'

We'd just rounded a bend. Ahead of us, at the side of the road, was a small cairn. And, on the top of it, somebody had placed the severed head of a rabbit. Ears sticking up.

'See, this is what I mean,' said Alan. 'It's not normal.'

'Define normal,' I said, because I was enjoying the conversation, but I also felt a bit out of my depth. Not least because my own granddad had been a dentist in the Midlands.

'Normal,' said Alan, 'is a thing you can tell normal people about. Without them thinking somebody should be locked up.'

I thought about this. On Luci's first expedition, he'd once told me, one of the rugby lads had found a sheep's placenta and picked it up on a stick. Gross, slimy, filmy thing. He'd threatened to flick it at people, and they all scattered, and eventually he had flicked it at Payne ('PAIN!'), that kid who once got knocked out by the hockey ball.

Payne was running away at the time, said Luci, but it caught him on the back of the head and wrapped itself around the front over his face, and he rolled down the hill clawing at it and suffocating inside it, like it was some sort of alien membrane. Eventually somebody had to ram a finger through the thing over his mouth so he could breathe. Or, at least, that was the story; and next to that, some rabbit's head on a pile of stones seemed small beer. And who were these mythical normal people Alan was on about, anyway? The guys from my old school, maybe? They'd never even have been here.

'It was probably dead already,' I decided. 'When they found it. Otherwise it would have run away.'

'Hopped away,' said Alan.

'You're being very suburban about this,' I said.

'Do they hop?'

'Not really.'

'What about when you shoot them in the other leg?'

'What's up,' I said, 'with you and Johnnie?'

'Och, just don't,' he said, and he looked poetically off at the hillside horizon, like he was Robbie Burns on a tea towel. And so we just trudged on, and for a while I just didn't.

'No, but I do want to know,' I said eventually. 'Because it's sort of becoming a massive pain in my arse. Because he's being weird and you're being weird, and it seems to me that you both need a pretty good reason to—'

'He asked me to help him kill Fusty,' said Alan. 'And also MacPhail.'

'Yeah, fuck off.'

Alan shrugged. 'I'm not joking.'

'Yeah, but you misunderstood,' I said. 'It was a joke. He can't have meant it.'

Then I thought back to the summer. And I wondered if I was totally sure that Johnnie hadn't sort of asked me to help him kill Fusty and MacPhail, too.

'He seemed quite upset with me,' said Alan mildly. 'Afterwards. Like I was letting him down by not being totally okay with it. Like I wasn't the friend he'd thought I was. He wanted to do Fusty first. Out in a field. At night. Make it look like suicide. Because he's still so upset about his best friend Douglas.'

'But Fusty wouldn't . . .' I said. 'I mean, he doesn't seem the sort that . . .'

Alan shrugged. 'Yeah, it's not a great plan. Apart from being, you know, psychotic. I'm not sure what he was going to do to MacPhail. We didn't get that far. Maybe take him out in the night, like a ninja.'

'He didn't mean it,' I said again. 'He was fantasising. It's like his whole thing about blaming them. Which I actually believed for a bit. Sort of. But it's nonsense, isn't it? He's just upset. Because of the house.'

'Enough with the fucking house,' said Alan. 'It's just a house.'

'It's not, though, is it?

'We're losing ours, too,' said Alan.

I looked at him.

'And I'm not planning on killing anyone,' he said. Then he sighed. 'Except maybe my dad.'

It was because of the recession, he said. I said I didn't really know what that was, and he said it didn't really matter what it was, but maybe I should read more newspapers. So, I resolved to start. The point was, he said, his uncle Marco, who owned all the restaurants, had run out of money, which meant his dad had to repay him this massive loan he'd borrowed in the 1980s, and his only way of doing that was by selling the house. So, I asked why Mungo had borrowed all the money from Marco in the first place, and Alan said it was because he didn't have any and never had.

'It's not so different,' he said, 'to Johnnie's thing. There used to be all this money and now there isn't because everybody has forgotten how to get it. Because it's been ages. Because you can't just march off and loot it from Burma any more. Or whatever. And now other people have it instead, and if you want some of it, then you have to give them all your stuff. Like art, but we already did that. So, now it's the house.'

He said this quite placidly, looking ahead, one foot after the other. If you hadn't known him, you wouldn't have thought he was bothered at all.

'Shit, man,' I said.

'It's only a house,' he said again. 'I'm not asking for sympathy. It's not like your mum.'

I had no idea why we were suddenly talking about my mum. It's not like we had to sell her.

Then Alan said his parents were splitting up, too. Although, he added, he expected that this was just because they couldn't afford a new house big enough for them both to ignore each other in, and it wouldn't really make much difference. And I thought of Moray Place, and the way it existed like two rival courts, with Mungo and his friends drinking red wine and baying on one floor, and Leonora and all the Italians drinking white wine and wafting perfume on another. And I thought of not going there any more, not on random afternoons or after parties or ever. No more smoking upstairs and then going down into some random hubbub to steal cheese. None of it. And, I dunno, maybe it was like my mum, a bit.

'She'll probably go back to Glasgow,' said Alan, of his own

mum. 'Dad's found a flat in Marchmont. Like a student. He's got some mad idea about starting a wine bar.'

'With your uncle?'

'God, no,' said Alan. 'I mean, he asked, but Marco won't touch him with a barge pole. I don't think anyone will. It won't work, will it? He's just going to potter around. With less and less. All those old jackets of his getting older and older. Face getting redder. Anything to pretend he's not normal.'

'Define normal,' I said again.

Alan snorted.

'You sound like you hate him,' I said.

Although then, as we rounded the next corner, we saw six boys from the year below, trudging slowly towards us under their massive rucksacks. Two of them were smoking, but one of them suddenly started pretending he wasn't. Alan was a prefect. You never knew.

'What the fuck?' said Alan. 'You're going the wrong way.'

They all looked at each other.

'We climbed a hill,' said one of them. 'It took ages. Max said it was a short cut.'

'Maybe we're the ones who are going the wrong way,' I said.

'I never go the wrong way,' said Alan. 'Morons. Turn around.

17

THREE DAYS AFTER WE left school, a bunch of us were invited to the leaving ball at Zara's school, up near St Andrews. Or rather, Alan was invited, and told to bring some boys who wanted to meet girls for some girls who wanted to meet boys. It's funny, I feel like I should have got to know Zara properly at some point, but it just never happened. She was always around, but I suppose she frightened me. People like her and Alan, I don't know, it's like they rule the world. Like, they clock each other, as people who can get things done, and the rest of us just get to orbit them. Right? Anyway, Alan got me, Johnnie and Barf to go, and after that he just asked around, getting Wee Geordie Meehan and some guy called James.

Johnnie drove. He and Alan seemed to have made up, and without anybody murdering anyone. I feel I should be able to tell you what had happened, but I don't actually know. All I can say is there had been one summer night, in the meandering lull after A-levels, when I'd slogged down to the Dump and found them there together, with Johnnie having climbed over the fence behind which backed onto that Musselburgh dogshit park. He looked different. His hair was down to his shoulders, and he wore army combat trousers, and he had all these muscles, I guess from working on the farm.

'Oh,' I'd said, delighted. And he'd beamed back, and all had been good in the world.

The rest of the world wasn't terrible, either. My dad was in the closing stages of parting company with the fucking butler show, having somehow held it together that far. This was definitely good news, but for now he was still stuck in Devon, where the latest series was shooting. My mum, meanwhile, was breathing away like an old pro. No tubes or masks or anything. She was smiling a lot and talking more than in ages. When I squeezed her hand, she squeezed back. Obviously, it wasn't as though she was about to leap up and start Riverdancing, or anything. Still, mainly because she now spent most of her time staring at the telly and sipping unmentionable goo, the doctors were saying that there was really no reason why she couldn't soon do that at home instead. Hence my dad wanting to be home, too.

Anyway, for the ball, Johnnie picked me up first, so I sat in the front. The roof was off the Land Rover and, one by one, the rest of them lined up side-by-side on the benches at the back. It was one of those still, yellow Scottish June afternoons. I kept laughing, looking back over my shoulder. Alan was handing out beers. Wee Geordie Meehan had a Scotland Rugby hat on down over his ears, with a bobble. As we came down the motorway slip road, I remember turning up the volume on the stereo, just as it hit the solo from Boston's 'More Than A Feeling', and Johnnie looking over, with a grin. And the hospital, the fucking butler and, I suppose, even Johnnie's dead brother all felt quite far away. It's pretty basic being a boy.

We were late, though. Like, really late. We told Zara we'd

had car trouble, but it was just that 'When I Come Around' had blown out the left-hand speaker, like it always did, and we'd had to stop in a lay-by to fix it, and the Juicy Fruit was all dry and old now, so it took a while. We all changed into our kilts and black-tie in a supermarket car park, and then ran through the streets to this community hall.

'You're a wanker,' said Zara to Alan. Her blow-dried blonde hair was enormous. 'We're about to eat. We thought you weren't coming.'

He apologised, and Zara dutifully produced the five girls for the other five guys. Mine was called Natalie, and she seemed nice, but I don't remember much about her at all. Which is awful, when you think about it, because maybe she'd had hopes and dreams of her own. Some mystery boy, who she'd been looking forward to, for weeks. Honestly, though, I don't. Although I do remember, afterwards, this shy, tiny girl stepping forwards and Zara peering at a list on a bit of paper and saying, 'Right, who is Wee Geordie Meehan?'

'Me,' rumbled Geordie, now in his kilt but still in his hat, too.

'But he's not wee,' said Zara. 'He's bloody massive.'

★

After the ball, there was an all-night party in a barn at a deer farm. A coach took us, so nobody had to drive. Johnnie and Alan were snorting speed, together like lovers reunited, so I left them to it and fell in with the rugby boys. 'Tomm-Oh!' they shouted sometimes, which was manageable. I drank a lot that night. Cans and cans, and then half a bottle of red wine. Somehow, they all thought I'd had sex with Angela. I didn't deny it. That was manageable, too.

There were huge haybales inside, sort of functioning as furniture. At one point seven or eight of us dragged one outside and set fire to it.

'Come on,' said this anxious girl I hadn't seen before. 'Guys. You can't do this.'

'Nobody minds,' I told her confidently.

'I mind,' she said.

'Fuck off?' suggested that guy Steve, and she got all tight-lipped and went away. Somebody asked who she was. Somebody else thought she might live here.

We dragged out more bales and sat on them. I remember a girl sitting next to me and talking to her, but my words sounded all booming and mushy, like my tongue didn't know what to do and my volume control was bust. I put my arm around her, but she moved away. Maybe I shouted something after her, couldn't say. Not long afterwards, anyway, she and another girl went into the Portaloo, maybe having bought some of Johnnie's speed. Steve and Glenn stood outside, rocking it. Then, as they rocked, I ran up and kicked away one of the breeze blocks, which meant the whole thing toppled over quite close to the fire.

'Tomm-Oh!' roared the lads, and the girls rolled out, sideways. Not blue. Different plumbing system, I suppose. Not long after that, I puked up all the red wine onto a pile of straw. At the time, I wondered if it was blood.

★

I was away a lot that month. I have memories, rolodexed into snapshots, but I'm not totally sure what goes where. Mysteriously parentless houses, huge vats of pasta. Long drives in various cars, sometimes Johnnie's, sometimes not. A party in a village hall. Another huge barn. Fifty kids in sleeping bags on the floor – that night? Another night? – while two of them right in the middle had loud and unashamed sex under a table-tennis table. Climbing a hill to see a sunrise, God knows who with. Passing Layman, on the other side of a chicken-wire fence, standing up and drawing his kilt closed while a nameless, faceless girl lay turned away and bare-backed in the heather. Him asking for a cigarette. Me passing one through a hexagonal, galvanised gap.

Tents outside a holiday cottage. Nowhere to shit. A night on a beach, shivering around a fire. On an island out west? Or near Aberdeen in the east? Couldn't say. Some fights. A fence ripped down in somebody's field, somewhere else, and set alight. Fighting off hangovers on the velour seats of Stagecoach coaches going from A to B. A dozen teenagers going through their pockets on a wet sunny street somewhere in the Borders, sniggering in loud voices outside a greengrocer about whether you could buy just one banana. Horrified locals stepping around us and saying 'excuse me' in voices that didn't sound like ours at all. You know. Stuff like that.

What I do remember is calling home, from a red phone box opposite a bus stop.

'Where are you?' said Annie, who answered.

'Wait,' I said. 'Where are you?'

'I knew it was drugs,' said Annie. 'You called us, dipshit.'

'But why are you in Edinburgh?'

Annie explained that she was in Edinburgh because she was from Edinburgh. Because she'd grown up there, with me. And because she sometimes came back to visit her beloved family.

'You should have told me,' I said.

'I did. You forgot. Where are you?'

I was in a little village. I looked out the nearest scratched little pane of glass towards the bus stop.

'Tighnabruaich,' I suggested.

'Argyll?' said Annie. 'Near Dunoon?'

'Maybe. There's this guy. He's got a cottage on the beach. Or his parents do. From Loretto. Or maybe Merchiston? I'm not sure. We came through from Glasgow. There's a bunch of us. Alan was here, but he had to go.'

Then Annie said our dad had no idea where I was or who I was with. And that she'd told him I probably had a secret girlfriend. Some posh girl in pearls in a big house.

'And he just can't wait,' she said quite maliciously, 'to meet her.'

'Oh my God, I hate you so much.'

Annie sniggered.

'Anyway, they don't even wear pearls,' I said. Thinking of Flora, and her hippie beads and amulets on leather thongs.

'They?'

'Girls,' I said. 'Who I know. Generally. Generically. Leave me alone.'

Then Annie said she was in Edinburgh until the weekend. So, maybe I could come home.

'I guess,' I said.

'I mean, you do still live here.'

'I guess.'

★

Also, there was the time we stopped off at the castle. This was weeks later, after I'd been home and left again. We were on the way to something in Edinburgh from some party on some lawn outside some big house outside some village outside some town. Wherever we had been, I also remember that Johnnie was late, so I'd gone into a barber shop and had the guy shave the sides of my head while I waited for him to turn up. I can't pretend it looked quite how I'd hoped. Less punk. More radiation.

I also remember that Dean was with him. Somehow, even with my new, stupid hair, I was less conspicuous than he was. He wore polo-shirts with the top button done up, tucked into stonewashed jeans. His brown hair was short and brushed directly forwards. He didn't talk about being in jail, and I didn't ask. He was good company, though, which was just as well because Johnnie abandoned us early on for some girl and didn't come back. I don't remember who she was, but I do remember that it made Dean my sidekick rather than his, and I have no memory of him leaving my side all night, except for once, when he needed a piss and went off to do it in a field because he thought it was rude to go wandering into a stranger's house, even if you were at a party on her lawn. Which I thought was pretty weird.

The next day we'd just dropped him off in Auchternethy when I noticed we were taking the small lane down towards the river, rather than aiming for the motorway into Edinburgh. And I wondered if we were going to see Johnnie's mum, although he said no, we were going to the castle.

'Oh,' I said, delighted, 'is she back?'

'Who, Flora?' said Johnnie. 'Aye. But I need to pay a visit on her dickhead cousin.'

'You aren't going to do anything stupid, are you?'

Johnnie nodded backwards. I swivelled to see into the back of the car.

'No gun,' said Johnnie. 'So, I suppose I'll just have to strangle him with my bare hands. Unless you'd rather I didn't?'

I looked at him.

'Idiot,' said Johnnie. 'What's wrong with you? It's just some papers he wants me to look at. Go see Flora. I'll pick you up after.'

Fusty would be in the estate office, he said, so he dropped me off on the Auchnastang driveway before burning off. The front door to the house was open.

'Hello?' I called cautiously from the gravel, and there she was, coming down the stairs. She was in hippie backpacker clothes, all baggy and green, and her hair was henna brown.

'Oh!' she said. 'It's you!' And then we hugged, and I noticed she smelled different. Exotic. Oiled. She took me through to the kitchen, and we drank some tea that wasn't proper tea that she'd brought back from India. It tasted like wood.

'Mmm,' I said, as if this wasn't totally horrible.

'I love it,' she said. 'I'm going to drink it forever.'

'I came with Johnnie,' I said. 'He's gone to see your cousin. Something about some papers? So, they're talking now?'

Flora shrugged. She wasn't really interested in any of that. She'd come home a fortnight ago, she said, because she'd wanted to meet the baby. Only then she'd left again and gone to Norfolk, so she'd really only been here a couple of days.

'There's a baby?' I asked.

'Little Wilbur. My baby brother. Didn't you know?'

I thought of her mum, back when I'd been here shooting. The way she'd looked bigger and softer.

'Oh yeah,' I lied.

We looked at her India photos. There she was, on a hillside, on a beach. In a fleece, a bikini, a sarong. There was her friend Lucy, and her other friend Katie, and maybe a few more people, all of whom I remember being called Lucy and Katie, too, but hey, a lot of people just were. There she was at a temple, all pointy stone, with some guy. And at a market, looking at the head of a goat, with the same guy again. There she was next to an elephant, more guy, this time with his arm around her shoulders. He was tall, floppy-haired and blond. I hated him.

'Yeah, so, I met a boy,' said Flora, putting her hand on my arm.

I thought about this. What was with the hand on the arm? Was I not also a boy?

'He doesn't look very Indian,' I said.

'He's not,' she said. 'He's called Patrick and he's at Edinburgh University.'

'Of course he is.'

'But he's also from London. And Norfolk. Which is why I was there. Digglesworth. It's amazing. Have you heard of it?'

'Vaguely,' I said, lying again.

'It's so beautiful. I was really upset we couldn't go to Kashmir, but Patrick said Digglesworth was almost as good, and I reckon it must be. People say Norfolk is flat and boring, but they haven't been. 'There's a lake.'

'But you've got your own lake,' I said. 'I mean, loch.'

Flora said yes, but Digglesworth had a proper one. And also Patrick's sister was a model and used to go out with Prince Edward.

'You've probably seen her in *Tatler*,' she said. 'At the parties.'

My God. It was like talking to my dad.

'And he's at Edinburgh!' she said. 'And I'm going to art college. It's fate.'

'You're in love,' I said, hating how it sounded.

'Don't be stupid,' she said, but obviously delighted.

Then I told her that Alan was going to Edinburgh, too, but she didn't seem very interested. Then I told her that I was still waiting to hear from Cambridge, and she said Patrick's little brother was going there, and maybe we'd be friends, and he was called Charles Digglesworth and I should look out for him. So, I asked how come they were from Digglesworth but also called Digglesworth, and she said their dad was Lord Digglesworth. And I said, wow, that was just a coincidence too far, and she didn't laugh at all.

★

Johnnie still wasn't back after half an hour, so we went out for a buzz around on the quad bike, before coming back to a house of screaming. The baby was up. It – I suppose the traditional term is 'he' – was in the kitchen, being bounced around on the shoulder of a harassed-looking girl in a high ponytail and a tracksuit, while Flora's mum shouted at her and told her to be better at things. Eventually it was taken off to a place called 'the nursery' with a bottle, and the other three of us went and joined Flora's gran in the conservatory, for tea. Actual cucumber sandwiches. I'm not even shitting you.

The old lady was in a wheelchair with a tartan rug over her knees. Flora's mum called her 'Mum', although she clearly wasn't her mum. They had the same perm, pretty much, but her jaw was purest MacPhail.

'Remind me,' said Flora's mum to me. 'Who are you?'

'You remember Tommo,' said Flora to her.

'Hello, Emma,' I said confidently because I remembered Alan calling her that.

'What have you done to your hair?' she said.

'It's an undercut.'

'Ghastly,' she said. 'Have we met before?'

'Um, I was here at Christmas. Shooting.'

'Oh, you're the boy who stays,' said Emma MacPhail, putting a sandwich onto her mother-in-law's plate.

'Only once,' I said. 'Last summer.'

'Or should I say,' she added sweetly, 'who tries to stay. In other people's houses. For as long as they'll let him.'

I opened my mouth and then closed it again. I think maybe it made a noise as it shut. A little pop. Up close, I could see that Flora's mum had freckles under her make-up. I had a sudden flash of her, not as a generic Labrador blonde, but as a scary redhead in deep cover. She was wearing a stripy top, like the French, which was casual but not half as casual as the nanny. She didn't look exhausted. She looked perfect, and busy, and like she had no time whatsoever for my shit.

'Um,' I said again. Flora seemed to be biting her lip.

'Oh!' said her gran suddenly. 'You're the butler boy!'

I shrugged. Unsure whether this was better or worse.

'The one on the train is my favourite,' she said, in a croaky voice. 'Such a *clever* butler.'

'I've never met him,' I said. The words replayed in my head, sounding mad.

Then she said my father must be jolly clever, too.

'Because he's from a very different background, isn't he?' she said. 'To the one he writes about. And you can only sometimes tell!'

'I guess he's more like the butler,' I said, feeling a bit annoyed now.

'Archibald,' said Flora's gran. 'He was our butler. Did you know him?'

'Oh, Mum,' said Flora's mum fondly. 'Don't be silly. Thomas has probably never met a real butler in his life.'

She passed me the teapot, and as I poured myself a cup of tea I noticed my hand was very slightly shaking. I'd forgotten they drank proper tea, though, so sloshed it out full of twigs and leaves. How could I have done this twice? There was a sieve thing on the table next to it, I noticed, in a little silver saucer. I looked into my cup and felt Flora's mum looking into it, too.

'Obviously it's a madhouse around here,' she said, dabbing her perfect lips with a napkin. 'With dear little Wilbur. So, I'm afraid there simply isn't any—'

'I was just with Johnnie,' I said. 'Burchill. I mean, I'm not . . . I wasn't . . . He was coming back. But.'

'I suppose Flora should give you a lift to the station,' said Flora's mum.

'Let me go to the loo,' said Flora, leaping up.

The three of us left in the room all looked at each other. I took a sip of my tea and felt grit on my tongue. I forced it down. I wasn't going to spit it out.

'So, you heard about her new friend Patrick?' said Flora's mum.

'Yes,' I said.

'It's such a relief,' she said, 'that she's finally making better decisions.'

18

I GUESS IT WAS a kind of limbo, the rest of that summer. The parties dried up, and I had very little to do except learn to drive and wait to find out where I was going to university. When are we talking? The beginning of August? I suppose. My dad's return home had been delayed, which meant my mum's had, too. Johnnie was doing his hick summer farm stuff, and Alan had gone to Italy on some crammer history of art course, which he said his dad had paid for with his mum's credit card, and which she felt too guilty about to cancel.

I could have gone down south to be with my dad, not that he ever offered, or stayed with Annie, who offered all the time. Or I could have invited myself back to Burnside, but Flora's mum had left me feeling uneasy about that sort of thing. So, I just stayed home. Feeling quietly heroic about being alone.

There were other people around, anyway. Mainly, I hung out with Claire and Gina, who were both working in this bookshop at the top of Leith Walk which had something to do with cookery. A cookbook shop? Is that a thing? Sometimes I'd meet them on their lunchbreak, and we'd meander into the Old Town to this place that sold baked potatoes, or sometimes get sandwiches from the deli next door and eat them sitting on that bogus Acropolis thing at the top of Calton Hill. We were all in limbo, in a way. Gina was about to go off on a gap year to Australia, from which she'd never return. Sorry, that sounds like she died. She just moved to Melbourne. Claire was waiting to find out if she had a place at the Sorbonne.

'It's funny,' I remember saying, up between the pillars, 'because when I met you, you always said "coffee" like you were French. And I thought it was a bit pretentious.'

'It was,' said Gina. 'She used to wear a beret.'

'Yes, but on the other hand,' said Claire pleasantly, 'bugger you both with a baguette.'

Then she asked if I'd heard from Alan. And I said yes, a bit, and I thought he was in Florence. And then I asked if he was being a bit of an arsehole.

Claire looked surprised. 'Why do you say that?'

'She's the arsehole,' said Gina cheerfully. 'He's weeping into his rigatoni.'

I didn't say anything.

'Wait,' said Claire, 'did you think he'd dumped me?'

I held up my hands.

'Or spaghetti,' said Gina, sounding annoyed. 'Rigatoni! What am I thinking? Bloody cookbooks.'

'I know he's your friend,' said Claire. 'And I love him. Honestly. But he's just such a useless waster.'

My God, I remember thinking. What must she think about the rest of us?

★

Eventually I passed my driving test, and Claire said her mum had asked if I wanted to come over for dinner to celebrate. I'd never met Claire's mum, so this seemed weird. But it wasn't like I could pretend to be busy.

They lived out in Colinton, in this long, low, white house with a double garage. Her little brother was there, too. He said almost not one word while I was there, and to this day I can tell you very little about him, although I do remember that he was called Colin, which given they lived in Colinton, I thought was pretty amusing. Although I reckoned somebody else would have pointed it out before.

I knew already that Claire's dad was an advocate, which is Scottish for lawyer, and that he worked mainly on something to do with the oil industry. This meant he was away quite a lot, like he was that night, although apparently only up in Aberdeen. Maybe because of that, I'd vaguely expected that her mum would be a bit like Alan's, all posh-lunchy and aloof. She wasn't like that at all, though. She was a doctor at the Sick Kids hospital on Sciennes Road and, the moment I walked in, she gave me a hug and told me to call her Alison.

'I've heard a lot about you,' she said, while Claire beamed.

'Me, too!' I said brightly, although this was a total lie. Or, if it wasn't, then I hadn't been listening. She had a nice voice, more Scottish than I'd been expecting, with a Morningside edge, but not enough to make your ears bleed. I suppose she looked a bit like Claire, although her long, loose hair was grey, and I guess she was about a head shorter.

'You two go amuse yourself,' she said. 'We're having stroganoff.'

I had no idea what we were supposed to do. If it had been Alan's house, we'd obviously have sloped off upstairs to smoke. At Johnnie's, we'd have popped out to kill something. Neither seemed to be on the cards. What did other people do in the evening? Little Colin from Colinton was watching *Blockbusters* in the living room. Should I do that, too? Had I known this stuff once?

Instead, we went to Claire's room, which was lovely: all tidy and crisp despite having sarongs on the walls and a paint-spattered easel next to the window. She lit a candle which smelled of vanilla and put on The Lemonheads, and then I sat on the very corner of her bed while she talked about how much she was looking forward to living in Paris. I remember asking if she was going to get a bicycle and a stripy top and put a string of onions around her neck, and she said, 'That's such a cliché,' and I said, 'Sorry,' but then she admitted that she was going to buy a bicycle and she had the top already.

Afterwards we did actually watch *Blockbusters* for a bit, but then her mum called us through to the kitchen for the stroganoff. Just me and Claire. Colin from Colinton had eaten after swimming.

'Do you know,' said Alison, after pouring me a glass of red and sitting down, 'I once went to your house.'

'Are you sure?' I said doubtfully.

'You weren't born. Nor was mademoiselle, there.'

'Oi,' said Claire.

'It was Hogmanay,' said Alison. 'Your parents had a dinner party. So glamorous.'

'I think you've got the wrong people,' I said politely, and although I hadn't actually been joking, she still laughed.

'I had this boyfriend,' she said. 'He was a journalist. Silly man. He knew your mum through work, and he was very taken with her. Your dad, too. A writer and a high-flying civil servant! Freshly down from London.'

'From Peterborough,' I said.

'No,' said Alison, 'I think they'd been in London, too. Although you'd know. There was a baby? Tiny, still. Your sister? But your mum made it look so effortless. Her clothes! She had a Diane von Furstenberg dress. You know, with the belt? I'd never seen one before.'

'Cool,' said Claire.

'Green,' I said, frowning, because maybe I remembered that.

'I think so,' said Alison. 'And the conversation! Books and politics, and back again. I'm not sure I said a word. I was a bit of a mouse. Fascinating people. What a wonderful house to grow up in.'

I stared at her. Those dim memories. Voices down the corridor. Clinking glasses. That time Mum had leaned over me in bed, that swinging red glass jewel. Maybe it hadn't just been once. Maybe I'd got that all wrong.

'So, give her my best,' said Alison. 'Although Claire says she's not well?'

'No,' I said.

'And that must be tough.'

I thought about this. I remember feeling a bit hot. I can't remember what I said. Something about the home being really quiet. About there being a lot of plastic. Something about basins.

'But she's in the hospital a lot,' I said. 'Right now, in fact. And my dad's away, too.'

'Yes,' said Alison.

'So, I guess . . . I mean, I'm like, you know, sort of free? And I can get up whenever. And eat whatever. And go out and stuff. And lots of people don't get to do that. And some people, like . . . Claire, remember when we went to Barf's?'

Alison seemed to be mouthing the word 'Barf's'.

'Well,' I said, 'it was, like, were his parents even there? Or were they not? Did anyone know? And I suppose, compared to that. Well. I'm really lucky.'

'Do you want some more?' said Alison, who sounded sad, for some reason.

'Yeah,' I said. 'Thanks. Wow, it's really good. I'm starving.'

★

Then my dad finally came home from Devon, and my mum came home from the hospital, and I promptly went to London. This was also the week that I got the results for my A-levels and Highers and found out I was going to Cambridge, after all. Just like Charles Digglesworth.

I went to London because Alan had been invited to a couple of parties. He didn't seem to know whose parties they were, or anybody else who was going, but that was hardly new. Also, he was allowed to bring a couple of friends, and a party was a party. So, I asked my dad if we could use his flat.

'Back up, son of mine,' he said, because it was lunchtime, which was exactly the right time of day for him still to be relatively chirpy. 'London, now, is it? For why?'

We were in his study at the back of the house, which was where he went to escape the armies of carers and lifters who drifted in and out to deal with my mum. Unlike the rest of the house, it didn't smell of antiseptic. It did smell of booze.

Anyway, London. I shrugged, irritated, because I didn't really know.

'It's like a club,' I said vaguely. 'Alan is in it because of his dad. Just since he left school. He's suddenly getting invited to loads of stuff. To meet people. And so girls can meet him.'

'Oh, this is priceless,' said my dad. 'Alan is a débutant?'

I stared at him.

'Or rather,' he said, 'a deb's delight! It's the season! The Beau Brummell of Moray Place!'

'You say the weirdest things. Anyway, they're moving to Marchmont.'

'Marchmont?' said my dad, sounding horrified.

I shrugged. 'Also, I met a woman last week. Claire's mum. You've met Claire. And she said she came here for a party in the 1970s. With you. And mum. One Hogmanay. And she said you were really interesting and glamorous. Although I think she might have got the wrong people.'

'Oh,' sighed my dad.

'Oh, what?'

'She's doing well. Your mum. Don't you think?'

I shrugged.

'Look, of course you can use the flat,' said my dad, sounding suddenly tired. 'Don't do anything stupid. Drugs and what have you. There isn't a cleaner at the moment. I'm afraid it might be a bit of a mess.'

★

It was. We took the train down on the Friday morning, feeling wild and adventurous at Waverley but frankly a bit timid by the time we got to King's Cross. The station was nuts, even more so than it had been when I came down at Christmas, full of all these people standing around for no reason I could understand. I guess we were more conspicuous as a group. Within minutes, this guy in a baseball cap had offered to sell us grass.

'No thanks, man,' said Johnnie, 'but it's good to know you're here.' And the guy looked at him incredulously, like he'd said it in Klingon. Then we went to the flat, and Johnnie said was my dad not actually that rich, then, because the street was horrible and the flat was as messy as he'd warned me it would be. Although Alan said that London was all like this.

The first party was an afternoon drinks party in a room in a very big house in a place that I have since come to understand to be Battersea. The invitation said *smart casual*, which was an imponderably terrifying phrase but apparently just meant you should look like Terry Wogan. So, we wore our school sports jackets with shirts and chinos. We were given champagne on the way in by this huge woman with hardly any hair and the poshest voice in the world.

The first thing she said to us was, 'Scottish boys! Now, you must meet some girls!' and then she introduced us to three of them, none of whom were dressed like Terry Wogan at all. Two were very small and wearing skirts and blazers, like they were going to an office, but the third was imposing and blonde and had this very grown-up, strappy cocktail dress thing on. She was called Candy.

'I know a dog called Candy,' I said politely, and it was all downhill from there.

Johnnie and I sloped off after an hour. Alan didn't mind. He'd shaved and brushed his hair; the clothes worked on him. He was enjoying himself. His voice had a new boom to it.

After the long walk back to Victoria, we took a tube to Camden. We had nothing else to do, and I'd read about it in music magazines. We ended up in this huge pub near the station, where some people were punks, some were in Adidas like Blur and some were in Day-Glo clubbing clothes, and absolutely nobody at all was in a tweed jacket and a nice shirt and their school shoes. Although maybe people thought we were Pulp fans.

'It's weird here,' said Johnnie, who had turned his collar up.

'It's amazing,' I said.

Then some guy with a nose ring gave us a flyer for a gig at another pub along the road which would give us our first drink half-price. So, we went to find it, past pubs blaring pop, pubs playing jungle, a heavy metal bar, lots of pubs playing music that sounded like The Kinks, and all sorts of everything else. We bought pizza slices for a pound and I burned my mouth. We never found the gig, although for a while we stood outside this massive club, where you could hear the techno from outside and see smoke and lasers from the door. Some beepy track I'd heard on the radio. I wanted to go in. It was a tenner entry, though, and we had to get back for Alan. So, we kept on walking and ended up in Camden Market, where I bought this really cool retro T-shirt with a picture of a tropical island on it, and Johnnie tried to buy hash but actually bought a lump of highly varnished wood and sulked about it all the way home.

'That's actually really nice wood,' said Alan, turning it over between his fingers back at the flat. 'I reckon you got the better of the deal.'

'I don't get it,' I said. 'You already had hash.'

'I thought London hash might be different,' said Johnnie, who was quite deflated.

At the party, said Alan, he'd run into Zara's cousin, that girl with all the hair who he'd snogged at that ball all those years ago. She had a boyfriend now, but he was okay, and their friends were, too. And after the drinks, he said, they'd gone on to Pizza Express.

'They'll be at the thing tomorrow,' he said. 'That'll be better. You'll see.'

'I don't even know why we're here,' said Johnnie.

'To meet people,' said Alan. 'To be people. Broaden your horizons, man.'

'You're going to end up like your dad,' said Johnnie.

'No, I'm not,' said Alan quite savagely. 'That's the whole fucking point.'

★

The party the next night was in Woking, which turned out to be one of those places that vaguely lies about being in London and totally isn't. There was a coach back, but we had to get ourselves there. We took a tube, then a train, then a taxi. We were all in black tie, and Johnnie and I were in kilts. That was pretty special. Turns out that walking through King's Cross in a kilt is a bit different to walking through Edinburgh in a kilt. Who knew? Johnnie brought a bottle of vodka for the trip.

Actually, it was outside Woking, I suppose, in this huge red-brick mansion surrounded by formal gardens. It was called Featherstonehaugh Hall, but you pronounced it

Fanshaw Hall because English people like fucking with you. Sort of like Barf's house might have looked, if it wasn't falling down. There was a marquee on one of the lawns, and champagne on the way in, and hundreds of people, all about our age. Nobody was in a kilt. The driveway was full of cars, including lots of really quite posh sports cars that people seemed to own, even though they were all about our age. I'm not particularly into cars, but I recognised one of them as a Porsche. It was yellow. Stretching away, there was a huge lake, shaped like a thermometer.

'Sorry,' I said, as we walked in, 'what actually is this place?'

'He's a viscount,' said Alan, who seemed cheerful. 'I think. His family has something to do with soap. People were talking about it last night. It's his eighteenth. I don't know him. He went to Eton. I think basically all the guys here went to Eton. You know I nearly went to Eton?'

'Why didn't you?' I asked.

'Because it's down here around somewhere,' said Alan, waving an arm around. 'And Mum thought it would be mental.'

Vaguely, I wondered if Charles Digglesworth would be there. Or, indeed, Patrick Digglesworth, but maybe he was too old. There were dodgems. Repeat: it was a party with dodgems. There was endless booze and endless food, too, from burger vans and hot dog stalls. The girls were amazing, stalking around between the house and the marquee in the sorts of dresses you see in magazines. I thought of the Pony Club Ball, and all those Edinburgh girls in their nice M&S. Then I thought of Flora and Trixie, and how different they had always looked from everybody else.

There was a band in the marquee, playing light rock

covers. 'Walking On Sunshine', 'Black Betty', that sort of thing. People were dancing, but Johnnie wasn't a big dancer, and I obviously wasn't going to dance by myself. Alan had introduced his new friends, as promised, but they hadn't seemed terribly interested in us, beyond the obligatory small talk about kilts and university.

'Marjorie and Katie,' said Alan, of a pair of looming beautiful giraffes, 'are coming to Edinburgh.'

'That's nice,' I said dutifully, and they swooned around above me, long necks level with my eyeline, besting me in the hunt for high and succulent leaves.

'I'm not going to university,' said Johnnie quite aggressively. 'Didn't see the point.'

'My dad said that,' said a red-faced boy in a floppy, hand-tied bow-tie. 'Better to go into business.'

'But you're going to Cambridge,' said a giraffe to him, her tongue not blue.

'Fucking hell,' said Johnnie and simply walked off.

'Oh, me too,' I said, watching him go, and then bow-tie said, 'Pembroke,' and she said, 'Trinity Hall,' and I named my college, too. Then he talked for a while about some particularly inspirational economics tutor who was there, in a manner which managed to sound both more informed and knowledgeable than I'd ever been about anything, but also, somehow, moronic. How do they do that? And then they all went off, and Alan, too, to find somebody else who was going to Edinburgh. Because she knew simply everybody, and her brother had the most splendid flat by Charlotte Square, and wasn't it all going to be fun.

I wandered and watched, but my heart wasn't in it. Normally I'd have put together a whole party taxonomy by now – those guys are losers, there's the nexus of cool, etc. – but here I didn't know how. I didn't understand the signals, the hair, the dresses. Plus, all the men were in the same clothes, with only the occasional flat collar/wing collar distinction going on, seemingly with no pattern at all. Once or twice there would be a white jacket, clearly on a dick, and occasionally some velvet; but most blended together, meaning their faces did, too – a sea of eggs. There were no other kilts. I felt like an inverse Morris Dancer. Also, whenever I spoke, I could hear this Morningside whine in my own voice. It wasn't the Scottishness that bothered me. Johnnie's Scottishness made him sound rugged, and even Alan's had a lordly edge to it, like he was related to people who captained submarines. I mean, he probably was. Mine sounded deferential. Butler class. I didn't like any of it at all.

I found Johnnie eventually at a bar on the lawn, and he was drunk. Not enough to make a scene, but enough for us to be the two pissed hobbits in the kilts. His ponytail didn't help. Nor my weird undercut. Nobody else had those, either.

Later, at about ten, the band quit and a DJ started up; just another tall, floppy-haired kid like the rest of the tall, floppy-haired kids, but this one had taken his bow tie off and put on a baseball cap. Now that jackets were off, I realised there was actually huge variation among the men, because they were all wearing those posh white shirts that covertly have colourful patterns swirling around on the backs and the arms. You know the ones? I'd noticed them at home, occasionally, and even pondered getting one. But now everyone was special, so nobody was.

The DJ's shirt was tie-dye on the back, which seemed to me to be vaguely taking the piss. He was playing techno.

Everybody on the dancefloor was whooping at him, like he was famous. Maybe he was in *Tatler*, with the Digglesworths.

'We have to get some drugs,' said Johnnie quite blearily but also decisively.

'Don't we have some already?'

'Proper drugs. Not hash. Ecstasy. Coke. Look at them. They're all on something. We just need to ask around.'

'I dunno, man,' I said, because I'd spoken to, like, three people all night, which made me feel that a sudden leap towards sourcing Class As might be a bit beyond us. Johnnie started asking people, but all the wrong people. Boys who might as well have had monocles and stock portfolios. Girls who looked like librarians. At one point, no kidding, he sidled up to a group of slightly older men literally in some sort of military dress uniform with brass buttons and stuff.

'What are you doing?' I said to him. 'They're in the army or something.'

Even Johnnie knew this was becoming a farce. It was like we were trying to buy smack in Niddrie dressed as circus clowns. Eventually I dragged him away across the lawn to the lake and made him sit down and smoke a joint with me. And he lay back on the grass and blew smoke, irritably, at the moon.

'Have you been to Barf's house?' he said.

'Is it bigger than this?' I said. 'Or about the same?'

'Or Layman's castle?'

I didn't know Layman had a castle.

'They're both shit,' he said. 'They're falling apart. Layman has a dungeon you can't go into without a gas mask on. Because of the mould.'

'Still,' I said. 'A dungeon.'

'Why aren't any of them like this?'

I thought back to what Alan had been saying, on our expedition from school. After we saw the rabbit's head.

'It's because everybody has forgotten how to get money,' I said. 'Because there aren't wars. And you can't just get it from Burma.'

'Fuck are you talking about?' said Johnnie, and I felt like my own dad.

'Anyway,' I said. 'The MacPhails' house is okay. How come they've got money?'

'Stole it,' said Johnnie. 'Stole it from me.'

You could hear the music even out here, only a little muffled. It sounded familiar.

'That's the track they were playing in Camden,' I told him, suddenly realising. 'In that club.'

'So?'

'Why would anyone be here,' I said, 'when they could be there? Why are we?'

Johnnie rolled onto his front. He pointed the joint towards the marquee, like it was a laser gun, tracing the movements of the people bounding in and out.

'Maybe this is how we look,' I said, 'to people who aren't us.'

'I really thought I'd be able to keep it,' he said. 'Even after Douglas. Even after MacPhail said I couldn't. But I can't find a way. I just don't know how. Nobody fucking helps, man. It's, like, who else do I have to shoot?'

'Else?'

'You know what I mean.'

'I thought you weren't going to shoot anyone,' I said. 'I thought that had just been, you know . . .'

'Pyscho Johnnie,' said Johnnie.

'Yeah.'

'I'm tired,' he said, and I didn't say anything, and not long after that I realised he was asleep.

★

It happened that night, but I didn't know. Not until I heard the message on the answerphone back in the flat the next morning. My dad had also called Alan's dad, who had called the viscount's dad, I expect quite excitedly, but nobody had been picking up. We'd come back on the coach, which dumped us in a place called Sloane Square. Alan at the back, with some people he now knew. Me and Johnnie at the front, him a mess, me a carer, letting him drool onto his scrunched-up Bonnie Prince Charlie jacket. Then a taxi, which cost an unreasonable bomb. Alan had been wired, thrilled, wanting to talk about this person and that. Johnnie had been comatose, wanting to puke but holding it together in case the driver kicked us out. I was too furious to speak. With both of them. About life. About everything.

I only saw the wee red light blinking on the machine the next morning. I was in my pants, having gone through to get a glass of water. Thinking of the argument we'd all had, eventually, the night before. Thinking vaguely of getting dressed pretty soon and going back up to Camden by myself, just for a wander around. Then I saw it, and clicked it, and the message played. And I dropped my glass and it smashed, cutting my feet, and it was like my legs just gave up and I was sitting on the floor. It wasn't like I was upset. Nothing like that at all. I just didn't want to be standing up any more.

'Shit,' said Alan, running in. 'What happened? Are you okay?'

'It's my mum,' I said. 'She's gone. I need to get home.'

19

WE BURIED HER TWO weeks later, in a horrible cemetery next to a huge place that sold carpets. I remember the carpets because I also remember having a horrible thought about whether they did much trade from people on the way home from funerals after some dead guy had really made a mess.

With my mum, it hadn't been dramatic. So long we'd spent at bedsides, in hospitals. Listening to machines that went 'beep' and trying to figure out what the beeps meant. Thumbing closed her eyes while they stared, blank and dry, at the ceiling. Thinking, 'Oh, so this is what the end looks like.' But, after all that, she died on a good day, attempting to drink a cup of tea. Like her throat had considered the options on her behalf and whether it ever wanted a bunch of tubes shoved down it again, and gone, 'Nope,' and just spasmed and closed. My dad was with her – he'd made the killer tea – and I'd thought he'd be distraught when I finally made it home. Instead, he was clear-eyed and sober, airing the house. No smell of antiseptic, nor even of wine. Just a normal house with one less person in it.

It was surprisingly big. The funeral, I mean. Not the house, although that felt bigger, too. There were colleagues at the cemetery, and Mum's old university friends up from London. Family, too, including my bonkers Aunt Julie and her tiny husband, Martin, who wanted to talk about sex all the time. Everybody hanging around outside the damp red stone chapel thing, doing sad-face under aggressively neutral Edinburgh skies. Where had they all been, I wondered, when she was still alive? My sister, Annie, was there, obviously, having come up with me on the train from London the day after she died, and then gone home, and then come back again. Both times she was with a guy called Tim, the boyfriend I'd been told about but not really paid much attention to the concept of. The first thing I noticed about him was how trendy he was, in thick, black-rimmed glasses and a Morrissey T-shirt, which was baffling to me. That was on the train, obviously. Not at the funeral. No.

Johnnie came with his mum, Jenny. 'Bit tactless to bring *her*,' I felt like saying, but he wouldn't have got it and neither would she. I spotted them just after we'd parked, hanging around outside the little chapel thing. On the one hand I was a little alarmed because the last time we'd properly spoken he had definitely been talking about shooting people again. On the other, I was really pleased to have some proper company, not least because the alternative would have been speaking to my mum's mad sister about something like fisting.

'I'm so sorry,' Jenny said, and she hugged me, and I remembered back to the first time she'd done that, and how it had made me miss hugging my own mum. How similar Jenny and Johnnie looked, I thought, both in long black coats, sharing eyes and noses, pretty much both with the same length hair. Jenny said they couldn't come back to the house afterwards because they had an appointment in Perth. Then she said she'd let us talk and stepped away.

Johnnie's body language was almost comically teenage.

Real *Kevin & Perry*, twisted-like-a-pretzel stuff. I'd always been able to imagine him fighting for me, defending me, hurling bricks for me or going over the top for me. Johnnie, one way or another, always with a gun. But this? This was his torture.

'She's furious,' he said. 'With me. Because we only found out when this was happening last night. Alan called.'

I nodded. Alan had gone back to London. He had a job at a posh estate agent, with some guy he'd met at the party, and couldn't get away. He'd called me, too. So had Claire, who was already in Paris.

'I'm sorry,' said Johnnie, 'but with my brother's funeral, my mum called everyone. To tell them what was happening. And I guess she did that with my dad's, too.'

'Right,' I said.

'And nobody called us.'

'I suppose my mum was a bit indisposed.'

Johnnie smirked. Then he put a hand over his mouth and looked so shocked with himself for smirking that I started smirking, too.

'These things,' he said. 'They're fucking nuts. We can't stay. I'm sorry. But also, I don't want to. Will you at least get pissed later?'

This hadn't occurred to me.

'Might do,' I said. 'It's all old people, though. Except for my sister's friends. And they seem to be mainly pregnant.'

'Ella's here,' said Johnnie.

'Ella?'

'Ella,' he said. 'Barf's Ella. From school. Look.'

★

A few months later, I'd find out that your standard Perthshire grave looks black because that's the colour of the soil. In Edinburgh, though, graves are red, like the crags on Arthur's Seat, and the chapel where they see you off, and the slabs of stone they put up to tell people who has gone. My mum's grave had a puddle at the bottom. Annie cried. I think maybe my dad cried, too. I didn't want to. I sort of felt it might make the puddle worse.

Afterwards, Ella came back to the house. My dad had wanted me to come with him and Annie, but there was also this ancient great-uncle of somebody's down from Newcastle that he had to worry about, and at the last minute there wasn't room. So, instead, Ella and I sat in the back of Aunt Julie's Honda, while mini Martin drove and she told us that my mother had been an incredibly passionate woman and that they'd always wondered if my father had been truly capable of satisfying her needs. And I wouldn't say it was the most excruciating fifteen minutes of my entire life, but it was probably up there at about number four or five.

Ella was being very polite. I remember she had this black skirt suit thing on, with a jacket, over incredibly clean Doc Marten boots. Her mad hair was all pinned up.

'Security is the denial of life,' she said to Aunt Julie, after quite a bit of this.

'What?' I said.

'It's Germaine Greer,' said Ella.

'Gosh, aren't you a clever one,' said Julie, and I felt like a little orphan boy packed off in the care of distant elders.

Afterwards Ella and I sat in the garden against the wall under the kitchen window, each with a plate of cold sandwiches and chopped-up sausage rolls. The window was open, and I could hear the buzzing hum from inside above our heads. Alan, it turned out, had called her, too. It was warmish, despite the grey. I'd loosened my tie. She'd undone her jacket. I know I just said you couldn't wear a T-shirt to a funeral, but she was wearing a black Ash one, which said 'Girl From Mars' on it. I'd never seen it at school. Maybe it was new. She actually came across to Edinburgh most mornings with her dad, she told me, because she had a job in a pizza restaurant under his office.

'I'm really glad you're here,' I said. 'It's all a bit much. I never knew she was so popular.'

'Well, she was an incredibly passionate woman,' said Ella.

'Oh God.'

'Sorry.'

Inside, I could hear Annie calling my name, sounding worried. I stood up, and the warm smell of humans and coffee came at me out the kitchen window like a floating duvet. From this angle, you could see how warped and water-damaged the wooden laminate counter was. I guess my mum hadn't been in the kitchen for a while. Annie was holding a big glass of red wine.

'Are you okay?' she said.

'Yes.'

'You should have one of these,' said Annie, waving her glass around.

'Right.'

'I've had three. I was going to drink tea. But I felt it was disrespectful.'

'Right.'

Then Ella stood up, too, and Annie said, 'Oh!' and backed away. Then we sat down again.

'Wine is actually not a bad idea,' I said.

'Are you, though?' said Ella. 'Okay?'

'I keep dreaming about her being alive. Like all this has been a big mistake.'

'That's probably normal,' said Ella confidently.

I took a breath.

'But it's not nice,' I said. 'In the dream. It's awkward. In fact, it's really sinister. Like there's something wrong with her that only I can see. Something missing. Like she's a monster. A rotting monster. And it's embarrassing, too, because it's happening now, so we've told everybody she's dead, and they've all been really nice, and now they'll think I've made a fuss about nothing. And so, she's alive, but I wish she wasn't, and I feel guilty about that; and she's like a fucking zombie, anyway, so I'm scared of her and feel guilty about that, too, and maybe it's all just because I don't want to have to do it all again. And, I dunno, is that normal when somebody dies? Because it seems quite a big deal if it is. And you'd think somebody might have said.'

'Actually, it really might not be normal,' said Ella.

'Right.'

'But, on the other hand, after my granddad died, I had this really clear dream about him cooking his own leg on a stove. In a huge pot. Like a kebab.'

'Wow.'

'Thank you,' she said.

'Did he only have one leg?'

'In the pot?' said Ella. 'In the dream? In reality? I'm not clear what you're asking me.'

'In reality.'

'Two,' she said. 'Normal, two-legged man.'

But it was definitely his leg in the pot, she added, because she'd recognised the big varicose vein he had under his knee, which she'd always seen sticking out from under his dressing gown. So, I asked what he was standing on, in the dream, and she said presumably the other one, although she didn't remember that too clearly because she'd only been ten at the time. Then she said she'd thought about it loads since then, and she reckoned it was just the mind trying to find something to latch on to because of the horror we felt at death, which was the worst horror in the world; and then there was the stuff which surrounded us while we were feeling it – which was just people being sad, and hugs, and platitudes – and there was a huge disjunction there, an incongruity. Which, she said, was probably why people liked horror films, too.

'Because the world has horrors,' she said, 'which feel like horrors and hurt like horrors, but don't look like horrors. And so, we need to imagine other things which do look more straightforwardly like horrors, or else it's all too complicated and we might go mad.'

'You are clever,' I said, 'but you're not very cheery.'

'The horror,' she said, 'the horror.'

And then she chuckled, and we sat there in the garden. And she held my hand until her dad turned up and it was time for her to go.

Afterwards, I went back through into the house, which was still quite busy, and I poured myself a glass of wine, and I imagined it was blood. Dead person's blood. Not necessarily my mum's. Anyone's. 'Cheers, Mum,' I said to her, and then I downed it and poured myself another. Then I wandered around, generally being charming. Annie had a few friends here, and they had become quite loud. Her boyfriend, Tim, looked worried. My dad wasn't drinking at all, but he seemed content, talking with men I dimly recognised from years ago. Cousins, aunts, relatives, they all loomed up at me, and they had bits of sandwich on their lips and wine stains on their teeth, and I looked at their rictus smiles and they were the monsters now, and I imagined them bigger, savage, vulpine, splitting their faces into the faces of cartoon beasts. Or they had coffee breath, but that was fine, too, because as I spoke to them politely of Cambridge and A-levels and schools and choices, I made the coffee smell of mud, red mud, grave mud, and I sucked it hungrily in. And then, really before very long, the last guests were leaving, and Boyfriend Tim and I half-carried Annie to bed, and then he and my dad and I sat around the kitchen table eating leftover sandwiches; and then Tim went to bed, and my dad did, too, and I said I would soon, too, but I didn't. Instead, I drank more blood and opened the back door and lit myself a cigarette, watching the smoke and thinking of wars and crematoria and cancer and all the other times that smoke, actually, was really bad.

'Own it,' I thought to myself. 'Balance it out.'

★

It was maybe ten days after that when Ella called up and roped me into working with her at the Game Fair. I was confused at first, because I'd never heard of game fairs, and every time she said 'game fair', I heard 'game show' and kept thinking of Bruce Forsyth. But then she explained that a game fair was actually a big festival thing for farmers and country types, full of guns and sheepdogs and fairground rides, and this year it was happening at a place called Craill, near Blairgowrie. She was going because the pizza restaurant she'd been working at this summer had a stall, and the owner was driving her up, and they needed another pair of hands.

The owner, it turned out, was Marco, Alan's uncle. He picked me up in his Range Rover; Ella and me were in the back, and some silent, spotty guy called Peter was in the passenger seat. He had a carphone, did Marco, the first I'd ever seen, and he spent the whole two-hour drive with it wedged under his chin, shouting about things like tax and mozzarella.

The game fair itself was nuts. We were in a valley in the shadow of a castle that looked like something out of Disneyland, the whole place was a mudbath, and every fucker had a dog. Marco had been towing a trailer with an unreasonably large red-brick pizza oven in it, and our first job was to manhandle the thing along muddy lanes between stalls, skidding around until we got to a big white gazebo thing that said MARCO'S ITALIAN on it. It took all four of us, and people kept getting in the way. There were old grey men in fleeces and jeans, but also people who looked like Alan's dad. There were women in tracksuits, but also women in Barbours and stripy shirts with the collars turned up. And none of them helped at all.

'Okay,' said Marco, 'give us an hour to set up. You two go have a wander.'

'Will we not get lost?' I said.

'I'll look after you,' Ella said.

It was pretty easy to get your bearings. The castle helped,

looming over us like we were medieval villagers. Actually, it was sort of amazing, these three grey-brown harled grey towers with pointy roofs, looking not unlike a triangle of giant toilet rolls in wizard hats. Slits for arrows, or maybe for eyes. Down below, everything was arranged around a big square pen the size of a tennis court with a scaffolding tower at one end. There were speakers on top of it, and a very Scottish-sounding man in it, chuntering away about things like horses and sheep dog trials.

'Gonnae be some braw coos the day!' he was saying. And we all love a braw coo.

Along either side, stretching away, were lines of stalls selling jumpers and fishing rods and quilted gilets and Victorian pots and dog beds and cheese and Aga utensils and basically all that other shit I kept seeing in all these kitchens I'd spent so much time in over the past few years. I guess it had to come from somewhere.

'Do you,' I said to Ella, 'come here often?'

'I've been to a few. But my parents loathe them.'

We tramped around. There was a stall selling Scottish tablet, which I quite fancied, but it was still only quarter to ten in the morning. At one point we passed a shotgun stall, the blue-blackness of a hundred guns on racks sucking in the light and turning it into a cave. There was farm equipment, quad bikes, hats. Salesmen shouting, bagpipes in the distance. A little fenced-off area, where bemused captive owls stood blinking at us all from T-crossed sticks.

Ella went off to queue for a coffee, and I stood on the main thoroughfare, staring. I couldn't help but notice that the Barbour people were a lot louder than the fleece people.

Often, they seemed to know each other. You'd see islands of them, converging. Handshakes, dog leads entwined. Also, I noticed one guy in a headband and a T-shirt who looked really strange because he also had on these mad, baggy, armoured trousers held up with braces, like he was a knight from space, half-undressed after a battle. He was drinking a Coke, and I stared at him for ages, trying to figure out what was going on. Then a battered Land Rover towing a trailer pulled up, and a girl with a shaved head hopped out the back of it and handed him the other half of a huge horned monster costume. Then she took out a plastic bucket and a placard which said *Save The Sumatra Rhino* on it.

The Land Rover trundled on and parked next to this painted gypsy caravan covered in a tarpaulin banner which said INFO. Two boys climbed out from the back, too, looking dishevelled and borderline crusty, notably different from everybody else. They were unloading beer barrels; the next tent seemed to be some sort of bar. One had shaggy hair and a beard under a beanie hat, and the other even had dreadlocks. I lit a cigarette and watched them for quite a while before I abruptly realised that the guy with dreadlocks was Johnnie.

'Hey!' I said, rushing over.

'Oh, hello,' said Johnnie.

'Cool hair. Why the hell are you here?'

'I'm helping.' Johnnie nodded his head backwards. 'I'm staying with Layman.'

Layman, I abruptly realised, was the guy in the beanie. I guess it had been a long summer.

'In the caravan?' I said, impressed.

'Um, no,' said Johnnie, and he pointed his thumb over his shoulder. 'In the castle.'

Now the driver of the Land Rover was out, too. He was in mustard cords and a smart shirt and jumper, and for a moment I assumed he must be Layman's dad. Then I saw he was only about twenty-five. Big red face and brown curly hair.

'Hello, hello!' he said. 'Are you Keith? From the bar?'

'I don't think so,' I said. 'I mean, no. I'm a friend of Johnnie's. From school.'

'Another reprobate! Good to know you. Jack Layman.'

'So, you're . . .?' I said, trying to figure this out.

'My brother,' said the other Layman, who was coming back for another barrel. 'Hiya, Tommy. Didn't know this was your sort of thing.'

'He gets around,' said Johnnie, and there was a bit of an edge there, for some reason.

'It's Tommo, by the way,' I said, and I shook the older Layman's hand, before a guy in a tracksuit who seemed to be the real Keith appeared, and Jack walked off, booming at him. Could they really be brothers? They were very different. One halfway to being a rock star, and the other looking like Rupert Bear. He was even wearing a cravat. He seemed guileless, like a big bouncing dog. Just knowing that he existed somehow made Will much less intimidating. All the same, with Jack gone, suddenly everything felt strangely formal and awkward.

'Anyway,' I said, 'thanks for coming.'

Layman looked confused.

'To the funeral, I mean,' I said to Johnnie.

'Right, yeah,' said Johnnie, and he seemed to gather

himself, somehow. 'Look,' he said, 'are you wanting to stay? Here? Because I'm sure that's fine, but—'

'Oh! No. I'm working. On the pizzas.'

I looked back and saw Ella standing in the thoroughfare, coffee in one hand, other on her hip, staring after me.

'Anyway,' I said, 'I'd better go.'

★

It was hard work. The gazebo was open, but the oven was hot as hell and the steam rose up from the damp mud, meaning that you didn't know whether you were sweating, absorbing or just melting. The customers came in waves, mainly the fleece people. Ella took the money, and Marco and Peter made the pizzas, whirling the dough and laying it out on a big table covered in flour. It was my job to scrape them up with a giant shovel thing and tip them into the oven. Then I had to scrape them out again. Before long all the hairs on the back of my right hand had singed clean away. Marco was in a chef's hat and a white apron, happy as Larry, so different from the trussed-up awkwardness I'd seen in Moray Place. We barely had time to talk.

'Take a proper break,' said Marco, at about 3 p.m. 'Both of you. Dinner rush soon.'

Leaving the sweaty stall gave me that disorientated, stumbling feeling, like when you come out of the cinema. Hot to cold. I had a big lumberjack shirt on, but I was shivering. Ella had a puffer jacket. Things were no less busy now, but the atmosphere was somehow wilder. We aimed for the bar, past the main forum, which now seemed to be hosting some sort of madcap race between a thousand tiny, yapping dogs. The same voice was blaring out from the speakers up the tower, but it had become a lot harder to understand.

'Yon wee dugs,' it slurred. 'Yon Linford Christie wee dugs man, aye?'

'Do you think he's okay?' I said to Ella.

'I think he's shitfaced,' she replied, and I had a vision of him sitting up there, all day, all alone, with only a diminishing bottle of whisky for company.

In the bar, we realised he wasn't alone. It was packed. Elsewhere there might have been jaunty dogs and people selling terrible handmade mugs, but here there was some proper, heavy drinking going on from plastic pint glasses on trays. I could see the appeal: grab a trestle table, designate a driver, while away the day. Actually, there were a few people I recognised, ruddy-faced boys who might have been at Barf's party. Also, at the bar, there was Fusty.

'Oh, hello,' I said.

He looked at me non-comprehendingly. He was hopelessly drunk. Bloodshot eyes. Something down the front of his shirt that could have been gravy, but could have been far worse.

'Are you okay?' I said. 'Who are you with?'

'Two pints of Stella,' said Fusty, trying to give me a tenner.

'Shall we wander?' said Ella, who had somehow got hold of our drinks already.

'Yes,' I said.

'Cunts,' said Fusty unexpectedly as we walked away.

Leaving the bar, though, was a mistake. The sky was grey now. Rain was spitting. Then, suddenly, it wasn't spitting, but pouring. People were running everywhere, tramping through mud. We were next to a game conservancy stall covered in pictures of red deer, so we cowered under the awning with our plastic pints. Then a red-faced man in tweeds stuck his head out and nodded inside.

'Do you want to see the gralloch?' he said. He sounded like he was from Newcastle. All the consonants were a mess.

'What's the gralloch?' I asked.

'You've never seen the gralloch?' he said. 'You must see the gralloch!'

Then he was gone.

'That was strange,' I said to Ella.

'Don't care,' she said. 'I'm drowning here. Take me to see the gralloch.'

So, we followed him in. There were seats in rows, maybe twelve of them, laid out for a show. Most were taken, but we found a couple at the back. At the front, there was a weird metal contraption like a gallows. A dead deer hung from it by what could have been its arms; think a prisoner in a Vietnam film, but with antlers.

Ella leaned over and whispered in my ear, hot breath tickling. 'Satanism.'

'Normally,' said the man from Newcastle, 'we'd do this on the hill. And not just because it gives the pony less weight to carry down.'

He told us he was Craill's head stalker. As in, stalking for deer. Not stalking for heads. He'd been a paratrooper, he said, but now he did this. Then he started telling us what 'this' was.

It was like he was a poet. It could be beautiful on a mountain, he said. The clouds came down from the sky and the steam came up from the peat. At first, you'd worry if they could smell you, even from the other side of a glen. Then you'd worry about sight. Then sound. You'd walk, he said, then you'd duck, then crawl. You'd wait for a clear shot. Never the head, because the head was tough; they could be wounded and run, and you'd have to chase. No, you'd go for just behind the front shoulder, because that was the heart. You'd breathe with the gun, and you'd squeeze.

I was entranced. The rain beat down; it was hypnotic. Ella was next to me, but I wasn't thinking of her. I was thinking of Flora and her mountains. Then Johnnie with his gun in his fields, as if his rabbits were the first steps into a whole culture, a whole hierarchy, with this at its peak. I thought of our school, and how it taught you war, and how this sort of did the same. How this whole day, in fact, could have happened hundreds of years earlier, but with swords and jousting in place of guns and game. Like this whole culture, with all its trappings, was training in disguise.

'Then,' said the man from Newcastle, 'the gralloch.'

With that, he pulled a knife from a scabbard at his side and plunged it into the dead deer's chest. Then he slashed down, and from out the belly tumbled this huge, wet white bag, followed by terrible grey translucent tubes.

'You rip it all out,' he said, with relish, 'and you leave it for the hooded crows.'

Then he nicked the side of the bag with his knife, and it split, too, showing wet grass inside, and the tent filled with a smell halfway between compost and a lawnmower.

'Okay, enough,' said Ella, standing up and pulling my arm.

'You did say you wanted to see the gralloch,' I said.

'These people are insane.'

'You sound like Alan,' I said.

273

★

By 6 p.m. people were leaving, although it took us another hour or two to clear up. Marco said he had people to meet, and there was a bus we could take to the station in Pitlochry. Or, if we preferred, there was a ceilidh in the village hall and we could hang out at that until later, when he'd be driving back to Edinburgh. So, with fifty quid each in our pockets, we opted for the latter. We were a team now. It felt pretty good.

First, he dropped us at the only pub, the Boggan House Hotel. We took a small, round table by the window. Ella went to the toilet and came back wearing make-up; she bought pints and chasers because, she said, we were in the Highlands now. I guess we were both pretty wired. It was like being on holiday. We talked about my mum for a bit, but mainly we talked about university. What it would be like, whether we'd keep in touch. Her brothers had applied for Oxford, she said, but neither of them had got in. There were two of them, both about thirty now. They'd both gone to Eskmount, which meant she'd always desperately wanted to go there for sixth form, too. Ever since she was small.

'Because,' she said, 'I'm an idiot.'

'Was it really that bad?'

'You were all so sweet and sensitive on your own. And then you get together and be nuts and arseholes.'

'Sweet and sensitive,' I said carefully, 'like Barf?'

'Yes!'

'You're pissed.'

'He wants to be,' she said. 'He just doesn't know

how. It's, like, everything he does, he's looking over his shoulder, at this idea of . . . of everything. And it's totally screwed.'

'Was I an arsehole?' I asked her. 'To you?'

'Totally,' she said and downed her drink and went to get some more.

Later, when the pub started emptying out, we followed the crowd down the road to the ceilidh. The stalker was there, him from the gralloch, on stage with his sleeves rolled up, playing the accordion. It was lovely, a real Ewok village vibe. Warm and buzzy, people of all ages. Locals, I suppose, but not the Barbour locals. Nor the fleeces, who I suppose had come from the cities, like us. A lot of the men were in tweed and checked shirts, but they had their sleeves rolled up and big shiny faces from drinking beer. There were teenage boys in jeans and tracksuits with hair like Dean, and girls in miniskirts like they thought they were in a club. In a small brown corridor, next to the toilets, there was a plaque on the wall which announced that Craill Hall had been *Gifted to the Village of Boggan by the Layman Family of Clan Wishart*. Although it seemed they were giving tonight a miss.

We bought beer at the bar and sausages in buns at this table next to it. The band played reels, but mad reels, not all stately and precise like at the balls I'd been to, but hectic and fast, with an edge of The Pogues. We danced.

'Were ye up at the fair?' said this scrubbed-looking guy during the eightsome reel. He was older than us, but not by much, dancing with a woman in big hoop earrings.

'We were doing the pizzas!' shouted Ella.

'Ah!' said the stalker, who was part of our set, and seemed

to have surrendered his accordion to somebody else. 'It's the lassie who puked at the gralloch!'

'I did not!' shouted Ella as he spun her by the arm. 'I just needed air!'

Then she was pirouetting in the middle, and the stalker was next to me in the circle. There was a woman on his other side, drunk and roaring in heels and a tight green dress. I guessed she was his wife.

'Glasgow?' he shouted at me.

'Edinburgh!' I shouted back.

'City folk,' he said, but nicely. 'Never seen that before, eh?'

'Oh, totally,' I said with manly confidence, 'but just with a chicken.'

Marco turned up at just shy of ten, and I was sorry to go. His Range Rover was around the back, so we followed him out and round the side of the village hall to the car park. There was a small group off to the side, and a smell of hash. And, as my eyes followed my nose, I realised the group was Johnnie and Layman, along with the guy and the shaven-headed girl who had been saving the Sumatran rhino.

'Oh!' I said, peeling off towards them. 'We never found you.'

'I'm sorry,' said Johnnie, who sounded wasted.

'We didn't see you inside, either. It's great in there.'

'Yeah, not quite my scene,' croaked Layman.

'But there's a plaque!' I said stupidly, and he shrugged. And, as I left them, I wondered why they'd bothered coming, if only to hang around outside. Although maybe, up there in their massive toilet-roll castle, they'd just felt a bit left out.

PART THREE

20

AT CAMBRIDGE, MY ROOM was in a modern quad, above a breeze-block barn that was the college bar. I lived above a party that happened every night. I bought old needle cords and tight T-shirts that I had carefully chosen to look like I'd owned them forever. Two days in, I noticed that only the hairy Dungeons & Dragons kids wore Doc Martens, so I bundled mine into my cupboard and wore Converse instead. The summer hung around and the days were balmy. There was a pond with ducks, and you could sit on a bench next to it smoking and nobody told you not to or wrote a letter about it to your parents.

I was watchful, but I knew how to be secretly watchful now, so I don't think anybody caught on. I made new friends and joined them in bitching about life in an institution, but I never meant it. What even to bitch about? Sometimes, everyone was cross about the latest transgression of the boat club or the rugby lads, who'd run around in their blazers, bellowing into their beer. It was nothing; mayflies after you've fought off bats. There was a tradition here, something about the most annoying first year being thrown in the pond. I don't remember if it happened, but if it did, it was nothing. Nobody stripped naked unless they wanted to. Nobody got bundled in a trunk and thrown down the stairs. You could make mistakes and correct them in a heartbeat, and I did, forever feeling faint disbelief that the penalties for missteps were all but non-existent. It was school-lite, an open prison after a pen. Maybe, I pondered, Eskmount hadn't been a training for dying in a war or governing Burma, after all. Maybe it had been a training for this.

I still read newspapers, like Alan had said I should, and I realised this meant you never ran out of things to say, as long as you were with other people who read them, too. Lots of people had taken gap years, teaching English in Łódź or Plovdiv, building latrines in Dharamshala or Bulawayo; that sort of thing. I hadn't, so at first I kept quiet in those conversations, because the alternative was just pretending, perhaps by making up a whole new African country. Gradually, though, I realised the geography was irrelevant. These were all just stories about independence, about being away from home, and I had no end of those. All those underpopulated houses, all those empty moonlit fields. I hadn't realised it was the sort of shit some people had to go to Indonesia for.

I wouldn't like to pretend I never screwed up, though, because I definitely did. Early on, I remember a conversation about death and killing. Some loud guy called Johann had killed a goat in Kinshasa and was boasting about it, because most people had never killed anything. I was stoned – I could roll joints, too, not flashy ones, just competent, then offer them up, not making a fuss – and I made the mistake of confessing that I'd killed more animals than I could remember.

At first, they didn't believe me. Then I talked a bit more, and they did. And I could see clearly, despite the weed, or perhaps because of it, that things were right on the edge of going terribly wrong.

'Honestly,' said this vegan girl called Naomi, who'd been notably spiky about this whole conversational topic from the start, 'do you know how fucked up this would all be if you weren't posh?'

'I'm posh,' said a West Londoner called Arabella. 'Don't blame this on being posh.'

Until all that death stuff, things had been going pretty well. Naomi loved the way I said her name because I did not yet know that English people don't say 'Naomi' as 'ni-oh-mee' but do something totally different, which sounds like a horse.

At that moment, though, I felt purest panic. Then, with a flash of inspiration, I dragged up some bits of Alan that I'd seen, and taken, and packed away for future use along with all those bits of everybody else. I used his incredulity and his weariness. His scornful urban bemusement. Then I told them about the chicken. Nobody had a story like the chicken. The sergeant major. The neck. The smell. The egg.

'That,' said Naomi, 'is nuts.'

Johann looked furious.

'Ha,' I thought. 'Stick your Kinshasa up your arse.'

★

I think it helped that I was Scottish. Not hugely Scottish, but Scottish enough to distinguish me from acres of other undergraduate public schoolboys, who wore shirts, and shoes that weren't trainers, and boomed, and weren't Scottish at all. It was easier, down here. You could be generically Scottish, without having to explain what school you went to and why; without feeling all apologetic and fraudulent in front of local people at a ceilidh after a game fair.

Thinking about it, I suppose almost nobody was quite what they were pretending to be. That's what you do at university, right? That's the point. Aside from the girls, my new best friend was a guy called Dave, who was the only person reading philosophy and from Chelmsford. Dave was gay, and to hear him then you'd have imagined that he'd always been exactly the same, all fearless with his vests and his Brett Anderson voice and his ethnic-looking earring in the wrong part of his ear. Only, was that right? Even Alan had changed, and this after already being Alan to start with. He was at Edinburgh now. I'd had a quick afternoon pint with him in the Halfway House just before getting the train south. He'd been in red jeans and a cashmere polo neck, and it had confused me terribly.

Anyway, that was me. I bought a bike in Market Square, some rusted blue hulk from a rip-off spiv. A week later it was stolen. A week after that, I'm pretty sure, I bought it again. The Indian summer passed to winter; my next big purchase was a big canvas coat with a fake sheepskin collar, as was the fashion. I'd turn it up against my face as I rode my daft bike down the ancient lanes to lectures, and then I'd sit there with Dave, not really listening, pulling synthetic sheepskin out of my beginner's stubble. And in the afternoons we'd smoke and drink tea and talk metaphysics, worrying about whether the present King of France was bald , or what it was like to be a bat.

At night, two or three times a week, we'd go clubbing,

or at least what passed for clubbing in the disused wine cellars of ancient Cambridge colleges. I knew, now, what Johnnie's farmboy friends had been yearning for, when they'd stood in front of his car and flicked the lights. I liked the strobe, the noise, the oblivion. Sharing drinks, girls shouting in your ears, measured looks under lashes, skin on skin. Apart from Dave, most of my friends were girls, and I'm honestly not sure I ever quite got over the sheer pleasure of being able to talk to them without three hundred schoolboys shouting about it in the background. It wasn't hard to be friends with girls, I realised now. You just had to not try to get off with them. It literally was that easy. Particularly when there were so many other girls to get off with instead. Sometimes, this led to waking early in some different room in a different, foreign college, to different posters on the wall and different, unknowable female cosmetics crowded around a different sink.

The first time it happened, I'd gone home with a geographer from Caius who had hair in buns like Björk and a plastic skirt. Not for one second, that night, did I feel like a nervy posh kid whose sexual experiences, to date, had largely been in country houses or barns. At 5 a.m., with her hair out on the duvet and her make-up off, she looked like a child. But I suppose I did, too.

I feel now that I remember walking back through Cambridge that morning. Maybe, though, I confuse it with a few other mornings. All mine. Fresh yellow sunlight slanting down, so far unseen by anybody but me. Walking down King's Parade, that time or another, I remember actually shivering with the deliciousness of it all. It was always my favourite, King's. So excessive, those golden

Gothic spires simply not messing around at all. 'I am an Oxbridge college,' it says. 'Fucking deal with it.' Sublime. Often, I'd find myself wishing Johnnie or Alan could be there, to see who I now was. Before being glad that they were not, or else I'd have still been somebody else.

It was on a rainy Sunday right before the end of that term, I think, that I came back in the late afternoon from a pub where I'd been watching *The Simpsons* with God-knows-who and found a note from Ella on the noticeboard I had pinned to my door. ON A RAG TRIP, it said. WILL BE IN THE ANCHOR AFTER LUNCH. Rag was a charity thing, and the Anchor was a pub by the river. I ran out and leapt on my bike, sluicing through the streets, but I got there just as she was leaving to catch the bus back to Oxford. There was a huge group of them, maybe twenty, and they were all literally walking out the door.

'I tried to call,' she said, 'but nobody answered.'

This wasn't surprising. There was one phone on my stairwell, shared by about thirty of us, but whenever it rang it was the annoying girlfriend of the vet on the ground floor. Nobody else bothered picking it up.

'Stay,' I said. 'Come on. Go back tomorrow.'

She shook her head. She had tutorials, she said, really early. She, too, I noticed, was wearing a big coat with a furry collar. Under it was the suggestion of something strappy and sparkly. Her hair was enormous, and her eyes were sparkly, too. She looked amazing, and she hugged me fiercely. I wondered if she was drunk. Behind her, this blond guy was hovering, about my height and wearing an Adidas top.

'Come on, hun,' he said. 'We'll miss it.'

'I can't believe I don't get to see you,' I said, feeling plaintive.

'I'll see you at home at Christmas,' she said, but she didn't because I only went back for a week.

★

In fact, I didn't really see anyone much, except for at Hogmanay. Alan had invited me to a party in this posh New Town club called Po Na Na. I was dressed all wrong, and for most of the night I didn't know a soul there except for him and Claire, who was back for the holidays with, of all things, a French boyfriend. He seemed nice, actually, a skinny guy in a hoodie with lots of curly hair, who seemed about as out of place as I was. Unfortunately, he was also called Thomas, which made things weirdly awkward for both of us.

Fusty turned up just before midnight, alone and more shitfaced than I'd ever seen him. Worse than the Game Fair, even, and the bouncer threw him out after about five minutes. Roughly, too. First, he had him by the lapels, up against a wall, and then he was pitched heavily through the door. I followed him out and found him puking against the back of a car. It was teeming with people out there. Edinburgh Hogmanay people. Oceans of them. I was glad of the stamp on my wrist from the club, or else I'd never have got back in.

'Hey,' I said, 'are you okay?'

'Fucker,' said Fusty and retched a bit more. He looked dreadful. His face was all blotchy and he smelled like an old sofa that had been pissed on by a cat.

'Fusty,' I said. 'Philip? It's me. Do you know who I am?'

'Same. Same as all the others. Bastards.'

Then he sort of slid down the back of the car, and when I hauled him back up again he took a swing at me. It wasn't even close but took me by surprise.

'Hey,' I said again, 'are you fucking mad?'

He just stood there in the street, all hunched and twisted, looking at me with loathing. I didn't know what to do. I'd have called him a taxi, even after that, but the roads were impassable with people. In the end, though, he just gave me a shove and staggered off downhill towards the New Town, like a sailor floundering across a yawing deck. I let him go. Never liked the guy, anyway.

I didn't last much longer. There was no sign of Johnnie, not that I could have imagined him there, anyway. Alan said he hadn't heard from him in months.

★

By spring, I had passably long hair and nobody had stolen my bike in ages. I drank tea and spoke to girls about their boyfriends, and then went out at night and met other girls, and then got up in the morning to go to lectures with Dave. I learned about Red Bull and Platonic Forms and never quite got the hang of ecstasy or the categorical imperative. This was life now.

There were some guys from our course from one of the more modern colleges up the hill, Robinson or Fitzwilliam, I forget which, and they lived in a house a mile or two out of town, and one night they had a party. They were proper stoners, this lot, and the theme of the party, or rather the rule, was that you had to wear a hat. I'd gone without, so I made do by getting a pot from their kitchen and strapping it to my head with masking tape under my chin. This was fine. There was this girl there, a very small blonde mathematician called Martina, who always dressed like a Spice Girl. We ended up sitting on the floor in the living room, with our backs to the radiator, having a very intense conversation about Tony Blair.

'He just smiles too much, and I don't trust him,' she was saying, and things to that effect, and I remember nodding so often and seriously and enthusiastically that the pot on my head clanged against the radiator so loudly and frequently that they had to turn the music up. I stayed late because I'd decided that Martina and I were not destined for friendship, but she'd drunk too much tequila and one of her friends had to take her home. So, I hopped on my bike and soared down past Castle Hill, through grey streets with grey mist rising off the grey Cam. And that was the night I found Flora asleep outside my door.

I didn't recognise her at first. Her head was down, and her hair was absolutely blonde now. She had a string bag between her feet, and she had an empty bottle of gin on her lap, dribbling its last drops into her denim skirt. I put a hand on her shoulder, and she started, looking up.

'Shit,' I said. 'What the hell are you doing here?'

'You *do* live here!' she said, but she was slurring. 'I had to call Alan. I wondered if you'd gone away.'

'Is everything okay?'

'It's Patrick.'

'Patrick,' I said, trying to remember.

'My fiancé,' she said. 'My ex-fiancé. We've split up.'

And then she started crying, and I could get no more sense

out of her at all. So, I helped her inside and put her to bed.

I slept on the floor, which wasn't super. In the morning, which wasn't much later, she still had her eyes closed, and I went out to get some sandwiches from Peppercorns, which was this place that sold baguettes across the street. There was a battered silver Fiat Panda parked weirdly around the back of college, with a parking ticket on it, and with a shock I realised it was hers. She still had her face to the wall when I ran back inside, but I had my licence now, so I rummaged through this little string shoulderbag that was lying on the floor until I found her keys. Then I took the car to the multi-storey in Market Square. It cost a bomb, but everybody said you could sneak your car out in the middle of the night by driving out the way you were supposed to drive in.

By the time I got back with the sandwiches, she had wet hair and was sitting on my bed wrapped in my towel.

'I found the shower,' she said. 'And I managed not to get locked out. Which I reckon is pretty good going.'

'What's going on?' I said, handing her a Coronation Chicken.

'I'm so embarrassed,' she said. 'Oh God. You'll think I'm insane.'

She'd been with Patrick, she said, in Norfolk. Apparently, it wasn't far away. In fact, it was so close that they'd been to Cambridge a couple of times before, to see Patrick's brother Charles. Who, until that very moment, I had forgotten all about.

'But you never came to see me,' I said, hoping I didn't sound plaintive.

'But I *wanted* to,' she said, putting a hand on my arm, and I found it so uncomfortable that I wanted to pull away.

She'd come down from Edinburgh the day before, she told me. Without Patrick, because he'd had a study break and had already gone to Norfolk. Her art school, in Leith, didn't have those, so she'd still had classes. Only then she'd thought, fuck it, and decided to come down and surprise him. And she did, because his parents were away, and she'd found him with a girl called Tabitha, who I might know from that Kula Shaker video (what?), who she knew for a fact was his ex-girlfriend, and not from that long ago, either.

'And she was in the kitchen,' she said furiously, 'and not wearing trousers. And he wasn't even sorry. And I said she had to go, and he said she didn't, and that I did. And he just seemed to find it funny. And I suppose that's why he never gave me a ring.'

'I didn't even know you were engaged,' I said. 'Aren't you a bit young?'

'It was a really tiny party.'

'Oh,' I said, and the silence threatened to become uncomfortable. 'Anyway, I'm really sorry. But that doesn't actually explain why you're here.'

Flora looked surprised. Then she said she hadn't wanted to drive all the way back to Edinburgh, and she couldn't face seeing anybody in London, either. But then, she said, she'd been coming towards the A1 and saw a sign for Cambridge.

'And I suddenly thought, Tommo! He knows about all of it! And so, I stopped to call Alan, to find out where you'd be. And to buy the gin. And here I am. Could I stay tonight?'

I shrugged, feeling that same old familiar sense of fraudulence.

'Sure,' I said.

★

She didn't have any clothes. She'd had a suitcase, she told me, but it had already been in Patrick's hallway when she'd run out, and she hadn't wanted to go back. I gave her some baggy jeans and an old lumberjack shirt, then turned my back while she pulled them on. Despite myself, I could see her reflection in the window. A flash of something, probably her back. I turned, and she said we should go out for a walk.

I took her through the shopping part of town, where in my presumably flawed memory every shop was a Clinton Cards. I took her to King's Parade, where it was all gown-hire shops and off-licences, and tried to explain how it looked in the dawn, when the light caught the mad yellow buttresses. Hoping that she'd ask what I'd been doing walking home in the dawn, but she never did.

I told her about the drum and bass nights in sweaty cellars, and about this huge night at the end of last term, when Dave and I had gone to this party thrown by a girl on our philosophy course we didn't really know, and it had been in this ancient library room in Girton College, which was miles away; and then there had been another party afterwards and we'd ended up on the roof of some huge block of flats knowing nobody at all. And the time this other girl who some other friends knew, a scientist from Queen's, had thrown a party to celebrate her twenty-first with the theme of space travel, only it was happening in a room above their formal hall, which was simultaneously hosting a medieval banquet, which meant that going downstairs to the chaotic unisex toilets meant spacemen mingling with monks in habits, and fifty different Barbarellas doing their make-up alongside serving wenches, and knights standing alongside men in green facepaint and novelty antennae on Alice bands at the urinals.

Along the way, I could feel something changing in her. Her voice changed, too. It grew less high, less precise. Less performative. She'd chuckle darkly and lean in towards me, like a conspirator. I'd grown so used to her talking and me just nodding that an actual conversation was almost a shock.

We wound up in the Anchor, like you always did. Probably, there was Oasis playing. There was usually Oasis playing. We drank pints of lukewarm IPA and ate crisps.

'God,' she said. 'I'm loving these clothes. It's like old me. Patrick got cross when I wasn't smarter.'

'Well, he sounds just lovely.'

'He was, at first. He was really into me. I think it was the whole Scottish shooting, fishing thing. The castle. But then he realised I wasn't going to be any use for any of that, and he got a bit mean.'

'I don't think I understand.'

'Yes, you do.'

'Really, though,' I said. 'I honestly don't.'

So, Flora said it was all about Wilbur, her baby brother. A boy, after three girls. So, now he was going to inherit everything, and she wasn't getting anything. And Patrick had never mentioned that at first, but now he mentioned it a lot, and now this.

'Shut up,' I said. 'You did not just get dumped because you aren't inheriting a castle.'

'No. I was never getting the castle. Philip was.'

Philip was Fusty, obviously. 'Because of his penis superpower,' I said, remembering.

'Yes,' said Flora. 'But I was getting Burnside.'

'Johnnie's Burnside?' I said, astonished.

'Don't call it that.'

The way she said all this, it was like she thought I already knew. Like she thought everyone knew. Like we all sat around talking about it, in our many Flora conversations. Like she didn't know, in fact, that I'd spent half my life trying to have Flora conversations, and nobody else was up for it. But the point was, she said, that MacPhail really had intended for her to inherit Burnside. Like, he was mainly buying it to build those houses, but that was definitely part of the plan, too. First, Fusty was going to live there as the heir, and when MacPhail died and primogeniture gave him Auchnastang, then Burnside was to pass to Flora. They'd talked about it, she said, a lot. Because, primogeniture or not, he wanted something to stay with his own blood.

'Only now,' said Flora, 'he's got better blood, hasn't he? Male blood. Darling little Wilbur blood. So, he gets everything. And I get nothing. Not Burnside, not Auchnastang. Not even, now, Digglesworth. Cheers.'

'And Fusty?' I said uneasily, remembering his drunken fury at Hogmanay.

'Yeah, well,' said Flora, 'nobody is going to want to marry him, either.'

★

That evening, we went down to the bar. It was packed, but she was noticed because new people always were. Also, I dunno, maybe it was me. Look, I'm not saying I wasn't cool. Please don't tell people I wasn't cool. Maybe, though, I wasn't so cool as to raise no eyebrows when I stepped into the bar with somebody like Flora. We'd stopped twice on the way home; once so she could go into Boots and buy make-up and women stuff, and once so she could go into the Macmillan charity shop and buy a fake lace vest and a fake leopardskin jacket. I could feel eyes on her, and I wondered if she could, too. We sat with some of the girls I'd hang out with, Naomi the vegan and this other girl called Clara, who had a biker vibe. They were polite but bemused. A friend from home, I said. A surprise. She'd just turned up.

We drank pints of beer in plastic cups, two, three, maybe four. Dave arrived, also in a vest and make-up, oddly enough. They were all going on to a drum and bass night in a cellar, and we tagged along. That, too, was packed, with condensation running down the walls. Here, the beer was Red Stripe in cans. We set up camp on a corner bench, and Flora disappeared. Just as I was starting to worry, I spotted her in the corner speaking to this terrible dickhead I knew from Queens' who had hair like Billy Idol and, I knew, sold speed. She'd bought some, wrapped up in a square of glossy Sunday supplement, and she started snorting it the moment she came back, through a fiver rolled into a tube.

'It's not my thing,' I told her.

'It's just like a coffee,' she said, so I dabbed a bit. Dave joined in. Clara had skunk because she was one of those girls you used to get who always did. At first, I'd smoked it like the hash we had back home, but it blew you away and I'd learned to be more cautious. Tonight, I didn't hold back and neither did Flora. I remember the music as Roni Size, but drum and bass in my memory is always Roni Size. I do know it was loud, thudding in my inner ear.

We moved on from Red Stripe to Red Bull and vodka. The night decomposed into the beat, and we danced in a throng, my T-shirt as damp as the walls, slick skin touching slick skin. I remember the sweat on her shoulders, the thin ropes of her hair flicking in the strobe. When the lights came up, the room looked like it had hosted a small war, and Flora looked like she'd fought hard and won it. Or, at least, she did to me.

Outside, the air was crisp and the steam rose from our backs. The group peeled off home, but Flora and I went down to the Cam, by the Mill, and smoked some more. Turned out she'd bought skunk, too. I remember jabbering and laughing. I had some theory, I think, about anonymity, about the Scottish middle classes coming to England and being able to vanish. Like expats going home. I think she might have been a bit too wasted to properly listen, though. Or maybe I was too wasted to properly speak. Or she just wasn't interested. We lay back on the grass and held hands and then she kissed me, her Red Bull tongue battling with my own. Then we stumbled home and properly fucked in my single bed, for the first time and the last. I don't actually remember so much about it.

★

The next afternoon, things were awkward. It was like she'd suddenly decided she didn't want to be there, but she also didn't seem to want to leave. She'd washed her shirt in the sink – a green gingham thing – and with her hair up in a ponytail she didn't seem like my Flora at all. We went out for a late breakfast, to a coffee shop on Mill Road, but I didn't have any money and my card was bouncing. She rolled her eyes and bought us croissants and black coffee and sat looking crossly out of the window.

'Is everything okay?' I said.

'Stop saying that,' she said.

I had a tutorial at about 4 p.m. that I couldn't miss, but the thought of wandering around Cambridge with her until then made me feel all cold and chilly and bleak. I wondered if we should buy newspapers, or go to the cinema, or maybe even if I should suggest that she actually leave. I thought of how long I'd spent dreaming of time with her like this, none of which was supposed to involve irritable espressos on a hungover Thursday afternoon.

'Look,' I said, 'I think you're allowed to be pissed off. About all of it. Wilbur. Patrick. All that. But I don't think it defines who you are.'

'And I don't think,' said Flora quite bitterly, 'that you have a clue.'

'I suppose it's worse for Fusty,' I said, mainly to upset her.

'He's a gross, fat bastard,' she said, with a savagery I hadn't heard from her before.

'Oh.'

'Did you know that he once pushed a girl down a hill in a Portaloo? Who does that?'

I said nothing at all.

'He was always a sleaze,' she said. 'Sometimes, it was like he thought he was going to inherit me, too. Dad might kick him out. He should. He's being unbearable about all of it.

He can go back to his weirdo parents. God, am I like them now? Just some spare fucking . . . person?'

'Maybe you can find somebody else with a big house to marry,' I said.

'Fuck you,' she said, and I could see that she was gripping her croissant so tightly that her knuckles were white. There were flakes escaping between her fingers.

'Sorry,' I said.

'Sometimes, it's like you don't understand anything at all.'

I put my hand over her hand. She was still gripping the croissant, so it wasn't ideal. Still, it seemed the right thing to do. She clearly didn't think so, though, and pulled her hand away. The croissant stayed, warm and mangled.

'I think,' I said, 'that you're being a bit melodramatic. Because you're upset. And you're sort of mixing everything together. And you feel like you're losing everything. But from where I'm sitting, you still have quite a lot.'

'Yeah, but what would you know? You never lost anything in your life.'

'Except my mum,' I said quietly.

'Excuse me?'

'My mum. She died last summer.'

Flora blinked. 'I heard about that. But it's not the same. That's normal. That's just . . . people die. That happens to everybody.'

'Oh.'

'It's not fair,' she said. 'This. Right now. What you're doing. It isn't fair.'

'I've got to go,' I said abruptly. 'I've got a tutorial. I'll see you back in the room.'

★

I didn't, though, because she wasn't there. And, after I'd waited a few hours, I went to look in the multi-storey car park in Market Square, and her car wasn't there, either.

The next morning, I called Auchnastang. MacPhail answered himself.

'Mr MacPhail,' I said. 'It's Tommo. Tom. Tom Dwarkin. Flora was here. In Cambridge. And now she's not. And I just wanted to check that she—'

'She was with you?' MacPhail interrupted.

'Yes.'

'She left Digglesworth for *you*?'

'Yes,' I said. 'I mean, no. She just came here. Because she was—'

'My wife was right,' he said. 'I thought you were harmless.'

'Excuse me?'

'Don't call again,' he said and put down the phone.

2 I

SUMMER SHOULD HAVE BEEN when Cambridge came into its own. There were exams to deal with, yes, but there were also afternoons of drinking in the field by the Mill pub, and long, mad expeditions in punts. Still, I wasn't quite feeling it.

Sometime in May, I had a visit from Alan, who had come down with a girl I didn't know, to see another girl and a guy I didn't know, either. Dave and I took a trip with them, out along the Cam through the Fens towards Grantchester. It wasn't a bad day, because there were strawberries and rosé wine and nobody fell in, but it still felt like there was an awful lot of stuff we weren't quite talking about. Plus, I dunno, somehow it didn't all make me feel tremendous. Alan's friends were emissaries of a Cambridge I didn't know so well, all long-limbed and glamorous, from one of the huge colleges like Trinity or St John's. I liked them, but I couldn't help noticing that even when visiting my world, Alan somehow had a knack of making me feel as though I was visiting his.

Do long summer evenings ever make you depressed? I know they're not supposed to. They do me, though, and I think it started then, after Alan had gone. The warmer the night, the greater the scented potential, the bleaker I felt. Maybe it went all the way back to those evenings at school that we'd spend at the Dump. And then later, the nights in the fields, the New Town, the big houses, the parties. The thrill of something at your fingertips, illicit and enviable, just about to be your own.

What, though, was I chasing now? In the evenings, like I said, Dave, Naomi and the rest would always be somewhere, but there were so many choices. The hugeness of it. Were we making the right choices, each and every night? How would we know? Even at the Mill, down by that field, I'd see other groups beyond ours, people I vaguely knew or had just often seen – beautiful people, Alan's people, interesting people – and I'd think, man, but I'm never going to get on top of all this. Each night, I knew, there were parties in terraced houses I didn't know, happening with people I'd never met, who went to colleges I'd never been to, and there just wasn't a way in. And that was just the start of it. Sports people, with their mad evening rituals; theatre people, with their long, lock-in parties at the ADC Theatre; Footlights comedy people, who everybody said were destined to be on telly ten years hence. Big names on campus, actress girls, politics guys, people with an air of semi-celebrity, who'd make a pub or a college bar hush just by arriving. This wasn't like Johnnie, Alan and Flora. This was so much worse. I'd never get to know them all.

The worst thing was, I didn't even really want to try. Because it didn't actually help, did it? Because I'd learned that, if I'd learned anything. Because the people you'd chosen, the nights you'd had, the world you'd cleaved yourself into, they never really cleaved into you. Not properly. Not so that you'd be subsumed into them forever, and that would be that, now relax. They just didn't. They marked you, shaped you, tattooed you, sure, and maybe you did the same for them. But you were still bloody you.

Only, what else was there? What else to aim for? That's what I couldn't figure out. Because in the end, and I suppose this was maybe what it was all about, you couldn't really escape the fact that the people you'd been born with couldn't exactly be relied upon to look after you for ever, either.

★

It was about a fortnight after Alan had been down, anyway, that Johnnie called. Or rather, that I called him, because there was a message telling me to on the noticeboard on my door. I toyed with not bothering. But I'd missed him, and I guess I'd missed the person he was calling, too.

'Why are you so hard to get hold of?' he demanded when I called him back.

I didn't really know what to say to that. I didn't want to tell him that it was probably because I spent my afternoons walking listlessly along the river, or my evenings getting solidly drunk next to it. So, instead, I told him that the vet downstairs had stopped answering the phone when his girlfriend had dumped him, and the rest of us on the staircase hadn't quite worked out a new system yet. Which, as it happened, was also true.

'Anyway,' I said, 'what is this weird phone number?'

We hadn't spoken in months. I'd been back at Easter, but only for a few days, helping my dad clear out the house because he'd had enough of Edinburgh and was planning to move full-time to King's Cross, with a view to eventually relocating up to Hampstead. He had a big

Volvo and one afternoon I'd driven into town with a big oak bookcase in the back, to see if I could flog it to one of the antiques places on Queen Street. On the way, I'd passed Alan's old house on Moray Place, and there was a new and very shiny brass plaque by the door which, when I pulled over for a look, said it now hosted an investment management company. I'd tried calling Alan that night, but his flatmates had said he was working in London. Then I'd actually called Johnnie's place, too, but Jenny said he was out working on the farm, and he'd never called me back. Then, after all that, I'd tried both Ella and Claire, but neither of them had been around, either. It had all felt a bit grim.

'It's a mobile phone,' said Johnnie, now.

'A fucking what? Are you a drug dealer?'

'Not currently. Everybody has them. You should get one. Look, I need you to come up. End of June. I've got a plan. And I need your help.'

'What sort of plan?' I said suspiciously.

'Murder,' said Johnnie. 'Or kidnap. Bursting into Auchnastang with an axe.'

'Heeeeeere's Johnnie!'

'Yes.'

'Like Jack Nicholson in *The Shining*,' I explained.

'Yeah, I've seen it. I'm not a moron.'

'Sorry.'

'A party,' said Johnnie. 'But it's a secret. Don't tell anyone.'

Interesting. Maybe I hadn't been forgotten, after all. 'But I don't understand. Why is it a secret?'

'You'll see. Alan's coming, too.'

'Who else?' I said, trying to summon some enthusiasm.

'Layman? Barf?' I didn't even ask about Flora. I didn't want to know.

'Shit,' said Johnnie. 'You haven't heard? It was in all the papers up here. Layman's in jail.'

He was, too. Because Johnnie might not have been a drug dealer, but Layman was. He'd been arrested leaving a house in Dundee with a locked red moneybox, and when the police broke it open, they found a grand's worth of ecstasy and another grand of those Klonopin things, like the one Johnnie gave me.

'It's nice you've all been having fun,' I said. 'Without me.'

'You what?' said Johnnie.

'Never mind,' I said. 'Why was he doing that? He's loaded. Isn't he?'

Johnnie said he thought he'd just been bored. He'd been selling in Edinburgh, mainly to Alan's crowd, and he'd been quite chaotic about it. Now he was doing six months in Perth. *The Scotsman* had gone big on it, on account of his dad being in the House of Lords, and they reckoned that made the judge extra harsh. Johnnie had been to see him last month. Jail had reminded him of school.

'Dean's coming, though,' said Johnnie.

'Well, he hasn't been in jail for ages. Look, what do you mean, don't tell anyone? How can it be a party if nobody knows about it?'

'You'll see,' said Johnnie.

★

The party was still a month away, though, and it was a month full of revision and exam halls, and then the mad release of May Week (which, of course, occurs in June). I suppose I perked up a bit. There were balls. They weren't like the sweaty black-tie Christmas ceilidhs of my youth. They were huge and outdoor and lasted all night; half-disco, half-fairground, with actual bands you'd seen on *Top of the Pops*, and you couldn't not be impressed. Basically like that big débutante party we'd been to with Alan, but bigger and better. All booze included. Our college wasn't having one that year, so a bunch of us bought tickets to the Jesus College Ball and spent endless hours drinking alcopops and feeling sick on the Ferris wheel and dancing to, I think, Dubstar. Or maybe Lamb.

Often they'd give free tickets to alumni celebrities, which meant whenever you saw somebody over thirty wandering around, there would be a decent chance that you'd dimly recognise them. Which was how, at about 1 a.m., I came to be standing at a urinal and staring at a middle-aged guy in a white dinner jacket and a Paisley scarf.

'Oh my God,' I said. 'It's you.'

'Having a good night?' he said, in one of those booming, plummy voices that only actors have.

'You ruined my childhood,' I said.

'Excuse me?'

'Airhellair!' I screamed, in his face.

'Fucking students,' said the butler, and then he shook his penis and left.

I stood there for a moment or two, and then I started laughing. And then I shook my own and went off to join Naomi and Arabella on the dodgems, feeling better than I had in weeks.

★

On the train north, maybe ten days later, I bumped into Barf. It took ages to get home from Cambridge, which is perhaps part of the reason why I so rarely did it. You had to go to Peterborough, wait an age and then get onto the East Coast Line from London. That's where he was. Sitting alone at a table for four, with a six-pack of Heineken, two cans gone. I hardly recognised him. He'd put on a lot of weight. But then I did a double-take and slid in across the table.

'You're at Cambridge,' he said.

'Yes. What are you up to?'

'Ach, you know,' he said, gesturing at the beer. So, I took one and cracked it open.

I did know, in fact, a bit. Ella had told me that his dad had died really suddenly just before Christmas. He'd had a heart attack, out in a barn, trying to lift an old stove. Barf knew about my mum, probably also through Ella, so we spent a while comparing notes on all that. Although for him, I realised, the death had just been the start of it.

'He'd been dead, like, a day,' said Barf heavily, 'when the lawyer came and told us that we had to sell the house. Like, there wasn't even a discussion. Even if he'd lived, the bank probably would have taken it, anyway. I mean, it was falling down.'

'I remember,' I said, thinking of the stairs that weren't there, and the floors you couldn't get to.

Barf said his dad had plans, always, about opening the place up to guests, or hosting weddings, or conferences, or building a golf course. It was a bit of a joke, though, because none of them had ever gone anywhere. There were loads of barns he could have died in, said Barf, because they were all full of ancient boilers, rusted farm equipment, or insane lumps of machinery for purposes long forgotten. In one, he said, there had been the body of a Second World War military glider. No wings, just the body, and nobody knew why. There were farm cottages, but they were mouldy and damp and falling down. There was a stretch of river which supposedly had salmon in it, and where Prince Albert was said to have fished in the 1850s, but the banks were now overgrown with nettles and gorse and basically inaccessible. There were rowing boats, but all bar one of them were rotten through. Barf had known all this, all his life, obviously, but he'd never given it much thought. And, after the lawyer had left, he took a big, long walk and looked at it all, seeing it all for the first time as his own problem.

'I mean, it was a fucking nightmare,' he said. 'Like, you could suffocate under it all. I couldn't breathe. I could have had a heart attack myself.'

'Shit, Barf,' I said.

I was still drinking his beer. We were somewhere near Darlington. The estate sold quickly, said Barf, to some Ukrainian who wanted it for the shooting. Because once, he said, it had actually been quite good for that, too, and particularly famed for whatever the hell ptarmigan were. Only now the pathways up the hill were all overgrown and the grouse butts had all fallen down. And within six weeks of his dad dying, he said, all the furniture had been all cleared out by an Edinburgh auctioneers, and so Barf loaded up his car with whatever was left and just drove away.

'And I'll never go back there,' he said simply. 'I couldn't

bear to. Mum moved down to Harpenden, near to her sister. That's where I've been. I'm living in Glasgow. Not sure why. Don't really know anyone. Can't really lie, Tommo. I'm a bit of a mess.'

'I know the feeling,' I said.

'Shut up, man,' he said. 'You seem fine.'

Pretty soon the beer was gone. We'd bought more from the buffet bar, and some tiny bottles of Famous Grouse (because Famous Ptarmigan wasn't an option), and we'd sat at our table drinking the Highland way, with a beer and a chaser on the go together. I guess that's where Ella got it from. It was a laugh, though. He cheered up, once we got past the shellshocked death and loss stuff. First, we talked inevitably about old mad stuff, parties and school. Barf had been in Pothle, a house with a reputation for being mad and savage, and from the way he told it, that reputation had been well deserved. They also, he told me, did that thing of putting people in trunks and sliding them down the stairs. And all the dunking in baths. But the one he kept thinking of now, he said, was this tradition of bigger kids putting smaller kids in duvets and hanging them out the window. Three storeys up.

'I heard about that,' I said. 'I thought it was a myth.'

'You never had it? Not even in the first year?'

'I wasn't there. Remember? I joined late.'

'Oh aye,' said Barf. 'You were new.'

'Weird how nobody really talked about it afterwards. Not properly. Once they were older.'

'Probably started doing it themselves,' said Barf. 'I did.'

By the time we got to Edinburgh, we had a proper booze buzz on. Neither of us was in a rush, so Barf got off the train, too, and we climbed the steps of Fleshmarket Close across from the station and went up to the Halfway House. I called my dad to say I'd be late, on the mobile phone that Barf now had, too. Really convenient, actually. More pints, more chasers. And it was only then, because I was now drunk enough not to care that it was for some reason a secret, that I asked him if he was going up to Johnnie's the next week. Although he said that he hadn't spoken to Johnnie in months.

'It's not that we've fallen out,' he said. 'It's Burnside and all that. It makes me feel a bit bleak. At least it only took us six weeks. Seems to be taking them years.'

I leaned over across the pub table. 'So . . . he said that he has a plan.'

'Aw, fuck,' said Barf. 'Not another one.'

'How d'you mean?'

Barf looked at me warily. 'You didn't know?'

'Oh, *that* plan.'

'I thought you were in on it,' said Barf. 'His whole thing about taking them out and shooting them. Fusty and MacPhail, too. He said he was going to tie them up, put them in the car and then drive them out to . . . ach, fuck knows. It was a mess.'

'Alan told me. But I thought he was just, you know, mouthing off.'

'Who knows? You know what he's like. Or was like. Or whatever. But no. I don't think he was. Alan definitely didn't think so. The guy had bags and a spade in the car. He had *twine*, Tommo. Like, I was humouring him, and then I suddenly wasn't sure. But I didn't . . . I mean, what are you going to do? He wanted us all to tool up, there and then. We were already pretty shitfaced. It was some weekend. How were you not there?'

I knew perfectly well why I hadn't been there. I'd been in Cambridge. Joining us for the murder, this weekend? Can't actually. Oxbridge interview.

'Anyway,' said Barf, 'Alan was *raging*. Started laughing at first, like I did. Then, when he realised he meant it? Fucking *exploded*. Told Johnnie he was a fucking joke and slapped him.'

'I didn't know any of this,' I said.

Johnnie had been holding the gun, said Barf, and for a moment he'd thought he might shoot Alan instead. Or maybe first. Like it was going to be a whole spree thing, like you read about in America. Instead, though, he'd just started crying.

'And then what happened?' I said, feeling like we were talking about complete strangers.

Barf said he didn't really remember.

'Oh, come on.'

Barf shrugged helplessly. 'I think we went back to the house and watched *Withnail & I*.'

We stayed in the pub a while longer, but I wasn't really into it. I just kept thinking back to all that, and the way nobody had quite told me about it. Wondering what I'd have done, if I had been there and Alan hadn't. And wondering, in a sort of inverse, guilty way, whether I'd slightly let Johnnie down by not being there. All that loyalty inside him, never repaid. The way he'd kill or die for you, and you totally knew it. And then he'd finally asked us all for something in return, the biggest thing imaginable, and nobody would do it. And I hadn't even realised I was being asked.

Eventually, I think, Barf caught my distance and said he was going home.

'I'll walk you to the station,' I said because that was the way to my bus, too. And as we walked, Barf talked about going to uni, or maybe to college to get some Highers first because he'd screwed them up at school. Or maybe travelling, or maybe starting a café or a pub. And I thought of what he'd said about his dad and all of his mad plans that never went anywhere, and I wondered if this was the same.

'Are you working?' I said. 'At the moment, I mean?'

'Nah. Although I should, shouldn't I? I mean, I've got some money. But still. Get a job. That's what people do.'

He said the word strangely. 'Job.' Like it was in quote marks, or it bewildered him.

'Barf?' I said, remembering that drunken Hogmanay. 'What actually did your dad do?'

'He didn't do anything,' said Barf.

22

I THINK I SAID already that my own village, now subsumed deep into Edinburgh, had originally been the first port of call when you left it. It has one remaining pub, which is ancient, and there's a weird little cottage down by the phone box with a plaque on it telling you that it was once a tavern where Bonnie Prince Charlie stayed the night before riding to war at Prestonpans. I hadn't thought of this in years, but I did that morning, ten days later, as I drove west, out along the bypass, over the Forth Road Bridge and up the M90 towards Burnside and Auchnastang. Man. The massive ball-ache of doing all this on a horse.

I was in my dad's Volvo. He'd hired a van that weekend, to take an apparently interesting sideboard up to somebody who might want to buy it in Fort William. This was the sort of thing he did now. I'd no idea why – it's not like he needed the money – but he seemed to be pretty cheerful about it and had a plan to stay in a nineteenth-century hotel up there that people who give a shit about nineteenth-century hotels apparently rated very highly.

The butler drama rolled on, without him or indeed the original butler being involved, but the cheques still rolled in. He was writing books again, I knew, but his major project these days seemed to be very slowly emptying the house and spreading its contents as widely around Scotland as humanly possible.

I'd spent the week following his instructions, which had mainly involved packing books into boxes. Remarkable how much research a mediocre writer of airport fiction had to do. For myself, there had been remarkably little left that I felt like salvaging. Some clothes, my guitar that had once been Luci's guitar, some letters, some books of my own. Weirdly, it was the little, worthless things that I found myself staring at. A used shotgun cartridge I'd found in my pocket after that day at Auchnastang. These old, lurid green laces I'd once had in my Doc Martens. A cigarette lighter, unremarkable and now long dead, but which I'd kept on my bedside table because I'd found it in my pocket the morning after that first party at that first house in Niddrie, in the house of that girl called Charlotte, and it had seemed, forever after, like a key to a better, magical world.

Anyway, there I was now, heading out over the Firth of Forth. Window down, fag on the go, crunching the gears. Thinking, all the way, about exactly what I was driving towards. A secret party? Who did that? Was it even a thing? Thinking of what Barf had told me about Johnnie's last plan, the one I'd only half-known about. Thinking of what Alan had said about it, afterwards, about Johnnie's disappointment with him. What was it he had said? 'Like I was letting him down . . . Like I wasn't the friend he'd thought I was.' So, was he now about to try it all again, with a different friend? Was *I* the friend he'd thought I was? Even though I'd let half the school drag him away and throw him in a bath. Or maybe that was all in the past, and Johnnie had mellowed. Was he, though, the sort of guy who mellowed? A mellow Johnnie? Did that make sense? Thinking all this, anyway, while actually quite looking forward to getting there. Because it probably *was* some sort of party, wasn't it, after all? And I hadn't been to one in a while.

Off the M90, to my surprise, I got lost. Twice, I looped into Auchternethy village and out again, crisscrossing over the river. At one point I found myself on a brand-new road, tarmac but not even any lines yet, going past a building site of new-build houses. In relief I decided this must be the field MacPhail had taken me to that time, except it wasn't. Nothing looked quite right. Mortifying. So much time in other people's cars. I thought I knew it around here, but I didn't at all. Imagine if I'd had to drive to Barf's old house. I'd have been screwed. I'd have missed Hogmanay all over again, even though it was currently June.

Eventually, though, I found myself on familiar lanes. A tree of old. Johnnie's lay-by. There were still pheasants flattened into frisbees on the tarmac around that blind corner, although I suppose they must have been new ones. Then the Burnside drive, although that didn't look quite right, either. The trees seemed to hang heavier; the track was more pitted and rough. There were pigeons on it, congregating, which seemed startled to see me coming. And then I saw the house, and it was like being kicked in the chest.

'Oh,' I said, and I stopped the car and got out.

It had always been a mess, Burnside, but at least it had looked loved. Now it looked broken. The privet bushes around the end of the drive were wild, unshaven green chins. The windows all had boards over them, save for one covered in a flapping tarpaulin. The deep, damp V-shapes in the yellow harl had grown deeper and damper, and there were weeds growing between the wide stone steps leading up to the front door. There were no cars. I walked around the back and saw that the door to the farrier barn, the one that Johnnie had once shot a fox in, had a big shiny chain and padlock over it. No cats there now, I guessed, nor chickens or horses next door, either.

The kitchen back door, the glass one we had always used to get in and out, had a board over it, too. Stuck on it, with a nail, was a note: AT THE COTTAGE. J.

It was very Johnnie to simply assume I'd know which cottage he meant, but of course I did. He meant the one we'd gutted that summer, with lovely old Archie, the one with the bees, where I'd learned how to use a hoe. Off the top of my head, I couldn't perfectly remember how to get there, either, but there was only one little track leading away from the house, so I knew it had to be somewhere down there. And indeed it was.

If Burnside had gone one way, the cottage had gone the other. I remembered it as a greying ruin, surrounded by nettles, but now the nettles were gone and the walls were a fresh white. There was a new roof on there, and new windows, too, still covered with cellophane. Parked out the front was Johnnie's Land Rover. So, I parked there, too, and cautiously pushed open the door.

'Morning,' said Johnnie.

★

He was bigger, bulkier. He still had the dreadlocks, now down to his elbows, but he had a full dark beard, too. T-shirt, combat trousers. A whirling tattoo around one arm, and tribal earring high in one ear, like Dave had. He hugged me, one-armed, and I felt his bicep curl around my back, a big, thick, knotted treetrunk of a thing. Then I followed him inside, and I felt myself grow cold.

The walls were plastered now, but unpainted and bare. The floor was covered in thick cellophane, of the sort that gangsters put down before a murder, all the way up to the foot of the stairs. In the middle of it stood a table and a chair. Sitting at the table was Dean, looking even more terrifyingly thin than ever before, and lying on the table was a large coil of rope, an axe, a box of cartridges and a shotgun.

'Okay,' I said, 'you have to tell me what I'm doing here, right now.'

'Have you not told him already?' said Dean, with a smirk.

'Not exactly,' said Johnnie.

'I think I can guess,' I said slowly.

'It's not rocket science,' said Johnnie.

'It's mad,' I said.

Johnnie said it might be.

'You're a fucking psycho,' I said. 'I can't let you do this. I'm going to warn MacPhail.'

'Oh no, you're not,' said Dean, standing up right next to me, with the gun now in his hands. He was wearing one of those T-shirts that change colour depending on your temperature. All pink around the armpits and the waist. Maybe getting pinker.

'Don't point that thing at me,' I said, sounding shrill.

Dean looked down at his hands, surprised. 'It's not loaded,' he said, but I could see his eyes flicker towards the cartridges on the table, so I stepped forward and punched him before he could reach for it. Not a good punch. My knuckles cracked. I didn't have time to close my hand.

'Bastard!' said Dean, astonished.

'Tommo,' said Johnnie, 'what the fuck are you doing?'

'No, what are you doing? Still with this shit? I'm going to the police.'

That was when Alan came down the stairs, hair all mussed up, yawning.

'All right, Tommo?' he said. 'What's all this?'

'You're here?' I said. 'You're all right with this? They're planning a murder.'

'You loony,' said Alan. 'No, they're not. They're planning a rave.'

★

That was Johnnie's story, too. It was happening in the farmyard. A proper one, like the ones you used to read about in the magazines, for which people were going to have to call other people, and instructions were to be given out from a payphone at a petrol station outside Lanark. That bit wasn't our problem; there were underground festival groups in Edinburgh, Glasgow, Perth and Dundee that Dean and Johnnie knew who were on top of all that. Our job was to set everything up. Fergus and Mark, from my rabbit hunt years ago, were coming over to man the decks. MacPhail had no idea, and wasn't going to be told, either, at least until it was too late. For

Johnnie, it was the last hurrah before his life at Burnside was over.

'But why are we here?' I asked. 'In this creepy cottage?'

'It's my mum's,' said Johnnie. 'She's moving in next month, with the girls. We don't have the house any more. We're renting in Perth.'

'But the floor.'

'They're still painting,' said Johnnie.

'But the gun,' I said hotly. 'Rabbits?'

'Myxomatosis,' said Dean conversationally. 'Not many left.'

'What are you talking about?'

'Rats,' said Johnnie. 'It's for rats. You nut.'

'Oh,' I said, and I sat down on the plastic floor, hard.

And at that point I would have sworn, quite wrongly, that nobody was going to get shot dead today at all.

★

They all took the piss, but not for long, because we had a lot to do. Dean was disarmingly good about it all. Apparently, it really hadn't been a very good punch. Johnnie already had the sound system and the lights, borrowed off the rave people in Glasgow and stashed in the locked barn. So, we all drove back there and lugged it out, bit by bit, into the biggest cow barn, the one where we used to kill pigeons. It was hard, heavy work, particularly as one of us always had to be up a ladder on the barn's roof, keeping lookout in case anybody came by.

Nobody did, though. These days, the farm was deserted. MacPhail had basically bought it, said Johnnie, but to do

316

that it had had to be bought first from all the stakeholders, himself and MacPhail included, and bound up in a company. And the company, right now, was in escrow, waiting for all the money to come in and out. Or something like that. In the future, anyway, it was barely even going to be a farm. Two more fields, and the farmyard itself, were going to be converted into housing estates. Iain Bonnar, Fusty's dad, didn't work for MacPhail any more; Johnnie reckoned they didn't even talk. Most of the animals had been sold off, and the main thing that MacPhail was planning on farming in the remaining fields was EU subsidies. In short, he was doing all the things you could do with a place like this if you had the sort of money to plough into it that Johnnie's family had never had.

We ran big, industrial cables from a power point to the end of the barn where the decks were going to be. We left Alan on the roof, for a bit, and used the ladder to replace all the lightbulbs with red and purple ones that Dean had brought, in a box. We set up speakers and a strobe and a bank of coloured spotlights. We dragged big trestle tables from the barns nearest the house, hosed them down and set them up inside. Then, maybe at about 2 p.m., Dean and Johnnie set off into Auchternethy to fill the Land Rover with beer, and Alan and I sat on the roof and had a spliff.

'Haven't touched this stuff in ages,' said Alan dubiously.

'I honestly thought it was a different sort of plan,' I told him. 'For real. Because I ran into Barf last week. And he told me about the last one. When we were at school.'

'But you knew about that at the time, surely?' said Alan.

'To be honest, I've never really known anything. I don't even know how Douglas died.'

'Well, that's not my story to tell.'
'No.'
'But I will.'

★

So, let's go back. Let's explain it all. It's 1993. As in, way back at the start. Right? It's colder than this, because it's only Easter, and the boys are roaming the farm in the Land Rover. Not Johnnie's Land Rover. The old one. The one they'd get rid of, afterwards, because of the brain.

Johnnie is there, and Dean, but so are Fusty and Douglas. This is an unusual grouping, but that's just how things have turned out. They're lamping for rabbits, but they only have a shotgun. No rifle. This means you have to get up close, and the bang scares them away between shots. There is no end of rabbits, though, so they always come back.

Douglas is driving. Fusty in the passenger seat. Riding shotgun, to use that phrase we continued to use – including even Johnnie – after the event. Johnnie is in the back with Dean and sulking about it. Actually, he was sulking already. He and Douglas have been bickering since he came home for the holidays; about Douglas taking over the farm, about MacPhail hassling them to sell it, about there not being enough money, about Johnnie not helping, about everything else they can think of. Two nights ago, Johnnie threw a potato at Douglas at the dinner table and the twins started to cry. As in, things are fraught. They've only ended up in the car together at all because Douglas and Fusty have bought some hash, which isn't like them, and neither of them know how to roll a joint. The hash that the police would end up inadvertently giving back to Johnnie, you'll remember, and which I shared at that party right back at the start. Dead Man's Hash. Yes.

Dean and Johnnie have been planning their own night of smoking down by the river, anyway, but Douglas and Fusty trundle past and pick them up. Dean is up for this because Douglas is older and has a status that Johnnie does not. Johnnie is sulking about this, too. They roam around. They shoot. Two or three rabbits end up on the front, next to the wheel.

Fusty has brought whisky, and they're all sharing the bottle, even Douglas, because nobody is planning on going near a public road. Johnnie wants to go to that steep road, the one by the hill that will later be a building site, the Plunge, and do the thing he likes to do in his little Renault, where you kill the lights and roll. Nobody else is up for this. Eventually they end up by the ravine, instead.

There is no system. It all depends on who is on what side of the car. Fusty has the gun, and Johnnie the bright, Batman search-beam light. They've both stepped out of their respective doors, focusing on two rabbits on a hillock maybe fifty feet away. Fusty is taking ages to decide which one to go for.

'Get a move on!' snaps Douglas, only the instant he says it, Fusty fires, pumps, then fires again. Two rabbits down, even though the second was running away. With a normal shotgun it would have been a left and a right, one barrel after the other, which would have been impressive enough. With the pump action, the illegal pump action, it's proper awesome Stallone shit. Neither are dead, though. Both are thrashing around. Fusty shoves the gun at Johnnie and runs over to them. Dean follows him. Johnnie does, too, pumping another cartridge into the gun, the illegal pumpy gun, but there's no need. By the time he gets there, Fusty and Dean have already done the thing with the feet and the ears and the necks. Crack, crack. So, Johnnie turns around and gets back in the passenger seat.

'What are you doing?' says Douglas.

'My turn,' says Johnnie.

'Just get in the back,' sneers Douglas.

'Fuck you,' says Johnnie, going nowhere.

'No, fuck you,' says Douglas, grabbing the gun off him. So, Johnnie grabs it back.

Maybe it's chance. Maybe he grabs a little too low. Maybe there's a split second where he knows exactly what he is doing and even wants to do it, hand twisted, finger flicking down, full of hate, remembering a click, once, in a barn. For the rest of his life, he will always wonder. Either way, it happens. There's a bang, so much louder than a gun normally sounds, and suddenly Douglas isn't Douglas any more. Like a turnip lantern. Although I feel we've covered that before.

★

Obviously that's not precisely how Alan told it, as we sat there on the roof. Some of it, he was sort of guessing, and other bits I've guessed, too. Neither of us were there, after all, and of the four of them who were, only one of them still does much talking. Some other bits, I've got from him. Still, I think it's about right.

'But I don't understand,' I said to Alan. 'That's not what it said in the paper. That's not what people know. It's not even what the police think. Is it?'

'MacPhail,' said Alan. 'They called him. Fusty had a radio. It was lambing season. He was up. And he came with Iain Bonnar. They pushed the car over the edge. And they cleared up the other three boys. Literally took Johnnie's clothes and burned them. Poured water over his head to wash out the bits.'

The bits, I thought.

'And then,' said Alan, 'they took him back to his house in Fusty's jacket and his pants. And he had to go to bed.'

'But the police . . .'

'Bonnar was the police. Remember?'

'But why?' I said. 'If it was an accident, why bother?'

Alan shrugged. Initially, he said, it was a legal thing, because the gun was MacPhail's, via Fusty, and it wasn't licensed and never had been because MacPhail was careless about that stuff, particularly with the local police in his pocket, via Bonnar. So, that could have been bad. In the years since, Johnnie had come to think that it might even have sent MacPhail to jail.

The thing was, it would also have sent Johnnie to jail. His hands on the gun, his fingerprints on the trigger. And, even right there and then, MacPhail had clearly realised that this presented an opportunity. Douglas, always, had refused to sell Burnside. But Douglas was gone. And now there was only this frightened, naked teenager. Who, reckoned MacPhail, might be a bit more pliable. As, indeed, he had been.

'Shit,' I said.

'Did you really not know?' said Alan. 'I just assumed. You guys were so close.'

I thought about this. 'I think that we weren't as close as you maybe thought we were.'

'Shut up.'

'I'm serious. It was like you just decided one day. Like you got the wrong end of the stick. I didn't mind. I was glad. It was the best thing that ever happened to me.'

'Don't be daft.'

'Anyway,' I said, 'I knew all the parts. Sort of. I just never knew them altogether. Or what they meant. And the bits I did know – I dunno, maybe I didn't believe them. Christ. How do you get through something like that?'

Alan didn't answer, and I turned my head, taking in the sweep of the fields around us. The sun was getting heavy. Not setting, as such, because it was only late afternoon, and June, and up here actual darkness didn't have a hope. It was molten, though. Red running gold. One way was the river and the butter-yellow fields of rape. The other, the valley and the hills and the turrets of Auchnastang peeking up, gateway to the Highlands. I thought, for the first time, of the two adjacent names: the Scots Burnside and the Gaelic to the north, so fitting as farmland gave way to peaks and moors. MacPhail in his castle. I remembered Johnnie shooting at it; a kid with his air rifle, the best he could do.

'I mean,' I said, 'what a bastard.'

'Hold up,' said Alan, nodding towards the road. 'They're coming back.'

★

Johnnie and Dean had bought a terrifying amount of beer. Mainly Tennent's, but some Skol, too. They'd had cans open, already, in the car. Alan stayed on the roof and started calling everyone he knew. Turned out he had a mobile, too. More in hope than expectation, I gave him Ella's number. Dean was fiddling with the electrics, nervous, not wanting to turn on the power and make it all go boom too soon. It made me think of all those nights in the Land Rover when we'd dipped the lights and hidden in barns from Iain Bonnar. And now we were about to turn the farm into T in the Park. Although Bonnar, said Dean, wouldn't be a problem, because he'd had a drink on for months now, just like Fusty, and never went out. The local police might come, especially if MacPhail called them. But Dean's rave guys in Glasgow had said the legal situation was pretty murky. If he didn't actually own the place yet, there might not be much he could do.

Anyway, Johnnie and I heaved the booze in, box by box, and stacked it on the trestle table. It was sweaty work. Then we went across to the tractor barn, to get these two huge blue oil drums, which he wanted to put all the cans in, on ice. They were cumbersome. You had to hug them, like a bear.

'How come you never thought of doing this when you were allowed to?' I said to him.

Johnnie grinned at me, face squashed against his barrel, gold-toothed, like a pirate. I can still see it.

'Better like this,' he said. 'Ruder.'

We were halfway across the farmyard. I put down my barrel.

'I don't get it,' I said.

Johnnie stopped.

'All the stuff MacPhail put you through,' I said. 'Alan and I were talking about it. Just now. And I don't know why you put up with it. You're a lion, man. You're not scared of anything. Why him?'

'Shit, Tommo, do we have to do this now? I'm having a good day.'

'Sorry,' I said, and Johnnie put down his drum, too.

'For my mum,' he said. 'Because it would have killed her. And my sisters. And also because he would have fucked us.'

MacPhail, said Johnnie, had made that pretty clear. Play along, cooperate, and his family would get some money and the cottage. And Johnnie would stay out of jail. Fight him, he said, and Johnnie's life would be over, and his mum would never forgive him, and then he'd ruin her, too, by dragging her into court and bleeding them dry. And they'd come out with less.

'I was just a kid,' said Johnnie. 'I didn't realise then how much trouble he'd have been in, himself. With the gun. Or that I'd have to lie to my mum. Forever. And how that would be. But, shit, maybe he was right. Maybe it was better this way. You seen Fusty lately? The guy is a mess. Maybe I'm better off out of all of it. Maybe he did me a favour.'

'I don't think so,' I said.

'Nobody knows,' he said. 'Just you, Dean, Alan and Barf. I never told anyone else. Not even Layman. Came close with Luci. Which is sort of amazing, actually, because there was a time when I was right on the edge of telling everyone. But it's done, now. It's over. And some days, I'm close to forgetting it ever happened. Even myself.'

'You never actually told me,' I said to him. 'Not exactly.'

'Of course I did. We used to talk about it all the time. More than I did with anyone. Man. You kept me sane. Now, are we done? Can we get these fuckers in?'

'Aye,' I said, and I heaved mine up and followed him into the barn and asked where he'd put the ice.

'Oh, man,' he said. 'We totally forgot about it.'

'I'll go,' I said.

23

I'M NOT ACTUALLY SURE what my plan was. It's possible I didn't really have one. But I looked at the cigarette between my fingers on the wheel of my dad's Volvo, and I saw how much it was shaking, and I knew there was simply no way that I was just going to get some ice. And so, at the top of Burnside drive, I didn't go right, towards the village. I went left, towards Auchnastang.

As I came up the drive, it all looked oddly different. I couldn't figure out why. A new fence, perhaps? Had there even been a fence before? There was a different Range Rover, not metallic red like I remembered, but black, like it belonged to a secret agent, or a rapper. Also, the castle stone looked lighter, brighter, like the New Town bricks suddenly had in Edinburgh, after they'd abruptly hosed away two centuries of soot and grime one summer when I was a kid. Perhaps the window frames had been painted, too. I thought of Barf's old house, all falling down, and Burnside, not far behind. This couldn't be more different. It gleamed. Had it just been powerblasted with money? I was up the drive and pulling in next to the steps when I suddenly realised that this wasn't all that had changed. The bastards had chopped down my sex hedge.

It was properly evening now, and as I stopped my engine, I could hear chattering birds. I suppose I was still buzzing from that earlier spliff. Maybe I shouldn't have been driving. I was intending, I think, to hammer on the door and face MacPhail down, tell him what I thought of him, something like that. I kept thinking of the last time I'd spoken to him, on the phone. The disdain in his voice. His disdain for me. The nerve of it. It was only now, though, that I thought of my dad and the way he'd described MacPhail as a shark. And I wondered if I was making a mistake.

Worse still, the door was open, so hammering on it wasn't really an option. Instead, I stuck my head inside and called out a tremulous 'Hello?' And, in the hallway appeared somebody who I took at first to be Flora's mum.

'Tommo?' she said, and I realised with a sort of muted shock that it wasn't Flora's mum at all.

'I need to see your dad,' I said, feeling immediately preposterous.

'Nobody else is here,' said Flora and, as she came into the light from the door, I could see that she was in this white blouse, maybe silk, and a gilet, and her blonde hair was now a bob to her ears, which had pearls in them. Yes. Pearls. It seemed inconceivable that I had ever thought us even potentially the same sort of creature. And then I suddenly thought, with a delicious malice, that I could maybe ruin her life.

'I heard something,' I said roughly. 'I just found out. And it's awful.'

Flora put a hand to her mouth. Not her own mannerism. Copied. Like the way Fusty had copied the pinch of his trousers. Really annoying.

'But we haven't even sent the cards out yet,' she said

coyly. 'There's an announcement next week in the *Daily Telegraph*. Are people talking already?'

'About what?' I said, completely taken aback.

'About me and Jack.'

'Who the fuck is Jack?'

So she said, 'Jack Layman,' and I just stared at her, and then she said, 'I think you know Will?' and I kept staring, and she said that it was a wonderful love story, actually, because she'd gone to Craill just after she'd last seen me, but Will hadn't been terribly nice, and then one day he'd left to go to Dundee and hadn't come back. And I said that was probably because he'd been arrested, and she agreed.

'And Jack was just so lovely. So supportive. And it all just makes perfect sense, doesn't it? And he's only a little bit older than us, although he seems so mature. I mean, Mummy was younger than me. And Daddy adores him. Darling, are you horribly upset? Because that's really sweet. But, I mean, we weren't ever—'

'Your dad blackmailed Johnnie. Over his brother. And he's a bastard. And you need to know.'

'Oh,' said Flora, and her hand went back to her mouth, and I noticed that her finger had a ring on it, with a diamond the size of a pea.

★

We sat in the kitchen. They'd done it up, I realised. It was modern now, all marble and chrome. She made tea, with that fucking little sieve, and I ignored mine completely and told her everything that both Alan and Johnnie had told me. Feeling bad about it because I knew Johnnie wouldn't want me to. But also feeling vicious as hell. And afterwards, for a while, she said nothing at all.

'The thing you have to understand,' she said eventually, 'is that not everybody can cope. With these places. Not everybody is cut out to make them work.'

I didn't know what she was talking about. I wasn't totally sure that she knew what she was talking about. From my bone china cup, I finally sipped my bone-cold tea.

It wasn't about inheritance, she said, but character. About some people having it, and some people not.

'And when they don't,' she said, 'things have a habit of righting themselves. That's what Daddy says. Like a train which wobbles on the tracks. The right people end up in the right places. They always have. And it can seem cruel, if it turns out you're not one of them. Like poor stupid Philip. Or Johnnie, who isn't really anything like his brother at all. And sometimes, when the wrong people don't know they're the wrong people, you have to help them along. It's perfectly fair, as long as you see the big picture. It's like evolution. Don't you see?'

I put down my cup with a clatter. Maybe it chipped.

'You knew,' I said.

Flora said they were moving into Burnside. Her and Jack. Until they inherited Craill, which could be ages.

'And by then, she said, 'maybe little Wilbur will want it. And on it goes. And all that is what you'll be messing up if you keep talking about this. That and Johnnie's life, too. Just so you can feel a part of something. When you aren't.'

'He was a kid. They rinsed the blood and skull out of his hair in a field and then dumped him at home, alone, to get up in the morning and bullshit his mum.'

'It wasn't easy for any of us,' said Flora. 'I'd been away. I was skiing. It was a big shock. But people die. It's normal. People with history know that.'

'You're a monster.'

'And you're a little boy, and you should go. Daddy and Jack will be back soon. They're out on the hill. They're awfully late, but I suppose that means they must have been quite far away when they got their stag. And they'll have had to drag it all the way home.'

'After the gralloch.'

'Well, yes,' said Flora, sounding surprised for the first time since I'd arrived.

You rip out the guts. And you leave them for the hooded crows.

★

After that, annoyingly, I still had to get ice.

Everything was closed in Auchternethy, so I kept on going to Crieff and then the outskirts of Perth. The impossible urbanity of it. How could it be? That you got field and hills in the world, but also garage forecourts. That the human eye could track a rabbit's tail, but also a red tail light. That there were people like Flora, but also people like everybody else. It was only when I found myself pondering whether you could get ice at a service station that I remembered making the same trip all those years ago on the night that Johnnie took acid. With a gun, I remembered, and with Mark and Fergus. They'd probably be there by now. All sorts of people might be. They'd be wondering where I'd gone.

Turned out you could get ice at service stations, after all, so I bought all they had, and it took me two trips back to the car to carry it all. Then I bought a bunch of cigarettes and Rizlas, too. Then I turned around. I had the music up because I was still shaking and wanted to drown myself out. It worked. The radio was playing pop crap, but the right pop crap, stuff with a beat, of the sort they'd played at parties half a decade before. The sun was almost gone now, but the sky was still a sort of slate blue, burnishing to gold on the horizon. As I turned back into the lanes before the farm, I cut the stereo and opened the windows, to let the wind buffet me in smothering, muted waves. Dean had been right; there really weren't many rabbits now. Time was, they'd have been all over the roads. Still, rabbits or not, I felt the Proustian rush of hedgerows in the evening. The trees were silhouettes, and the air smelled of mud and forgotten promise. I felt muted myself, and it was a relief. And then the rhythm of the wind took shape, I passed Johnnie's lay-by, and I realised I could hear a beat.

There were a surprising number of cars already in the farmyard, maybe fifteen. I parked right by the barn and lugged out a few bags of ice, hearing the music boom. I'd expected things to still be at that awkward, excruciating early stage, where the music feels too loud and nobody wants to dance, and you get that self-conscious feeling that makes you want to sack the whole thing off and go home to bed. It wasn't like that, though. There was a proper buzz. I wondered how long it would take for the police to come.

'Took your time,' said Johnnie, when he saw me sitting on a crate outside and smoking a fag.

'Sorry, I had some stuff to do.'

'And just how was Flora?' he said, amused.

'Pretty normal.'

Johnnie said Dean had a guy coming with some pills and powders, and did I want any? I said probably not, unless I needed to stay awake. To my surprise, Johnnie said he didn't do that stuff any more, either. Not judging, just didn't want it. He said he'd gone to a thing up in Aberdeen with Dean a few weeks ago, and he'd been driving, so he'd stayed clean, and it had made him realise how much you missed when you didn't. I asked about hash, almost affronted, and he shrugged and said sometimes, but not much, and certainly not tonight because he had his medical next week for the army.

'For the fucking what?'

'Black Watch,' he said. 'Mind those guys who used to come and talk to us for the CCF? They reckon I could be an officer.'

'Have you lost your mind?'

'It's cool. Always thought about it. What else am I going to do? Hardly want to stay here.'

'Sheesh,' I said. 'I'm sorry, man. About all of it.'

Johnnie did his pirate grin again. 'You seem to be having quite an emotional day.'

'Yeah.'

'I'm okay,' he said. 'My mum's okay. It's all okay.'

And I put my arm around his shoulders, and he put his around mine, and we both squeezed, and I remember the feel of him – the muscle, unhurtable, immortal – and I remember thinking, 'Shit, okay, maybe it is.'

★

Within an hour and a half, it was heaving. Strobes, lights, arms. So many cars outside. Forty? Inside, at least a hundred people, maybe more. Lots of students, probably, but there were kids in their teens and a few of those thin, older, weathered-looking people you always used to get in techno clubs back then, who were for some reason always dressed a bit like jesters. Most of them I'd never seen before but, dotted around, was the odd face I knew. Friends of Alan's from Hogmanay. Claire, who I used to know so well, here with a group, kissing me on the cheek and then pirouetting away. Jamie, who I'd known once as Layman's friend, now with a goatee beard. Perhaps Charlotte, that Edinburgh girl with the massive house, where all of this began. There was also this very familiar-looking guy – thin, almost beautiful, quite androgynous – at the centre of a group of proper clubbing people, with neon clothes and bleached hair. I couldn't swear to it, but I think he might have been Peter, my arranged marriage from the Normandy Club. Although I was a couple more joints in, by then, and maybe I was doing that thing where every face does its best to tell you a story you know.

Two younger girls, though, I definitely recognised. Not old enough to be there, really; no more than fifteen. They were running around, spinning, loving it, and I stared at them for an age before I realised they were Marianne and Tabitha, Johnnie's twin little sisters. It had been years, but they knew me, too.

'Of course I remember *you*,' said Tabitha, tiny and perfect with smoky eyes, and I was struck by how much she looked like her mum.

'Holy *shite*,' said golden Marianne, in this gravelly, very

Scottish-sounding voice. Honestly, it was all I could do to resist telling them they'd grown.

Darker skies. Pigeons coming across the fields towards the barns to roost, then thinking better of it. The DJs were good, throwing out all manner of beepy nonsense. Alan had his shirt off, tied around his waist. Some girl he knew had tequila; she was handing out tiny plastic glasses and filling them up from two bottles in holsters like guns. Were we now a promotional opportunity? Another girl I didn't know was in her bra on the shoulders of some guy. She had one of those glowsticks that climbers use on the end of a string, and she was whirling it around her head. For a while, I nodded up and down alongside Dean and some of his friends. He was really going for it, drenched with sweat, T-shirt now pale and soaking all over. He had a little bottle of poppers, which he'd pass over every now and then, and I'd take a sniff and feel that thing where it's like somebody has threaded a throbbing rope between your ears and used it to lift you a foot off the floor. In a lull, I asked him if this was his life now, full-time drugs, clubs, parties. Although he said no, only at weekends, because he was mainly now managing a team of eight selling life insurance for Scottish Widows.

And still the cars came. Small ones, mainly, Fiestas, Polos, Corsas, Renaults, like Johnnie's one we drove around these very fields. It still wasn't dark, because it was June and scarcely got dark, but it was definitely night, with the scores of people now milling around outside becoming silhouettes when the strobe throbbed out the door. The smoke, the smell, the laughter, a thin, sudden arm around my waist from behind.

I spun, and it was Ella, smirking. I gaped. I can still see her, exactly as she was then; she had one of those tight Adidas T-shirts on that girls used to wear, white, with darker piping around the arms and neck. Crossing her shoulders were the straps of a tiny rucksack, too small to hold an apple.

'You came!' I said.

'I brought people,' she said, nodding her head towards a group which included Geordie Meehan, of all people, now a bear in a baseball cap, and her friend Catherine, who had never liked me, but who seemed to be smiling at me all the same. I hugged Ella and took her hand, leading her outside towards the crates. Beaming, jabbering, thrilled fit to burst.

★

There was a proper toilet in the farmyard, which wasn't wildly pleasant, but at least meant that nobody had to get rolled down a hill in a Portaloo and turn blue. Ella was off queuing for it when the black Range Rover from Auchnastang arrived, and out stepped Flora and Jack Layman.

I didn't approach them. I didn't do a thing. Genuinely, I wasn't even sure if they represented a problem. In fact, they seemed almost enchanted. Him particularly, giving off the vibe of a Tory MP inspecting the local fête. I remember it, and I can't overstate it: he had a Barbour on and a tweed cap. I half-expected him to start shaking people's hands. They walked right past me, as if I was anybody.

'Who are they?' said Ella, appearing by my side.

'Local landowner.' I said, vaguely.

'Oh.'

'Actually, it's Flora,' I said, 'who I used to know.'

'Her?' she said, surprised, and I shrugged, and that was when I saw Fusty walking up the farmyard behind them, coming from God knows where and holding a gun.

Was it all slow motion from then on? That's what's supposed to happen, and I can understand why. I do seem to remember an impossible amount from the few short minutes that followed. On the other hand, though, it all seemed to happen at light speed, too fast for me to even move.

Fusty was shouting. I couldn't make it out at first, although the music was having one of those quieter bits that happen before the louder bits, which meant the words were gradually getting clearer. Something about land. Get off my land. God, the cliché of it. Most people hadn't noticed him. Others seemed to be smirking. A guy who looks like Fusty? Shouting, 'Get off my land'? Holding a shotgun? It seemed like a joke, right up until the moment he fired it, straight up into the sky. Like a sheriff silencing a rowdy Wild West town.

Flora turned, Jack turned, everybody turned.

'Dickhead,' said somebody scornfully.

Fusty's face was red, redder even than everybody else's in the light bleeding from the barn. He was wearing a jacket, shirt and tie. Preposterous. The collar was up, and his hair was everywhere. He looked insane. I should do something, I remember thinking. He's ten feet away. It's a shotgun. Double-barrelled. Which means he's only got one more shot. Then I could get involved. That's what I'll do. Ten feet. One more shot, then I'll be a hero.

But he didn't fire, and I didn't move. He just kept shouting, although now Flora was shouting, too.

'Go home,' she was saying. 'My dad's coming. And Iain Bonnar.'

Such a weird way to say it. Not, 'And your dad,' but, 'And Iain Bonnar.' No dad for Fusty.

'Get off my land!' shouted Fusty again.

'It's not yours,' said Flora, in disgust.

Then she started to shout something else but stopped when Fusty put the stock of the gun up to his shoulder and levelled it directly at her. Now Flora's mouth hung open. Jack's, too. Both like dark tunnels. Pitch black. Darker than the sky. You couldn't hear music at all now. Just, from the barn, the sound of people going 'wooo'.

'It should be,' said Fusty.

And then, from behind me, came Johnnie. Striding up between them. Not looking angry. Not even looking annoyed. How did he look? I have never stopped wondering. It's the image of his face I'll have forever, but I can't figure it out. Maybe amused?

'It's not yours,' he said. 'And it's not hers, either. It's mine. And you both fucking know it.'

And then Flora looked at Johnnie, as if confused, and then Ella, right in my ear, said, 'Oh no.' And then Fusty shot Johnnie, right in the face, and the music was suddenly deafening, and Flora was shrieking, and Jack Layman was spinning away, holding one eye. And now I did move, finally, but towards Johnnie, who was on his back in the farmyard mud. Dreadlocks splayed out behind him. And some horrors, I realised then, you don't have to dream.

24

A SMALL BOY SLIDES in a trunk down a staircase. He batters the lid, thinking of coffins, and when he gets out at the bottom maybe he's become somebody else. Right? He is hung from a window in a duvet cover, has a jug of food thrown over his head and gets hurled into a freezing bath. When a flying apple hits a milk jug, he learns, you turn over a table and start flinging spaghetti. On an ash lagoon, next to a sign which says, DANGER OF DEATH, he learns to run across a crust of mud. You can see, I suppose, how that leads to a brick to the face. What about a shotgun blast, though? Does it lead to that?

What if, though, he's spent all his time in a place where the names of the dead are inscribed on the walls? Hundreds of them, carved in solemn script and then painted over in gold; names and ages, and virtually every one of them dead before the age of twenty-two. When you learn – no, learn won't do it; when you *breathe* – when you breathe in the belief that this is the highest calling there could be? To fight and kill and be dead by twenty-two? When that, looking back, is the only certainty that has been given to you by an environment that, should you follow any other path, will make no sense at all? What if you are taught to kill a chicken, and are shot at in a hut? Does that factor in, too?

And what if, at home, you are the last in a long line of

people who have triumphed over other people, their own siblings and kinsmen, in ways long forgotten? Because you must be, because you wouldn't be there if they hadn't. And what if, at the same time, you are learning how it feels to have the cold metal of a gun barrel in one hand, and the warm wood of its stock in the other, and the thrill of that wood going to your cheek, and the way to hold it, not too loose but not too tight, either, so the gun can buck and you don't get a fat lip? For play, as your ancestors did, too, and theirs, right back to a time that they learned bow and sword skills and jousting instead. You are guns who are people, and people who are guns. Weapon-ready, bred to tackle the trenches only with a revolver and a whistle, and to turn the former on anybody less weapon-ready than you. What happens, though, when there are no trenches? Where does it all go? This is what I asked myself back then. This is what I still ask myself today, when I think about it, although I honestly rarely do.

★

Five years have passed, although it feels like longer, especially when I'm in Edinburgh. Perhaps it's not so different, but it feels it to me. It's the other side of a millennium, and Scotland is building a parliament. When I'm back, which isn't often, it feels to me as though the sort of people I used to know – with their farms and shabby castles and looming Edinburgh townhouses – have somehow retreated. Something has replaced them: brick people, not stone people; people more varnished pine than polished oak. And the sort of person I have become – a London Scot, a Burns

Night Scot – doesn't seem to have much to do with that. Nor, often, seem to want to.

At first, when I went up, I'd stay with Johnnie's mum and his sisters. She's in East Lothian now; a nice enough house in a wee place called Drem. I think it reminded us all a bit too much of being in court, though, so I stopped doing that. I still write to her sometimes. Tabitha, I know, is in Edinburgh, learning how to be a doctor. Marianne is down here, about to graduate from something intimidating to do with politics at UCL. She'll go far, that one, and every time I see her I'm a little more terrified. I should see her more.

Philip MacPhail never did buy Burnside. There had always been stories about him, like my dad said, rumours about what he did, and what Iain Bonnar did for him. That Bonnar's son should have shot a boy dead on land MacPhail was buying – a boy whose own brother had died a few years before – well, even some of the London papers cared about that. Even before Fusty went to HMP Perth – where he still is – he'd lost whatever backing he had for the Auchnastang housing development. That meant the farm sale stalled, too. In the end, it was sold to that Icelandic billionaire who invented those string-pull packets you get cheese in. You know the one. The family got more money, but the last I heard, he wasn't even farming it. Just letting it grow wild, reintroducing beavers and stuff. I think the house was pulled down.

I know this last bit thanks to Dean. I saw him six months ago, when he was down here for a conference at the London ExCeL. We had a drink, and he paid, and I felt pretty shabby. His dad still lives in Auchternethy. A couple of years ago, he told me, MacPhail had a heart attack, or a stroke, or whatever, and these days the Auchnastang stairs have a lift on them. There's a factor running the estate now because MacPhail can't and Wilbur is just a kid, but it's not in great shape, apparently. Some people wonder whether the Icelandic guy might buy it, too.

Dean also told me that Flora and Jack Layman were in the toilet-roll castle at Craill. This, though, I knew already, thanks to an article in a Sunday colour supplement, which I read because – madly – the place is now being used as the main location in an ITV adaptation of another one of my dad's books. I think my dad has been up there a couple of times, but we haven't really talked about it, so I don't know if he's met them. There were two blonde kids in the photos, both girls. Flora, almost matronly, with an actual perm. Jack in his pirate eyepatch, actually quite dashing. His parents are still around, but they've moved into some wee cottage, so the new generation can take over. No idea where Will is now. No mention of him. And the book, by the way, isn't about a fucking butler. The hero is a village doctor. He has a big black leather case, and everything. It's totally different.

★

So, no, I don't think about it often. Next week, though, I'm going up. Although obviously not to Craill, and not to Burnside, either. What's happened, see, is that Alan and Claire have rented a wee house on Skye, and they've invited Ella and me to come along. I know nothing about the house, but also I know everything. Because it will have ramshackle walls and floors, and a big old kitchen table, and a woodshed, and a hearth inside with a curling stone next to it. I mean, won't it? Doesn't it have to? And it won't be a wild week, what with their baby, but I find I'm wildly excited about it, all the same. The hills, the air, the long nights; all these things I haven't touched in years. I suppose there may be rabbits, too, but I expect we'll leave them alone unless we're eating one. Alan has an idea to open a restaurant up there, with a young chef he's met in Glasgow and backing from his uncle Marco. I like the idea of him living there. I like the idea of always having somewhere to go.

We're driving, anyway. Feels like cheating to fly. Alan says we can have his spare room in Hillhead the night before, and Ella's parents are still in Bearsden, but I've a real urge to go through Edinburgh. Maybe a hotel, or maybe we could stop off in Drem and see Jenny Burchill. Well, we'll visit, at least. She won't remember Ella, but I think they'll get on. Wherever we stay, I do know that I'll veer off once we're over the bridge and go to see Johnnie in the Auchternethy cemetery, next to his dad and his brother. I feel I should sit by his grave and smoke a joint, but I don't really know where to get one. Also, that would mean Ella having to drive afterwards. God, the things we used to do.

The funny thing is, I reckon I can already tell exactly how I'll feel when we leave him. Down here, he feels far away; like I said, I often don't think of him at all for weeks, maybe months. Up there, though, with peaks folding away out the window, even before we get on little lanes with hedges and ditches at their sides, even before we reach whatever cottage Alan has found and smell the smoke from the chimney, even before all that, it seems impossible that it won't feel like he's with me, anyway. Perhaps in one of his moods, or perhaps as excited as I am, but there, for certain, all the same.

It makes me think, now, how often I took those trips for granted. How I thought, or knew, or thought I knew, that there would always be the next place, as open as the last; a whole doomed world teetering on the edge of an entropy I recognised even then, and perhaps even revelled in, but without ever quite grasping what entropy entails. And it has taught me, I suppose, that you can't cling on to things that are crumbling. Because you will break your nails, and you will fall, and then you will look back up and wonder how it can be that something which once seemed as solid as stone itself is now barely there at all.

ACKNOWLEDGEMENTS

Thanks to Francisca Kellett, my wife, the first, last and perfect reader of everything. Thanks to Jamie Crawford at Polygon, who seemed to get exactly what this book was supposed to be from the very first moment I told him about it. Thanks to Edward Crossan, also at Polygon, to whom I will forever owe a pint in the Tilted Wig.

Thanks to my agent Clare Conville for her faith and patience, and thanks to Damian Barr, without whom I might at one point have thrown the whole damn thing on a fire. Thanks to John Witherow and Craig Tregurtha at *The Times* for some vital time off. Thanks to Caitlin Moran and John Niven for being there with cigarettes and good advice whenever I was in need of either.

And thanks, most of all, to Alex B., Jon U., Eddie M., Donald S., Andrew W., Wally T., Angus H., Joe M., Struan E., Johnny B., Hamish M., Max A., Will VW., Iain H. and plenty of others, none of whom are actually in this book, I swear, but all of whom are there in spirit on every single page.